We get married and raise the baby together."

To his chagrin, Jenna laughed. Not just laughed but snorted and snuffled with it, as if she couldn't contain her mirth at all.

"It's not so impossible to think of, is it?" he demanded.

"Impossible? It's ridiculous, Dylan. We barely even know one another."

He nodded in agreement. "True. That's something easily rectified."

All humor fled from her face. "You're serious, aren't you?"

"Never more so."

"No. It would never work. Not in a million years."

"Why not? We already know we're—" he paused a moment for effect, his eyes skimming her face, her throat and lower "—compatible."

"Great sex isn't the sole basis for a compatible marriage," she protested.

"It's a start," he said, his voice deepening.

is a Dy

EXPECTING THE CEO'S CHILD

BY
YVONNE LINDSAY

Published in Great Britain 2014
by Mills & Boon, an imprint of Harlequin (UK) Limited,
Eton House, 18-24 Paradise Road, Richmond, Surrey, TW9 1SR

© 2014 Harlequin Books S.A.

Special thanks and acknowledgement are given to Yvonne Lindsay for her contribution to the DYNASTIES: THE LASSITERS miniseries.

ISBN: 978-0-263-91469-6

51-0614

Harlequin (UK) Limited's policy is to use papers that are natural, renewable and recyclable products and made from wood grown in sustainable forests. The logging and manufacturing processes conform to the legal environmental regulations of the country of origin.

Printed and bound in Spain
by Blackprint CPI, Barcelona

New Zealand born, to Dutch immigrant parents, **Yvonne Lindsay** became an avid romance reader at the age of thirteen. Now, married to her "blind date" and with two fabulous children, she remains a firm believer in the power of romance. Yvonne feels privileged to be able to bring to her readers the stories of her heart. In her spare time, when not writing, she can be found with her nose firmly in a book, reliving the power of love in all walks of life. She can be contacted via her website, www.yvonnelindsay.com.

To my dear friend Rose-Marie, who has known me since we were both teenagers—thank you for always being my friend and an especial thank you for calling florists in Wyoming for me! :) I owe you, Smithy!

One

Jenna puzzled over the complex wreath design a family had requested for their grandmother's funeral the coming Wednesday. She just about had it nailed; all she needed to confirm with the wholesale suppliers was that she'd be able to get the right shade of lilacs that had been the grandmother's favorite.

The sound of the door buzzer alerted her to a customer out front. She listened to see if her new Saturday part-time assistant would attend to the client, but the subsequent ding of the counter bell told her that Millie was likely in the cool room out back, or, unfortunately more likely, outside on the phone to her boyfriend again.

Making a mental note to discuss with the girl the importance of actually *working* during work hours, Jenna pushed herself up from her desk, pasted a smile on her face and walked out into the showroom. Only to feel the smile freeze in place as she recognized Dylan Lassiter, in all his decadent glory, standing with his back to her, his attention apparently captured by the ready-made bouquets she kept in the refrigerated unit along one wall.

Her reaction was instantaneous; heat, desire and shock flooded her in turn. The last time she'd seen him had been in the coat closet where they'd impulsively sought refuge—to release the sexual energy that had ignited so dangerously and suddenly between them. They'd struck sparks off one another so bright and so fierce it had almost been a relief when he'd returned to his base in Los Angeles. Almost.

Jenna fought the urge to place a hand protectively across her belly—to hide the evidence of that uncharacteristic and spontaneous act. She'd known from the day her pregnancy was confirmed that she'd have to tell him at some stage. She hadn't planned for it to be right now. At first she'd been a little piqued that he'd made no effort to contact her since that one incredible encounter. She had half understood he'd been too busy to call her in the aftermath of his father's sudden death during Dylan's sister's wedding rehearsal dinner. But afterward? When everything had begun to settle down again?

She gave herself a mental shake. No, she'd successfully convinced herself that she didn't need or want the complication of a relationship. Especially not now and especially not with someone as high profile as Dylan Lassiter. Not after all the years of work she'd put into rebuilding her reputation. She'd made a conscious choice to put off contacting him, too, and despite the slight wound to her feminine ego that he'd obviously done the same, she would just have to get over it because she sure as heck had plenty else to keep her mind occupied now.

"Can I help you?" she said, feigning a lack of recognition right up until the moment he turned around and impaled her with those cerulean-blue eyes of his.

Air fled from her lungs and her throat closed up. A perfectly tailored blue-gray suit emphasized the width of his shoulders, while his white shirt and pale blue tie emphasized the California tan that warmed his skin. Her mouth dried. It was a crime against nature that any man could look so beautiful and so masculine at the same time.

A hank of softly curling hair fell across his high forehead, making her hand itch to smooth it back, then trace the stubbled line of his jaw. She clenched her fingers into a tight fist, embedding her nails in her palms as she reminded herself exactly where such an action would inevitably lead.

He was like a drug to her. An instant high that, once taken, created a craving like no other. She'd spent the past two and a half months in a state of disbelief at her actions. She, who'd strived to be so careful—to keep her nose clean and to fly under the radar—was now carrying the child of a man she'd met the day it was conceived. A man she'd barely known, yet knew so much about. Certainly enough not to have succumbed the way she had.

It had literally been a one-night *stand,* she reminded herself cynically. The coat closet hadn't allowed for anything else. But as close as the confines had been, her body still remembered every second of how he'd made her feel—and it reacted in kind again.

"Jenna," Dylan said with a slow nod of his head, his gaze not moving from her face for so much as a second.

"Dylan," she replied, taking a deep breath and feigning surprise. "What brings you back to Cheyenne?"

The instant she said the words she silently groaned. The opening. Of course he was here for that. The local chamber of commerce—heck, the whole town—was abuzz with the news. She'd tried to ignore anything Lassiter-related for weeks now, but there was no ignoring the man in front of her.

The father of her unborn child.

A noise from the back of the store made both of them

turn around. Oh, thank God. Millie had finally deigned to show up and do her job.

"Ah," Jenna said, fighting to hide her relief. "Here's Millie. She'll be able to assist you with any requirements you might have. Millie, this is Mr. Lassiter, he's opening the Lassiter Grill in town. Please make sure you give him our best service."

She sent Dylan a distracted smile and turned to go, only to feel him snag her wrist with warm strong fingers. Fingers that had done unmentionably wicked things to her and whose touch now sent a spiral of need to clench deep inside her.

"Not so fast," Dylan said, spinning her gently back to face him again. "As capable as I'm sure Millie is," he continued, flashing a smile that had the impressionable teen virtually melting on the spot, "I'd prefer to deal with you directly."

"I'm sure you would," Jenna answered as quellingly as she could. "But Millie is available to help you with your inquiry. I am not."

Her heart rate skipped up a beat as a hint of annoyance dulled his eyes.

"Scared, Jenna?"

His low tones were laced with challenge. Jenna stiffened her spine.

"Not at all, just very busy."

"Not too busy, I'm sure, to catch up with an old *friend.*"

Hot color stained her cheeks. They weren't anything near approaching friends. She barely knew him any better now than she had the day they'd met—the day they were so drawn to one another that flirtation had turned to touching, and touching had turned to impassioned, frenzied lovemaking in the nearest available private space.

A butterfly whisper of movement rippled across her lower belly, shocking her into gasping aloud. Of course—the moment she'd been awaiting for weeks, her baby's first perceptible motion, would have to happen with its father standing right here in front of her.

Dylan's fingers tightened on her wrist. "Are you okay?"

"I'm fine," she said hurriedly. "Just very busy."

"Then I'll only take a few minutes of your time." He gave her a searching look. "Your office?"

Her body wilted in defeat. "Through here."

He released her wrist and she felt the cool air of the showroom swirl around her sensitized skin, as if her body instantly mourned the loss of contact, his touch. She found herself rubbing at the spot where he'd held her, as if she could somehow rub away the invisible imprint he'd left upon her.

Stop being ridiculous, she growled silently. *He was nothing to you before, aside from an out of character dalliance, and he's nothing to you now.* Logically she knew she couldn't avoid him forever. Despite the fact he was based in L.A., with the new restaurant opening here in town they were bound to cross paths again sometime. It might as well be now.

The tiny fluttering sensation rippled through her belly again, reminding her that there was a great deal more to consider than just her own feelings about seeing Dylan Lassiter. Thankfully, he hadn't noticed that her petite frame carried a new softness about it now. That her figure, rather than being taut and flat, was gently rounded as the baby's presence had suddenly become more visible at thirteen weeks.

She hadn't shared news of her pregnancy with anyone yet, and had no plans to start right now. Instead, she'd sought to hide it by changing from her usual style of figure-hugging attire to longer, more flowing lines.

As they entered the tiny office she used for administration, she gestured to the chair opposite her desk and sank, gratefully, into her own on the other side. Instead of taking the seat offered to him, Dylan sat on the edge of her desk. She couldn't help but notice the way the fine wool of his trousers skimmed his long powerful thighs, or how the fabric now stretched across his groin.

Her mouth suddenly felt parched and she turned to reach for the water jug and glasses that she kept on a credenza behind her desk.

"Water?" she offered with a croak.

"No, I'm fine, thank you."

She hastily splashed a measure of clear liquid into a glass for herself and lifted it to her lips, relishing the cooling and hydrating sensation as the drink slid over her tongue. After putting the glass down on the desk, she pulled a pad toward her and picked up a pen.

"So," she said, looking up at him. "What is it you want?"

He reached out and took the pen from her hand, laying it very deliberately down on the notepad. "I thought we could talk. You know, reminisce about old times."

Heat pooled at the apex of her thighs and she pushed her chair back from her desk. Anything to increase the distance between them.

"Look, you said a few minutes, and frankly, that's all I had. Your time's up. If there's nothing business related you need to discuss…?" She hesitated a moment, her temper snapping now at the humor reflected in his eyes. "Then you'll have to excuse me so I can attend to my work."

Dylan's sinfully sensuous lips curved into a half smile.

"You're different, Jenna. I can't quite put my finger on it, but I'll figure it out."

She fought back a groan. The man was all about detail. She knew that intimately. If she didn't get him out of here soon he was bound to notice exactly what it was that was different about her. She wasn't ready for that, not right now, anyway. She needed more time.

Before she could respond, he continued, "I want you to do the flowers for the opening. Wildflowers, grasses, rustic—that kind of thing. Can you do it?"

"I'll get my staff on to preparing some samples for you on Monday. I take it you'll be around?"

His smile widened. "Oh, yes, I'll be around. And your staff won't be handling this for me. You will."

"My staff are well trained and efficient—"

"But they're not you—and I *want* you."

His words hung in the air between them. She could feel them as if he'd actually reached out and touched her.

"You can't have me," she whispered.

"Can't I? Hmm, that's a darn shame," he said. "Because then I'd have to take my business elsewhere."

His words, so gently spoken, sent a spear of ice straight through her. It would take only a day for the news that she'd turned his business away to get through town. Less than that again before more people would follow his cue and take their business to other florists, as well. She'd fought long and hard to get a reputation as the leading florist in town and she wasn't going to lose it just like that.

She bit the inside of her cheek as she swiftly considered her options. Well, option. She really had no other choice but to take his business. Refusing it, with the associated fallout when word got around that she'd turned down a Lassiter—well, it didn't bear thinking about. However, the benefits would roll in pretty quickly when it was known that she'd done the flowers for the opening. There was nothing some of the better-heeled members of Cheyenne society loved more than following a trend set by the Lassiter family.

"I may be able to carve out a little time," she hedged, not wanting him to see how easily he'd forced her to capitulate. "Do you have particular designs in mind?"

"Tell you what. Why don't we discuss this further over dinner tonight."

"I'm sorry, I have plans for tonight." Plans that included a long soak with her feet in a tub filled with warm water and Epsom salts, followed by a home pedicure while she could still bend down and reach her toes. "Perhaps you could give me your contact number for while you're here. I'll call you when I'm free."

He gave her a narrow-eyed glance, then lazily got to his feet, reached into his back pocket for his wallet and slid out a card. She went to take it, but he didn't immediately let it go. Instead, he tugged it closer to his body, thereby tugging her a little closer, too.

"You'll call me?"

"Of course. We're closed tomorrow, but I'll check my schedule on Monday and call you then."

"I'll look forward to it," he said with a lazy wink and released the card.

She followed him from the office into the showroom. Even though she'd worked here since she was a teenager, she was still attuned to the sweet, luscious fragrance of the blooms she had on display. The various layers of scent filled the air with a strong feminine presence. A complete contrast to the powerful masculinity that was Dylan Lassiter.

Jenna held the front door to the store open for him.

"Thanks for stopping by," she said as he stepped past her and onto the sidewalk.

Just as he did, a large delivery truck passed on the street. The subsequent whoosh of warm air hit her full on, the gust plastering her short-sleeved tunic against her body. Dylan didn't miss a trick. His eyes drifted over the new fullness of her breasts, then lower, to where her waist had thickened, and to the gentle roundness of her tummy. He stared at her for what felt like an aeon before his eyes flicked upward to her face.

What she saw reflected back at her had the ability to nail her feet to the ground, right where she stood. She'd read about his convivial side, his laissez-faire attitude to life and his ability to continually land on his feet even as he eschewed traditional choices. Conversely, it was widely known that he was a perfectionist in the kitchen, which took a keen mind and grim determination.

The expression that he presented to her belonged to a different man entirely. This was the face of the CEO of the Lassiter Grill Corporation, not the playboy, not the one-time lover. No, this was the face of a man who had a question and, she thought with a shiver, would do whatever it took to get his answer.

"Looks like we have a bit more than just flowers to discuss. I think we'd best be having that dinner mighty soon, don't you?"

He turned on the heel of his hand-tooled boot and strode toward a dark SUV parked a few spaces down the street. She couldn't help but watch the lithe way his body moved. Jenna closed her eyes for a second but still his image burned there as if imprinted on her retinas. And she knew, without a shadow of a doubt, that her time for keeping this baby a secret had well and truly passed.

Two

Dylan swung his SUV into the traffic and fought to control the anger that roiled inside him like a building head of thunderclouds.

She was pregnant. No wonder she'd been as skittish as one of Sage's newborn foals when he'd arrived. He was probably the last person on earth she either expected, or wanted, to see.

His baby? The timing would be about right—unless she was the type of woman who indulged in casual assignations with just about any man she met. The thought made her stomach pitch uneasily. He needed to know for sure if their encounter had resulted in pregnancy. God, pregnancy. A kid of his own. And with her.

It wasn't hard to recall how his eye had been drawn to her that cool March Friday. He'd wanted her, right there, right then.

He remembered his first sight of her as she flitted about like some exotic bird, her attention solely on the flower arrangements she'd designed for his sister, Angelica's, wedding rehearsal dinner—a dinner that had ended before it began when his adoptive father, J.D., had collapsed with a fatal heart attack—for a wedding that had been called off, permanently now it seemed.

The building had been full of people doing what they did best, but Jenna stood out among them all in her jewel bright colors. An effervescent energy simply vibrated off her. Their initial banter had been fun and she'd given as good as she got. But the real craziness had started the moment he caught her hand in his and pulled her into an alcove where he kissed her, so he could see for himself if she tasted as intoxicating as he'd imagined.

She'd spun out of his arms the instant he'd loosened his hold on her but the imprint of her slight frame against his body had stayed with him through the course of the next hour, until he'd known that one kiss was definitely not enough. Satisfied the catering team in the kitchen knew what they were doing, he'd hunted Jenna down as she'd applied the finishing touches to the floral design she'd created for the entrance to the Cheyenne Depot—a historic railroad station that had been converted into a popular reception hall. Hunted her down and entrapped her in his arms for what he'd planned to be just one more kiss.

One more kiss had turned into a frenzy of need and they'd found their way into the coat closet at the front of the building. In its dark recesses, they'd discovered just what level of delight they could bring each other to.

He'd never been the kind of guy who waited for anything to come to him. No, he always went out and got it. And he'd certainly gone out and gotten her—both of them swept along on a tide of attraction that still left him breathless whenever he thought about it. He'd had casual encounters before, but this had been so very different. But then his father had died and his world had changed.

By the time the formalities here in Cheyenne had been taken care of, he'd had to race back to L.A. to continue his duties as CEO of the Lassiter Grill Corporation. Hassling Angelica for the contact details of the florist she'd used for that night—a night from which repercussions continued to cause his sister pain—had seemed a cruel and unnecessary thing to do. Besides, he'd had enough on his plate with work. Now, it seemed, he had a great deal more.

His inattention to the road forced him to jam on his brakes when the traffic ahead slowed suddenly. He swore softly. Two hours. He'd give her two hours to call him about dinner—max. If she hadn't phoned by then, he'd sure as heck be calling her.

In the end it was fifty-eight minutes exactly before his cell phone began vibrating in his pocket. He took it out, a smile curving his lips as he saw the name of her store come up on the screen.

"I was thinking we could make it tonight," he said without preamble. "My place, seven o'clock."

"Y-your place?"

He rattled off the address. "You know where it is?"

"Sure. I'll find it," she answered, her voice a little breathless.

"Maybe I ought to pick you up. Don't want you changing your mind at the last minute."

"I won't, I promise. I'll see you at seven."

She hung up before he could say another thing. His mouth firmed into a grim line as he slid his phone back into his pocket. It was a rare thing indeed to find a woman of so few words. Even when they'd first met they'd been bigger on action than conversation.

That was certainly going to change. He had a list of questions as long as his arm and he wasn't letting her go until she'd answered every last one.

One thing was certain. If she was carrying his child, he was going to be a part of that baby's life. Losing his own parents when he was young, then being raised by his aunt Ellie and her husband, J. D. Lassiter, Dylan knew just how important family was. He'd been too young to remember his mom and dad properly, too young to mourn more than the sense of security he'd taken for granted from birth. After his parents died, however, that all changed, until Aunt Ellie and J.D. stepped in and ensured that he, his brother, Sage, and sister, Angelica, never wanted for a thing. Even after Ellie Lassiter passed away, her sister-in-law, Marlene, had become a surrogate mom to them. It had been family that had gotten them through.

Now, with J.D. gone, too, the whole concept of family was even more important to him than ever. His brother thought he was nuts putting so much store by it. At constant loggerheads with J.D. and determined to make his own place in the world, Sage had always insisted that the only family he needed was Dylan. As close as they were, Dylan had always wanted more. And, if Jenna Montgomery's baby was his, it looked like he might be getting it.

Jenna reluctantly got ready to go out to Dylan's place. He was a complication she would rather ignore right now, but clearly, he wasn't about to let that happen. She quickly showered, then took her time rubbing scented moisturizer into her skin. So what if she had just shaved her legs— they needed it. She certainly hadn't done it for *his* benefit.

Nor had she applied the makeup she barely ever wore anymore for him, either. She was doing this all for herself. Pure and simple. If it made her feel good, feel stronger, then she was doing it. The same principle applied to the clothes she'd chosen to wear tonight. The royal purple stretch lace dress flattered her figure, even with the additional curves that now showed. It empowered her, as did the black spike-heeled pumps she teetered on.

She paused for a moment to assess herself in the mirror. Too much? Her eyes scanned from her dark brown hair, worn loose and flat-ironed dead straight, to her shiny patent leather shoes. She swiveled sideways. This was a total contrast to the kind of thing she'd worn in recent weeks. And, yes, it was definitely too much—which was why she wasn't going to change a thing.

She grabbed her purse from the bed and told herself she was not nervous about this meeting. That's all it was. A meeting. She'd tell Dylan what she'd been planning to tell him all along, and that would be that.

She wouldn't be swayed by the depth of his blue eyes, or the careless fall of his hair, which always looked as if he'd just tumbled from bed. She knew he was handsome; she'd fallen prey to that so easily. She also knew he was successful and intelligent and had a charm that could melt a polar ice cap. But she'd be immune to all that now, too. At least she hoped she would be.

She'd had weeks to think about this. Weeks in which to decide that while Dylan should know about his baby, she was most definitely bringing it up on her own. She knew full well what not to do when raising a child. Her own parents had been the prime example of that. No, her baby would want for nothing. He or she would grow up secure in the knowledge of Jenna's love and protection.

A man like Dylan Lassiter, with his cavalier lifestyle, a girl for every day of the week, every week of the year, not to mention his celebrity status, which ensured he traveled constantly, did not fit into the picture at all. She'd taken a walk on that wild side of his and yes, she had enjoyed every precious second. But life, real life, had to be lived in a far more stable and measured way. She owned her own home and had a business that was doing well.... With a few economies she could and would do this all on her own.

With those thoughts to arm her, she locked up and

walked out to her car. Checking the map one more time, she headed north to the address he'd given her, on the outskirts of town.

Doubts began to assail Jenna as she pulled in between the massive gated pillars, each adorned with a wrought-iron, stylized *L,* at the entrance to the driveway. The drive itself had to be several football fields long. She knew the family was wealthy, but seriously, who did this? Who kept a property this immense when they spent only about two months of every year living here? The Lassiters, that's who. It was a stark and somewhat intimidating reminder of the differences between herself and Dylan, and it struck a nervous chime deep inside her.

What if he used his money and his position to make things difficult for her? She had no idea what he was really like, although she remembered, without the slightest hesitation, how he'd felt and how he'd tasted. He was forbidden fruit. The kind of man every woman, no matter her age, turned her head to watch go past. The kind of man every woman deserved to savor—as Jenna had—at least once in her lifetime. But he wasn't a forever kind of guy. She'd been thankful he hadn't contacted her after their…their…*tryst,* she reminded herself again. She definitely wasn't looking for the roller coaster ride or the intrusive media publicity a relationship with him would offer.

Almost everything she knew about Dylan Lassiter she'd gleaned from social media and word of mouth around town—of which there was plenty. He'd basically gone wherever whim had taken him, spurning the opportunities and advantages afforded him by his adoptive father, and refusing to go into the family business or even attend college. Jenna sighed. What would it have been like, she wondered, to be able to be so carefree? She knew he'd traveled widely, eventually training in Europe as a chef and then coming back to L.A. and building a solid name for his skills, together with a certain celebrity notoriety at the same time. His life, to her, just seemed so...*indulgent*.

Her upbringing had been as different from Dylan's as a bridal bouquet was from a sizzling steak platter. And from her perspective, while there was plenty about Dylan Lassiter to recommend him to anyone who liked to run fast and loose, there was very little to recommend him as father material.

That said, this baby was *their* creation. Dylan had rights—and she had no plans to stand in the way of those. But she also wanted her child to grow up secure, in one place, with a stable and loving parent. Not used in a tug-of-war between parents, as she had been. Not dragged from pillar to post as her father moved from country to country, then state to state in pursuit of some unattainable happily-ever-after. And certainly not implicated by her father's fraudulent schemes or left abandoned at the age of fifteen because her sole surviving parent was doing time in jail.

No, Jenna's baby was going to have everything she hadn't.

She gently applied the brake and her car came to a stop outside the impressive portico. She rested a hand on the slight mound of her belly, determined not to be totally overwhelmed by the obvious wealth on display before her. This baby had rights, too, and yes, he or she was entitled to be a part of what stood before Jenna. But right now she was the baby's only advocate, and she knew what was best for him or her. And she'd fight to her very last breath to ensure her child got exactly that.

She grabbed her bag and got out of the car. The front

door opened as she walked toward it, and Dylan stood on the threshold. Jenna's heart did that little double skip, just as it had the very first time she saw him. It was hard to remain objective when the man stood before her. He'd tamed his hair slightly, giving him a more refined look, and he'd changed his suit for a pale blue cotton shirt that made his eyes seem even bluer than before.

"You found the place okay?" he asked unnecessarily as she ascended the wide steps.

"Hard to miss it, don't you think?" she replied, not even bothering to keep the note of acerbity from her tone.

She didn't want him to think even for a minute that he had the upper hand in this meeting. He inclined his head slightly, as if acknowledging she'd scored a valid point.

"Come on in," he invited, opening the door wide. "You must be ready to put your feet up after working all day. Can I get you something to drink?"

"Just mineral water, if you have it, thanks."

She hadn't drunk alcohol since she'd known she might be pregnant. In fact, there were a lot of things she didn't eat or drink as a result of the changes happening deep inside her body.

"Sure, take a seat," he said, gesturing to the large and comfortable-looking furniture that dominated the living room off the main entrance. "I'll be right back."

He was as good as his word. She'd barely settled herself against the butter-soft leather of a sofa big enough to sleep on before he was back with two drinks. An ice-cold beer for himself and a tall glass of sparkling water for her.

"Thank you," she said stiffly, taking the glass from his hand and studiously avoiding making eye contact.

But she couldn't avoid the slight brush of fingers, nor could she ignore the zing of awareness that speared through her at that faint touch. She rapidly lifted the glass to her lips to mask her reaction. The bubbles leaping from the water's surface tickled her nose, further irritating her. She swallowed carefully and put the glass on the coaster on the table in front of her.

Dylan sprawled in the seat opposite, his large, rangy frame filling the chair. His gaze never left her face and an increasingly uncomfortable silence stretched out between them. Jenna cleared her throat nervously. Obviously, she was going to have to start this conversation.

"I—I wanted to say how sorry I was about your father's passing."

"Thank you."

"He was much respected and I'm sure you must miss him very much," she persisted.

"I do," Dylan acknowledged, then took a long draw of his beer.

Damn him, he wasn't making this easy for her. But then again, what had she expected?

"He'd have been proud of the new restaurant opening here in town," she continued valiantly.

"That he would."

"And you? You must be pleased with everything being on time."

"I am."

A muscle tugged at the edge of his mouth, pulling his lips into a half smile that was as cynical as it was appealing. Jenna suddenly had the overwhelming sense that she shouldn't have come here. That perhaps she should have waited a day or two before calling him. Hard on its heels came the contradictory but certain knowledge that she definitely should have been in touch with him long before now.

Was this how a mouse felt, she wondered, just before a cat pounced? Did it feel helpless, confused and frightened, with nowhere to look but straight into a maw of dread?

She watched, mesmerized, as Dylan leaned forward and carefully put his beer on the table. He rested his elbows on his knees, those sinfully dexterous hands of his loosely clasped between them. Warmth unfurled from her core like a slowly opening bud, and she forced her eyes to lift upward, to meet the challenge in his.

She fought to suppress a shudder when she saw the determination that reflected back at her. She reached for her water and took another sip, shocked to discover that her hand shook ever so slightly. She dug deep for the last ounce of courage she possessed. Since he was determined to make this so awkward, she'd find some inane way to carry the conversation even if it killed her.

"Thank you for asking me to dinner tonight. It's not every day I'm catered to by a European-trained celebrity chef."

She was surprised to hear Dylan sigh, as if he was disappointed in something. In her?

"Jenna, stop dancing around the issue and cut to the chase. Are you pregnant with my baby?"

Three

Dylan cursed inwardly. He'd been determined to be charming. He could do charming with his eyes closed and both hands behind his back. So why, then, had he so ham-fistedly screwed up what he'd planned to be a relaxing evening of fact-finding with a woman he'd been fiercely attracted to from the second he'd first laid eyes on her?

It was too late now. The words were out and he couldn't drag them back no matter how much he wanted to. He huffed out a breath of frustration. Jenna looked about as stunned by his question as he was at actually blurting it out that way. Damage control. He desperately needed to go into damage control mode, but try as he might, he couldn't think of the words to say. What he wanted was the answer. An answer that only Jenna Montgomery could provide.

Beneath his gaze she appeared to shrink a little into the voluminous furniture. She was already a dainty thing—her small body perfectly formed—but right now she was dwarfed by her surroundings and, no doubt, daunted by the conversation they were about to have.

Dylan knew he should try and put her at ease, but the second she'd alighted from her car he had felt the shields she'd erected between them. It had aroused a side of him he hadn't displayed in years, made him deliberately un-

cooperative as she'd tried to observe the niceties of polite conversation. It had driven him to ask the question
that had been plaguing him since that gust of wind off
the road had revealed changes in her slender form that
were too obvious to someone who knew that form as intimately, even if fleetingly, as he had.

"Well?" he prompted.

"Yes," she said in a strangled whisper.

Dylan didn't know what to say. Inside he felt as if
he'd just scored a touchdown at the Super Bowl, but he
also had this weird feeling of detachment, as if he was
looking in on some other guy's life. As if what she'd
just said wasn't real—didn't involve him. But he was involved, very much so. Or at least he *would* be, whether
she liked it or not.

"Were you going to tell me sometime, or did you just
hope that I'd never know?"

As much as he fought to keep the hard note of anger
from his voice, he could feel it lacing every word. It left
a bitter taste in his mouth and he struggled to pull himself under control. He didn't want to antagonize her or
scare her away, and it wasn't as if he'd made an effort to
get in touch with her again before today. This was way
too important, and at the crux of it all an innocent child's
future depended on the outcome of tonight.

"I meant to tell you, and I was going to—in my own
time. I've been busy and I had a bit of a struggle coming to terms with it myself. Getting my head around how
I'm going to cope."

Jenna's voice shook, but even though she was upset,
he sensed the shields she'd erected earlier growing even
thicker, her defense even stronger.

"And you didn't think I should have known about this
earlier?"

"What difference would it have made?"

Her words shocked him. What difference? Did she think that knowing he was going to be a father made no discernible difference to his life, to how he felt about *everything?* Hell, he'd lost his own father only a couple months ago. Didn't she think he at least deserved a light in the darkness of mourning? Something to get him through the responsibility of having to get up every day and keep putting one foot in front of the other, all because so many other people depended on him to not only do exactly that, but to do it brilliantly—even when he wanted to wallow in grief?

"Trust me." He fought to keep his tone even. "It would have made a difference. When did you know?"

"About three weeks after we—" Her voice broke off and she appeared to gather up her courage before she spoke again. "I began to suspect I might be pregnant, and waited another week before going to my doctor."

Dylan sucked in a breath between his teeth. So, by his reckoning, she'd had confirmation that their encounter had resulted in conception for plenty of time. She could have shared the news—no matter how busy she was.

Damn it, he'd used a condom; they should have been safe. But nothing was 100 percent effective, except maybe abstinence. And there was one thing that was guaranteed, when it came to Jenna: abstinence was the last thing on Dylan's mind.

Even now, as quietly irate as he was right this second, she still had a power over him. His skin felt too tight for his body, as if he was itching to burst out and lose himself in her. His flesh stirred to life even as the idea took flight. Desire uncoiled from the pit of his belly and sent snaking tendrils in a heated path throughout him.

No one had had that power over him before. Ever.

Yet this diminutive woman had once driven him to a sexual frenzy that had tipped over into sheer madness. She still could.

A ringing sound penetrated Dylan's consciousness, a much needed reminder of the here and now and the fact that Jenna sat opposite him, quite a different woman from the one he'd so quickly but thoroughly made love to two and a half months ago.

"I'll be right back," he said, surreptitiously adjusting himself as he rose from the seat. "I need to check on something in the kitchen."

After a quick examination of the beef bourguignonne simmering on the stovetop, and checking that the rice in the cooker was fluffy and ready, he grunted with satisfaction. They would continue this discussion at the table, where, hopefully, he'd find his manners again and stand a better chance of hiding the effect she had on him.

He returned to the living room and painted a smile on his face.

"Dinner's ready. Would you like to come through to the kitchen? I thought we could eat in there, if you're comfortable with that."

"Since I usually eat standing up at the store or off a tray on my lap when I'm home, just sitting at a table sounds lovely."

She stood and smoothed her clothes, her hand lingering on the tiny bump that revealed a child of his now existed. It hit Dylan like a fist to the chest. His child. Someone of his blood. Everything else in his life right now faded into the background as that knowledge took precedence. Now there was another generation to think about, to protect and to teach.

The thought filled him with a new sense of purpose, of hope. The past five years had been challenging, the past couple of months even more so. But this baby was a new beginning. A reason for Dylan to ground himself in what was good, and to put some much needed balance back in his life, balance that was sadly lacking. This baby, his son or daughter, was a lifeline out of a spiral of work and hard play that had threatened to consume him. One way or another he would be a part of his child's world—every single day if he could, although that would take some engineering with him based in L.A. and Jenna here in Cheyenne. Whatever the logistics, he was prepared to work this situation out. He just needed to be certain that Jenna felt the same way.

She crossed the room to where he stood, and he put his hand at the small of her back and guided her through to the kitchen. He felt her stiffen slightly beneath his touch, and heard her breath hitch just a little. Knowing she wasn't as unaffected by him as she pretended went a long way toward making him feel better about the semi-erection he was constantly battling to keep in control.

He seated her at the square wooden table in the kitchen and gestured to the vase containing a handful of wild-flowers he'd found on his four-acre property when he'd gone to walk off some steam this afternoon.

"They could probably have done with your touch," he said as he turned to the oven to take warmed plates out and lay them on the table.

"They look fine just the way they are," Jenna commented.

But as if she couldn't resist, he saw her reach out and tweak a few stems. Before he knew it, the bouquet looked a hundred times better.

"How do you do that?" he asked, bringing the Dutch oven filled with the deliciously fragrant beef across from the stove.

"Do what?"

"Make a jumble of weeds look so good."

She shrugged. "It's a knack I picked up, I guess."

"What made you decide to work with flowers?"

"I didn't, really." She sighed. "They kind of picked me."

"Not a family business, then?" he probed, curious to discover just how she had ended up under Mrs. Connell's roof.

Jenna gave a rueful laugh. "No, not a family business at all, although once I started working at the store it felt like home to me."

There was a wistful note in her voice, one he wanted to explore further, but found himself reluctant to. There was time enough to find out all her secrets, he told himself.

He spooned rice from the cooker onto the warmed plates, and put them on the table.

"This looks great," Jenna commented, leaning forward to inhale deeply. "And smells even better. To be honest, I think your skills with food far outweigh mine with flowers. I can barely reheat a TV dinner without burning something."

Dylan feigned horror. "Wash your mouth out. TV dinners? You're going to have to do much better than that for the baby."

He reached for a ladle and spooned a generous portion of the beef onto her plate before serving himself. When she didn't immediately pick up her fork, he sat back and looked at her. Her lips had firmed into a mutinous line and there was a frown of annoyance on her forehead.

"What did I say?"

"I didn't come here to be told what to do. Maybe it's better if I go."

She pushed back her chair a little, but before she could go any farther he reached out and grabbed her hand.

"Okay, truce. I will try not to tell you what to eat, but you have to admit, for me it comes with the territory. It's what I do. It's in my nature to want to feed people well."

It was also in his nature to want to lift her from her chair, march her to the nearest accommodatingly soft surface and relive some of the passion they'd shared. She looked down at where his fingers were curled around her wrist, and he slowly eased his grip and let her go.

"As long as we're clear on that," she muttered, scooting her chair closer to the table again and lifting her fork.

She scooped up a mouthful and brought it to her lips. His brain ceased to function as she closed her eyes and moaned in pleasure. Other body parts had no such difficulty.

"That's so good," she said, opening her eyes again.

For a second Dylan allowed himself to be lost in their chocolate-brown depths. Just a second. Then he forced himself to look away and apply himself to his own meal.

"Thanks, I aim to please," he said with a nonchalance he was far from feeling.

It didn't seem to matter what he did or what he said, or even how she reacted to any of it—he was drawn to her on a level he'd never experienced before. Sure, that could play to his advantage, but he had the sneaking suspicion that Jenna Montgomery was a great deal more hard-headed than her feminine presence at his table suggested.

"Home grown?" she asked, spearing some beef and popping it into her mouth.

For a second he was distracted by her lips closing around the fork, then the enticing half smile they curved into as she tasted and chewed.

"Yeah, from the Big Blue. Nothing but the best."

"Your cousin runs it, doesn't he? Chance Lassiter?"

"And very well, too. It's in his blood."

And therein lay the rub. While he and Sage had been raised Lassiters, they weren't Lassiter by birth. Not like Chance, not like their sister, Angelica. It was one of the reasons why this baby meant so much more to Dylan than he had ever imagined. This child was a part of his legacy, his mark on the world. It was all very well gaining fame and fortune for doing something you excelled at and loved, but raising a child and setting him or her on a path for life—nothing compared to that.

"Have you thought about what you're going to do when the baby is born?" he asked, deliberately changing the subject.

"Do?"

"About work."

"I'll manage. I figure that in the early stages I should be able to keep the baby at work with me."

He nodded, turning the idea over in his mind. "Yes, sure—initially. I think that would be a good idea."

"I'm sorry?"

He looked at her in puzzlement. But his confusion didn't last long.

"What you think should matter to me, why, exactly?"

He let his fork clatter onto his plate. "Well, it is my baby, too. I have some say in what happens to him or her."

Even though he'd tried to keep his voice neutral, some of his frustration must have leaked through.

"Dylan, as far as I'm concerned, while you have rights to be a part of this baby's life, it doesn't mean you have a say in how I bring it up."

"Oh? And how do you see that working? Just let me jet in every now and then, have a visit and then jet out again?"

"Pretty much. After all, you live most of the time in L.A., or wherever else in the world you're flying off to—not here where the baby and I will be. Obviously, I won't stand in your way when you want to see him or her, though, as long as it's clear I'm the one raising the child."

That was not how things were going to happen. Dylan's hands curled into fists on the table and took in a deep, steadying breath. "That's good of you," he said, as evenly as he could. "Although I have another suggestion, one that I find far more palatable, and which will be better for all of us."

She looked at him in surprise. "Oh? What's that?"

"That we get married and raise the baby together."

To his chagrin she laughed. Not just laughed but snorted and snuffled with it as if she couldn't contain her mirth.

"It's not so impossible to think of, is it?" he demanded.

"Impossible? It's ridiculous, Dylan. We barely know one another."

He nodded in agreement. "True. That's something easily rectified."

All humor fled from her face. "You're serious, aren't you?"

"Never more so."

"No. It would never work. Not in a million years."

"Why not? We already know we're…" he paused a moment for effect, his eyes skimming her face, her throat and lower "…compatible."

"Great sex isn't the sole basis for a compatible marriage," she protested.

"It's a start," he said, his voice deepening.

Hot color danced in her cheeks—due to anger or something else? he wondered. Something like desire, perhaps?

"Not for me it isn't. Look, can we agree to disagree on

the subject of marriage? I've already said I won't stand in your way when it comes to seeing the child. Can we leave it at that for now?"

"Sure, for now. But, Jenna, one thing you will learn about me is that I never give up. Especially not on something this important."

Four

Jenna's heart hammered a steady drumbeat in her chest. He looked deadly serious. This wasn't how she had imagined their meal together going, not at all. She certainly hadn't imagined that he'd spring an offer of marriage on her like that.

Sure, there was probably a list as long as her arm of women who would jump at the opportunity. But she wasn't like that. And she'd meant it when she'd said his life was in L.A. and not here, because it *was.* While it was true that he'd been in Wyoming more often lately, it was only because of the new Grill opening in town. Once that was up and running he'd be straight back to the West Coast. Back to his high life and being featured in the celebrity news with his beautiful women.

No, marriage to Dylan Lassiter didn't even bear thinking of, she decided as she forced herself to take another bite of the melt-in-your-mouth perfection of the meal he'd prepared. He might be spending more time in the boardroom these days, she mused, but he hadn't lost his knack in the kitchen.

Maybe it would be worth marrying him just to have meals like this every day, she thought flippantly. An image of him barefoot and in the kitchen, wearing an apron and not much else, hovered in her mind, sending a pull of longing through her.

No, get a grip on yourself, she chided silently. She'd never settled for anything less than perfection when it came to a relationship. It was why she so rarely dated. That was why her behavior with Dylan back in March was such an aberration.

Once people began to notice her pregnancy, she had no doubt there'd be a whole ton of questions asked. Uncomfortable questions. Her hard-fought-for privacy would be invaded—her reputation open for all of Cheyenne to discuss. It shouldn't bother her, but it did. She knew what it was like to be the focus of unwanted attention, and she'd worked hard to stay out of the public eye ever since.

"I'm glad you acknowledge that our child is important. I happen to agree, which is why I'm not going to rush into anything or make any decisions today," she finally stated.

"You're important, too, Jenna," he answered softly.

For a second she felt a swelling in her chest—a glimmer of something ephemeral, an intangible dream emerging on the periphery of her thoughts. Then reality intruded. She shook her head.

"Don't lie to me, Dylan. We both know that since March neither of us has made any attempt to contact or see one another, until today. In fact, if you didn't have the restaurant opening coming up, we probably wouldn't even be here right now."

"I don't know about you, but I've thought about that evening a lot."

Jenna couldn't stop the warm tingling sensation that spread from the pit of her belly at his words.

"Don't!" she blurted.

"Don't what? Don't admit that we were blisteringly good together? Tell me you haven't thought about us, about what we did—and haven't wanted to try again. Even just to see if it wasn't some kind of weird fluke."

"I—"

Her throat closed up, blocked by a swell of need so fierce it overwhelmed her. She forced herself to erase the visual image that now burned in the back of her mind. An image he'd put there without so much as a speck of effort because it was always there, always waiting to be brought out into the light and examined, relived. She squirmed on her seat, suddenly uncomfortable, aching. For him. For more.

"Fine," she muttered curtly. "We were good together, but that's no basis for a future. We are two totally different people. Our lives barely intersect."

"That's not to say that they couldn't. Don't you want to just try it?"

He looked so earnest, sitting there opposite her at the table. It would be all too easy to give in, but she'd worked too hard for too damn long to even consider giving up her hard-won freedom, not to mention her hard-earned respect from the community.

She herself had been the product of a hurried marriage, one that hadn't worked on any level and had led to hardship and unhappiness for all concerned. She would not inflict that on her baby. No matter how enticing that baby's father was. No matter how much she wanted him.

What did he know of marriage, of commitment? Their own liaison was a perfect example of the impulsive life he led. See something? Want it? Have it, then just walk away without a backward glance. She couldn't risk that he'd do that with their child, let alone her. Not now, not ever.

"No," she said firmly. "I don't. Please don't push me on this issue, Dylan."

"Okay," he acceded.

She felt her shoulders relax.

"For today," he amended.

And the tension was right back again. He cracked a smile and she was struck again by his male beauty. There was not a thing about him, physically at least, that didn't set her body on fire. As to his morals, well, that was something else entirely. But her behavior didn't reflect so well on her, either, she reminded herself.

"Don't look so serious, Jenna. We'll declare a truce for this evening, all right?"

His voice was coaxing, warm. And almost her very undoing.

"Truce, then," she agreed, and applied herself again to her meal.

It truly was too good to ignore and, much as she hated to admit it, he was right that she should be eating better. Weariness had been quite an issue for her, and while prenatal vitamins and supplements were helping, nothing really substituted for a healthy diet and plenty of rest.

"More?" Dylan asked when her plate was empty.

"I'm stuffed," she said, leaning back in her chair with a smile on her face. "That was excellent, thank you."

"Just part of the package," he said with a smile. "So, are you too stuffed to think about dessert? Can I tempt you with some raspberry and white chocolate cheesecake?"

"Tempt me? Are you kidding? Of course I want dessert."

When he took the dish from the refrigerator she almost dissolved into a puddle of delight.

"You made that, too?" she asked as he sliced a piece for her. She reached out and nabbed a white chocolate curl from off the top, laughing as he went to slap her hand away and missed.

"Not me personally this time. It's one of the desserts

we're trialing for the steak house," he said, sliding her plate toward her. "I picked it up this afternoon."

She spooned up a taste and then another.

"Good?" Dylan asked.

"Divine. Don't talk to me, you're messing with my concentration."

He laughed aloud and the sound traveled straight to her heart and gave it a fierce tug. *Oh, yeah, it was all too easy to think you could fall in love with a man like Dylan Lassiter,* she told herself. He was the whole package. Not just tall, dark and handsome, but wealthy, entertaining to be with and bloody good in bed. Well, in a coat closet, anyway. And then there was the near orgasmic cooking.

Don't go there, she warned herself. But it was too late. Arousal spread through her like a wildfire. Licking and teasing at her until she felt her breasts grow full and achy, her nipples tightening and becoming almost unbearably sensitive against the sheer fabric of her bra. She knew the very second Dylan's line of vision moved, the precise moment he became aware of her reaction.

"Remind me to feed you cheesecake more often," he said, his voice slightly choked. "I'm going to make coffee. Can I offer you some, or a cup of something else, maybe?"

"Hot tea, please," Jenna answered, fighting to get her wayward hormones back under control.

Dylan stood and turned away from the table, but not before she noticed he wasn't exactly unaffected himself. So it seemed the crazy attraction between them showed no sign of abating. What on earth was she going to do about it?

Nothing. Abso-freaking-lutely nothing at all. They'd get through the rest of this evening. They might even discuss the baby a little more. But they were not going to do a single thing about this undeniable magnetism between them. After all, look where it had led them the last time.

Dylan ground fresh coffee beans and measured them into his coffeemaker, taking his time over the task. This was getting ridiculous. Why couldn't she see just how suited they were to one another? Why wouldn't anyone want to take that further? Her physical attraction to him was painstakingly obvious. Not that he needed any help in that department, but it was a natural trigger for his own.

There was a lot to be said for being a caveman, he thought as he switched on the electric kettle and heated the water for her tea. He'd never before felt so inclined to drag a woman by her hair into his lair and keep her there—making love to her until she no longer wanted to leave. He gave himself a mental shake. No, that image was completely unacceptable. He liked his women willing. He'd never used force or coercion before and he wouldn't start now—no matter how tempting Ms. Jenna Montgomery made the idea seem. Somehow, he had to make her see that they'd be good together. Good enough for marriage and raising a kid.

He heard the scrape of her spoon on the plate as she finished her cheesecake, and he returned to the table with their hot drinks on a tray.

"Shall we take these back through to the living room?" he suggested.

"Sure."

She got up to follow him and his eyes drifted again to her belly, to where his baby lay safely nestled. It roused something feral in him. Something he'd never experienced before today. Something he knew, deep in his heart, would never go away. He knew it was possible to love another person's child—knew it from firsthand experience, from *being* that child, from being loved. For some reason, though, knowing it was his son or daughter she carried made Dylan feel as if he could give a certain superhero a decent run for his money in the leaping tall buildings department.

He also knew he'd do anything, lay down his life if necessary, to provide the best for his kid.

Jenna returned to her seat on the sofa and Dylan sat next to her, a sense of satisfaction spreading inside when she didn't scoot away from him.

"When's the baby due?" he asked, after taking a sip of his coffee.

"First week in December, all going well."

"A baby by Christmas," he mused aloud, struck by how much his life could change in a year.

"Life will be different, that's for sure."

"So what have you planned so far?"

Suddenly he needed to know everything she'd already done, and what she wanted to do for the rest of her pregnancy. This should involve him.

"Well, I've started getting a few things for the spare room in my house, you know, to turn it into a nursery. I found a bassinet at a yard sale last weekend. I'm going to reline it and get a collapsible stand. That way I'll be able to use it in my office at the store as well as at home, until the baby gets a little bigger."

Dylan suppressed the shudder that threatened to run through him at the thought that his child would have secondhand anything. Did that make him a snob? Probably. He and his brother had shared things as they grew up, and there'd been nothing wrong with that. It didn't stop him from wanting to race out to the nearest store and buy all new equipment for his child, though.

Jenna, sensitive already, obviously picked up on his thoughts. "What's wrong? You think our baby is too good for a secondhand bassinet?"

"Actually," he started, thinking he needed to tread very carefully, "I was thinking more along the lines of what I could do to help out financially."

If she was scouring yard sales, maybe she was a bit stretched when it came to money. She had the store, but also had her own home. Financing both took a lot of hard work and determination. And dollars and cents.

"I can manage, you know," she said defensively.

"The point is you don't have to *manage*," he said. "I meant what I said when I told you I'm going to be a part of this baby's life, and I don't just mean the occasional visit. I'm happy to support you both."

She looked as if she was about to bristle and reject his words, but then she slumped a little, as though a load had been lifted from her slender shoulders.

"Thank you." She sighed softly. "It won't be necessary, but I do appreciate the offer."

"Hey," he said, taking one of her hands in his and mentally comparing how small and dainty it felt in his much larger palm. It roused a fierce sense of protection inside him. One he knew would be smacked straight into next week if he showed her even an inkling of how she made him feel. "We got into this together, and that's how it's going to stay."

She looked up at him, her dark eyes awash with moisture. "Do you think we can do that? Stay friends through this?"

"Of course we can."

"It's not going to be easy."

"Nothing worthwhile ever is," he commented.

At the same time he promised himself that no matter

what, she would not be doing this on her own. And one way or another, he'd get her to change her mind about marrying him. Now that he had her back in his life, he didn't want to let her go again. There was a damn fine reason why he hadn't been able to shake her image from his thoughts every single day. Now he had every incentive to find out exactly what that reason was.

Five

By the time Jenna rose to leave, weariness pulled at every muscle in her body. She was grateful tomorrow was Sunday. A blessed day of rest, with time to weigh up everything that had happened since Dylan Lassiter had walked back into her life. Maybe she'd get to work in the garden for a while, too—she always found that restful. Or even a lazy stroll around the Cheyenne Botanic Gardens might be nice.

"It's late," she said, stifling a yawn. "I'd better get home. Thank you for tonight. I mean that."

"You're welcome," Dylan replied, getting to his feet and putting his hand at the small of her back again.

Despite her exhaustion, her body responded instantly. It would be so easy to give in. To turn toward him, press her body against his large hard frame and sink into the attraction between them. To allow him back behind the barriers she'd erected when the reality of their encounter had hit home. Instead, she put one foot in front of the other and headed for the door.

"Are you okay to drive?" he asked, a small frown of concern causing parallel lines to form between his brows. "I don't mind dropping you home. I can always bring your car to you tomorrow."

"No, I'll be all right. Thank you."

"You know, independence is fine and all that, but accepting help every now and then is okay, too."

"I know, and when I need help, I'll ask for it," she answered firmly.

She could feel the heat rolling gently from his body, bringing with it the leather and spicy wood scent of his cologne. It made her want to do something crazy, like nibble on the hard line of his jaw, or bury her nose in the hollow at the base of his throat. Man, she really needed to get out of here before she acted on those irrational thoughts.

"Thanks again for tonight," she said.

"You're welcome. We still have plenty more to discuss. Okay if I get in touch?"

She hesitated, wishing she could say no, and knowing she needed to say yes. Given the way he tugged at her, emotionally and mentally, she knew it wasn't going to be easy sharing a baby with him. Jenna settled for a quick nod and all but fled down the stairs. But he was right at her side, so that when she got to her car it was his hand that opened the door for her. He leaned down once she was settled inside.

"Red fluffy dice?" he asked with a chuckle when he saw the things dangling from the rearview mirror of her ever-so-practical station wagon.

"I have dreams of owning a red convertible one day. *Had* dreams," she corrected.

With the baby on the way, that was one dream that would have to be shelved for a while. Maybe even forever.

"Classic or new?" Dylan persisted.

"Classic, of course."

He gave her a wink. "That's my girl."

She felt an almost ridiculous sense of pride in his obvious approval, and forced herself to quash it. It didn't matter whether he approved of her dreams or not. They weren't going to happen, not now. She was doing her best to hold everything else together. Luxury items were exactly that: luxury. An extravagance that was definitely not in her current budget.

"Well, good night," she said, staring pointedly at his hand on the door.

To her surprise he leaned down and reached for her chin, turning her head to face him, before capturing her lips in an all too short, entirely too sweet kiss.

"Good night. Drive safe," he instructed as he swung her door closed.

Her hands were shaking as she started the car and then placed them on the wheel. As she drove around the turning loop to head down the driveway, she sought refuge in anger. He'd done it on purpose, just to prove his point about compatibility. The thing was, she *knew* they were compatible sexually. Now they had to be compatible as parents. Seemed to her they'd definitely missed a few steps along the way, and now there was no going back.

His proposal of marriage was preposterous. She sneaked a glance in her rearview mirror at the two-story house, fully lit up from the outside and looking as unattainable as she knew a long-term relationship with a man like Dylan Lassiter was, too. Jenna forced her eyes forward, to focus on the road ahead, and her future. One where she'd have to fight to keep Dylan Lassiter on the periphery if she hoped to keep her sanity.

By the time she rolled her car into her garage and hit the remote to make the door close behind her, she felt no better. Seeing Dylan again had just put her well-ordered world into turmoil. She'd had enough chaos to last a lifetime. It was why, when she'd been placed with Margaret Connell after her father was jailed, she'd put her head down and worked her butt off to fit in and to do things right. Mrs. Connell's firm but steady presence had been a rock to a fifteen-year-old teetering on the rails of a very unsteady life.

Mrs. Connell had not only provided a home for her, she'd provided a compass—one Jenna could live by for the rest of her life. The woman had also provided a sense of accountability, paying Jenna a wage for the hours she spent cleaning up in the florist shop after school and learning how to put together basic bouquets for people who came in off the street and wanted something quick and simple.

By the time Jenna had finished high school, she'd known exactly what she wanted to do. She'd put herself through business school, spending every spare hour she wasn't studying working in the flower store, which she'd eventually bought and made her own. Mrs. Connell was now enjoying a well-earned retirement in Palm Springs, secure in the knowledge that all her hard work, both with Jenna and the business, hadn't been in vain.

Jenna calculated the time difference between here and Palm Springs. It probably still wasn't too late to call Mrs. Connell, and she so desperately needed the guidance of someone else right now. Someone older and wiser. Someone stronger than she was. But that would mean disclosing how she'd gotten herself into this situation. Telling someone else about behavior that she wasn't terribly proud of. The last thing Jenna wanted to hear in her mentor's voice was disappointment.

She climbed out of her car, went inside the house and got ready for bed. For all that Dylan had said about wanting to be a part of everything, she'd never felt so alone in her life, nor so confused.

Would he be so keen, she wondered, if he knew exactly who she was and what her life had been like? It was hardly the stuff of Disney movies. Her father had come home from work one day when she was nine, to find Jenna alone after school—her mother having abandoned them to sail, from New Zealand and her family, with the outgoing tide and pursue her dream of being a singer on a cruise ship. He'd pulled up stakes by the time Jenna was ten, and taken her to his native U.S.A., where he'd told her again and again that they'd strike it lucky any time, and that happily-ever-after was just around the corner for them both.

Unfortunately, his idea of luck had been inextricably linked to fleecing older, vulnerable women of their wealth, and using his looks and charm to get away with it. Until one day he'd gone a step too far.

Jenna pushed the memory to the back of her mind, where it belonged. She'd learned the hard way what it meant to be an unwitting public figure, and how cruel the media could be. Given the Lassiter family profile, any relationship between her and Dylan would be bound to garner attention—attention she didn't want or need. For her own sake, and that of her unborn baby, she would do whatever it took to keep a low profile.

She slid between the 800-thread-count bed linens she'd happily picked up in a clearance sale, and smoothed her feet and legs over the silky soft surface. She might not be in his league financially, but she didn't do so badly. She could provide for her baby, who certainly wouldn't want for anything. So what if some of their possessions were a little care-worn or threadbare or—Jenna grimaced in the dark, remembering Dylan's reaction—secondhand. She would manage, and her private life would remain that way: private.

* * *

Dylan whistled cheerfully as he drove away from the classic car dealer, relishing the sensation of the wind ruffling his hair. The thrum of the V8 engine under the shiny red hood before him set up an answering beat in his blood. Today was a perfect day for a picnic and he had just the partner in mind to share it.

After swinging by the Grill to make sure everything was running smoothly, he put together some food and drink, checked the GPS on his phone and headed toward Jenna's address, which he'd happily plucked from a phone book. He was curious to see where she lived—where she'd planned to raise their baby. *Planned* being in the past tense, because now that he was on the scene, he didn't intend for them to live apart. All he needed to do was convince Jenna.

When he turned into her driveway he had to admit he was surprised at where she lived: it was a new neighborhood, the streets lined with modern homes. Skateboards, bikes and balls littered the front yards. He could see why she'd be comfortable here. Even though he hadn't seen anyone yet, there was a sense of community and projected longevity about the area.

He saw curtains in windows on either side of her house twitch as he turned off the ignition and sat a moment in the car. A smile played at his lips. Neighborhood watch, no doubt. It was good to know Jenna had people looking out for her when he wouldn't be.

Dylan got out of the car. He couldn't wait to see her face. He strode up the path that led to the front door and pressed the doorbell. Nothing. He waited a minute and tried again.

"You looking for someone?" A woman's voice came

from over the well-trimmed hedge on one side of Jenna's property.

"Yes, ma'am," he answered with a smile that wiped the distrustful look off her face in an instant. "Is Jenna home?"

The woman blushed prettily. "She's gardening out back. Just follow the path around the side of the house and you'll find her."

"Thank you."

Clearly, he'd passed muster. He jangled the car keys in his hand as he made his way around to the rear of the house. It only took a minute to find her. She knelt by a raised bed of roses, pulling vigorously at the weeds and dumping them in a bucket beside her.

"That looks suspiciously like hard work. Need a break?"

Jenna jumped at his voice and looked up, using the back of her hand to push a few loose strands of hair from her eyes.

"No, thank you. This job isn't going to do itself."

"Why don't you get someone else in to help?"

"Because first, I don't have money to throw around like that, and second, I enjoy it."

His eyes swept across her face, taking in the smear of dirt on her flushed cheek and the dark shadows that were painted beneath her eyes.

"If you tell me what to do, will you let me help for a while so I can take you out to play after we're done?"

She looked startled for a minute. "Seriously?"

"Yeah, of course I'm serious."

She pursed her lips a second, making him wish he could taste them again. Last night's chaste kiss had done nothing but ignite a desire for more.

"You don't really want to garden, do you."

It was a statement, not a question. He shrugged. "I'd be lying if I said I did. But I'll do what's necessary to achieve my objective."

Jenna narrowed her eyes. "And your objective is…?"

"Taking you out to lunch."

"I'm not dressed for lunch."

"That's okay, I prepared a picnic."

A wistful expression replaced the wariness in her eyes. "A picnic? I've never been on one of those."

He couldn't hide his shock. "Never?"

She shook her head.

"Then let me be the one to remedy that for you." He stepped closer and took her hand in his, stripping off her gardening glove before doing the same with the other hand. "The weeds will still be here when we get back."

"Unfortunately."

"Then worry about them later. Come with me," he coaxed. "Now."

For a second she chewed at her lower lip, her gaze fixed on her hand still held in his.

"Shouldn't you be at work? The grand opening's not all that far away now, is it?"

"No, it's not. I've already been by the Grill today. Everything's under control. Besides, I'm the boss—when I say I need a bit of time out, I take it. So, are you coming?"

"Okay. But let me freshen up first."

"No problem. I'll meet you out front."

As much as he was itching to step inside her small home, to see what things she'd chosen to surround herself with, he sensed he'd pushed enough for one day. That she'd agreed to come out on the picnic with him was a coup in itself, and he'd take that victory before reaching for the next one.

"Give me ten minutes, then," she said, already walking toward the screened back door.

"No problem. Take all the time you need."

The door slammed behind her and he took a moment to look around the garden. Here and there were splashes of color, interspersed among some midsize trees. It was a good backyard, as backyards went. But it wasn't where his kid would grow up playing. Kids needed space—and he'd be providing it. Eventually.

Inside Jenna quickly changed from her tattered and dirty gardening gear into a T-shirt and jeans. To her surprise, she couldn't fasten the top button on her jeans, which was something she'd been able to manage, barely, last week. That was one thing pregnancy definitely guaranteed—change, and plenty of it.

She washed her face and smoothed on some tinted moisturizer. It would probably be too much to apply her usual makeup, but she wasn't going out with Dylan without feeling at least a little in control. She attempted a quick brush of her hair, but it was impossible to smooth the tangles that a sleepless night had wrought, so instead she carelessly swept it up and secured it with a few pins, then tied a scarf around her head.

Surveying the results in the mirror, she allowed herself a grin of approval. Her T-shirt was long and loose-fitting, her bra made of sturdier material than last night's. She'd be fine.

It took only a few seconds to lock up and head out the front door, but the instant her feet hit the porch she came to an abrupt halt. There, in her driveway, sat the car that had featured in all her fantasies. It was as if Dylan had reached into her mind and extracted the information himself, she thought, as she surveyed the fire-engine-red Ca-

dillac convertible with whitewall tires and the top down.
It was her dream car—right down to the red fluffy dice,
twins to her own, hanging in front.

Dylan straightened from where he leaned against the
passenger door, and flashed her a smile.

"You like it?"

Jenna forced herself to walk toward him, still locked
in a state of disbelief.

"I love it. What…? How…?" She shook her head. "Did
you hire it for the day or something?"

"No," he said. "After you mentioned it last night I
thought I'd look around online. I saw it this morning
and bought it."

"You *bought* it? Just like that?"

He lifted the keys and dangled them in front of her
face. "You want to drive?"

"Do I!" She snatched the set from his hand and tossed
her bag in the back before racing around to the driver's
side. She threw herself into the seat and ran her hands
over the steering wheel and the dash. "I can't believe it.
You really bought this today?"

Dylan seated himself next to her with another one
of those smiles that made her insides melt. "Sure did.
Shall we give her a run? I was thinking we could head
out to the Crystal Lake Reservoir, find a nice spot and
have our picnic."

It was at least a forty-minute drive to get there. She'd
love every second of it.

"Let's get going then," she said, smiling back at him.

He stared at her, the smile on his face changing, his
expression becoming more serious. He lifted a hand and
touched her cheek with one finger.

"You're so beautiful, you know that?"

Jenna didn't know what to say. Her stomach clenched

in reaction to his touch, to his softly spoken words. She wanted to refute it, but at the same time wanted to hold those words in a safe place in the corner of her heart, forever.

Dylan let his hand drop, breaking the spell. "C'mon," he said, "let's get this show on the road."

The engine's powerful roar when it turned over sent a shiver of happiness up her spine.

"I still can't believe you bought this," she said as she backed out the drive and onto the street. "That's just so impulsive."

"Why shouldn't I?" He shrugged. "I bought it for you."

Six

Dylan watched as her expression turned from one of sheer glee to one of horror. She jammed on the brakes, throwing him slightly forward.

"Whoa, there. Easy on the brakes, sweetheart."

"Tell me you didn't do that."

"Didn't do what?"

"Buy me this car."

"If I did, I'd be lying."

"I can't accept it." She shook her head vehemently. "That's just crazy."

"It is what it is."

But he was walking on thin air. She was out of the car—leaving the engine still running, the driver's door open—and standing on the sidewalk, her arms wrapped around herself in protection as if warding off some terrible pain.

Dylan shot out of the car and closed in on her, but she put up her hands, halting him in his tracks. What had he done? He could see her shaking from here.

"What is it? What's wrong?"

"You're trying to buy me, aren't you?" Her voice quavered and her face was pale. "Trying to make me do what you want."

"Jenna, the car's a gift."

"Some bloody gift!" she snapped, her eyes now burning as she looked at him squarely. "I know what a car like that is worth. You don't just buy one in the morning and give it away by the afternoon."

"Jenna, I'm hardly a poor man. I want to see you have nice things."

"Why?"

He was confused. *"Why?"*

"Yes, why? Why me? Why now? As I said last night, we hardly know each other. We had sex *once*. We're having a baby. That's it. That's all there is to us, and now you're buying me a Cadillac?"

"Maybe I'm buying it just because I can. Maybe I need to prove to you that I can provide for you, that you don't need to do all this on your own, that you don't need to keep pushing me away. Yes, we're having a baby— *together*. I know we're doing this all back to front, but I want to get to know the mother of my kid. I want to see if we can be a couple."

Jenna's eyes flicked away from his, but not before he saw the sheen of tears reflected there. Before he could close the distance between them, the first drop spilled off a lash and tracked down her cheek. She lifted a hand and furiously scrubbed it, and those that followed, away.

"I don't want the car," she said adamantly, through clenched teeth. "I will not be bought."

"Fine. I'll take it back tomorrow. But can't we just enjoy today? Take it for a spin. Enjoy it while we can?"

He tentatively put his arms around her, pulling her closer. She lifted her chin and blinked away the moisture in her eyes. She was one tough chick, that was for sure.

"Just for today?" she asked, her voice tight.

"Sure, if that's what you want."

"So it's not mine anymore?"

"Nope."

He felt a pang of regret that he'd have to say goodbye to the big red beast, but if that's what it took to begin to win her trust, then that's what he'd do. Jenna looked past him at the car and he could see the longing in her gaze. Even though she wanted it, she would still refuse it. Her moral ground remained solid, even in the face of a desire so hungry she was almost salivating with it.

"Jen?" he said, noticing that he wasn't the only one with eyes on her right now. In fact, not only were curtains twitching, but there were faces appearing at windows, too.

"What?"

"I don't want to rush you, but shall we go? We're providing a bit of a show here."

"Oh, God," she groaned. Her lips firmed and she drew in a breath. "Fine, let's go then. But you can drive."

He didn't argue. Instead he guided her around to the passenger side of the car and helped her into her seat before closing the door and heading to the driver's side.

"You okay?" he said, reaching across the car to squeeze her hand.

"I'm fine. Just go, will you?"

"Whatever the lady wants."

The trip to the reservoir was accomplished in silence. Dylan kept throwing surreptitious looks at Jenna during the journey and was relieved to note the tension in her body had begun to ease as they headed out of Cheyenne. As they wound along the route that led to the reservoir he kept an eye out for a place with a vantage point overlooking the lake. He gave a grunt of satisfaction when he found just the spot, and brought the car to a stop beneath some trees.

Through a gap between the trunks, the lake gleamed like highly polished mirrored glass, reflecting the surrounding rock formations and flora in a perfect echo of their surroundings.

Dylan got out of the car and opened the trunk, unloading a large rubber-backed blanket and a picnic hamper. He passed the blanket to Jenna.

"Here, find us a spot. I'll bring the food and drinks."

She took it without a word and headed a little closer to the water. When he joined her she'd spread it out in a sunny spot in a small clearing.

"I…I'm sorry. For before," she said in a stilted tone. "I'm sure my reaction probably appeared over the top to you."

"A little, but that's okay. No apology needed."

"No," she said vehemently. "You were trying to be nice and I threw it back at you. I just…"

She averted her gaze out over the water, as if searching for something to draw strength from to help her get her words out. Dylan waited quietly, watching the internal battle reflected on her face.

"I just don't like it when people think they can buy someone else with things, or when other people accept them."

Dylan scratched his jaw as he played her words over in his mind. Sounded as if there was a story behind that statement. Would he ever hear it from her? He hoped so.

"Fair comment," he answered, putting the hamper and the small drinks cooler down at the edge of the blanket. "And duly noted for future reference."

"You're mad at me, aren't you?"

"Not mad. Disappointed, maybe, that you don't feel you can accept the car from me, but hey, I'm a big boy now. I'll get over it."

And, he added silently, *I'll find a way through that wall of yours, one day.*

He opened the cooler and handed Jenna a bottle of mineral water before snagging one for himself.

"Italian?" she asked, looking at the label. "Is there anything you do normally?"

"Define *normally*."

She chewed on her lower lip a moment before speaking. "Well, inexpensively, then."

"Why should I?"

"Because one day you might wish you had, for one. What if the bottom drops out of steak houses and the Lassiter Grill Corporation goes down with it?"

Dylan shook his head, a smile playing around his mouth. "It'll never happen. People like food, especially good food. Plus, they're more conscious these days of how their food is raised. The cattle on the Big Blue are free range and grass fed. Only nature's goodness. The beef served in the Grills is the best in the country, probably the world, and I ensure our staff and our dishes live up to that promise."

"You're very confident."

He paused a moment, thinking about it. "Yeah, I guess so. I haven't always been this way. Being raised by J.D. made a big difference, though. It took a while, but we got there."

"You lost your parents quite young, didn't you?"

"Sage was six and I was four. I don't remember too much about them, but Sage—" Dylan sighed "—he took it real hard. Kind of put himself in opposition to anything J.D. said or suggested from day one."

"I always wished I had a brother or sister," Jenna said wistfully, taking a sip of her water.

He found his gaze caught by her actions, riveted by the movement of her slender throat as she swallowed.

"Only child?"

"Only and lonely," she said lightly, but even so, he heard the truth behind her words.

"Where did you grow up?"

"All over. I was born in New Zealand and grew up there before my mom and dad broke up."

"New Zealand, huh? I thought you had a bit of an accent."

"Hardly," she snorted. "When we heard my mom had died, Dad packed us up and brought us back here to the States. Any accent soon got teased out of me at school."

"Back to the States?"

"My father's American. We traveled a bit and eventually I got to settle here in Cheyenne. The rest, as they say, is history."

Painful history by the sound of things. What she didn't say spoke louder than what she did. Dylan turned to the hamper in a bid to break the somber mood that had settled over them. He reached past the cooling pads he'd packed around the food and lifted out a couple covered containers. He popped the lids off, revealing in one, sandwiches made with freshly baked whole grain bread, and in the other, a selection of sliced fruit.

"I can promise you I prepared these myself and that I carefully studied what you can and can't eat in pregnancy," he said, putting the dishes down between them on the blanket.

Jenna picked up a sandwich and studied the filling. "You mean you washed and dried the lettuce in here yourself?"

"With my own fair hands," he assured her with a grin. "But don't tell any of my kitchen staff that or they'll expect me to do everything myself."

They ate in companionable silence and Dylan quietly cleared up when they were done.

"Tell me why you've never been on a picnic before," he suggested, interrupting her contemplation of the lake's beauty.

She remained silent for a while, and so still he began to wonder if she'd even heard him.

"I guess I just never had the opportunity before," she eventually said, but he could tell she was leaving plenty out of that trite little answer. "It's nice, though. Thank you."

He'd have to be satisfied with that, he told himself, and filled in the gap in conversation that followed with his own tales of the times he and Sage had raided their aunt's kitchen to take a picnic outdoors. He loved it when he made Jenna laugh. It lifted the shadows from her eyes and showed a different side to her than the one that constantly met him head-on and tried to thwart his every attempt to spoil her.

It wasn't much later that Jenna lay down in the sunshine and closed her eyes. She was asleep in seconds. The day's temperature was still pretty mild, but the wind had a bite in it, so Dylan got his sweater from the trunk of the car and gently put it over her as she slept.

He stretched out beside her, wishing they had the kind of relationship where he could pull her into his arms, curl around her body and keep her warm with his heat alone.

All in good time, he assured himself. All in good time.

Jenna woke with a shiver as a shadow passed over the sun. She opened her eyes to see a cloud sailing overhead. She realized that she had something covering her and lifted it to see what it was. Dylan's sweater? When had he done that? A warm sensation filled her at his consideration.

For a minute or two she just lay there, absorbing the

sounds of the insects and birds, and relishing the peaceful surroundings, before she became aware of a deep steady breathing that came from close by. She turned her head and saw Dylan lying on his back beside her. Well, that answered one question, she thought. He didn't snore. His arms were bent up under his head and even in sleep the latent strength of his biceps were obvious. She observed the steady rise and fall of his chest. His T-shirt had risen above the waistband of his jeans, exposing just a hint of his lower belly.

At the sight of his bare flesh a tingle washed through her, and her fingertips itched to reach out—to touch and trace that line of flesh with the faint smattering of dark hair. She didn't dare give in to the temptation, though. Things were already incendiary between them. They didn't need any further complications and right now, to her, a relationship with Dylan was a complication she'd rather avoid.

She looked past him to the Caddy, sitting in all its shiny glory under the trees.

What kind of man did that? she asked herself. Who on earth bought a classic car on a whim for someone he barely knew from Adam, just because she said it was a dream of hers? The thought triggered a memory of the day her dad had come to pick her up from junior high. They were living in Seattle at the time and he'd rolled up in a brand-new 5-series BMW, looking like a cat that got the cream.

Soon after, she'd met the reason behind the car. His latest conquest had bought it for him when he'd admired it one day as they'd passed a dealership. It was payment, he'd said flippantly, for services rendered. Jenna hadn't fully understood, at the time, just what he'd meant by that. Just as she'd never understood, until she got older, why all the women he dated had at least ten, sometimes more, years on him. Or why he was always turning up with expensive things. Even back then it had made her uncomfortable. It hadn't seemed right, especially when her dad never appeared to hold down a real job. But her father had just laughed off her concerns when she got brave enough to broach them.

He'd never stayed with anyone for long. All of a sudden she'd wake one morning and they'd be on the move again. Sometimes clear across the country in pursuit of his next happily-ever-after. She'd had no idea that even while he was dating one woman, he was casually grooming up to five others via the internet. Nor did she know that when they'd moved to Laramie when she was fifteen, and she'd shaved her head as part of a school-run fund-raiser for one of their cancer-stricken teachers, that her father would use that picture to create a whole new set of lies to fleece his victims with.

Lies that eventually saw him hauled off to jail for fraud and caused her to be placed here in Cheyenne with Margaret Connell. Jenna squeezed her eyes shut. She didn't want to think about that time—about the gross invasion of her life by the media, the reporters who'd accused her of being complicit in her father's schemes. She'd been just a kid, with nowhere and no one else to turn to. When child services had taken her, she'd wondered if she was going to end up in prison, too. After all, she had no one else. Her mother was dead. They'd learned she'd died less than a year after she'd left them, choking on her meal aboard ship. And there'd been no other family to come in and pick up Jenna's fractured life.

Mrs. Connell had been a much-needed anchor and a comfort. For the first time in her life Jenna had been able to stay in one place for more than what felt like five minutes. It hadn't broken her reticence about making friends, though. Even now she found it a struggle to get close to anyone. She'd learned growing up that it was better that way, better than having to say heart-wrenching goodbyes every time her life turned topsy-turvy again.

She studied Dylan's strong features. Even in sleep he looked capable, secure in his world. What would it be like to take a chance on him? To just go with the flow and let him take control of her and the baby's worlds?

Even as she considered it, the idea soured in her mind. And what about when he lost interest and moved on? she asked herself. As her father had moved on so many times? As Dylan himself had moved on from various publicly touted relationships in his life? She wouldn't do that to her child, or to herself. They were both worth so much more than that.

Self-worth. It was a hard lesson to learn, but it was one Margaret Connell had reinforced every day Jenna had lived under her roof. It was why Jenna could never accept anything that was a facsimile of a real life, or a real love. She'd been there already and she still bore those scars. Probably always would.

Dylan's eyes flicked open and he turned his head to look at her. "Nice sleep?" he asked with a teasing smile.

"Mmm, it was lovely. Thank you for this. It was a great idea."

"Even though we had to do it in that?" He nodded over toward the Cadillac.

"Yes." She heaved a mock long-suffering sigh. "Even though we had to do it in that."

He rolled onto his side, facing her. "You certain you don't want it? You're allowed to change your mind, y'know."

"No, thank you. I don't want it. Besides, there's no anchor point for an approved child restraint," she said soberly, reminded anew of how much her life, her dreams, would change in a few short months' time.

"Good point. Maybe I'll keep it for date nights."

Jenna felt her entire body revolt at the statement. Here she was contemplating approved child restraints for *their* baby, and he was busily planning his next night out with some woman.

"*Our* date nights," he specified with a wicked grin that told her he knew exactly what she'd been thinking.

"We won't be having any of those," she said in an attempt to suppress his humor, especially since it was humor at her expense.

"I think it would be good for our kid to see our common interests don't just revolve around him or her. I've seen too many couples lose sight of what they feel for one another when they're crazy busy with their kids and with work. They lose themselves, and worse, they lose each other."

His words, spoken so simply, ignited a yearning inside her that made her heart ache. He made it sound so simple. But she knew to the soles of her feet that life just wasn't like that.

"You're forgetting one thing," she murmured. "We aren't a couple."

He leaned a little closer. "We could be."

And with that, he inched a tiny bit nearer and closed his lips on hers.

Seven

The second their lips touched, Dylan knew it was a mistake. If only because they were in a public place and there was no way he could take this all the way. Not here, not right now—even though his body demanded he do so. He should have waited until they were behind closed doors. Someplace where they could relish their privacy and take the time to explore one another fully. Enjoy one another without fear of discovery.

It didn't mean he couldn't make the most of the moment, though, and he slid his hand under Jenna's head, cradling her gently as he sipped at the nectar of her mouth. Her lips were soft and warm, pliant beneath his. A rush of need burst through what was left of his brain, urging him to coax, to plunder, to take this so much further than a kiss. But he held back.

He wanted her, there was no denying it. But he was prepared to take this slowly—as painful as that would be—if that was what he had to do to convince her he was serious.

Jenna's hands lifted up to bracket his face, and he took that as permission to use his mouth to tease her some more—to open her up and taste her, their tongues meshing, their teeth bumping. How he wished he could see all of her, and touch and taste every inch.

She was pregnant with his child and he'd never seen her naked. Just the idea of it made his nerves burn with raging heat, and urged him to go further. But still he held back, eventually forcing himself to ease away, to create at least a hand span of distance between them. It wasn't enough. There could be an entire continent between them and it wouldn't deaden how he felt about her. How much he wanted her.

"Think about it," he said, rolling away and standing up.

"Think about what?" she asked, looking up at him with a dazed expression in her eyes.

He fought back a smile. Maybe that's all he'd have to do to convince her they should get married. Kiss her senseless until she simply said yes.

He offered her a hand and helped her to her feet, then picked up and folded the blanket, slinging it over one arm. "Us. Together. You know—a couple."

She started to shake her head, but he reached up and gently took her chin between his fingers.

"Think about it, Jenna. At least give me a chance to prove to you how good we could be together. Not just as lovers, although I know that will take us off the Richter scale—again. But as a couple." His hand dropped to the slight mound of her belly. "As a family."

Before she could respond, he grabbed the cooler and turned and walked to the car. He didn't want to see rejection in her eyes. Not when he'd realized, even as he spoke, just how much he wanted this. He'd lost his parents when he was only four, Aunt Ellie—his adoptive mother—only three years after that. He was luckier than most. He'd had four parents in his lifetime, five when he counted Marlene as well, and each one had left an imprint of devotion. An imprint so indelible it had made him promise himself that, when he eventually had a family, he would be a part of his children's lives. They would know the security of parents who loved them unreservedly. He'd had that, and he would walk over flaming gas ranges if necessary, to make sure his kid had it, too.

Jenna appeared beside him, handing him the now empty hamper as he stowed the cooler and blanket in the trunk.

"Will you at least consider it?" he asked, closing the trunk with a solid thud.

She looked up at him, vulnerability reflecting starkly at him from those dark brown eyes of hers. "Okay."

One small word and yet it had the power to change everything about the life he lived, about the choices he'd made. It should be daunting and yet it made him feel excited on a level he hadn't anticipated. Made him almost feel a sense of relief that he could, maybe, stop searching for that one ephemeral thing that he'd always felt was missing from a life rich in so much already. The thing he'd sought in travel and women and had yet to find. He shoved his hands in his jeans pockets to hold himself back, to stop himself from giving in to the impulse to grab her and twirl her around with a whoop of satisfaction.

"Thank you."

The drive back to her home was completed in silence but it was a comfortable one. With one hand on the wheel, he'd reached across and tangled his fingers in hers for most of the journey. It wasn't something he'd ever stopped to consider before with anyone else but, right now, he felt as if the connection between Jenna and him had solidified just that bit more. And it felt strangely right. By the time he dropped her off and saw her into her house he was already formulating plans for tomorrow. Plans that most definitely featured Jenna Montgomery.

Monday morning, the smell of fresh paint and new carpet filled Dylan's nose the moment he strode in through the front door to check on progress at the restaurant and was pleased to see the delivery of the new furniture was well under way. He stopped a second to inhale the newness, the potential that awaited. The excitement that had thrummed quietly inside of him built to new levels. It was happening. He'd felt excited about each of the previous three Lassiter Grills to date but this one was even more special to him than the others.

Hard on the heels of his excitement came a thrust of regret that J.D. couldn't be here to see their dreams become a reality. It was still hard to accept that his larger-than-life, hard-as-nails father figure was really gone. At moments like this, it was that much worse.

God, but he missed that man. And as much as he grieved for J.D. with a still-raw ache, he owed it to the old man to make sure that everything about this new restaurant would match, if not eclipse, their existing venues. That meant keeping up his hands-on approach to business and proving that J.D.'s faith in making him CEO of the Lassiter Grill Corporation was well founded.

With a nod of approval, he walked past the massive polished wood bar to the double doors that led into the kitchen. As much as he loved the front of the restaurant, this was the hub of what made the Lassiter Grills great. This was where he belonged, amongst the stainless steel countertops and the sizzle and steam and noisy organized chaos of cooking. The last of the equipment had been installed a week ago and his team had spent the past week trialing the signature dishes that would be specific to the Cheyenne steak house, along with the much loved menu that made the Lassiter Grills so popular in L.A., Las Vegas and Chicago.

It was ironic, Dylan thought as he surveyed the hand-picked team, that he'd spent the better part of his adult years running away from responsibility and family commitment and yet in the past five years he'd embraced every aspect of both of those things. Clearly, he was ready to settle down.

The very idea would have sent a chill through him not so long ago but over the past few months, well, it had tickled at the back of his mind over and over again. Maybe it was losing J.D. so suddenly that had made him begin to question his own mortality and his own expectations of life. Or maybe he was finally, at the age of thirty-five, mature enough to accept there was more to life than the hedonistic whirlwind that had been his world to date. It was a sobering thought.

Satisfied that his staff had it all under control, he drove over to Jenna's store. He pushed the door open and stepped in, his nostrils flaring at the totally different scents in the air, compared to those back at the Grill. As before, there was no one in the front of the store, but he could hear off-key humming coming from out back. The humming came closer and he saw Jenna walking through, carrying an armload of bright fresh daisies. She'd pulled her hair into a ponytail today, lifting it high off her face and exposing her cheekbones and the perfectly shaped shells of her ears. He imagined taking one of those sweet lobes between his teeth and his body stirred in instant response.

"Oh, I didn't hear you come in," she said, placing the flowers on the main counter.

"No problem. I haven't been waiting long."

He studied her carefully. She looked tired, a little pale.

As if she'd had about as much trouble getting to sleep last night as he had. He couldn't help himself; he lifted a hand and skimmed the back of his fingers across her cheek.

"You okay? You're not overdoing things, are you?"

She pulled away from his touch. "I'm fine, Dylan. Trust me, I won't do anything to harm this baby. I may not have planned for it, but now that it's a reality, there's nothing I want more in my life."

There was a fierce undertone to her voice that convinced him she was telling the truth. It didn't stop him worrying, especially when she bent to shift a large container filled with water to another spot on the floor.

"Here," he said, brushing her aside. "Let me do that for you. I thought you had staff to help you."

Jenna stood back, a quizzical expression on her face. "I do, but they're part-time. I open and close the store each day."

"Then let me do the heavy stuff today."

"No problem, but I'll be back to doing it again tomorrow. Unless you plan on being here for me every morning to help me rearrange everything in the store?

"If that's what it takes," he said as he straightened. "Or I could arrange that you had someone here first and last thing to do this if you'd rather."

She shook her head, a rueful smile pulling at those kissable lips of hers. "I'd prefer to do it myself."

"Hey, can you blame me for wanting to take care of you? You're carrying precious cargo there."

A wistful expression settled on her face. "Yeah, I am, aren't I? But I still have a job to do. Now, I guess you're here to see what I've worked out for the flowers for the opening? I've sketched a few ideas and also thought I'd put something together quickly with what I had out back."

She grabbed a square of burlap and some twine, and

wrapped them around a plastic-lined cardboard base. She then moved around the store, selecting stems of greenery and laying them on the counter next to the daisies. Before his eyes, she used the assortment of items to create a vision of beauty.

"Hmm, needs some berries, too, I think," she muttered, more to herself than anything. A second or two later she turned the arrangement around to face him. "There, what do you think?"

He eyed the compilation of color and texture and decided he liked it very much. She had a genuine talent for this. There was nothing generic about what she'd created. She'd taken his minimal instructions and put together what he'd wanted without his fully understanding it himself.

"That's great. So these would be for the tables?"

She nodded. "And then I'd do something bigger, maybe in a crate propped on some hay bales, in the foyer. What do you think?"

"I think you're an artist."

She gave a little shrug. "I have a knack, I guess."

"Don't sell yourself short, Jenna." Dylan cast his eye over the arrangement again. "I'm thinking, though, that the colors need to be bolder. These might disappear in the decor. Why don't you come back with me to the restaurant for lunch? You can get a better feel of what I mean."

"You're going to feed me again? Three times in three days? This is getting to be a habit."

"We need live subjects to try the menu, and some of our waitstaff need the experience, too," he explained, even though it was more a case of now that he'd seen her again, he didn't want to let her out of his sight. "You'd be doing me a favor."

He didn't fool her for a second, that much was obvious

from the smile that spread across her face. "A favor, huh? Well, since one of my workers is due in shortly, I think I'd be able to slip away for an hour for lunch."

"Just an hour?"

"I do have a business to run. Besides, won't it be better for your team to get used to working with customers who are in a hurry?"

"Good point," he acceded, even though he wished he could just whisk her away for the afternoon and keep her to himself.

"I'll come at one, okay? I have some orders I need to put together for our delivery guy and—" she glanced at her wristwatch "—I need to get to work on them now if they're to be ready on time."

"That's great. I'll be waiting."

Jenna watched him leave, surprised at herself for agreeing to lunch today. Despite all her tossing and turning last night, and her resolve to try and keep things purely business between them, it appeared she wanted to see him again more than she'd realized. True, this visit was under the guise of checking the decor of the restaurant, but the prospect of spending more time with him, even if only an hour, made her bubble inside, as if the blood in her veins was carbonated.

Valerie, her assistant, came in through the front door.

"Wow, tell me the guy just leaving wasn't an apparition."

"Oh, no." Jenna smiled. "He's quite real."

"Just my luck to be running late today, or I could've served him."

Jenna looked at her long-married friend, a mother of four, and raised a brow. "Seriously?"

"Well, a girl's entitled to her dreams, isn't she? He

looks vaguely familiar. What did he want? Please tell me he wasn't ordering flowers for his girlfriend."

"That was Dylan Lassiter," Jenna said with a laugh, "and he's ordering flowers, through us, for the latest Lassiter Grill opening."

"He is? Wow, that's got to be good for business. You think they'll keep us as a regular florist? It'd be a fabulous lift for our profile."

"I haven't discussed future work with him, but we have a good start. Which reminds me, if I don't get my work out of the way this morning, I won't be able to make it to the restaurant for our next meeting at one."

"I could always go for you," Valerie suggested with a wink.

"I'm sure you could," Jenna said, still laughing, and imagining Dylan's face if she took Valerie up on her offer. But an unexpected surge of possessiveness filled her. She didn't want anyone handling Dylan's requests but herself. Dragging her thoughts together, she briskly continued, "C'mon, help me with these orders before Bill gets here for pickup."

The balance of the morning flew by. While she worked, Jenna considered the ramifications of having a regular corporate account with the Lassiter Grill. The exposure for her business would be great, there was no denying it. She made a mental note to raise the subject with Dylan, and went to get ready for their lunch date.

She was running late by the time she arrived at the restaurant but luckily found a parking space just around the corner.

Dylan was waiting by the front door as she jogged up the sidewalk.

"I was beginning to think you'd stood me up," he said, opening the door for her and guiding her inside.

"Just a busy morning, that's all."

"We have company for lunch. My brother, Sage, is joining us, together with his fiancée, Colleen."

Jenna immediately felt at a disadvantage. "Oh, I wish you'd said so. I'm not dressed for company."

Dylan turned his gaze to her and she felt him assess her from top to toe. "You look mighty fine from where I'm standing."

Heat bloomed in her chest and flooded all the way up to her cheeks. Great, now she'd look like a little red fire engine when introduced to his family.

"I mean it, Dylan," she said awkwardly.

"So do I. Seriously, you have nothing to worry about. They're my family and they'll love you any way you're dressed."

He grabbed her hand and led her inside. Her eyes darted around the dining room, taking in the design features that were such an integral part of the pictures she'd seen of each Lassiter Grill. While the building had a stone exterior, the interior walls were log lined. Her eyes roamed over the high ceilings, hung with massive iron fans, and down to the wooden plank floors. A huge floor-to-ceiling stone fireplace held a place of dominance in the center of the restaurant. What they'd sacrificed in space they'd more than made up in character. She loved the ranch-style atmosphere. It was realistic without being over the top. An idea popped into her head.

"I've been thinking about the opening and about how you'll dress the tables for the night," she began.

"Uh-huh?"

"What do you think of burlap table runners on white linen?"

He paused a moment, considering. "That sounds like a good idea. D'you have pictures of what you're thinking?"

She nodded.

"Good, we can talk about them after lunch. C'mon over and meet my brother."

Her nerves assailed her and she tugged at Dylan's hand, making him stop and turn to face her.

"Do they know?"

"Know?"

"About us, about the baby."

"Not yet. Do you want to tell them?"

She shook her head vehemently. It was enough that Dylan knew, but she wasn't ready to share the news with others.

"Okay, but they're going to find out sooner or later," he warned.

"Just not yet, okay?"

They crossed to the table where the couple were seated. Sage rose to his feet as they approached. Slightly taller than his brother, with medium brown hair sprinkled with a touch of gray at the temples, he looked like a man used to being in control. He also didn't seem like the type you could hide anything from for long, and the way his gaze dropped to her hand clasped in Dylan's larger one, and then back to his brother's face, told her he saw a great deal more than what lay on the surface. She pulled free of Dylan's grip as a frisson of unease wended its way down her spine. She so wasn't ready for this.

"Jenna, this is my brother, Sage, and his fiancée, Colleen. Sage, Colleen, this is Jenna Montgomery."

"Pleased to meet you," Jenna said, taking the bull by the horns and stepping forward with her hand outstretched. "Dylan's asked my firm to do the flowers for the opening. I hope you don't mind my crashing your lunch, but he wanted me to see the restaurant before we confirmed a color palette."

She knew, as soon as the words left her mouth, that she'd overcompensated. As if sensing her discomfort, Colleen rose from her chair with a welcoming smile and shook Jenna's hand.

"I'm pleased to meet you. Didn't you do the flowers for—"

"Angelica's rehearsal dinner, yes," Dylan interrupted, his swift interjection earning him a curious glance from his brother.

"I was going to say for a friend of mine's dinner party a couple of weeks ago," Colleen corrected smoothly, still holding Jenna's hand. "She was thrilled with what you did. I know you'll do a great job for Dylan."

Jenna began to feel herself relax as Colleen took over the conversation. It didn't mean that Sage stopped his perusal of her, but she allowed his fiancée to distract her as they turned the discussion to the pair's upcoming wedding and what the best flowers and style of bouquet might be. Across the square table, Dylan and his brother bent their heads together in deep discussion. Despite the differences in their coloring, their eyes were very much the same and the shape of their jaw and their mannerisms spoke of their strong familial connection.

Dylan looked up and flashed Jenna a smile before shifting his attention back to his brother, and she felt herself relax a little more. Colleen was very easy to talk to, and by the time they'd ordered off the menus and awaited their meals, Jenna found herself beginning to enjoy the other couple's company. Sage, while appearing a little standoffish at first, was clearly very much in love with his fiancée, and Jenna had to quell a pang of envy.

What would it have been like to meet Dylan and let a relationship with him progress the way most normal couples started? She shoved the thought aside for the piece of mental candy floss it was. She couldn't afford to indulge in thoughts of what might have been. She had been dealt large doses of reality in her lifetime, and coping with those, while keeping her wits about her, was paramount.

When their orders came Jenna applied herself vigorously to her serving of smoked baby back ribs with fries and grilled corn on the cob, which certainly beat a hasty sandwich grabbed in between customers at her shop. It felt strange being the only diners in a restaurant, waited on so industriously by the staff there, although the other three seemed to take it in stride. Jenna took her cue from Dylan and tried to act as if she was used to this kind of thing.

About thirty minutes later, when Sage made his apologies and rose to leave the table, Jenna decided she should do the same.

"No, wait for me here while I see Sage and Colleen out," Dylan insisted. "We still have those colors to discuss, as well as the table dressing you mentioned."

She nodded and turned her attention to the glass of mineral water Dylan had ordered for her. The water reminded her she needed to find the restroom. She got up and moved to the front of the restaurant, but before she could reach the facilities she overheard Sage talking to his brother.

"She's pregnant, Dylan. I hope you know what you're doing."

"I know she's pregnant. It's my baby."

"It's what?" Sage couldn't hide the shock in his voice.

"It's my baby and I'm going to marry her."

"Don't be a fool, man. It's not like you were even dating. You don't *know* her or anything about her. You don't even know for sure if the baby's yours—it could be anyone's. Shouldn't you at least wait until it's born, so you can do a paternity test?"

The sour taste of fear filled Jenna's mouth. This was exactly what she'd hoped to avoid. She didn't need Sage's censure or his implications. Yes, she had behaved like a tramp that Friday evening back in March. But so had Dylan. It was unfair that there was always one set of rules for guys and then another for women. The fact remained that they were dealing with the outcome of their dalliance, but the last thing she wanted was for it to become common knowledge. Not when she'd worked so hard, for so long, to wash away the taint of her father's behavior from her life.

She was where she was and who she was despite her upbringing. And, dammit, she would make a great mother even if juggling her business and motherhood would be a challenge. Jenna knew, to her cost, that life wasn't about easy solutions. It was about making the right choices and working hard to hold on to them.

"I don't like your insinuation, brother. Be very careful what you say about Jenna. I plan to marry her and I will raise my kid with her."

Dylan's tone brooked no argument and Jenna's spirits lifted to hear him defend her.

"Look, I didn't mean to offend you, but let's be realistic about this. At least have her investigated. If you won't, I will."

Ice cold sensation spilled through her veins. Investigation? It wouldn't take much to unearth her past, a past she'd fought hard to put behind her. Dylan's voice was raised when he answered his brother.

"I am being realistic about this, Sage. You know what family means to me. You know what *you* mean to me. I am not walking away from my son or daughter, and I'm not walking away from Jenna."

She held her breath through the tense silence that developed between the brothers, but she couldn't help but shift slightly. She really needed to pee. Her movement must have made some sound, because Dylan turned his head, his eyes spearing her where she stood.

"Um, I was just looking for the restrooms?" she said, horribly uncomfortable that she'd been caught standing there, eavesdropping.

"Through there," he said, pointing.

She scurried in the direction he'd indicated. After she relieved herself, she washed her hands under cold water, and then assessed her reflection in the mirror. She'd faced condemnation before and survived. It wasn't pretty, but she'd do it again if she had to. She dried her hands and returned to the restaurant. Dylan stood waiting for her.

"I'm sorry you had to hear that."

"It's okay. It's only what everyone will think, anyway." She brushed it off, but a note of how she was feeling must have crept into her voice.

"Jenna, I—"

"Look, let's just leave it, okay? Thank you for lunch. Now that I've been here I think I'll have a better idea about what you'll need for the floral designs, and I agree, bold and strong colors will be best." She flicked a look at her wristwatch. "I need to get back to the store."

"What about the other matters we were going to discuss?" he asked, searching her eyes. But she found herself unwilling to meet his.

"I'll email you."

"That sounds suspiciously like a brush-off." He cupped her shoulders with his big strong hands, the warmth of them swiftly penetrating the thin knit jacket and silk blouse she wore. "I'm not giving up on us, Jenna."

"Dylan, there is no *us*."

"I refuse to accept that," he said succinctly. "And one thing you need to know about me is that when something or someone is important to me, I never give up. You are important to me, Jenna Montgomery. Don't doubt it for a second."

When had anyone ever said anything like that to her before and meant it? She'd tried these past few days to keep Dylan at a distance, emotionally at least, but those few words wedged a tiny crack in the shell that had formed around her heart and began to split it apart. And when he lowered his face to hers, and caught her lips with his own, she felt herself reaching up to meet him halfway, as needy as a flower seeking rain on a drought-parched prairie. Wanting his promises, wanting his attention as she'd never wanted anything from anyone before.

Eight

Two days later Dylan paced the confines of his L.A. office. He was restless. Something had shifted inside him last Monday at the new restaurant. From the second he'd seen Sage take in Jenna's presence at his side and come to the correct conclusion about her pregnancy, he'd known he would defend her to anyone for any reason. For all time.

During his training in France he'd heard people refer to a *coup de foudre*—love at first sight—and he'd eschewed it for the fantastical notion it was. But thinking about that split second when he'd first noticed Jenna back in March, it was the only way to describe how he'd felt and behaved that night. It certainly described how he felt now. His family would just have to struggle to understand. Hell, even he struggled to get a grip on just how much one woman could turn his world upside down.

Since he'd walked back into her world five days ago, his every thought had been consumed by her, his every action taken with her in mind. Now, instead of focusing on the business and meetings to discuss the commencement of their planned East Coast expansion that had called him back to L.A., he was resenting the fact that it had taken him away from Cheyenne—away from Jenna.

He'd called her last night, but he'd sensed a reserve in her again, as if overhearing Sage's words had somehow erected an invisible wall thwarting the tentative connection they'd been building on. If only Dylan hadn't been forced to let her leave on Monday. If only he'd been able to pursue that kiss they'd shared at the restaurant just a little further. Instead, she'd all but fled from him and he'd had to let her go, his cell phone ringing in his pocket even as he watched her flee.

It was as if she was too scared to trust him, too scared to allow him into her life. But there was more to it than that. So many more layers to Jenna Montgomery that his hands itched to peel away. He'd have to bide his time, though, at least until Saturday, when he was due back in Cheyenne.

Dylan came to a halt at his office window and looked down over the sprawling metropolis that was Los Angeles. This had been his home, his city, for the past five years, and he'd fit in here. After training and cooking in restaurants in continental Europe and the United Kingdom, he'd been ready to come back to the States, ready to take on his next role in his career. But with J.D.'s death he'd been forced to take stock, to reevaluate his belief system and what was important in his life.

Right now, he missed Cheyenne. More to the point, he missed a certain woman who lived there. The perfect solution would be to take her and simply transplant her here into his life, his world. But even he knew that wouldn't be fair to her. She had a life in Cheyenne, a business and a home. Until he'd shown up in her store, she'd had everything worked out quite perfectly, Dylan had no doubt.

He forced his mind back to work, back to the task at hand. He'd get through these days because he had to, and because, ultimately, doing so would let him return to where he most wanted to be right now.

His phone chirping in his breast pocket was a welcome interruption to the frustration of his thoughts.

"Lassiter," he answered, without checking the caller I.D.

"Hey, Dylan, it's Chance. How are you?"

"I'm good, thanks, and you? How're things at the Big Blue?" Dylan smiled as he spoke. A call from his cousin was always a welcome break from everything else.

"I'm thinking of putting a barbecue together for Saturday. Think you could handle someone else's cooking for a change?"

Dylan laughed out loud. "Sure. For you, anything."

"Great. I was also thinking you might have a certain someone you'd like to bring along with you?"

"You been talking to Sage?"

"I might have."

Dylan could hear the smirk that was undoubtedly on his cousin's face.

"Chance—" he said, a grim note of warning in his voice.

"Hey, I promise I'll be on my best behavior, truly. I just want to meet her."

"And if she doesn't want to come?"

"I guess I can probably feed you, anyway," Chance drawled teasingly as if doing so would be a great hardship.

"That's big of you."

"But I'm sure, with your charm and skills, you'll manage to get her to come along."

"I'll let you know. What time do you want us?"

"Let's make it early. Hannah is visiting with her little girl, Cassie. She's the cutest tyke."

Since the discovery that Chance had a half sister—his father's secret daughter—the family had been getting to know one another, with great results. Now Hannah was engaged to Logan Whittaker, the lawyer who had been responsible for finding her when the contents of J.D.'s will had become known, and their family continued to expand. It was a good thing, Dylan thought privately.

"You getting ready to settle down, cuz?" It was Dylan's turn to tease now.

"Not likely," Chance replied, "but it's hard not to love her. She's a good kid. Anyway, come around six."

Dylan did a little mental calculation. By the time Jenna closed shop on Saturday and he picked her up, they could just about make it.

"We might be a little late," he said, "but we'll be there."

"Great, I'll let Mom know. She loves having family over. The more the merrier, right?"

Right, Dylan thought grimly as he disconnected the call. Now all he had to do was convince Jenna she wanted to meet more of his family, when all they probably wanted to do was subject her to the third degree. Damn Sage and his flapping mouth. Still, when push came to shove, his family was the backbone of who he was today, and Dylan wanted Jenna to see that, to be a part of it and to want their baby to be a part of it also. This gave her a perfect opportunity to see just what his family's lives were like.

Dylan had never been happier to leave L.A. and take the flight that brought him back to Cheyenne. As he pulled up in his SUV outside Jenna's house, he saw her at the front door before he could even get out of the car. He'd toyed with bringing the Caddy—he hadn't quite been able to bring himself to part with it just yet—but he knew it would probably make her uncomfortable. Besides, with the temperatures tonight set to drop to around fifty degrees, they'd probably welcome the climate control in the SUV instead.

He got out from behind the wheel and walked around to open her door for her, his eyes drinking in her appearance. He hadn't seen her for four days, but it felt like four weeks. Was it his imagination or was her tummy just that tiny bit rounder, her breasts that much fuller? Everything inside him tightened up a notch.

"Hi," she said, ducking her head as if she was a little shy.

"Hi back," he replied, bending his head to kiss her on the cheek. She blushed a pale pink when he did. He loved that he could do that to her, unnerve her like that. "I missed you."

She flicked her gaze up toward him and he saw her bite her lip, an action that sent heat rushing to his groin.

"I missed you, too."

She sounded puzzled by the fact and it made him quirk his lips in a smile. Dylan handed her into her seat and closed the door, suppressing the urge to punch the air and give a primal whoop of satisfaction. Progress. At last he was making progress.

He filled the time during their thirty-mile drive out to the Big Blue with what he'd been doing in L.A.

"So your sister lives in the house in L.A., too?"

"Yeah. Dad bought the property about twenty years ago and Angelica has really made it her own. She has a knack for decorating, for making a place feel like a home." He sighed inwardly. "It's always good to see her, but she's been pretty angry since Dad died. Things are strained between all of us."

"Angry?"

"Yeah." Dylan suddenly wished he hadn't brought the

subject up, but it probably deserved airing. "Dad was pretty old-fashioned, but I always thought he was fair. What he did to her when he left a controlling share in Lassiter Media to her fiancé, rather than to her, was a slap in the face. It's really upset her, especially since she'd basically been the one running Lassiter Media up until J.D.'s heart attack."

"Wow, I can see why she'd be upset. Is that why the wedding got called off?"

Dylan nodded. It still made him sick to his stomach. "Lassiter Media was Angelica's life, and now she's left wondering if the whole reason Evan asked her to marry him was so he could gain control of the company. Not exactly the basis for a good start to marriage."

Jenna was quiet for the rest of the journey, until Dylan reached across the center console and laced his fingers through hers.

"You okay?" he asked, flicking her a glance.

"Just a bit nervous."

"Don't be. Chance is a great guy."

"Who else will be there?"

"His mom, Marlene—she'll love you, don't worry. And his half sister, Hannah, is visiting with her daughter, Cassie. And look, we're nearly there."

He pulled in through the gates to what had, in his mind, always been home. After his parents died, J.D. and Ellie had brought him and Sage here to the ranch. Originally, the main house had been far more modest, but as the Big Blue had become more successful, it was replaced by the two-story wood-and-metal structure they were now approaching. Wraparound porches with hand-hewn wooden railings graced both levels.

"Wow, this is quite a place," Jenna commented, sit-

ting up a little straighter in her seat. "You and Sage grew
up here?"

"Lucky, huh? Just think, all this land and these big
wide-open spaces for two little boys to burn their energy
off in. I had a great childhood."

It occurred to Dylan that she hadn't talked much about
her own upbringing. Aside from knowing she was born
in New Zealand and had, for the most part, grown up in
the U.S., he still had a lot to find out about her.

They got out of the car and walked up to the entrance.
Dylan pushed open the front door and guided Jenna inside, yelling out a "hello" as he did so. Footsteps sounded
in the hall and an older woman came forward.

"Dylan! Great to see you!" She enveloped him in a
huge hug.

"Aunt Marlene, I'd like you to meet Miss Jenna Montgomery. Jenna, this is my aunt, Marlene Lassiter."

"Mrs. Lassiter, I'm pleased to meet you."

"Oh, go on now, we don't stand on ceremony here.
Call me Marlene and I'm going to call you Jenna. Head
on through. I've still got a few things to see to in the
kitchen. Hannah and Cassie are outside on the patio and
Chance is fiddling with the grill, as if he thinks he knows
what he's doing."

"No Logan today?" Dylan asked.

Marlene shook her head. "No, he called me to apologize and say he'd been called out of town for legal work
for some high-profile corporate client but just between
you and me I think he's ducked away to avoid the wedding planning." She finished with a wink and a sparkle
in her eyes that took the sting out of her words. "So, go
on outside. They're waiting for you."

Jenna appeared to hold a little tighter to Dylan's hand.
He guessed it was a bit overwhelming when you came

here the first time. He looked around the house he'd grown up in. Maybe the second time, too. Out on the patio she seemed to relax a bit more. The expansive gardens stretched out before them.

"Is that a pond?" Jenna asked.

"It's a saltwater pool designed to look like a pond. When Sage and I were younger we used to swing from a rope tied to a branch on that tree there—" he gestured to the limb in question "—and drop into the deep end."

"Wow, you really had it all, didn't you?" she said, almost to herself.

A little girl bounced toward them, her bright red hair hanging in disordered ringlets around her pretty face and her green eyes sparkling with mischief.

"You're my uncle Dylan, aren't you? But Mama says you're more like a cousin something-removed. What's that?"

"Cassie! Let Dylan and his guest say hello to the rest of us first, before you start bothering them," a woman's voice called from the patio.

Dylan watched as Chance's half sister, Hannah, rose from her seat and came over to greet them.

"Hi again," she said to him before turning to Jenna. "I'm Hannah Armstrong."

"Jenna Montgomery," she said. "Is that your daughter? She's adorable."

Hannah beamed with pride. "Yes, that's my little treasure. She's quite the character. Here, you leave Jenna with me and go and see what Chance is doing over by the grill."

Dylan gave Jenna a glance to see if she was comfortable with that. She inclined her head slightly.

"Sure, I'll be fine," she said, but he could see by the pallor of her cheeks that she was still a little nervous, as if, given the right provocation, she'd turn and run like hell back to Cheyenne.

"I'll say hi and then I'll be right back."

"It's okay," Hannah assured him in her gentle voice. "I won't bite."

Jenna let Hannah draw her over to where she'd been sitting a moment ago, and they relaxed in the late afternoon sun.

"I'm gonna help Grandma with the horse derves," Cassie announced importantly, before skipping back inside the house.

"Wow, she's full of energy, isn't she?" Jenna commented, her lips still pulled into a smile over the little girl's mispronunciation of *hors d'oeuvres*.

"Sure is. Has been like that from the day she was born. Never a dull moment with her around, and I wouldn't have it any other way."

There was a steely vein of pride running through Hannah's voice. One that made Jenna press her hand on her lower belly. Yes, that's how she felt, too. As scary and unknown as what lay before her was, she wouldn't have it any other way, either.

"It's so beautiful here," she remarked, looking around again, trying to take it all in.

"I know. When I first saw the place it totally blew me away."

"You didn't grow up here?"

"No, I'm from Boulder, Colorado. But I'm getting married next month and Cheyenne will be our permanent home after that. In the meantime, Cassie and I are staying here. She's loving having an uncle she can twist around her little finger, not to mention a Grandma who just adores her."

Jenna tried to put all that information together, but something was still out of sync in her mind. "Marlene's not your mom?"

"It's complicated. Chance and I share a dad," Hannah explained with a wistful smile. "But they've all been so welcoming since we found out about one another. Especially Marlene, which was so much more than I could have hoped for."

"They seem very tight-knit," Jenna observed, watching Dylan and Chance laughing together over something one of them had said.

"But inclusive at the same time. Don't worry." Hannah patted Jenna's hand. "I wondered what I'd be letting myself in for, but they made me welcome from the start. You'll fit right in."

Would she? Her heart yearned for stability; she'd created as much as she could herself by working hard and buying her own home. She was almost fanatical about establishing roots, about grounding herself in familiarity and routine after her younger years filled with instability. From what she saw here, the Lassiters were clearly just as invested in permanence.

"Here you are, ladies. Some icy cold lemonade for you, honey," Marlene said to Jenna as she returned, putting a tray with a couple of frosted pitchers and some fresh glasses on the table in front of her. "And margaritas for us."

Jenna felt uncomfortable. So they knew already that she was pregnant. She murmured her thanks and watched Cassie carry a tray with inch-high edges to Chase and Dylan.

"Used to be a time she'd serve me first," Hannah commented with a rueful smile. "But now it's all about her uncle."

"She might have him wrapped around her pinky," Marlene observed, "but it's mutual. It's good to have a child around here again. It's been too long since those boys were growing up."

The older woman turned to face Jenna, a warm glow lighting her hazel eyes. "How are you keeping with the baby, Jenna? Well, I hope?"

Jenna's upset that news of her pregnancy had preceded her must have been evident on her face.

"Oh, I'm sorry, hon. Is it supposed to be a secret? Chance told me and I just thought the whole family knew."

Jenna hastened to reassure her hostess. "No, really, it's okay. I'm just not used to people knowing just yet." She smiled to soften her words. "As to how I've been? I've been pretty lucky. A little nausea in the early stages but my main problem has been tiredness."

"You're in your second trimester now, aren't you?" Marlene asked. When she nodded, the other woman said, "You should notice you're feeling better again soon. This is where you get to experience all the fun of a pregnancy, without the sickness or the aches and pains. Is your family looking forward to the baby's arrival?"

Jenna squirmed a little. She was totally unused to someone being so inquisitive, though friendly. "I don't have any family locally," she settled on saying—unwilling to admit to anyone here that her father was doing time at the state penitentiary in Rawlins.

"Oh, you poor girl," Marlene clucked sympathetically. "Never mind. If you'll let us, we'd be glad to help you out. If you have any questions, anything at all, you just ask away."

"Thank you." Jenna blinked back the burn of tears at the kindness of Marlene's unexpected offer. Her eyes

hazed over again and she lifted a hand to wipe at the
moisture that began to spill.

"Don't you worry, honey," Marlene said softly as she
handed Jenna a crisply laundered, lace-edged handkerchief. "We'll take good care of you."

Jenna wiped her eyes and fought to get her ridiculous emotions under control. She was a virtual stranger
to these people. Yet because of one impulsive accident,
they were prepared to open their hearts to her. She'd been
so closed up, so reluctant to let anyone in, that she felt
slightly off-kilter at the prospect of even thinking of accepting help and support. She didn't deserve this. Didn't
deserve their trust or their generosity.

Even so, the idea of it dangled before her like a tantalizing, yet forbidden, fruit.

Nine

Dylan looked over to where the women were talking. Something tightened in his chest when he saw Jenna's expression and recognized the distress on her face. He went to step toward her, but was arrested by Chance's hand on his shoulder.

"Don't," his cousin said.

"She's upset. She needs me."

"Mom will look after her. Trust me. She'll have everything under control."

Dylan watched as Jenna recovered her usual poise. And as the women seemed to grow closer and enjoy one another's company, their laughter floated toward him on the light evening breeze.

"Do you want some more horse derves, Uncle Dylan?" Cassie asked from beside him, shifting her weight from one leg to the other.

"No, thank you," he replied, squatting down to her level. "But thank you for taking such great care of us. How about you offer some of those to the ladies?"

"Okay!" the little girl said brightly.

He watched as she strutted importantly to the table where the women sat. A sense of wonder stirred deep inside him. Would his kid be a boy or a girl? Would it one day be right here, playing on this patio like he had?

"So when did you knock her up?" Chance's voice interrupted his reverie.

Dylan's hackles rose. He didn't care for his cousin's turn of phrase. "I don't think that's any of your business."

"Of course it is. Sage thinks it isn't yours—that she's maybe pulling a fast one on you."

"Sage should keep his thoughts to himself," Dylan growled. "It's mine. And so is she."

His cousin nodded, clearly satisfied with that response. "You going to be a hands-on dad?"

"Every chance I get," Dylan replied emphatically.

Chance looked pensive. "I often wonder what life would have been like to have grown up with my own dad around longer, y'know?" His father had died when Chance was eight years old. He, too, knew what it was like to grow up without his natural father.

"Yeah. It's why I'm going to be there for my kid, through thick and thin."

"And Jenna? How does she feel about that?"

Dylan took a swig of his beer and rolled the brew over his tongue for a moment before swallowing. "She's coming around to the idea," he said with a grin.

Chance gave him a punch on the arm. "Thatta boy. Besides, with all you can offer, why would she refuse?"

"That's the thing. She doesn't seem to want what I can offer. She's fierce about her independence, and from what I can tell, she's worked hard for it. I just need to convince her that it's okay to share the load."

"Well, good luck with that. I'd rather rope a steer in a bad mood than try and convince a woman of anything."

"Good point," Dylan concurred, before gesturing to the platter of raw steak waiting to be cooked. "Hey, you going to do anything with those or are you waiting for them to cook themselves?"

The seriousness of their discussion broken, they turned to the matter of cooking the meat. But a niggling thought remained at the back of Dylan's mind. What if Jenna wouldn't let him in? What if she wouldn't share the load? What then? He knew he could use his power and his money to get what he wanted, but the very idea soured his stomach. No, he wanted her to come to him willingly and wholeheartedly. Not because she had to, not because she was being coerced. But because she wanted to as much as he wanted her.

It was late when he drove Jenna home. Dylan had fully expected her to want to leave soon after they'd enjoyed their meal, but it seemed that the longer she spent with his family, the more she wanted to stay. It made him begin to hope that she could see herself being a part of his own close circle. Part of his life.

"Thank you for taking me tonight. I really enjoyed it," she said softly.

"It was my pleasure. I'm glad you came."

"They're all so lovely. And Cassie's so sweet. I loved how she crawled into your lap after dinner and just fell asleep there."

He'd loved it, too. Had welcomed the little girl's trust in him. It had been a precious gift, and he'd missed the weight of her little body when Hannah had eventually lifted her and carted her off to bed. It made him yearn even more to be a father, to cradle a child of his own in his arms.

"Kids are special. No doubt about it."

Dylan drove onto Jenna's driveway and got out to walk her to her front door. He waited on the porch as she fitted her key in the lock, the breeze bringing a teasing hint of her fragrance toward him. Roses. She always carried that sweet scent on her. It suited her. The flower was so beautiful yet could be prickly at the same time.

She pushed the door open and hesitated a second or two. He saw her shoulders lift and then drop, as if she'd drawn in a deep breath.

"Jenna? You okay?"

She turned to face him. "Do you…?"

She bit her bottom lip, the action having the exact same effect on him as it had the other day. Fire licked along his veins as he waited for her to finish her sentence.

"Do you want to come in for a nightcap?"

Hell, yeah, a little voice all but screamed at the back of his mind. He didn't want tonight to end. She'd softened, somehow. Her defenses seemed lower than before. He pushed the screaming voice aside. He needed to tread softly. He certainly didn't want to scare her or damage the tentative closeness that had grown between them tonight.

"One more drink and I'll be over the limit to drive," he said quietly—asking her the important question without putting it into so many words. He'd go if that's what she wanted. He wouldn't be happy about it. But he'd go.

Jenna took a step closer to him and placed her hand on his chest. "Then perhaps you should stay."

His breath caught in his lungs. Could she feel his heart all but leap from his chest at her words? "Perhaps I should," he managed to reply, and hooked an arm around her waist.

They headed in together. He let her go as she walked around her sitting room, flicking on the occasional light.

"I'm not even sure what I have in the way of spirits, but I'm bound to have some wine. Would that be—?"

Her voice broke off as he caught her hand and drew her to him.

"I don't really want a drink, Jenna," he said, his voice a low rumble.

"You don't?"

"No, I just want you."

"Oh."

It was all she got time to say before he kissed her. The taste of her lips almost blew his head off and ignited the slow-burning embers within him to flaming, ravenous heat. His kiss was hungry, demanding, and to his delight she met his need with corresponding passion. Her hands slid upward, from his chest to his neck, then cupped the back of his head, not letting him break the kiss.

"Bedroom," he demanded against her mouth, not wanting to remove his lips from hers for even a second.

She pointed down the hallway. "At the end, on the right."

He scooped one arm behind her knees and the other behind her back and lifted her, holding her body against his. She snaked an arm around his shoulders and caressed his cheek with her free hand, as if she was as reluctant to break their connection, their kiss, as he. He covered the short distance down the hall and pushed the door open with his foot. Her bedroom was small, with minimal decoration. Simple in its design. A plainly covered bed took up most of the space, a solid plank of blond wood serving as a headboard.

Dylan let Jenna slide to her feet.

"I want to see you this time," he growled, moving away from her for the brief second it took to switch on the bedside lamp.

He turned back to her and reached to lift her loose-fitting tunic from her body. His mouth dried at the sight he revealed, his untaken breath burning in his chest. Her skin was smooth, with the lightest touch of summer in its tone. He let his gaze track down her throat, across her shoulders and to her breasts, which spilled from the lacy cups of her bra.

"I told you you were beautiful. I was wrong," he said, his voice thick with emotion. "You're so much more than that."

His hand reached out to trace a faint blue vein on her breast, and he heard her sharply indrawn breath. He followed the line to where it disappeared beneath the pale blue scalloped edge of her bra.

"I'm going to kiss you there," he promised, lifting his eyes to hers—his stomach clenching at the heat he saw burning back at him. "But first, I'm going to see all of you."

He took his time removing her sandals and slim-fitted capris until she had only her bra and panties left. Fine tremors quivered through her body as he let his hands drift up her arms to her shoulders. Her skin was so soft, and sweetly fragrant, and he trailed fine kisses along her shoulder and then up the side of her neck.

"Let me get the bed ready," she said as he nibbled on her earlobe, just as he'd imagined doing a few short days ago.

"It looks pretty damn ready to me," he said when she pulled away with a small laugh.

Still, he was happy to use the time she took turning down the comforter and tugging back the sheets to shuck off his clothing—something he managed with record speed. His erection strained at the cotton of his boxer briefs and he rubbed his hand down his aching flesh. Soon, he promised himself, soon. But first there were more important things to attend to. Such as examining the woman in front of him from head to foot. Getting to know what made her breathless with desire. Making her scream with pleasure such as she'd never experienced before.

Jenna lay down on the bed and held out a hand to him. He took it, stretching out next to her and marveling at how perfectly formed she was. He traced the curve of her collarbone again—such a delicate line—and followed his touch with the tip of his tongue. She rewarded him with a sigh of pleasure so he did it again, his tongue lingering in the hollow just at the base of her throat. Her pulse leaped against him, as avid and hungry as his own.

Dylan continued his voyage of discovery, his fingertips tingling as they met the swell of her breasts. He swept over their shape before letting his hand travel to her shoulders, slipping first one, then the other bra strap down, and reaching beneath her to unsnap the clasp.

"Should I be worried that you did that so easily?" Jenna teased, but then her voice ended on a gasp as he traced the pale blue line of her vein to where it collided with the dark pink distended nipple.

"Never," he said, before using the tip of his tongue to meet that pink tip.

She shuddered beneath him. "Do that again, please?"

"Your wish is my command," he promised, and did as she asked.

Her moan of delight drove a fierce spear of lust straight to his groin, but he forced himself to ignore it. To dwell instead on her pleasure, on her. He took his time with the rest of her body, lingering over her breasts, her ribs, her belly button, and then moving down to the small firm swell of her belly.

His hand hovered there and he willed the connection between them to go beyond skin, beyond sensation. His baby. His woman. His life. He pressed a kiss against her skin, his hands now skimming her panties, tracing the outside edge of the fabric where they met the top of her thighs. Her legs trembled at his touch, her pelvis thrusting upward toward him. He cupped her, marveling at the heat and dampness that collected at her core.

"Dylan, please!"

He pressed his palm against her, felt her shudder against him.

"You're teasing me. It's not fair," she cried, her voice a strangled sound.

"All's fair," he said easing her panties down her legs and punctuating his next words with firm kisses on her thighs, then the junction where they met. "In." Kiss. "Love." Kiss. "And." Kiss. "War."

His mouth found her center and he saw her hands knot into fists on the sheets as his tongue flicked against her glistening sex. The scent of her was driving him crazy. A delicious blend of rose and musk.

He couldn't stand it a second longer. He had to have her, be inside her, be one with her. He shoved his briefs down and settled between her legs, feeling her jolt as he nudged the blunt tip of his erection at her entrance. She lifted her hips in welcome and he slowly let himself be absorbed by the tight warm heat of her body. Slowly, so slowly, until he was buried in her. Until he was exactly where he needed to be.

His hips flexed and she met his movement with her own, her inner muscles holding and releasing him in time with their actions. Her irises darkened to near black, clouded with the fog of her desire. He tried to make it last, to make it even more special, but when her body began to pulse around his, when her eyes slid closed and she released a keening cry as her body shuddered toward its peak, he lost control—his hips pumping until he, too, reached his climax.

Lost in the power of wonder and emotion that swept over him, Dylan let his body take him on the ride as he crested wave after wave of pleasure. His entire frame shook with the force of what he'd just undergone—with the perfection of how it had felt. He rolled to one side and gathered Jenna against him, waiting for his heartbeat to return to anything approximating normal.

It was a long time before he could speak.

"I think we just proved our first time wasn't an aberration," he said with a huff of breath. He felt her chuckle ripple through her.

"Yes, I think we did."

He could hear the humor in her voice, humor mixed with a languid satisfaction that made him feel even better, knowing he'd contributed to her well-being. Everything was right in this moment. Perfect. He knew he'd never tire of this. Of the feeling of her in his arms, of the curve of her sweet bottom beneath his hand. Of this sense of connection he'd never shared with another woman.

He wanted this—forever, with her. It took all his self-restraint not to press her again to agree to marriage. To agree to committing to one another forever.

Deep down he knew she still had reservations. Understandable, given the short length of time they'd actually known one another. But they had the rest of their lives to discover all those finer points that kept a relationship interesting. What they shared was a gift beyond compare. He should know—he'd sought perfection wherever he went in whatever he did.

Jenna Montgomery was that perfection for him. He just needed to convince her of that fact.

Ten

Jenna could hear Dylan's heart racing beneath her ear, and her lips curved into a smile. He might be the CEO of the Lassiter Grill Corporation, he might be a world-renowned chef and playboy, but underneath it all he was still just a man. A pretty damn fine one, that was for sure. And, right now, he was hers.

Her man forever? She was beginning to believe it could be true. She'd loved spending time with him and his family this evening. Could she find the courage to reach out from behind her safe fortress and grasp what he offered? Only time would tell.

Dylan's fingers traced a lazy trail from her hip to her shoulders and back again, his touch setting off tiny shivers beneath her skin. She stretched beneath his touch, like a cat, almost purring.

"Tell me what you like," he asked softly. "This?" He firmed his touch. "Or this?"

"Hmm, let me take about the next twenty minutes or so to get back to you on that," she replied.

He laughed and the sound filled her heart with happiness.

"Twenty minutes? That's quite a commitment."

"It might be," she said, realizing that if she really wanted this—really wanted *him*—she needed to take the bull by the horns and open up to him.

But whenever he started talking about commitment it still struck a knell of fear inside her. He knew virtually nothing about her but the face she presented to him right here, right now. The person she was today was a far cry from the person she'd been eleven years ago.

Pretty much everything about Dylan and his life was an open book. Yes, he'd had sorrow in his life with the death of his parents and then his adoptive mother, and more recently, J.D. But with each loss, he'd had the advantage of family, of someone else willing to step up to the plate and fill that yearning hole in his life.

With the loss of his parents it had been J.D. and his wife, Ellie. With the death of Ellie, Jenna had learned tonight, Marlene had stepped into the breach to provide mothering to Dylan and his brother. What had Jenna ever had growing up, except a will for survival? That will had gotten her through her parents' arguments, their one-up-manship and then her mother's desertion.

It had gotten her through the news that her father was taking her to America, away from everything and everyone she'd ever known or allowed herself to anchor to.

Did she dare anchor herself to Dylan?

"You're thinking so hard I can just about hear the cogs turning in your brain," Dylan said teasingly. "Wanna share?"

She began to say no, but then realized that this was a perfect opportunity to give him some of her truths. What he did with it would define what happened between them in the future.

"I was just thinking about how different our lives were, growing up."

"How so?"

"You had such stability, such strength behind your

family. It's like everyone has a place and they fit there, y'know?"

"Uh-huh. It's not always a bed of roses but we get along pretty well."

"Pretty well?" she said, tweaking one of his nipples with a pinch that made him yelp.

"Okay, very well. But we work at it."

"That's part of what I mean," she said, smoothing her hand over his chest to soothe his injured flesh. "You do work at it, together. I guess I've never had that sense of community within a family. From what I know, my parents were both only children, and their parents died before I was born. It should have made them closer to one another, but instead it always felt like they were tearing each other apart."

"Doesn't sound comfortable, for them or for you."

"No, it wasn't. It was confusing, unstable. I never knew from one day to the next if they'd be happy and loving or morose and picking a fight. When my mother left us, I almost felt a sense of relief, y'know? But by the same token I was distraught because she didn't take me, too. Dad said she felt like we were holding her back."

Dylan sighed. "That was unfair of him for saying it and, if it was true, of her for feeling it. You can't do that to a kid. Your job as a parent is to nurture, to support and love your children. Yes, that means putting your own needs last a lot of the time, but I reckon there's a time and a place for everything and everyone, and when your kids are young it's *their* time, *their* place."

Jenna closed her eyes as a swell of something rich and true buoyed up inside her. His words were so simple, yet they rang with such a deep certainty about what was right and wrong. Tenets she held dear to her own heart.

"Well, obviously they didn't feel that way."

"Do you stay in touch with your dad now?" Dylan asked.

Jenna shook her head. She didn't want to tell Dylan that her father would be locked up behind bars for at least another two years. He'd probably have been out on parole by now if the prison staff hadn't discovered he'd begun grooming wealthy widows for future cons during his computer time inside.

"No. We lead totally separate lives. To be honest, I don't want anything to do with him," she said emphatically.

"Will you tell him about the baby?"

"No. I don't want him anywhere near us."

"Family is family, Jen," Dylan said, still stroking her skin, his actions soothing the anger that had risen in her as they discussed her dad. "I wouldn't be where I am now without mine."

She laughed, but it was a bitter sound. "Nor would I. But I've learned the hard way that just because someone is family doesn't mean they have your best interests at heart. My foster mum gave me more care and stability than my parents ever did. Thanks to her, I've learned to do very well on my own and I like it that way. I work hard, and what I have is my own. Okay, so I can't provide luxuries like saltwater ponds with swinging ropes, or private jets and silver spoons. But I can provide what counts—stability and constancy in a loving home. I've set down roots here. I finally belong somewhere and I'll protect that, and my baby's right to that, with every last breath in my body if I have to."

Dylan was silent for a while, but then he spoke. "And do you see any room for me in that life of yours?"

She rolled on top of him, her legs tangling with his

and her hands on either side of his face as she rose up to kiss him.

"That depends," she said, pulling away so they were inches apart.

"On what?"

"On whether you plan to keep telling me what to do, or whether you want to be an equal partner in what happens in our baby's life."

Tiny twin frown lines appeared between his brows as he looked into her eyes. "I can do partnership," he said carefully. "But I'd rather do marriage."

This time, when he said it, it didn't send quite the same shaft of anxiety through her. Instead, she felt a sense of curiosity—a need to take his suggestion and examine it more closely instead of rejecting it out of hand.

"I'll think about it," she said, hardly believing it herself as the words fell from her lips.

"Thank you," he answered simply.

His strong, warm arms closed around her and she caught his lips again, letting herself and her fears go in his touch until once more they were lost in each other.

The air had grown cool around them and Dylan shifted to drag the covers up over their naked forms. Jenna had fallen asleep almost immediately after the second time they'd made love, but he'd continue to lie there turning over her words.

Her family had hurt her, had made her doubt and fear closeness. Chipping away at her barriers would take time and care. And love? Yes, and love. Love and dependability. Those had been the backbone of his upbringing. He wanted those attributes to be the backbone of his kid's upbringing, too, and to do that he needed to woo Jenna with those promises. He'd known all along that courting her would be a challenge. They'd done everything from back to front, for a start. But he'd get there, he decided as he finally drifted off to sleep. What he and Jenna had between them was far too important. Failure was not an option.

In the morning Dylan eased himself from the bedsheets without disturbing her. Dragging on his jeans, he padded through to her kitchen to see what he could rustle up for breakfast. He eyed her appliances with interest. Everything was new and in near pristine condition. Either she was a fanatical housekeeper or she didn't do a great deal of cooking in here. From what she'd said about TV dinners, he suspected it was the latter.

He opened her fridge and confirmed that she didn't do a great deal of cooking. His brow furrowed as he considered his options. A quick check of the vegetable drawer revealed a red pepper that was just about past its best by date, and some fresh mushrooms. He made a sound of satisfaction. Further rummaging in the kitchen uncovered potatoes and onions in matching earthenware containers.

So, with these items combined with the eggs in the fridge, he could do a Spanish omelet with red pepper and a side of fried mushrooms. His mouth was already watering at the thought. But when it came to slicing the potatoes, he eyed Jenna's knives in despair and wished he was in his own kitchen with his quality steel blades honed to perfection. Still, he'd made do with worse, he thought, testing the blunt edge.

He fried the potato and onions together in a pan while he went to work slicing mushrooms and beating the eggs. By the time he was ready to turn the halved omelet onto two warmed plates he heard a sound in the hall.

"Good morning," he said as Jenna stumbled into the kitchen, wrapped in a fluffy long bathrobe.

She looked as though she'd forced herself awake. Her hair was mussed and her eyes had a sleepy look about them that almost made him abandon their breakfast and take her straight back to bed to wake her up properly.

"Good morning," she said as she went over to the fridge and grabbed a bottle of water and screwed off the cap. "Something smells good. Are you feeding me again?"

"Spanish omelet. You hungry?"

She groaned. "Hungry? I'm always hungry lately."

"Then," he said, scooping up the sliced mushrooms he'd fried in a little butter, and sharing them between their plates, "you'd better wrap yourself around this."

She gave him a puzzled look. "You did this?"

He waggled his fingers in front of her. "With my own fair hands."

"Did I actually have the ingredients or have you been out?"

He laughed. "You had everything here. I haven't left you for a moment."

Nor did he plan to for the rest of this weekend, or any of the time he had free until the official opening of the Grill next week.

"Hmm," she said, quickly setting the small table she had in the dining area and transferring their plates onto the table. "Maybe you should give me some lessons."

His mouth quirked in a smile. Lessons? Oh, yeah, he'd love to do that. His mind filled with the possibilities, starting with Jenna wearing an apron…and nothing else.

"Sure. Shall we start today?"

"I was kidding, but if you're serious…"

"I never kid about food."

"Okay, today would be fine."

"Good, I'll take you back to my place. We'll have more to work with there."

She returned his smile and he felt as though the sun had just risen again. "Thank you, I'd like that."

Dylan heard his phone beep. "Excuse me a second," he said, sliding it from his pocket and checking the display.

It was a message from Felicity Sinclair, Lassiter Media's queen of PR, confirming her arrival in Cheyenne tomorrow morning. He tapped in a quick acknowledgment and turned his attention back to Jenna.

"Sorry, work," he said by way of explanation.

"Do you always work on weekends?"

He shrugged. "When it's necessary. With the Grill opening next week everything has become more time sensitive. That was just a text from our PR executive. She's flying in tomorrow. I'll bring her by your store and introduce you."

"That'd be nice. Hopefully, she can make sure that Connell's Floral Design's logo is featured prominently in your advertising," she said with a cheeky smile.

Jenna leaned forward as she scooped up a mouthful of omelet, her action making her robe gape open enough to give him a glimpse of one pink-tipped breast. Any thoughts of work and the people associated with it flew from his mind as he allowed his gaze to drift over her. She continued eating, oblivious to his perusal, until her plate was empty and she lifted her attention to him—and realized just what had caught his attention.

Her eyes darkened, as they had last night, and her cheeks became tinged with pink.

"Not hungry?" she asked, her voice a little husky.

"Starving," he replied, putting his fork down and pushing his plate away.

He eased from his chair, dropping to his knees and

sliding one hand inside her robe to cup her breast. Her nipple instantly tightened against his palm.

"Ah, now I see why you're feeding me so well," Jenna said, drawing in a deep breath. "You want to keep my energy levels up."

"Among other things," he drawled, letting his thumb graze back and forth over the taut nub that just begged him to take it in his mouth.

Never a man to ignore his instincts, Dylan did just that. Jenna's fingers tunneled through his hair, holding him to her as he nibbled and sucked her flesh.

"Well, it's a good thing I've eaten then," Jenna managed to say before he pushed aside her robe and lavished her other breast with equal attention. "Because I have a feeling I'm going to need the extra calories."

"Them and more," he murmured against her skin.

They didn't get out to his place until well after lunchtime and by then they were both famished again, for each other and for more sustenance. How they even made it into his high-tech kitchen bemused him, when all he wanted to do was take Jenna to the dizzying heights they'd shared, over and over again.

Instead, he supervised her as she put together a simple lunch for them both. Jenna surveyed the assembled ingredients on the island in the center of the kitchen.

"You always buy this extensively from the grocery store?" she commented as she tore up some romaine lettuce and threw it into a bowl.

"When I'm in the mood for Greek salad, yeah. What's wrong? Didn't your family ever cook?"

As soon as the words were out of his mouth he wished them back again. He already knew talking about her family created an invisible barrier between them, one he'd unwittingly put back in place.

"I can remember baking cookies with my mom once or twice when I was little, but aside from that, nothing really. Dad was big on takeout, or eating out. He often wasn't home for meals anyway, so I just learned to make do."

It was what she didn't say that struck him. How old had she been when she'd been left to fend for herself come mealtimes? Dylan moved around the granite-topped island and slid his arms around her waist, pulling her gently back against him.

"I'm sorry," he said, pressing a kiss against the back of her neck. "I didn't mean to bring that up."

"It is what it is," she said, studiously concentrating on slicing the red onion and then the red and green bell peppers she'd laid out in a row on the countertop in front of her.

"Here, do you want me to do that?" he offered, wanting to do anything to change the subject and shift her focus to something else.

"Actually, no. I'm enjoying this. I never thought I would, but it's true."

She flung him a smile over her shoulder and kept chopping and slicing until the bowl was filled with the earlier ingredients, together with tomatoes, olives and cucumber. Her hand hesitated over the feta cheese.

"It's okay," Dylan said. "I checked. It's made from pasteurized milk."

"Are you sure?"

"Hey, leave it out if you want to. It's not a food crime." To save her the hassle, he swept the packet up and put it back in the fridge, substituting it for a sliced cooked chicken breast. "Use this instead. There's no reason why we can't play around with tradition."

"Thanks," she said. "I'm sorry, I just don't want to do anything that will potentially harm the baby. He or she is all I have."

She placed one hand on her belly and Dylan could see the love in her face. He put his hand over hers. "You have me now, too. I want you to remember that, because I'm not going anywhere, Jenna. Not unless you're coming with me."

Eleven

She wanted to believe him. With all her heart she wanted it to be true. But she'd heard such platitudes from her father's mouth all the years she'd spent with him. He'd used them with her and also with his many lady friends. He'd always made it sound so sincere, as if the words truly came from his heart, but they'd come from a place far more closely associated with his wallet.

"Seeing is believing," Jenna said, trying to keep her words light. But she knew they'd struck to Dylan's core.

"You don't believe me?"

He reached to take the knife from her and turned her to face him. His hands framed her face and forced her to maintain eye contact with him.

"I didn't say that, exactly," she hedged, knowing to the depth of her soul that she wanted to be certain of him, to be able to trust what he said without looking for an ulterior motive.

Still, aside from the baby, and obviously the incredible sexual chemistry they shared, what else was there? A marriage took so much more than those two things. Her parents had been the perfect example of that. A marriage needed commitment, togetherness and mutual minds. What motive could he have to want to be with her? It wasn't as if she had something he needed. He had it all and then some.

"Jenna, I meant what I said. Yes, I know we haven't known each other all that long and, yes, we've gone at this all the wrong way. If I could, I'd turn back the clock and take the time to woo you, to prove that you can rely on me. Something brought us together, I firmly believe that. And we're meant to be, Jenna."

"I wish it could be that easy." She sighed.

"It can be. If you just let it."

"I'm trying, Dylan, honestly I am. I…I want to trust you."

"Then that's progress. I'll take it. We're halfway there, right? C'mon, let's get this salad finished and I'll show you around the house."

The next morning Jenna was happily reflecting on her day with Dylan when Valerie knocked on her office door and popped her head in.

"You have visitors. Mr. Drop-Dead-Gorgeous and a woman who looks as if she walked straight off Rodeo Drive. They make a nice couple," Valerie said, closing the office door behind her as she returned to the showroom.

A couple? Jenna didn't think so, not after the very thorough loving Dylan had given her yesterday. But even so, she felt a twinge of jealousy and insecurity. This PR chick, whoever she was, was certainly more suited to Dylan's world than Jenna ever could be. And she'd lay odds that she didn't have any dark or shameful secrets lurking in her past, either. Insecurity made Jenna uncomfortable as she rose from her desk and checked her appearance in the mirror that hung on the back of her office door.

Well, there wasn't a hair out of place and her makeup hadn't disappeared since she'd lightly applied it this morning. There was nothing else to do but go out and face them.

Her heart skipped a double beat when she thought about seeing Dylan. He'd been so attentive yesterday and had made her feel so incredibly special. She wished she was the kind of person who could simply embrace that and not constantly read between the lines of everything he said and did for an ulterior motive.

There was another knock at her office door.

"Jenna?"

It was Dylan. She pasted a smile on her face and reached for the handle. She felt her heart thump as she saw him. He was all sartorial corporate elegance today, dressed in a charcoal-gray suit, white shirt and striped tie. Her eyes skimmed past him to the tall, slim, golden-haired woman who was examining some pink holly-hocks. No wonder Valerie thought they made a cute couple. With the woman's tailored suit and high heels—Louboutin by the looks of them—she and Dylan looked as if they'd stepped out of the pages of *Forbes Magazine*. Jenna tugged at the loose-fitting tunic she'd teamed with a pair of stretch pants this morning, and wished her wardrobe had extended to something a little sharper for this meeting.

"Good morning," she said as brightly as she could.

Dylan didn't waste a second. He surprised her by swooping down and planting his lips on hers. Jenna put her hand on his chest to steady herself as her blood instantly turned molten. Two seconds in his presence and she was already starry-eyed. Man, she was so gone.

"Now it's a good morning," he said with a smile that crinkled his eyes at the corners. He linked her arm through his and drew her to his side. "Come over and meet Fee."

As he mentioned the other woman's name, she lifted her head and smiled in Jenna's direction. She took a few steps toward them, her hand outstretched in greeting.

"Hi, I'm Felicity Sinclair, but call me Fee," she said warmly. "Are these your designs? They're fantastic," she said, gesturing to some of the more artistic pieces the store had on display.

"Yes, mine and Valerie's," Jenna said, feeling a little more charitable toward the newcomer.

"You'd be very popular back home. I wish we had someone like you doing the flowers for our offices and functions. Dylan tells me you've got everything under control for Saturday's opening?"

"Yes, would you like to see a mock-up of the table settings?"

The next twenty minutes passed swiftly as Jenna went over her plans for the floral displays at the restaurant. By the time they left she felt a whole lot more confident in herself and her ability to hold her own with women like Fee Sinclair.

Dylan whispered in her ear as they were leaving, "Ready for another cooking lesson tonight? I was thinking of something along the lines of dessert, maybe with chocolate sauce?"

Fire lit inside Jenna, flooding her limbs and making them instantly feel heavy and lethargic. Her cheeks flamed in turn, earning her a considering glance from Valerie.

"Sure, your place or mine?" she asked, keeping her voice low.

"How about your place. It's closer to here for you in case we oversleep in the morning."

She nodded, not trusting herself to speak. He kissed her again, taking her in a hard and swift embrace that promised everything, but left her hanging in a daze of sensual awareness that clouded her already foggy mind.

"See you after work," he said, ushering Fee from the store.

After the front door had closed, Valerie zoomed straight to her side.

"And just when were you going to let me in on the secret?" she demanded, waggling a playful finger in Jenna's direction.

"Secret?"

"You and Mr. Drop-Dead-Gorgeous. You never told me you were an item."

Jenna smiled. "An item?"

"Sweetie, I saw the way he looked at you." She fanned herself theatrically. "And the way he kissed you? Well, suffice to say it had my hormones racing, and it wasn't even me he was kissing!"

"We're friends, Valerie. Good friends," she amended.

"He's your baby's daddy, isn't he?"

Jenna felt her cheeks drain of color. Aside from Dylan, and obviously his family, no one else was supposed to know yet that she was pregnant.

"I've had four kids of my own, remember. I know the signs. Look, I can understand you wanting to keep it quiet, especially with him being a Lassiter and all," Valerie continued. "I just wanted to say, good on you, girl. You work so hard, it's about time you had a bit of play. If there's one thing life has taught me, it's to grab what's offered and make the most of every darn second. You never know what's around the corner."

Valerie's words continued to ring in Jenna's ears as she forced herself to focus on her work for the day. Was she being a fool for trying to play it safe with Dylan? For not jumping, boots and all, into a future together? She didn't doubt he'd take care of her, but did she want to be taken care of? She'd fought to be independent, to be able to stand on her own two feet. Did he accept her as an equal? She weighed the thoughts in her mind, along with the realization that she was learning to trust him, to accept who he was. Could she take that final step and agree to marry him?

"So, what did you think?" Dylan asked as he drove Fee back toward the restaurant.

"Of the designs or of Ms. Montgomery?" she asked with a twinkle in her eye.

"Both. Either. Hell, I don't care." Dylan laughed. "By the way, I'd like you to see that her store gets linked to the Grill in the advertising push over the next few days."

Fee raised her eyebrows but took out her planner and made some notes. "Sure, no problem. The floral work is going to be fantastic—a perfect complement to the opening and the restaurant in general. About Jenna—she seemed familiar to me for some reason. I can't figure out where from. I'm not sure if it's her face or her name."

"She did the flowers for Angelica's rehearsal dinner. Maybe that's where you remember her from," Dylan said offhandedly.

"No, I don't think it's that. Not to worry, it'll come to me soon enough."

At the restaurant Dylan found it difficult to remain focused. All he wanted to do was race back to Jenna's store and sneak her home. Fee kept him occupied for the better part of the day, though, walking him through a couple of interviews she'd scheduled for tomorrow, among other things, and by the time he left the restaurant he was itching to get to Jenna's.

He'd barely thrown the car into Park when the front

door opened and she stood on the porch, waiting for him. He couldn't hold back the smile of satisfaction that wreathed his face. So, she'd missed him today as much as he'd missed her. That was definitely a step in the right direction. He snagged the bag of groceries he'd picked up on the way over, and raced up the path, sweeping her into his arms and delivering a kiss that he hoped showed how much he'd looked forward to seeing her again.

When he set her back down she looked a little starry-eyed, but a stab of concern pierced him when he saw how pale she was.

"C'mon, let's get you inside and off your feet. You look as if you've been overdoing things today."

He shepherded her through to her living room and sat her down on the long sofa, making her laugh when he picked up her feet and swiveled her around so she was fully reclined.

"Dylan, don't. It's not necessary. I just had a full day, that's all."

"And now you can relax. I'm here."

He said the words with a quiet authority he didn't really feel. In fact, with Jenna, he was never too sure just how close he was to overstepping the mark. He wanted to take care of her, to lift her problems from her slender shoulders and onto his broader ones. Especially when he saw her looking like this.

Despite her protests, he noted that she didn't make an effort to move off the couch, so he took the groceries through to the kitchen and poured her a glass of water, bringing it back immediately.

"Did you get off your feet at all today?" he asked, sitting at the end of the sofa and picking up one of her feet in his strong hands.

He began to massage her arches, and smiled when she groaned in delight.

"Oh, that feels good," she said, effectively dodging his question. "I'm thinking of keeping you on if you can promise you'll do this for me every day after work."

"You only have to say the word and I'm yours," he answered.

"The word?"

"Yes. And in case you've forgotten, that would be a yes to the will-you-marry-me question."

He deliberately kept his tone light.

"Okay, duly noted, and I consider myself fully informed," she teased with a tired smile.

Dylan picked up her other foot and began to massage it, as well, watching as she let her eyelids drift closed. When he stopped she didn't even move, so he gently placed her foot back down on the sofa and rose to go and prepare their evening meal. It worried him that she was so tired. Was that normal? He needed to do some research or talk to a doctor or someone. Maybe Marlene could help, or Hannah. He made a mental note to call the ranch in the morning, and then eyed the ingredients he'd bought for dessert before deciding to put them away for another time.

He worked quickly and efficiently in Jenna's kitchen, combining ingredients to form the spinach and pesto stuffing for the plump, free-range chicken breasts he'd purchased. He placed them in a shallow glass casserole dish, on top of quartered red potatoes that he'd tossed in olive oil. Then he smothered the breasts with the leftover stuffing before placing the lid on the dish and sliding it into the oven.

Just as he turned back from the oven, Jenna's home phone began to ring. He cursed the noise it made and dived for the handset on the kitchen countertop, hoping he'd get it before the sound woke Jenna.

"Hello?"

"Um, hello. Have I dialed the right number? Is this Jenna Montgomery's house?"

Dylan recognized Valerie's voice from the store.

"Yes, it's Dylan Lassiter here. Jenna's resting."

"Oh, good. I was just calling to see if she's okay. She took a dizzy turn in the shop today, and while I tried to encourage her to head home early, she flat out refused. Tell her that I've arranged for someone to keep an eye on the kids for me, so I'll open up for her tomorrow, would you? She can come in a bit later."

Dylan promised to pass the message on and placed the phone back on its station. A dizzy spell? No wonder she'd been looking pale. Clearly, she was overdoing things. His gut twisted in frustration. He was in no position to tell her what to do, but every cell in his body urged him to take charge and to make it clear that her health, and that of her unborn baby, should take greater precedence over her work.

But he was beginning to understand what her work meant to her. Without the support of family, she'd grown up missing the markers of encouragement and success that most other kids enjoyed. He thought about what he'd had growing up, and how he'd had the luxury of traveling and finding his niche in the world. How he'd taken all that for granted.

There were still huge gaps in what he knew about Jenna's past, not least of which being how she'd gone from living with her father to living here in Cheyenne with Margaret Connell. Dylan could only hope that eventually she'd trust him enough to tell him everything, to help him know her that much better so he could prove to her that spending the rest of her life with him was the best thing she could do for them all.

"Was that the phone?"

Damn, the call had disturbed her. By his reckoning she'd had only about twenty minutes or so of sleep, and judging by the darkness that underscored her eyes, she needed a whole lot more than that.

"Yeah, it was Valerie. She phoned to check up on you and to say she'd open for you tomorrow."

"She doesn't need to do that. I'm perfectly capable of opening the store myself. She has four kids to juggle in the morning," Jenna protested. "It's why she starts later."

"Clearly, she's juggled them so she can help you out. Why didn't you tell me you weren't feeling well today?" he asked, coming back into the sitting room and parking himself on the sofa again.

He lifted her legs and positioned her feet in his lap. Jenna got a defensive look on her face.

"I felt fine. I'd been bending down and when I stood up I just got a little bit dizzy. That's all."

"Have you felt dizzy before?"

"No, never. Seriously, I'm fine. Please don't fuss."

"Maybe I want to fuss over you," he countered. "Maybe I think you need a little fussing in your life."

She gave him a reluctant smile. "Oh, you do, do you?"

"Tell me, when was the last time anyone paid attention to you, real attention of the spoiling variety?"

Her grin grew wider. "I think that would have been last night, in bed, when you—"

"That's not what I mean, and you know it. Jenna, sometimes it's okay to let someone into your life, to let them share the load. I want that someone to be me."

Her face grew serious again and for a while she was si-

lent. When she spoke, her voice trembled ever so slightly.
"I want that to be you, too. I just—"

He leaned over her and placed a finger on her lips.
"No, don't justify anything. I'll take what you said and I'll
hold on to that for now, okay? Remember, I'm not going
anywhere. I'm right here for you, whether you think you
need me or not."

Twelve

Jenna stretched against the sheets in Dylan's bed, relishing the decadent luxury of the high thread count cotton against her bare skin. Last night they'd been out to the Big Blue for a family dinner, where the Lassiters had celebrated Hannah's engagement to Logan Whittaker. Again she'd been struck by the genuine love and warmth shared within the family. Love and warmth that had included her.

The siren call of being a part of all of that, the whole family thing, was growing louder in her mind, especially when combined with Dylan's attentiveness to her since Monday. He'd remained true to his word and shared her load; to be more accurate, it felt as if he'd shouldered the whole thing. Jenna still found it hard to accept gracefully, but she was learning. God, how she was learning. He'd delivered breakfast in bed each morning before driving her to work, his argument being that he didn't want her to suffer a dizzy spell while driving. And he'd collected her at the end of each day, to return to his or her home for dinner and to sleep.

And sleep they had. He hadn't made love to her since last weekend, insisting instead that she rest, and somehow, cradled securely in his arms each night, she'd slept better than she ever had before. She'd been unable to argue in the face of his logic, and had promised to follow up with her doctor if she felt the slightest bit dizzy again.

It was a novelty being so thoroughly spoiled. She couldn't remember a time in her life when she'd ever felt so pampered.

Or so loved.

He might not actually say it in so many words, but with every meal, every gesture, Dylan was using his attentiveness and care to prove that he'd meant what he said about wanting to be there for her in everything. Maybe they really could make this work, she thought, stroking the small mound of her belly through the sheets. Maybe they really could be a family.

She looked up as Dylan appeared in the doorway to the bedroom. He looked so sexy in just a pair of drawstring pajama bottoms slung low on his hips. His jaw was unshaved and his hair disheveled, and she had never wanted a man more in her life than she wanted him right now.

"How are you feeling this morning?" he asked, putting the tray with her breakfast on a bedside table and sitting down on the bed next to her to kiss her good morning.

"Fantastic," she answered with a smile. She raised a hand to trace the muscles of his chest, letting her fingers drift low over his ridged abdomen until they teased at the waistband of his pants. "In fact, any better and I think I'd be dangerous."

"Dangerous, huh?" He smiled in return.

She nodded. "I think I should show you how dangerous. Actions always speak louder than words, don't you think?"

Jenna rose up onto her knees, letting the sheet fall away from her body and exposing her nakedness to his hungry gaze. The look on his face empowered her. He made her feel so beautiful, so sexy, so very much in love. The realization should have hit her like a blow, she thought, but it felt right to admit it. To play around with the idea in her mind and to accept that with Dylan she could let go of the rigid control she'd developed to direct her life.

She pushed him back down on the bed, tugging at the drawstring of his pants and pushing the fabric aside to expose him to her gaze, to her fingers, to her lips. Then she showed him, slowly and lovingly, just how much he'd come to mean to her—imbuing every caress, every stroke of her tongue, with all that she felt and all that she wanted for the future. Their future.

Afterward, as they lay side by side, spent, their heart rates slowly returning to normal, Jenna looked across at the man who'd inveigled his way behind her defenses and come to mean so very much to her.

"Yes," she said simply.

Dylan's eyes narrowed and he looked at her intently, rolling onto his side. "Yes? Is that what I think it means?"

She nodded, suddenly shy and a little bit scared. This was letting go of her last vestige of control. But it would be okay, wouldn't it? With Dylan?

He reached for her hand and linked his fingers through hers before drawing them to his lips and kissing her knuckles.

"Thank you," he said with a reverence that brought tears to her eyes.

"Do you think your family will be okay with it? I mean, we haven't known each other all that long."

"They'll be more than fine, don't you worry. I'd like to announce it soon, though. No more secrets. What about at the opening the day after tomorrow? Everyone who matters to us will be there. Okay?"

No more secrets. Yet she still held one very close to her

chest. One that might change the way he thought about her forever. What the hell should she do? Tell him, and hope like mad that it wouldn't make any difference? Or keep it hidden away where it would hopefully never see the light of day ever again? It was impossible to know, but at least she didn't have to make a decision right now. After all, hadn't she just made the biggest decision in her life by accepting Dylan's proposal?

There was a time and a place for everything, and right now was not the time for the past. Right now was all about the future.

She slowly nodded. "Okay."

"Then I'd like you to wear this."

He slid open a bedside drawer and removed a pale blue ring box. Jenna's heart raced in her chest. Was that what she thought it was? Dylan slowly lifted the lid and showed the contents to her. A giant solitaire diamond, set high on a band embedded with smaller diamonds, winked at her in the morning light.

"Dylan, are you sure?"

He lifted the ring from its cushion and reached for her left hand, sliding the ring firmly onto her finger.

"I've never been more sure of anything in my life."

Dylan glanced around the restaurant. It looked, in a word, *perfect*. Jenna and her weekend girl, Millie, had delivered the table centerpieces, and they'd just left after putting together the massive tiered floral design in the foyer. Jenna had come up with an idea to use three up-ended logs of different lengths, and cunningly secured them so they wouldn't fall over. Her colorful floral displays cascaded over the logs in a tumble of nature's beauty.

It had given him a new appreciation for her talent as a

floral designer, and made him realize there was so much more to her than simply her ability to tweak a few wildflowers in a vase and make them look appealing. An ember of excitement burned deep inside him. He couldn't wait to announce to all the world tonight that she was his, that they were to be a family.

Today really was turning into the culmination of so many years of hard work, so many of his dreams. God, he missed J.D. and wished the old man could have been here to witness it all. He'd been at Dylan's side for the opening of each of their previous Grills. Dylan had to hope J.D. was here with him in spirit today. He would have been so proud.

"Dylan?"

Sage's voice interrupted him, dragging his attention back to the here and now. Dylan turned with a welcoming smile, surprised to see Sage here. But the serious expression on his brother's face wiped his smile clean away.

"Problem?" he asked.

"Mind if I talk to you for a minute?"

"Sure, fire away."

"In private?"

Dylan looked around at the hive of activity that buzzed about them. Waitstaff scurried back and forth, checking that the tables were all set to perfection and that every glass glistened. Through the serving window a similar hum of commotion came from the kitchen. If they wanted privacy, they'd need to go into his office.

Once they were inside, Sage made a point of closing the door behind him.

"What is it?" Dylan asked, getting the distinct feeling that he wasn't going to like what he had to say.

"Look, I don't quite know how to begin this."

"How about at the beginning," he prompted.

Sage's expression was stony. He drew in a deep breath before speaking. "I got that report back."

"Report?"

"The investigation into Jenna."

Dylan's blood hit boiling point in an instant. "You had no right—!"

"I had every right, as it turns out," Sage interrupted. He shook the contents of a large envelope onto Dylan's desk.

"What's all this?" he demanded, even as his eyes skimmed the words on one of the sheets that had fanned out.

Thief of Hearts! a headline proclaimed. The story went on to detail the trail of heartbroken victims a scam artist had left in his wake across the length and breadth of the country. Dylan continued to skim the article until his eyes jolted to a halt on a name: James Montgomery.

"Just because this guy shares her surname doesn't mean there's any connection," Dylan said, even though he had the distinct impression he was now grasping at straws.

Jenna had said she didn't see her father anymore. No wonder, if he'd been caught, tried and incarcerated for perpetuating such calculated crimes against innocent and vulnerable women.

"Keep reading. You ought to know," Sage said.

A knock sounded at the door and Fee popped her head inside.

"Am I interrupting?"

"No," Sage said before Dylan could answer. "Come in. You need to know this in case there's any fallout tonight."

"Know what?" she asked, coming into the room and closing the door.

"It seems my little brother's girlfriend is not who she appears to be."

"You don't know that," Dylan argued.

"Don't be so quick to judge me, Dylan. There's one thing I do know. That baby she's carrying *is* most likely yours. My investigator couldn't turn up any dirt on her in all the time she's lived in Cheyenne. Which begs the question, why did she suddenly latch on to you? Did she plan to get pregnant all along?"

"You bast—!"

Dylan lurched closer to his brother, only to have Fee step in between them. She looked from one man to the other.

"Guys, this isn't going to get physical, is it? I'd rather not be forced to explain black eyes at the opening tonight."

Her words compelled Dylan to relax the fists he hadn't even realized he'd made.

"You overstepped the mark, Sage," he growled.

"Can you blame me for wanting to look out for you? Read the articles then make up your own mind."

Through the fury that clouded his thinking, his brother's concern for him filtered through.

"Fine," he agreed, his jaw clenched tight.

"I'll leave you to it. Fee, you might need to read those, too." As Dylan began to protest, Sage overrode him again. "If my guy could discover this information, bear in mind others could, too. People who might want to cause trouble."

After Sage turned and left, Fee let out an audible breath.

"Wow, that was intense. What's it all about?"

Dylan swallowed back the bitter taste that had risen in his throat. "Some information he has on Jenna."

"Jenna? Really? Should we…?" Her voice trailed off as if she wasn't sure if going any further would be stepping on his toes.

Dylan sighed. "Yeah, we should. Here," he thrust half the papers in her direction. "Read."

Dylan finished reading the article he'd already started, feeling a sense of anger rising against Jenna's father for his callous behavior toward the women involved. Many of them were widows, women who'd lost their husbands and had sought male companionship, even love, only to find their bank accounts emptied and a pile of debt left in his wake when Jenna's dad left them. Imagine if something like that had happened to his aunt Marlene? Anger welled inside Dylan like a boiling cauldron.

He resolutely picked up the next article. Daughter In On It? questioned the headline. A photo of Jenna, much younger than she was now and with her head shaven beneath a tight headscarf, dominated the page. Even though she couldn't have been older than fourteen or fifteen, her beauty was easily apparent—perhaps even more so as she'd had no hair, so that the picture highlighted her large brown eyes and sweet smile.

Dylan's anger burned into a glowing mass of molten rock as the facts were grimly detailed. Jenna's father, the so-called Thief of Hearts, had used this photo of her and created an online fund-raising profile, saying she was dying of cancer and that they'd needed funds for her treatment. Dylan could barely believe what was there in stark black-and-white. While it was never proved that Jenna was a willing accomplice, questions still remained as to the depth of her involvement in that specific scam, as well as what had happened to all the money her father had conned out of his targets.

The article further revealed that as a minor, under the

care of the state when her father was sent down, Jenna would be put into foster care. That certainly explained how she had arrived in Cheyenne and ended up under Margaret Connell's roof—even though Mrs. Connell had never been known to foster anyone before then. Dylan reached for the printed single page report that summarized the investigator's findings. It went into interesting details about her financials. She'd attended the University of Wyoming without incurring any student loans and she'd also used a large cash deposit when buying her own home. A business loan had helped her buy the florist business. On their own, he could understand and accept each point, but the report raised far more questions than it answered. Like, where had Jenna gotten the money to attend university and buy her house?

Dylan reread the paragraph of the second article that talked about the sum of money that had been donated toward Jenna's "treatment." It was a hefty sum, reflective of the good will that had been shown by their community, and then abused and stomped on by her father. Apparently, the fund had been augmented by a six-figure donation from the woman Jenna's father had been known to be seeing at the time. Somehow, though, before the full investigation into her father's behavior, all that money had been withdrawn from the account set up in Jenna's name, and no amount of investigation had been able to reveal what had happened to it.

By the time he and Fee had finished reading the papers, a worried frown creased the PR manager's brow.

"Do you want to can the Q&A this evening?" she asked. "It might be best."

"It would be a complete break in our usual format. Wouldn't it raise even more questions if we do that?"

Fee pursed her lips. "You're probably right. I guess

we'll just have to hope that we can steer off any awkward questions, though I have to admit, I'm worried. As Sage said, if he could get this information, so can anyone."

Again that sense of being duped hammered at the back of Dylan's mind. It was information he'd have discovered himself if he'd been more diligent. If he hadn't been so swift to see only what he'd wanted to see.

"Let's just deal with it if it arises. Jenna's involvement in her father's scams was conjecture only."

Even as he said it, he felt his own doubts rise in his throat to choke him. Fee worried at her bottom lip with her teeth as she scanned the papers one more time.

"Are you sure that's how you want to handle it? In fact, are you sure you even still want Jenna there tonight?"

No, he wasn't. What he wanted was answers from Jenna. Answers he should have had from her before now. The fact she'd hidden all this from him hurt at a level he didn't want to discuss right now.

"Again, that would probably raise more questions than if she wasn't there. So, yes, I'm sure," he said firmly.

"Okay, then. I'll see you tonight."

Fee rose and left the office. He'd go to Jenna right now, he decided. He had to talk to her, to ask her for the truth behind this whole story. Determined to have this out with her face-to-face, he started to rise from his chair.

A loud crash sounded out in the kitchen, and within seconds a rapid knocking started at his door.

"Chef! Chef! We have a problem!"

Dylan groaned out loud, knowing that whatever was happening outside was far more urgent than talking to Jenna right now. He had more than a problem, he thought, as he shot from his office and into the kitchen to deal with the latest crisis. He had potentially opened up his whole family to someone who could be an accomplished scammer. One to whom he'd be inextricably connected for the rest of his life through their child. One who'd inveigled her way into his heart so securely that even entertaining the suspicion that she'd been a willing accomplice in her father's scheme caused a physical pain in his chest.

Sage had cautioned him about racing into this full-on, and Dylan hadn't listened. Had he been thoroughly duped? Had her playing hard to get all been part of her act? He didn't want to believe it could be true, but a devil of rationality perched on his shoulder told him he needed to consider all his options before taking this any further. As far as he knew Jenna had lived an exemplary life here in Cheyenne. Finishing high school, attending college, working hard and buying a home and a business. On the surface, it all looked so perfect. Too perfect maybe?

"Chef! We need you."

The shout spurred him into action. Right now, the kitchen was his priority; unfortunately, just when it looked as if his life was jumping out of the frying pan and into the fire. Deep down, though, Dylan couldn't help feeling a sense of betrayal. The other night, when she'd finally accepted his proposal, they'd agreed—no more secrets. And if this wasn't a breach of that agreement, he didn't know what was.

Thirteen

Jenna stepped from the car Dylan had sent for her, her gown falling around her in a delicate swirl of fiery-orange. The halter neck and empire waistline drew attention away from her bump, although she doubted she'd be able to continue to hide it for much longer. She thumbed the diamond ring on her finger with a small smile. Once their engagement was public knowledge it would be okay to let the news of their baby leak out.

She ducked her head shyly as some of the assembled media took her photo as she walked toward the front door.

"Name please, miss?" the stylishly suited young man at the door asked, before referring to his clipboard and ushering her through when she'd told him.

Dylan was part of a receiving line in the entrance. She drank in the sight of him in a dark pinstripe suit that looked as if it had been tailored specifically for him.

He was hers. The idea filled her with a sense of completion she could hardly dare believe. She really was the luckiest woman on earth. After all she'd been through, he'd become her light in the darkness. Her true north.

He looked up and she beamed at him, covering the carpeted distance between them as quickly and gracefully as her high heels would allow.

"Dylan, this looks amazing!" she breathed as she reached his side and lifted her face for his kiss.

She was surprised when his lips just grazed her cheek, but put it down to the swell of people pressing behind her as they came through the main entrance.

"I won't take up your time," she said quickly. "I'll leave you to your duties."

"No, wait just a second." Dylan caught her by the hand and turned to the man beside him.

"Evan, could you look after Jenna for me? Just until I can get free, okay?"

"Sure, absolutely no problem whatsoever."

"Jenna," Dylan continued, "this is Evan McCain, CEO of Lassiter Media. He's come in from L.A. for this evening. You'll be in good hands."

Jenna had recognized the ex-fiancé of Dylan's sister, Angelica, the minute she'd walked in the door, and said as much.

"It's good to see you again, Evan. I'm glad you could make it," she added.

"I wouldn't have missed it for the world." He smiled, his hazel eyes crinkling at the corners. "So, shall we go and see what the waitstaff are serving on those ridiculously large trays they're carrying around? I don't know about you, but I'm starving."

He offered her his arm and Jenna took it with a smile. She glanced back at Dylan, who was watching her with that little frown between his brows.

"I'll be fine. Just looking forward to when you're free," she said with a small wave.

He gave her a nod and turned his attention to the next newcomers in the line, welcoming the mayor and his wife with his accomplished smile and polite patter. As Evan led her away toward the dining room, Jenna couldn't help but feel that something was amiss. Aside from getting the message, through Fee Sinclair, that he'd be sending a car for her instead of picking her up himself today, she'd not had a single call from him. That in itself had been unusual.

Still, she silently reasoned, he was under a lot of pressure for tonight. In her call, Fee had mentioned the accident one of his staff had suffered in the kitchen earlier today, and Jenna knew he'd stepped into the breach. Did that explain the undercurrent of tension she'd felt? She hoped that was all it was, and that once he knew everything was running smoothly for tonight he could relax.

There was a loud murmur of activity at the entrance and Jenna turned her head in time to see Angelica Lassiter arrive, accompanied by a striking man. Tall, with dark brown hair and eyes that appeared to miss nothing, he looked incredibly handsome and yet had an air of ruthlessness about him that set her on edge. On his arm, Angelica looked absolutely stunning. Her shoulder-length hair was swept up into an elegant chignon that exposed the delicate line of her neck.

Jenna could feel Evan's tension as he watched his ex-fiancée's entrance. "Him? Of all the people she could have come with, she chose him?" he muttered.

"Who is he? I don't think I've seen him around here before," Jenna said, allowing Evan to turn her away from the newcomers and toward a waitress carrying a tray of canapés.

"No, you wouldn't have. No disrespect to you, but you don't move in Jack Reed's exalted circles."

Jenna couldn't help but recognize the bitterness in his voice. Evan continued, "He's from L.A., and has a hard-earned reputation as a corporate raider—all of which makes me wonder why he's even here. Unless Angelica did this to deliberately annoy me."

Jenna's first instinct was to refute what Evan had said.

She'd met Angelica again at Hannah and Logan's engagement dinner, and Dylan's sister had been gracious and charming. She certainly hadn't struck Jenna as malicious, even though there was clearly some undercurrent between Evan and Angelica's date. But then a tiny voice reminded her of something Dylan had said several days ago, about how upset Angelica had been when her father had cut her out of Lassiter Media in his will, leaving the controlling share to Evan.

"Well," Jenna said quietly, "I guess whatever the reason, the best thing for now is to make do with my company and show her that you don't mind who she's shown up with."

"Make do? Having your company is far better than making do," he said with a charming smile that lit up his face. "I apologize if I made it sound any other way."

Jenna laughed, the sound drawing the attention of the newcomers—in particular Angelica, whose set expression and sharp-eyed glare at Evan showed she was about as happy seeing him here as he was in seeing Jack Reed at her side. A swell of people moved between them, breaking the moment, and Jenna felt a wave of relief sweep through her.

Evan led her through the room, circulating among the gathering guests. The crowd consisted of Lassiters and members of the local chamber of commerce, interspersed with a few celebrities and a smattering of media. Jenna received many compliments on her floral displays and, from the number of business cards she was given and was asked for, would be rushed off her feet with work in the coming weeks. Things were really looking up, she thought, as everyone was invited to take their seats.

Evan showed Jenna to a seat at a table near the large stone fireplace in the center of the restaurant. The placeholder next to hers showed Dylan would be seated on her right, and Evan slid into the chair at her left. It took some time for the room to settle into quiet and for everyone to be seated. The lighting dimmed until only a podium near the front was well lit. She smiled through the gloom as Marlene and her date, Walter Drake, whom Jenna had also met at Hannah and Logan's engagement dinner, sat down opposite her.

Dylan took the floor, introducing his new Lassiter Grill team with pride. Jenna squirmed with excitement. Any minute now he'd be closing up the official business and inviting her to join him to share their news—their happiness—with everyone assembled. It felt odd, after so many years of keeping her head down and struggling to remain unnoticed, to be looking forward to being the center of attention. But as she watched the man she loved with all her heart standing there in front of everyone, she knew she could do anything in this world as long as he was by her side.

She thumbed the engagement ring he'd given her two days ago, and felt a swell of love build inside. She'd never been happier than she was right at this moment.

Dylan wound up the formal section of the evening, thanking everyone for being there, and asked if there were any questions from the floor. He smoothly fielded a number of questions relating to the restaurant before the tone began to swing toward a more personal note.

"Dylan, you've been spending a lot of time in Cheyenne lately. Aside from the restaurant, is there something or some*one* else responsible for that?" one of the female reporters asked with a sugary sweet tone.

Dylan nodded his head. "I've been seeing someone, yes, that's true."

The same reporter asked, "Are you going to tell us who that someone is?"

Fee, standing slightly to one side of Dylan, whispered something in his ear. He nodded and addressed the reporter.

"Jenna Montgomery. Many of you will know her already. She's responsible for the stunning floral designs here tonight."

A prickle of unease crept across Jenna's skin. That was it? Nothing about their engagement? She thought tonight was when he'd wanted to make the announcement. To shout it, loud and proud, that they were getting married and having a family together.

A different voice, a man's this time, rang out.

"Is it true that Jenna Montgomery is pregnant with your child?"

How on earth had some journalist heard about the baby?

Dylan kept his composure. "That is true," he answered smoothly as if the news was of no consequence.

The same man persisted. "Are you and your family aware that the woman carrying your baby is the same Jenna Montgomery who faked terminal cancer to help her father swindle nearly a quarter million dollars from a fund set up in her name eleven years ago?" the reporter persisted.

The room exploded in an uproar. Jenna felt the world tilt and a sensation like icy cold water ran through her veins. Through the haze of terror in her mind she heard Dylan's voice asking for calm. As the room once more fell quiet, Jenna found herself—like pretty much everyone else there—hanging on a thread waiting to find out what he would say.

"Yes, I am aware of Jenna's past and of the unproved

charges against her." He paused and whispered something to Fee, who went immediately across the room to two men standing to the side in dark suits. Together with them, she walked toward the reporter who had asked the questions. Dylan turned his attention back to the assembly as the reporter was quietly ushered from the restaurant. "Now, if there are no more questions, let's enjoy dinner."

An eerie silence filled the room like a vacuum as all eyes turned to Jenna. Across the table, Marlene looked at her in concern, a question in her eyes that Jenna had no wish to answer right here and now—or ever, if it could have come to that. She wanted nothing more than to run, and glanced around the room for the nearest exit, feeling like a cornered creature with nowhere to hide. Beside Marlene, Sage Lassiter's eyes bored into her as if he could see right through her to the woman he'd thought she was all along.

Her gaze flittered past them all, frantic to find a compassionate face, but everyone simply looked at her in a blend of shock or accusation. Here she was, a viper in their midst. Someone they'd accepted, welcomed— someone they really shouldn't trust.

Eventually, she looked at Dylan, silently begging him to believe in her. To *know* that she had been an innocent party in all that had happened. She should have told him long before. Her silence now made her appear complicit. Finally, his eyes met hers and she felt every last glimmer of hope for a future together fade into nothing. In his gaze she saw no trace of the teasing lover who'd shared her nights, nor the conscientious and caring soul who'd paid such devoted attention to her this past week. No longer was he the man who'd determinedly suggested marriage and then cajoled her into love—into believing in a time ahead where they could be happy together, be *parents* together.

A shudder rippled through her body, numbness taking her over until it was a struggle to draw in a deep enough breath. This was her worst nightmare. Her darkest, most shameful secret had been exposed to everyone here. People she admired and had come to trust. People who had come to trust her. Now that trust was crushed to smithereens, her hard-won reputation scattered to the corners of the county. She'd truly thought she'd managed to put all that behind her, but now, well, nothing could ever be the same again.

Dylan's eyes flicked from hers to someone else nearby, and seconds later she heard Felicity Sinclair's voice in her ear.

"Come, let me take you home. This can't be good for you or for the baby," she said in her capable, no-nonsense manner.

"Th-thank you," Jenna said gratefully, rising to her feet as Dylan continued to field a melee of questions from the media who'd been asked to cover the opening.

Fee guided her past the beautifully dressed tables— tables Jenna had helped decorate herself, in excited preparation for tonight—and the accusatory stares of the people gathered here punctured her as though each one was a spear of loathing. She couldn't believe how her world had turned on a dime, from one filled with joy and expectations to one where the future once again appeared bleak and lonely.

It seemed like forever, but eventually they were at the front of the restaurant and out the main doors. Fee ushered her immediately into a waiting car. Jenna didn't even stop to wonder how the woman had arranged for the driver to be there so quickly. Instead, she sagged against the seat, locked in a cocoon of loss, as Fee slid into the seat beside her and instructed the man to take them to Jenna's home.

Fee's hand slipped into hers. "Take a deep breath, Jenna. And another. Okay? Leave it to Dylan. He'll take care of everything."

How could he take care of everything? Why would he even want to? Jenna squeezed her eyes shut, but his image still burned there, especially the look on his face just before Fee had led her from the restaurant. The numbness that encased her slowly began to recede—replaced instead by a tearing pain deep inside her chest.

"It's going to be okay," Fee soothed. "You're out of there now."

Sure, they were out of there, but nothing was ever going to be okay again. Jenna had seen the questions in Dylan's eyes, the hurt and mistrust that had replaced the warmth and the love she'd already grown accustomed to seeing in him. Inside she began to mourn what they would never be able to share again.

She should have known better than to hope, known better than to reach out and take what he'd offered her so tantalizingly. She thought about all she'd undoubtedly lost. His trust, their future, his family. She would miss it all. Would she ever be able to look at him again and not see the accusation in his eyes? The knowledge that, of all the things she'd shared with him, that piece of her past was the one she should have shared first?

A discreet buzz came from Fee's delicate evening bag and she slid out her phone.

"Yes, we're on our way to her house."

Jenna could make out a muffled male voice at the other end.

"She's okay, for now. I'll stay with her until you can

come, just to be sure." Fee popped her phone back into her bag. "Dylan will be over as soon as he can get away."

Jenna nodded, but knew it wouldn't make any difference. What they'd had would be gone now. A man like him—a family like theirs—didn't need the notoriety that being with someone like her would bring. She'd known that all along, and yet she'd foolishly dared to dream it could be different.

Now, she knew, it would never be.

Fourteen

Dylan parked at the curb outside Jenna's house, leaving the driveway clear for the limousine that remained parked in the drive. He nodded to the driver as he walked past and up to the front door.

Fee opened it before he could knock.

"How is she?" he asked, his voice tight.

"She went to lie down as soon as we got here. Do you want me to head back to the Grill now?"

"If you don't mind. I guess you've probably already worked out a strategy to cope with any fallout over tonight?"

Fee smiled. "Of course. Leave it to me. This will blow over, you know. It won't affect the Lassiter Grill Corporation. If anything, the notoriety might even be good for you."

It might not affect the company, but it certainly affected everything else that was important to him, he thought as he escorted Fee out to the limousine. He watched as it drove away, and then turned and went back inside Jenna's compact home.

She was standing in the living room when he got inside. He was shocked to see how her dark eyes stood out in her eerily pale face. She hadn't changed from the gown she'd been wearing tonight, and it looked crumpled. His eyes drifted over her graceful shoulders, over the fullness of her breasts and lower, to where his baby nestled inside her. His gut twisted.

"Are you all right?" he asked, concern for her and the baby uppermost in his mind.

"A bit upset," she said, her hand fluttering to her belly. She gave a humorless laugh. "Actually, a lot upset."

He wasn't surprised. It had been a shock for him, too. First of all to discover that secret in her past, and then to have it laid out in front of everyone at the opening tonight.

Why had she kept it hidden from him? She could have told him at any time over the past few days, especially once she'd agreed to plan a future together. Did she honestly think that if she was an innocent party, he'd have felt any differently about her? Hell, she'd been so young she *had* to be innocent. Even if she'd participated in the scam, surely she would have been compelled to do so by the one person who was supposed to have been taking care of her.

Unless the real answer was all too damning. In general, people didn't hide the truth—which left an alternative that Dylan found distinctly unpalatable.

"It is true?" he asked. Everything depended on her answer.

"What part, exactly?"

He bit back the frustration that threatened to overwhelm him. How could she be flip about this? How could she continue to avoid telling him what he needed to know?

"All of it? Any of it?" He bit out the questions.

"There is some truth to it," she said softly, ducking her head.

"So you were involved."

Something passed across her face, something he couldn't quite define.

"Yes," she said, lifting her chin and meeting his scrutiny. "I was involved, but not voluntarily. I didn't know what my father was doing."

Could he believe her? He wanted to, but all the evidence, especially her silence on this very matter, suggested he shouldn't.

And it still didn't answer the question why she hadn't told him.

"What about me?" he asked.

"What do you mean?"

"What am I to you?"

"Dylan!" She sped across the carpet to stand directly in front of him, placing a hand on his chest. "You know what you are to me. You're my lover, the man I want to marry. You're the father of my baby. The man I love."

It sounded so sincere, and yet there were still shadows in her eyes. Truths that couldn't be told because maybe they weren't truths, after all. The questions that had been tumbling around in his mind all day were as irrational now as they'd seemed when they'd first evolved in his brain. Yet they still spewed forth from his mouth before he could have time to weigh them properly.

"Did I come across to you as an easy mark? Is that what it was? Did you see me at the rehearsal dinner setup and target me then? Or maybe the idea came to you later, when you discovered you were pregnant. Was that it?"

He saw her flinch beneath his onslaught. Felt her pull her hand away from his chest, and in its place felt coldness invade that part of him where his heart had beat steadily for her.

"I can't believe you'd think that of me," she said, her eyes wide with horror.

"Seriously, Jenna? We agreed, only two nights ago, no more secrets. What am I supposed to think?"

She stiffened her shoulders. "I can't tell you what to think. Look, perhaps it would be in the best interests of everyone concerned, especially your family and the Lassiter brand, if we didn't see one another again. I won't stand in your way when it comes to access to the baby, I promise you that. It's what I expected to do from the first, anyway."

She took one step back, then another, her fingers frantically working off the engagement ring he'd chosen with all the love he carried for her in his heart. She dropped the ring onto the occasional table beside her.

"Take it," she said bluntly, determination overlaying the anguish that still reflected in her eyes. "Just take it. I don't want it anymore."

He looked at the ring sitting on the table—its beauty an empty symbol of all his hopes. He scooped it up and put it in his suit pocket and turned and walked away.

"Fine. Since you still can't be honest with me, I'll go," he said bitterly. But nothing was fine at all. At the door he hesitated and turned back to face her. "You know what the worst thing about all of this is?"

She stared back at him, mute.

"The worst thing is that you wouldn't trust me enough to tell me the truth. I love you, Jenna. I really thought you'd learned to love me in return. Last chance. Tell me the truth."

She shook her head, her arms wrapping around her body, her cheeks glistening with the tears that ran freely down her face. Every instinct in his body urged him to go to her, to take her in his arms and to tell her that they could still work this out. That everything would be okay.

"Please," she said, her voice thick and choked. "Let yourself out."

She wheeled on her feet and fled down the hallway toward her bedroom. A second later he heard the door slam in finality. Raw pain, the likes of which he'd never known before, clawed viciously through him. Somehow he managed to walk out the door and get to his SUV. He sat there in the dark, staring at her house for a full five minutes, before starting the car and driving away.

Anger bubbled up from beneath his agony. Why couldn't she just tell him? Why couldn't she share that part of her that had now effectively driven them apart? Dammit, she'd chosen doing what was right for his family—even the Lassiter brand—over sharing the truth with him. What about his feelings? Didn't she care about them? Didn't she care that she'd let them both down?

Somehow he drove back to the restaurant, where the opening night party was still in full swing. He slid in through the rear entrance, but Sage caught him when he was in his office, about to put Jenna's ring in the safe.

"You all right?" his brother asked.

"No, I'm not all right," he growled, one hand swinging open the safe's door while the other closed in a fist around the ring in his pocket. It cut into his palm and he welcomed the pain. It matched how he felt inside. He flung a glance at his brother. "So, are you going to gloat? Tell me you were right all along?"

Sage shook his head. "You didn't see her face when that reporter threw that question at you. She looked as if her entire world had blown up."

"Her fabricated world, you mean," Dylan said bitterly.

"No," Sage said firmly. "Her real world. Maybe I was too hasty in showing you that report. Maybe we should have delved a bit deeper first. I agree," he said in response to his brother's snort of disgust, "it was my idea. But, Dylan, you didn't see how tonight affected her. Give it a few days. Go back to her. Talk it out."

He shook his head. "Not going to happen. She doesn't want to see me anymore."

He pulled his fist from his pocket and uncurled his fingers from around the ring, exposing the glittering piece before hurling it into the back of the safe and slamming the door shut.

"I didn't mean to hurt you, Dylan. You deserved to know the truth. But think on this. If she really was what those articles say she is, she'd still be wearing that ring."

Dylan weighed his brother's words. "You're probably right," he said with a sigh. "But until she's prepared to be open with me, I can't see us working this thing out. Besides, she'll probably never forgive me for what I said."

"What exactly did you say?"

"I asked her if I was her latest mark. I couldn't help it. It just came out. I was so mad that she'd kept something so important from me. Nothing about her life adds up, Sage. Nothing. Not unless she really was a part of her father's scheme and has been happily living off those proceeds all this time."

He didn't want to believe his own words, but without proof, without Jenna's own testimony, how could he think anything different?

Jenna walked on aching legs to her office to tally up the day's receipts. So much for today's cashless society, she thought, as she extracted the float to go back into the cash register, and then counted the notes to go to the bank the next morning.

She'd been beyond worried that after the disaster of Lassiter Grill's opening night, her business would slowly dwindle and die off. Instead, the opposite had been true. She'd barely been able to keep up with demand, and had been forced to increase her orders from the wholesalers. She and Valerie had been swamped working on special orders, and the foot traffic coming in through the front door had doubled over the previous week.

"Why don't you let me finish that up," Valerie offered as she entered the office. "You look dead on your feet."

"No, I'm halfway there already," Jenna insisted, even as a wave of weariness swept through her.

It wasn't the first time this week she'd felt weak and slightly disoriented. Considering she'd barely been able to force herself from bed each morning, or to eat or drink properly, it really was no wonder. Logically, she knew she had to look after herself, to look after the baby. But just now everything to do with herself fell into the "too hard" basket. She was glad they were crazy busy. At least at work she could get lost in the oblivion of one order to fill after another.

Valerie sat in the chair opposite Jenna's desk and studied her. "Have you heard from him yet?"

"What? No, I haven't. And I don't expect to, either."

"Never?" Valerie sounded regretful.

"Never, at least not directly," Jenna responded. She could hear the flatness in her voice and tried to inject some life back into it. "It's better that way."

"I don't see how. You're still pregnant with his baby. That takes two."

"Valerie, please. This week's hard enough as it is," Jenna implored her friend. "Can you just let it go?"

Valerie studied her from across the table. "Not when you look the way you do. I'm sorry, but I care about you. In fact, no. I'm not sorry. I *care* about you, Jenna. I've watched you go all the way from sweeping floors to taking this business over from Margaret and getting us to where we are today. You're bright, you're clever—but most of all you're honest. I know people have been saying things about you, and yes, I remember the stories about your dad from back when. It's shameful what he did to you and it's shameful that it's coming back to haunt you. You're not the person they said you are. The past belongs right there, in the past. I believe in you, Jenna. I just wanted you to know that."

Jenna gave the other woman a weak smile. "Thank you. I appreciate it."

"But it's not enough, is it? You still love him."

Jenna felt the all too familiar burn of tears in her eyes. She resolutely blinked them back, again. "That doesn't matter. What matters is this little person in here." She patted her tummy and was rewarded with a ripple of movement.

"Honey, trust me, it matters. You're killing yourself over this."

Of course it mattered. It mattered enough that barely a minute went by without her thinking of Dylan. Without seeing again and again the pain she'd inflicted on him and the disappointment that had been etched on his face before he'd left her on Saturday night. She drew in a deep breath. It would get better, eventually. She had to hold on to that thought.

Valerie persisted. "I think you should see him. Talk this out some more."

"He's gone back to L.A. At least that's what I heard."

"So pick up a telephone."

"No, really. It's over, Valerie. If I can accept that, I think you should, too. In fact, I'd appreciate it if you didn't mention it again."

Never would be too soon, Jenna thought as Valerie reluctantly agreed to her request.

"At least come to my house tonight for dinner. You can put up your feet. I'll make sure the kids wait on you and I'll cook you up one of my famous chicken casseroles."

"It sounds lovely, but to be honest, I'm beat. I just want to go home and go to bed."

"And have something to eat," Valerie added.

"Yes, yes, and have something to eat." Jenna gathered up the cash and checks and handed Valerie the float to put back in the cash register. "I'll do the banking on my way in tomorrow. Will you be okay to open up?"

"Sure. With my eldest and her best friend happy to mind the younger kids for a few extra dollars while they're on summer vacation, life's a whole lot less chaotic for me in the mornings. Don't rush in."

"I'll be here just after nine, I hope. We have another big day ahead."

"Which is exactly why I don't think you should be rushing around," Valerie teased with a laugh.

"Okay, okay. Don't you have enough mothering to do with your kids?"

"Hey, once a mother, always a mother."

Valerie went to put the spare cash in the register and then walked out the back with Jenna. "You take care tonight," her friend said, then got in her car and drove away with a cheerful wave.

Jenna watched her go with a wistful smile on her face. She'd never stopped to think all that much about Valerie's life beyond what she saw on the surface—married for sixteen years, with four great kids. Jenna was hit with a near overwhelming sense of envy for the simplicity of Valerie's world. For the security within it. She tightened her grip on the steering wheel and breathed in deep. She could do this. She'd been on her own for a long time now and she didn't need anyone else.

But even as she thought it, Dylan's face swam into her thoughts and with it a feeling of loss so devastating it made her head swim. She leaned back on the headrest and dragged in one breath after another until the woozy sensation left her. Then she turned on the ignition and put her car into gear, easing it out of the parking lot and onto the street, heading home.

She'd get through this. She just had to.

Fifteen

She was dragging her feet from the moment she got up the next morning. It was as if no matter how much time she spent in bed, or resting, it was never quite enough. Jenna surveyed the miserable offerings of food she had left in her fridge. Nothing worth eating for breakfast, she realized. She'd pick something up at a drive-through on the way to the store. She filled her traveling cup with drinking water, picked up her bag and went through to her garage.

Just as she pressed the garage door opener a wave of vertigo hit, and she put out a hand to the doorjamb to steady herself. It took about a full minute to pass.

"Pull yourself together," Jenna chastised herself out loud, adjusting her bag on her shoulder and stepping toward her car. "You ate a decentish meal last night. You can survive until after the bank."

She took a sip of her water, then another. There, she was feeling better already, she told herself, and walked the short distance to her car.

Driving to the bank, she felt fine. She found a parking spot close by and then went inside to wait for a free teller. Despite the early hour, it was busy for a Thursday. She hadn't been waiting terribly long before she felt the earth tilt beneath her feet once more.

"Not again," she muttered under her breath.

"What's that, miss?" said the older man in the line ahead of her.

"Oh, nothing, sorry."

"Are you sure? You look a bit—"

That was all Jenna heard before the blackness came out of nowhere to swallow her whole. She never even felt it when she hit the floor, nor did she hear the concerned cries from the people around her.

"You look like crap, man," Dylan's second in charge, Noel, said as he came into his office on Friday morning.

"Why, thank you," he replied in a voice loaded with sarcasm.

Truth was, he knew he looked like crap. Felt it, too. Since leaving Cheyenne he'd felt as if something—or more precisely, someone—was calling him back. He'd tried to tell himself he'd done all he could, that he'd overseen the opening to the best of his ability and that he'd left things in his executive chef's and restaurant manager's capable hands. Hell, he wouldn't have hired them if they weren't up to the job in the first place. It was time to pour himself back into what his job called for here in L.A.

Even so, his mind kept turning over that last conversation with Jenna, and with it, all the questions that remained unanswered between them. He'd done some more research and discovered that her father, James, had quite the reputation with the ladies. Exactly when he'd started fleecing them for every penny had been unclear, but when a couple of widows had begun comparing notes about their new beau over a game of bridge at their country club one afternoon, they'd seen and heard enough from one another to realize they were dating the same man.

After pressure from their families, they'd been the ones to bring the original complaints to the police, instigating the investigation into James Montgomery's habits. An inquiry that had unearthed a string of similarly swindled lovers in his past. Women who'd been too embarrassed to bring their situation to the attention of their families, let alone the authorities.

It made Dylan furious to think of so many innocents being duped by the charmer. A man whose first priority should have been the care and raising of his daughter. Dylan didn't understand how anyone could be so remiss in his duty to his own flesh and blood.

Speaking of *his* flesh and blood, he wondered how Jenna was doing. She'd be sixteen weeks along by now. When had she been due next for a scan? He huffed out a sigh and forced himself to relax his hand around the Montblanc pen he was strangling to death over the papers he was supposed to sign, and which Noel was waiting so patiently for.

"Your EA asked me to bring these in to you," Noel said, putting some pink message slips on Dylan's desk.

His eye scanned the papers, but it wasn't until he picked up the Cheyenne area code on one that he sat up and took notice. It wasn't like Chance to call him here at the office; his cousin usually called him direct on his cell phone, Dylan thought as he flourished his pen across the necessary pages and then passed the stack of documents over the desk to Noel.

"Was there anything else you needed from me today?" he asked the younger guy.

"No, I'm pretty sure we're up to date with these," he said, flicking through the pages. "I'll call you if anything arises from them."

"Thanks." Dylan nodded absently. He checked his cell

phone as he picked up the office handset to dial home. Two missed calls from Chance—yesterday. Whatever it was, it had to be urgent. His cousin picked up on the second ring, his voice gruff.

"Chance Lassiter."

"Hey, just the man I wanted to speak to. How come you're not working?"

"I wish I wasn't working. I'm going through the ranch accounts before handing them over to the accountant. But that's beside the point. Where have you been, man? I've been trying to get hold of you since yesterday."

"I had my phone on Do Not Disturb and forgot to change it back. What's up?"

"Have you heard about Jenna?"

Dylan stiffened in his chair. "Heard about her? Why? What's happened?"

"She collapsed in the bank yesterday morning. They had to rush her to the hospital."

"She collapsed? Do you know why?"

Dammit, he shouldn't have left Cheyenne. He shouldn't have walked away from his responsibilities to his unborn baby or to its mother.

"Mom called the hospital as soon as she heard, but they wouldn't give her any information other than to say Jenna was stable."

Stable was good, wasn't it, he consoled himself. At least she wasn't in serious or critical condition. "Has anyone tried to contact Jenna directly?"

"Sure. But her cell must be turned off. A woman called Valerie answered at the store, but she was about as forthcoming as a clam when Mom asked after Jenna."

Dylan mentally calculated what he had to complete today to be able to get back home to Cheyenne. Home. When had L.A. stopped being home for him? he wondered briefly, and then realized it never really had been. Sure, it was where he lived, but it wasn't where he belonged. Right now he belonged back in Cheyenne.

"I'll be there as soon as I can. Thanks for the heads-up, Chance."

"I knew you'd want to know. Hey, man. You're going to sort this out, aren't you? The rest of us don't care what happened to her in the past, or what she was involved in. We do care about who she is now, and she's going to be the mother of one of a new generation of Lassiters. She's one of us, whether she wants to be or not."

"Yeah, I'm going to sort this out," Dylan said, ending the call. *Somehow.*

But it was as if the world conspired to prevent him from getting to Cheyenne, from getting to Jenna and finding out what was wrong with her. He was as gnarly as a wildcat with a thorn in its paw by the time he dumped his remaining work onto Noel and instructed him that if anything else urgent came up, he'd have to handle it himself. To the younger guy's credit, he didn't so much as blink.

Dylan's executive assistant filled him in on the booking details for the flight she'd just managed to squeeze him onto at short notice. It would mean a stop in Denver, but at least he'd arrive in Cheyenne before midnight tonight. He cursed the fact that the company jet was down for routine maintenance. While he waited at the airport, he called the hospital and asked to be put through to Jenna, but was surprised to be told she'd already been discharged. That meant she had to be home, right?

In the departure lounge he tried her home phone number, but there was no reply. He tried her cell—again, no reply. He looked at his watch; her store would just about be closing. He dialed the number, only to hear the final boarding call for his flight. A security guard gave him a strange look as Dylan muttered a string of curses before grabbing his briefcase and heading to the gate. He'd have to stow his impatience and his concerns until he got to Wyoming and could see her for himself.

A delay in Denver saw his flight into Cheyenne land well after midnight. Dylan was chafing at the bit to drive straight to Jenna's house, but logic and reason told him that would be stupid. If she was home, she'd be sound asleep by now. The morning would have to suffice.

Once he arrived at his house Dylan shrugged out of his suit jacket and tore off his tie. He poured himself a generous measure of aged Scotch and threw himself into one of the large chairs in the living room. Sleep was the furthest thing from his mind right now. From the moment he'd received the news about Jenna, his primary focus had been on getting here. He hadn't really stopped to think about what he'd do when he arrived. Sure, he wanted to see for himself that she and the baby were okay, and he most definitely wanted to know what had caused the collapse that had sent her to the hospital in the first place. But what then? What came after that?

He still had questions to which she was the only one who held the answers. It had hurt him deeply when he learned she'd been holding back and made him say things he never would have under normal circumstances. But then again, their circumstances had never been normal, exactly, had they? That said, he'd been upfront about his desire to want to take care of her from the beginning. To build a future for her and their baby. Seeing her again, after their first encounter, had proved to him that their attraction was definitely not the kind of thing that crossed a person's path more than once in a lifetime. In fact, for many people, it never entered their life at all. He'd believed, down deep in his soul, that she was the one for him. Had that changed?

Aside from his natural concern for her, how did he feel now? Had knowing what lay in her past changed his emotions when it came to Jenna Montgomery? He took a sip of his whiskey and rolled the liquid around on his tongue before swallowing it. The answer to his question took a long time coming. No, he didn't love her any less. Sure, he was stung that she hadn't told him, but it didn't change how he felt about her at his core. He'd accused her of not trusting him with the full story about her past, but wasn't he just as bad not trusting her when she had told him she hadn't been knowingly involved in the cancer scam? Had he been so hurt by her withholding the truth that he hadn't even wanted to listen—had somehow wanted to punish her for that secret and therefore hadn't been prepared to believe her?

This past week had been hell without her. Without hearing the sound of her voice, the husky timbre of her laughter, the delicious hitch in her breathing when he kissed her intimately.

Could he imagine life without her? Hell, no, he couldn't. Every night since the opening he'd tried to see how his future would evolve without Jenna being an intrinsic part of it, and it had been a dark and harrowing place. He wanted her. More than that, he loved her with a passion so great he knew he could never settle for anyone else but her. Ever.

Which left him in a difficult position. He'd known from the start that their relationship was fragile, that it needed careful tending to bring it to its fullest and most exciting best. Had he crushed that tender seedling when he'd asked her if she'd thought him to be an easy mark? Could they revive the bond between them? She'd looked so battered, so bruised. He'd been so locked in his own anger and disbelief at what he'd perceived as disloyalty, not to mention dishonesty. He still wanted to know the truth, the full truth this time. They couldn't move forward until everything had been laid bare between them.

What was it she'd said, exactly? That she couldn't believe he'd think that of her. Somewhere along the line he'd earned her confidence, which was a far cry from where they'd been that day he'd swanned into Connell's Floral Design and back into her life. And, with a single comment, he'd destroyed it. But trust was a two way street. If she couldn't be 100 percent honest with him, too, then they didn't stand a chance.

He had his work cut out for him if he wanted to get her to open up to him fully, that was for sure. But he was driven to succeed in this, to surpass his success in everything else he'd wanted in his life to date. She'd said she wouldn't stand in his way with the baby, but he wasn't satisfied with that. He wanted them both.

What Chance had said resonated with Dylan. Whatever she'd done or been involved with in the past wasn't who she was now. Why should it matter? She was the mother of his baby. She was the woman who held his heart. That was all that counted. The rest, well, he'd deal with it one way or another, provided she'd let him. The morning couldn't come soon enough.

It was only ten o'clock and already Jenna was exhausted. Millie hadn't shown this morning, too hungover, if the garbled text message she'd sent had been anything to go by. Had Jenna ever been like that? she wondered. No, of course not. She'd been too busy trying to be invisible, yet invaluable at the same time.

A call to Valerie, to see if she could come in, even if

only for a couple of hours, had revealed that during the night she'd fallen victim to an apparently short-lived, but virulent, stomach virus that was ripping through their household. There was no way she'd come in and risk infecting Jenna, even if she could tear herself away from the bathroom right now.

Jenna had assured her tearful friend that she'd cope— after all, they'd completed most of the work for today's wedding client yesterday and by working back about three hours last night—but her head swam a little and she leaned against the counter, taking a swig of her water bottle and reaching for the salty snack the doctor had told her to introduce into her diet. She certainly didn't want a repeat of what had happened the day before last, and especially not at a time when she was on her own at the store. She'd had three bouquets to finish for the wedding today—now thankfully completed. With no Millie and with Valerie laid low with that stomach virus, it was all up to Jenna to handle those last-minute things, the things she'd counted on Millie helping her with so she wouldn't overdo it, she thought with a grimace. Not to mention walk-ins.

She heard the buzzer out front in the store. Ah, good, hopefully that'd be her wedding people in to pick up their table arrangements and the bouquets and boutonnieres. She forced a smile onto her face as she left the workroom.

Her smile faded the instant she saw who'd arrived.

"What are you doing here?" Dylan demanded. His face was a taut mask of control but she could see fire glinting in his eyes.

Jenna took a step back. "Where did you expect me to be? And what business is it of yours, anyway?"

"It's my business because that's my baby you're carrying. I went around to your place this morning, expecting to find you there, but you weren't."

"Well, obviously," she said drily, even as her heart rate picked up several beats at seeing him again.

"Why aren't you at home, resting?"

Oh, so he'd heard. She sighed.

"I just fainted, that's all." Jenna reached toward some roses she had on special in a tubular vase next to the cash register, and tore away a few damaged petals.

"Why? Have you been looking after yourself?"

"You're not my mother," she snapped. "I'm perfectly capable—"

"Don't give me that, Jenna," he growled. "I've seen inside your refrigerator. I know you don't cook for squat. Why were you hospitalized?"

"My blood pressure's a little low, that's all. I have to be careful not to let myself get dehydrated, and they recommended I up my salt intake. So you see, there's nothing to worry about."

"And the fall? You didn't hurt yourself?"

"No, and the baby's fine, too. Seriously, Dylan. I'm okay." Someone else came in through the front door. Ah, the father of the bride to pick up the flowers. "I'm also very busy, so if you'll excuse me?"

He didn't leave. Not through her discussion with her customer, nor when it came to helping the guy load the flowers into his van. Dylan even had the temerity to insist she stay in the store and sit down while he helped instead. She was seething by the time he came back inside.

"I don't need babying and I don't appreciate you coming in here telling me how to do my job."

"You're working far too hard. Aren't you supposed to have help here today? Where's Millie?"

"She couldn't make it, and…oh, there's a customer."

He waited while Jenna dealt with the woman. Then helped the client out to her car with the flowers she'd ordered.

"What do you mean, Millie couldn't make it?" he asked the second he and Jenna were alone again. "Don't you have backup?"

"Well, yes, sometimes Valerie will come for an extra day, but she's sick and she's already been doing most of the heavy stuff for me since my little incident."

"Little incident?"

Jenna could see he wasn't impressed by the terminology.

"Look, I fainted at the bank. The staff called an ambulance because that's their procedure. I was checked into the emergency department, and kept overnight for observation. I was rehydrated and then released in the morning with a set of instructions that I promise I've been following." *Mostly.*

It was as if he could hear her thoughts.

"Not completely, if I know you. What are your plans for lunch today?"

"I was just going to grab a sandwich—"

"How, when you can't leave the store unattended? How are you supposed to have a decent break if you don't have an assistant?"

"Well, I didn't know that she wouldn't be here until I got in this morning, did I?"

"Are you expecting any more customers today?"

"There are always a few walk-ins on a Saturday, but I have no more orders to fill."

"Good, then you won't mind me doing this."

He strode out back and she heard him locking the back door.

"What are you doing?" she asked.

"Get your bag."

"I won't do any such thing!"

"Fine. I'll do it myself." He shot through to her office and came out with her handbag slung over his shoulder. She'd have laughed at the sight he presented if she hadn't seen the look of absolute determination on his face.

"Dylan…" she started, but her words trailed away when he swept her up in his arms and carried her out the front door, hesitating only a second to turn the sign around to Closed. The door banged shut behind them.

"Key," he demanded, and she reached into her bag for her set, and while he still held her in his arms, turned the lock.

A group of people began to gather on the sidewalk.

"Hey, look at that! Isn't that Dylan Lassiter?"

"Yeah. Go, Dylan!"

To her chagrin, he flung them a beaming smile and began to walk toward his SUV, parked a few spaces down the street. As he went, the crowd grew larger, and began to applaud and cheer. Someone raced up to open the passenger door for him and another cheer rose into the air as he gently slid Jenna onto the passenger seat, before reaching around her to secure her seat belt.

Jenna was certain her cheeks were flaming. Dylan closed her door and marched resolutely around to the driver's side.

As he got into the car she flung him a murderous glance.

"This is kidnapping, you know."

"I know," he responded succinctly, right before he reached out to cup the back of her head and draw her to him.

Sixteen

His lips closed on hers with familiarity and yet with a sense of newness and wonder that tantalized and terrified her in equal proportions. On the sidewalk, the crowd went wild. Dylan broke away and reached for the ignition. For a second Jenna thought to protest once more, but the set of his jaw convinced her any argument would fall on deaf ears. She'd have to wait until he got her to wherever they were going.

It didn't take long to figure out. She recognized the route out to his home immediately.

"Dylan—" she started.

"Don't mess with me, Jenna. We'll talk when we're home."

He said it with such strength and distinctness it echoed in her mind. His home was in L.A. now, but from his tone it sounded as though he'd chosen the word quite deliberately. As if he meant to stay here. Her heart leaped in her chest even as her stomach dropped. The prospect of seeing him more often would be both torture and an illicit pleasure at the same time. She'd told him all along that she'd give him free access to their baby, so did this mean he meant to make his visits more frequent? Another more frightening thought occurred to her. Did he mean to get permanent custody? He had the funds at his disposal, and the family support.

She shoved the idea from her mind as quickly as it had bloomed there. He'd never once spoken along those lines. Why would he start now? Her thoughts flew back to last Saturday night at the opening—to the exact moment she'd felt her world come inexorably apart, like a dandelion destroyed in a powerful gust of wind. She simply couldn't go through all that again.

When they arrived at the house, he surprised her by parking in the garage rather than out front. She was even more surprised to see the red Cadillac gleaming under the overhead lights in the four-bay garage.

"You kept it?"

"I couldn't let it go," he answered simply as he lifted her from her seat and into his arms again. "A bit like you, really," he added cryptically.

He carried her inside to the casual family room off the massive kitchen, and put her down on a long L-shaped couch in the corner.

"Stay," he commanded, then wheeled around to the kitchen and went straight to the fridge, where he started pulling things out. In no time, he'd made a couple sandwiches on what smelled like freshly baked bread. He came back over to her and put a plate on her lap. "Eat."

She looked at him in annoyance, tempted to tell him where to stick his sandwich. But her mouth watered at the sight of it and she knew she needed to eat. Heck, she wanted to eat this layered concoction filled with freshness and flavor.

Once she'd finished, he took her plate, poured a glass of mineral water and handed it to her.

"Yeah, yeah, I know. Drink," she said, her voice dripping with sarcasm. This dictatorial side of Dylan was already starting to get old. "I am capable of taking care of myself, you know."

He just looked at her, his derision clear in those blue eyes that seemed to be able to stare straight through her. She couldn't hold his gaze. She might be capable of taking care of herself, but being capable and actually doing it had been two very different things.

"Things are going to change, Jenna," Dylan said, once she'd drained her glass and he'd taken it from her. "You are too important to me to leave either your health or the baby's to chance. You could have really hurt yourself in that fall, and what if it happens again?"

"It won't. I'm more aware of how I'm feeling now, and despite what you might think, I plan to take better care of myself." *It's just that everything else in the past two days has gotten in the way,* she added silently.

"Planning isn't good enough. You need more help if you're going to look after yourself properly."

"I know," she admitted. It was something she'd thought about a great deal this morning. One other person could make all the difference.

"So you'll hire more staff at the store."

Jenna's mind raced over the logistics of employing another full-time staff member—with wages, insurance and paperwork—and how that would upset her careful budget.

"At my expense—I insist on it," Dylan continued.

"Oh, no," she resisted firmly. What if he then decided to try to call all the shots when it came to her business? "Besides, it's not that easy to find a good florist. They don't just grow on trees, you know." The ridiculousness of that statement struck her at about the same time it struck him, and they both laughed. The sound lightened the mood, clearing the air as if by magic. Jenna let her barriers down. It *would* be great to hire another florist, someone who was innovative with design, yet didn't mind throwing together the traditional bouquets and arrangements that remained the backbone of her business.

"I'll look into it," she acceded.

"Thank you. I appreciate that you won't just get some walk-in off the street, and that in a business the size of yours, finding the right person might take some time. Can you get a temp until you find the right one? Do they even have temps for this kind of work?"

"I'll find out on Monday."

"I could do that for you," he offered.

"I said I'll do it and I will." She didn't want to relinquish an ounce of control to him if she could help it. This was her business and while, yes, he had a very valid point about her needing help, she would be the one looking for that help. Not him. Besides, didn't he have enough on his plate already? Jenna swung her feet to the floor and started to get up from the chair.

"Right, now that we have that sorted out, perhaps you could take me back to work."

"No."

Dylan stared back at her, his feet planted firmly on the floor and his arms crossed in front of him as if he was some kind of human barrier.

"Dylan, please. You've fed me, again. I've rested. Now I really need to get back."

"We need to talk."

"We've talked," she pointed out. "And I've agreed to get more help at the store. I thought—hoped—that would settle your concerns."

"On that score, yes. But there's a whole lot we didn't discuss last weekend that needs to come out in the open."

Jenna felt a fist close around her heart. So, they were back to her father. Would she never be free of his crimes?

Dylan reached out and took her hands in his. "I reacted

badly last Saturday. It hurt more than I wanted to admit when I learned you'd withheld stuff from me and in turn I hurt you back. I'm sorry for that. But I need to know everything. If you can be honest with me, Jenna, I believe we can work things out. Don't you want to at least try?"

She studied his beautiful face for a long time. He looked tired, with lines of strain around his eyes and those parallel creases between his brows that told her he was still worried, deep down. Could she do it? Could she share her shame with him and come out on the other side intact? There was only one way to find out.

"Okay," she said softly, dipping her head.

He let go of one hand to tip her chin back up again.

"Don't hide from me, Jenna. Don't ever hide."

Tears filled her eyes, but she blinked them back and drew strength instead from the reassurance in his voice.

"At first it was okay when Dad packed us up and brought us here to the States. We settled in Austin, Texas, where he was originally from. He met a lady, fell in love, but when it ended he just packed us up again, and off we went, somewhere else."

"It must have been hard, shifting around like that," Dylan sympathized.

"It was. I'd just get settled somewhere and the same thing would happen all over again." Jenna sighed. "I retreated into myself more and more, made friends less and less. His girlfriends started getting older and wealthier, and he started receiving more extravagant and expensive gifts from them. I would, too, because he always introduced them to me—maybe having me there in the background gave him some degree of respectability. They were usually nice to me, some more than others.

"One of them in particular, Lisa Fieldman, was especially lovely and she lasted the longest of all his girlfriends. There was a stage when I began to wonder—to even hope—they'd get married. That I'd have a mom again. She used to say she'd always wished for a daughter and that we'd do together very nicely.

"Lisa always had time for me and showed an interest in whatever I was doing. She even got my dad to come along to a school recital I was in when he'd never been to one before. I can still remember the big wink she gave me when I saw them in the audience. Lisa gave me a stock portfolio for my thirteenth birthday. She told me it would be something to fall back on—my 'rainy day fund.' I had no idea what that was and promptly forgot about it. I vaguely remember Dad trying to cajole her for control of it straightaway but she was adamant its management remain in the hands of her investment advisers. That was probably when Dad realized that she could see right through him. Despite that, I'm pretty sure she loved him, faults and all, but she wasn't a complete fool and kept a pretty tight rein on her finances. Of course, by the time the penny dropped for Dad and he realized he couldn't get any more out of Lisa, we moved on. It just about broke my heart. I'm pretty sure it broke hers."

Jenna paused a moment to swipe at her eyes.

"Your dad sounds like a real piece of work."

Jenna gave him a wry smile. "You have no idea. Anyway, I'd forgotten about the portfolio until I turned eighteen and some lawyer tracked me down to say it was mine to do with what I wanted. I couldn't believe it. Suddenly, I had funds that if I managed them carefully, could see me set up for life. I cashed in enough so I could get my degree without a student loan, and I kept working weekends at the store to meet my other expenses. I eventually sold off the balance a couple of years ago and used it toward buying my house."

She felt Dylan shift at her side and she gave him a piercing look. "You thought I'd somehow used the money my father swindled to buy my house, didn't you?"

He had the grace to appear shamefaced. "It was starting to look that way. The sums just didn't add up."

She nodded. "Yeah, I guess you're right. Anyway, I was able to use the house as collateral to borrow the money I needed to buy out Margaret when she was ready to retire. The repayments make things tight, but as long as I can keep afloat I'll get there in the end. The business will be all mine."

"That security is important to you," Dylan commented. "Owning your own home, your own business. Being answerable only to yourself."

Jenna nodded. "It became everything to me. It's the antithesis of what my life had been like up until my father was put in jail and I was sent here to Cheyenne to live."

"You were in Laramie when your father was investigated, weren't you? How did you end up here?"

Jenna rubbed at the mound of her belly absently. "Dad's arrest was national news and Lisa heard about it. Despite Dad ditching her the way he did and all that he'd put her through, she was still fond of me. Turned out she had a recently widowed college friend who lived here. That was Margaret. Lisa contacted her about taking me on. It was only supposed to be until I was eighteen, when I was theoretically supposed to be cut loose, but we got on well. I worked hard and she appreciated that. Plus, I also loved working with her and with flowers. We ended up being a natural fit. I have so much to be grateful to Lisa for, but I'm particularly grateful to her for using her influence to convince the authorities to send me to Margaret.

"Being here was a gift that I certainly wasn't going to

throw away. It gave me a chance to start over in a town where people barely knew of me. I hated every second of the publicity that surrounded my father's arrest. It was even worse when the media began to point a finger at me, saying I'd been complicit in his behavior. If I was guilty of anything, it was of ignorance. Maybe by the time I was fifteen I should have been asking questions about how he made so much money when he never appeared to work, but my head was filled with school and teenage stuff, so it never occurred to me to question any of it.

"One of my teachers got sick with cancer and the student council came up with the idea of a sponsored head shave to raise money to help her family out while she had treatment. When my dad saw me he was horrified at first. But then he took some pictures of me while I was visiting my teacher in the hospital. Without my knowledge or consent, he used those pictures to create a fake profile online, and used his imagination for the rest. It didn't take long for investigators to clear me of any involvement, but mud sticks and for me it stuck hard."

She thought back to that time when she'd been too afraid to leave the house and face the media assembled outside. Her father, then out on bail and awaiting the case to be brought before court, had simply taken it all in his stride, even laughing and joking with the reporters when he'd gone out. But for Jenna, who was still growing her hair back, every moment at school had become a trial by her peers, each day more unpleasant than the last.

"When Margaret placed me in school here I just did what I'd always done. Kept my head down and focused on my grades. By the time I attended the University of Wyoming people had begun to forget. Sure, I crossed paths with a couple of the kids I'd gone to school with in

Laramie, but time has a really good way of blurring the edges of people's memory."

Jenna studied Dylan's face again, and was grateful he'd listened without passing judgment. When given the chance, she'd grabbed the opportunity to forge a new life for herself, with both hands holding on tight. Sure, in hindsight she could see that her father had always believed he'd tried to do his best by her. That he'd obtained all those things under false pretenses was his cross to bear, not hers. Jenna knew that now. It didn't mean that she forgave him for it, but it was who he was.

"As to the money he raised, I have no idea where it is. He managed to hide it somewhere. No doubt he'll use it to seed his lifestyle when he gets out and the instant he does I hope the police will be back onto him. I'm sorry I didn't tell you all this before," she said softly. "I should never have accepted your proposal without doing so, but I guess a part of me was scared that you'd believe the worst of me when you knew."

"And then I did, didn't I?" he said ruefully. "Or at least it probably looked that way to you, huh?"

"In part. You have such a wonderful family, Dylan. I sullied them and your opening night at the Grill by bringing my life's ugliness into it."

"No, don't say that. What you went through made you who you are now. And we love you for it. All of us."

She searched his eyes to see if he was telling her what she thought, and hoped, he was saying. Sharing her past with him had made her feel lighter inside, as if it was no longer her burden to carry alone.

"Yes, Jenna. I do love you. I shouldn't have walked away from you last weekend. I was so angry and so hurt when I learned you'd kept such an important piece of yourself from me. I shouldn't have reacted the way I did.

You needed strength and support from me, and I didn't give it to you. But if you'll let me try again, that's what I'm offering you now.

"Everything, Jenna. My heart, my soul, my life. Knowing what you went through in your past just makes me want to create a better future with you, one for all three of us," he affirmed, placing his hand on her belly. "So I'm going to ask you again. Jenna Montgomery, will you marry me?"

Seventeen

Dylan's heart beat double time as he waited for her answer. He wanted this, her, the baby, more than anything he'd ever wanted his whole life. His happiness and his future hung now on Jenna's reply.

When it came, her simple *yes* was the most magical word he'd ever heard.

"I promise to make sure you never regret it," he vowed as he leaned forward and took her lips in a kiss that transcended every previous contact they'd ever had before. Nothing stood between them now. Their lives and their love were laid bare to one another.

"I know I never will, Dylan. You offer me so much, it makes me wonder what I offer you in return," she said uneasily as they broke apart.

"Everything," he said, and it was heartfelt. "I thought it was just a fluke, the way you made me feel the first day I met you, but you never left my thoughts. Through J.D. dying, through Angelica's wedding being called off… even when I was working hard on the Cheyenne Grill's opening, you were always there."

Dylan shifted on the couch so he could pull her into his lap, one arm wrapped around her while his other hand rested on the mound that resulted from their first meeting.

"I couldn't stop thinking about you, either," Jenna

admitted with a rueful smile. "It was…quite uncomfortable at times. I knew you were back in Cheyenne on and off, while the restaurant was being built. I guess I was a bit like a crazy teenager with a crush, hoping I'd get a glimpse of you. Your world, your background, is so different to mine. I convinced myself that you were unattainable for me, that our lives were too far apart and that I was happy not to hear from you or get in touch with you myself. But then I discovered I was pregnant, and it made me reassess everything. Made me wonder if you'd even be interested. After all, it's not like we got to know each other before we—"

"Shh," he said, pressing a short kiss to her lips. "So we didn't do things the conventional way. That doesn't mean we can't be as old-fashioned as we like, if we want to be, for the rest of our lives. Let's not wait to get married. I want us to be together, as husband and wife, as soon as we can."

"But what about where we're going to live? I—"

"I've been thinking about that. I have a strong team at my back. I can afford to work from here in Cheyenne, at least until the baby's born. After that, we can decide what we're going to do next, although I'd like to think I can make the move home permanent. I'd like to see our baby raised here, closer to my family's roots. So, what do you say? How does next Saturday sound?"

"Are you sure? That's a lot of organizing in a short period of time."

"We can do it, if we want to. I have contacts in the catering business," he said with a cheeky grin, "and I know someone who has a real way with flowers. If you're okay with it, I'd like to keep it small and invite family and close friends only. What do you think?"

She nodded. "That sounds perfect. Do you think we

could get married out at the Big Blue? It's an important part of your past and your family. I think it would be so special to be married there, where you grew up."

"I think that would be perfect," he said, kissing her again. "And I'm sure Chance and Marlene would be thrilled. So, shall we do it? I'll get the license on Monday and we can be married by the end of the week."

"I can't believe it's true, that it's really happening."

"Believe it, Jenna. Believe me. You are all I've ever wanted, you and our baby. I had some wonderful examples of love growing up. First my parents, and then J.D. and Ellie. Losing Aunt Ellie crushed J.D. He never stopped loving her until he drew his last breath.

"Even as a kid, I knew I wanted to know that kind of love with another person. I'm thirty-five years old, Jenna, I was beginning to think that kind of love wasn't out there for me, and God only knows I looked. I never expected to find it, to find you, right here under my nose in Cheyenne. And now that I have you, I'm never going to let you go."

"I'm going to hold you to that, Dylan Lassiter. Every day for the rest of your life," she promised, her eyes burning fiercely with her love.

"I can't wait."

It was a dazzling afternoon out at the Big Blue. As Dylan had expected, Marlene had taken the initiative and organized the wedding with the flair and efficiency he'd always known her to have. Strange how he'd thought he'd be wildly excited about today; instead, he was filled with a deep sense of rightness and calm. Everything he'd ever done to this point in time had led to this moment, this day, where he would declare his love for Jenna in front of their nearest and dearest.

He looked out the window of the second floor of the house and down toward the garden, where a hastily erected bower of flowers on the patio marked the spot where he and Jenna would become husband and wife very soon. A handful of waitstaff from the Grill circulated among the small gathering with trays of drinks and hors d'oeuvres, and he knew his executive chef had taken over Marlene's expansive kitchen to create a wedding supper that would rival anything he'd ever done before.

A knock sounded at the guest room door and his sister stepped inside. A smile wreathed Angelica's beautiful face, but he could see the concern in her eyes.

"Hey," she said, moving across the room to give him a quick hug.

"Hey, yourself," he answered. "I'm glad you could make it."

"Well, it was rather short notice, Dylan. Seriously," she teased, "a girl needs time to plan for these things."

"I figured if the bride could be ready in a week, our family and friends could, too."

"Good point," she said, stepping back and assessing him thoroughly. She flicked a tiny piece of lint off the lapel of his suit. "Speaking of which, this wedding is all rather sudden, don't you think? To be honest with you, I can't believe you're actually going through with it. Are you absolutely sure you're doing the right thing? It's no small step you're taking."

"I've never been more certain of anything in my life."

"Dylan, you don't have to marry her to be a father. You know that, don't you?" she pressed. "We hardly know anything about her."

"I know all that I need to know for now. I look forward to spending the rest of my life discovering the rest. As to not having to marry her—Angelica, I want to. I want her to be my wife more than I've wanted anything else in the world. It's a destination that I know, deep in here—" he thumped his chest "—we would have come to anyway. Having the baby, well, that just speeds it along."

"What if things go wrong?" she persisted. "Even when you think you know a person…"

Angelica's voice trailed off, leaving her bitterness and anger toward her ex-fiancé to hang in the air between them. Another knock at the door interrupted what Dylan was going to say, and Sage came into the room.

"You scrub up pretty well," he teased his younger brother.

"You don't look so bad yourself," Dylan replied, taking comfort in the usual banter.

"I never expected you'd beat me down the aisle," Sage commented lightly. But then his face grew more serious. "It's not too late to change your mind."

"Not you, too," Dylan groaned. "Look, guys, I appreciate the concern, but I know I'm doing the right thing. She's going to be one of us now. I'd like you to respect that. Can I have your promise you won't say anything about it again, please?"

Angelica and Sage each agreed, and the conversation turned to other matters.

Sage spoke first, directing his attention to their sister. "Since the three of us are together, I wanted to discuss the rumors that you're moving forward with contesting J.D.'s will."

"You're not still going ahead with that, are you?" Dylan asked.

"Of course I am," Angelica said with a stubborn look that the brothers knew all too well. She might have all her mother's beauty and grace, but deep down inside she was

J.D.'s daughter through and through. "As I recall, Sage, you were originally the one to suggest it."

His eyes reflected his frustration with her. "Yeah, but I also realized early on, and advised you, that continuing with the idea would prevent J.D.'s other wishes for inheritance from happening. Did you really want to see Marlene unable to live here? Or for any of the other bequests to be frozen while you battled this out? I thought you understood that it was more important to observe J.D.'s wishes in the end than to persist in something that's only going to cause bigger and bigger problems."

"Oh, sure." Angelica laughed, but the sound was insincere. "Nothing like the good ol' boys backslapping and agreeing to hush the little woman on her ideas, right? We all know Lassiter Media should have been mine. I did all the hard work. I picked up and carried on when Dad started to pull back from the day-to-day operations. Me! It's my baby and I want it back."

Dylan interrupted before things could get any more heated. Sage was right, but he could see where Angelica was coming from, even if he believed she was wrong. "I would have thought you'd want what's right for Lassiter Media. We all know that while we didn't agree with everything J.D. did, he was a brilliant businessman. He made his decision. Think of the wider picture, Angelica, if you even can anymore. You've become so dogged about this that your behavior is damaging the company. Is that what you want?"

She sighed and her shoulders sagged beneath the couture gown she wore. "No, it isn't what I want at all, but I have to fight for what's right. For what's *mine*."

Dylan put an arm around her. "We're going to have to

keep agreeing to disagree on this, Ange. This obsession isn't good for you, isn't good for any of us."

"That's easy for you to say," she retorted. "You got what you wanted."

"And I'd walk away from it all today if I knew that was what was best for the corporation."

The air was thick with the conflict until Angelica shook her head. "Let's not talk about this today, okay? We're here to celebrate you getting married."

The men grunted their assent, but Dylan knew the subject would not be forgotten. It was far too important to simply try and sweep under the rug. But for now, they could pretend there was nothing contentious simmering between them. He looked out the window once more, noting that the white folding chairs on the patio were filling with guests.

"Let's go do this," he said with a smile at his siblings.

Downstairs there was a hum of excitement in the air, yet it did little to ruffle the calm that wrapped around Dylan like a cloak. He'd spent every day in the past week looking forward to this moment, and finally it was here. Everything was coming right in his world, and he only hoped his sister could one day be as happy as he was.

Dylan took his place under the floral bower and smiled at the celebrant they'd booked to conduct the ceremony. Then he turned and looked down the aisle at the eager faces of the people he loved most in the world. All except for one, and she'd be coming from the house any moment now.

Jenna had elected to walk alone toward him, stating that she'd stood on her own two feet for so many years, she didn't need anyone to give her away. She was coming to this marriage freely and wholeheartedly. In response,

Dylan had elected not to have a best man, although they'd asked Sage and Valerie to be their official witnesses.

After a flurry of activity at the doors leading onto the patio, Marlene appeared with Cassie, who was dressed in mint-green organza and carried a basket of petals. Marlene flung Dylan a smile and gave him a thumbs-up. Until then, he hadn't realized he'd begun to feel nervous. No, it wasn't nerves, exactly, it was more anticipation. He couldn't help it; a big smile spread across his face.

Marlene took her seat and the music began. Cassie skipped her way down the aisle, throwing handfuls of petals on the ground, in the air and toward anyone who looked her way. Everyone was quietly laughing by the time she took her seat beside her mother.

And then silence fell upon them all as Jenna stood framed in the doorway. Dylan's breath caught in his chest as his eyes drank in the sight of her. Dressed in a simple white gown, with a broad satin sash under her breasts that lovingly contoured her slightly swollen belly, she looked radiantly beautiful. Her dark hair was swept up on her head, with tendrils drifting loose to caress the sides of her face and throat, and the diamond drop earrings he'd given her last night sparkled in the late afternoon sunlight. If he could have frozen this one moment in time forever, he would have. She was perfection, and she was about to be his.

Their gazes met and held as she began to walk slowly toward him, a smile on her face and her love for him beaming from her eyes. Then, finally, she was at his side, where she belonged for the rest of their lives.

The celebrant began to speak, and Dylan and Jenna made their responses, pledging their vows to one another. And Dylan knew, without a doubt in his heart, that he now had the family of his own he'd always wanted.

And as they turned to the assembly of guests as husband and wife, he looked at everyone's loving faces and knew this was the family he, Jenna and their baby deserved.

* * * * *

"I need to go."

Dylan had the good sense to look abashed. "Sorry. I didn't see you standing there. Did you sleep well?"

The expression of every woman within earshot was the same. Shock. Dismay. Vested calculation.

Mia wanted to tell them not to worry, but it didn't seem the time. She held out her arms for the baby. "I'll take her. Thanks for dinner. I'm surprised to see you looking so comfortable and domesticated with a baby. Or was that nothing but an act for your groupies?"

His eyebrows rose to his hairline, but still he didn't surrender the baby. "The little Mia I knew was never sarcastic."

"The little Mia you knew wouldn't say boo to a goose. I'm not a child anymore."

He stared at her. Hard. The way a man stares at a woman. "No, you definitely are not."

* * *

Baby for Keeps
is part of the No.1 bestselling miniseries from
Mills & Boon® Desire™—Billionaires and
Babies: Powerful men wrapped around
their babies' little fingers.

BABY FOR KEEPS

BY
JANICE MAYNARD

MILLS &
BOON

® and ™ are trademarks owned and used by the trademark owner and/or its licensee. Trademarks marked with ® are registered with the United Kingdom Patent Office and/or the Office for Harmonisation in the Internal Market and in other countries.

Published in Great Britain 2014
by Mills & Boon, an imprint of Harlequin (UK) Limited,
Eton House, 18-24 Paradise Road, Richmond, Surrey, TW9 1SR

© 2014 Janice Maynard

ISBN: 978-0-263-91469-6

51-0614

Harlequin (UK) Limited's policy is to use papers that are natural, renewable and recyclable products and made from wood grown in sustainable forests. The logging and manufacturing processes conform to the legal environmental regulations of the country of origin.

Printed and bound in Spain
by Blackprint CPI, Barcelona

Janice Maynard is a *USA TODAY* bestselling author who lives in beautiful east Tennessee with her husband. She holds a BA from Emory and Henry College and an MA from East Tennessee State University. In 2002 Janice left a fifteen-year career as an elementary school teacher to pursue writing full-time. Now her first love is creating sexy, character-driven, contemporary romance stories.

Janice loves to travel and enjoys using those experiences as settings for books. Hearing from readers is one of the best perks of the job! Visit her website, www.janicemaynard.com, and follow her on Facebook and Twitter.

I dedicate this book to children everywhere who think they are not smart. Don't ever believe it! It's a great big world out there. Follow your dreams…always!

One

Saturday nights were always busy at the Silver Dollar Saloon. Dylan Kavanagh surveyed the crowd with a gaze that catalogued every detail. The newlyweds at table six. The habitual drunk who would soon have to be booted out. The kid who looked nervous enough to be contemplating the use of a fake ID.

Around the bar—a winding expanse of wood that dated back to the 1800s and had been rescued from a building in Colorado—the usual suspects ordered drinks and munched on peanuts. The tourists were easy to spot, not only because Dylan knew most of the locals, but because the out-of-towners scanned the room eagerly, hoping to spot celebrities.

Western North Carolina's natural beauty drew people for many reasons. Families on vacation, for sure. But the state was also a hot spot for location scouts. Dylan's home, the elegant town of Silver Glen, was no stranger to famous faces. Just last week one of Hollywood's iconic directors had wrapped production on a civil-war picture.

Dylan shrugged inwardly. He had no interest at all in the famous or the infamous when it came to the world of filmmaking, no matter how many A-listers dropped by for a drink or a meal. Once burned, twice shy.

Suddenly, he realized that he had unconsciously been watching something that sent up a red flag. The woman at the other end of the bar was knocking back drinks at an alarming rate. He frowned, surprised that his head bartender, Rick, hadn't already cut her off.

Working his way behind the bar, Dylan inched closer to Rick. Two other servers were helping out because things were so hectic. And that wasn't counting the three waitresses handling food orders out on the floor.

When Dylan was in earshot of his employee, he tapped him on the shoulder and muttered, "You need to pull the plug on the lady in pink. She's had enough, I think." The woman exhibited an air of desperation that didn't mix well with alcohol.

Rick grinned, his big hands busy filling drink orders. "Not to worry, Boss. She's drinking virgin strawberry daiquiris."

"Ah." It was blisteringly hot outside, an airless summer evening that justified anyone having a cold one...or two or three. The AC was working very well in here right now, yet the woman swallowed her icy drinks with reckless precision. With a nod, Dylan moved away, aware that he was creating a traffic jam in the narrow space.

Rick, who was two decades his senior, cocked his head toward the door. "Go home, Boss. We got this." The big, burly man with the country accent was perfectly suited to his job. And he was a pro. He and the rest of the staff didn't need Dylan hovering and giving the impression he didn't trust them.

But the truth was, Dylan loved the Silver Dollar. He'd bought it as a twenty-year-old kid, and after renovating the old building from the ground up, he'd opened what was to become one of Silver Glen's most thriving businesses.

Dylan had been a wealthy man when he bought the bar. And if the place ever went belly-up, he'd be a rich man still. As one of the Kavanaghs, the family that put Silver Glen on the map back in the mid-twentieth century, Dylan could easily afford to spend his days and his dollars on idle living. But his mother, Maeve, had brought up all seven of her boys to respect the value of a hard day's work.

That wasn't why Dylan was hanging around the Silver Dollar on a Saturday night. He had put in plenty of hours this week. The reason was far more complex. This bar was proof—hard-core evidence—that he wasn't a total failure in life. Despite his youthful stumbles, he had made something of himself.

He didn't like thinking about his adolescence. Parts of it had been a nightmare. And the ugly reality that he was never going to match his older brother in academic achievement had tormented him right up until the day he admitted defeat and dropped out of college.

The truth was, he felt more like himself here at the saloon than most any other place. The Silver Dollar was laid-back, sometimes rowdy, and always interesting. It felt comfortable. Nobody here knew about his failings. No one, even the locals, seemed to remember that Dylan had been metaphorically voted "student most likely to be a bum."

He'd absolutely hated not being able to master the required subjects in school, but he had masked his anger and frustration by building a reputation for insolence, irresponsibility and wild partying.

Only when he had found this old building disintegrating and in disrepair had he finally settled down and found his passion. Like the building, there was more to Dylan than met the eye. But he'd had to prove himself. So the Silver Dollar was more than a project. It was his personal declaration of independence.

Besides, Dylan was *between relationships* at the moment, and he'd rather be here mingling than sitting at home watching summer reruns. He was a people person, plain and simple. That brought him back to the puzzle of the woman in pink.

Ignore her. Rick was right. Dylan *should* go home. As much as he enjoyed spending time at the Silver Dollar, there was more to life than business. Before he departed, though, he knew he had to check on his unusual and intriguing customer. When the stool beside her became available, Dylan took it as a sign. He had Irish blood running in his veins. Sometimes the universe pointed toward a clear and obvious path.

It wasn't strange to have a single lady drinking at the bar. But the ones who did were usually trolling for a pickup. This slight, harried-looking woman seemed to be encased in a bubble of solitude, her eyes focused on her drink. Quietly, he sat down to her left and only then saw what he hadn't been able to see from his previous vantage point.

She was holding a baby.

An infant, to be exact. Cradled in the woman's right arm, resting in her lap, was a tiny, sleeping child. A girl, if the little pink ribbon stuck to her one curl of dark hair was any indication.

Already regretting his impulse, Dylan assessed the situation instantly, realizing that more was at work here than a woman needing a drink. If he were smart, he would back away. His impulse to wade in and help people often went unappreciated, or even worse, blew up in his face.

When the woman didn't so much as acknowledge his presence, even though they were sitting practically hip to hip, his gut told him to stand up and walk away. He would have. He should have. But just then the slender female plopped her glass on the bar, hiccupped and gave one of those little multiple-hitching sighs that said louder than words she had been crying, was about to cry or was trying *not* to cry.

Female tears scared the crap out of Dylan. He was no different than any other member of his sex in that regard.

He had grown up without sisters, and the last time he saw his mother cry was at his dad's funeral years ago. So the urge to run made complete sense.

But something held him in his seat. Some gut-deep, chivalrous desire to help. That, and the faint female scent that made him think of summer roses blooming in the gardens up at the Silver Beeches, his brother's ritzy hotel on top of the mountain.

Still debating what he should say or do, he paused for another careful, sideways glance. His mystery lady was sitting down, so it was hard to gauge her height, but *average* was his best guess. She wore khaki pants and a pale pink, button-down shirt. Dark brown hair pulled back in a ragged ponytail revealed her delicate profile and a pointed chin with a bit of a stubborn tilt.

Something about her was very familiar, perhaps because she reminded him of the actress Zooey Deschanel, only without the smile or the joie de vivre. The woman at Dylan's side was the picture of exhaustion. Her left hand no longer held a drink, but even at rest, it fisted on the bar. No wedding ring. That, however, could mean anything.

Stand up. Walk away.

His subconscious tried to help him, it really did. But sometimes a man had to do what a man had to do. Grimacing inwardly, he leaned a bit closer to be heard over the music and the high-decibel conversations surrounding them. "Excuse me, ma'am. I'm Dylan Kavanagh, the owner here. Are you okay? Is there anything I can do to help?"

If Mia hadn't been holding her daughter, Cora, so tightly, she might have dropped the sleeping baby. The shock of hearing Dylan's voice after so many years burned through her stupor of despair and fatigue and ripped at her nerve endings. She had walked into the Silver Dol-

lar because she heard he was the owner and because she
was curious about how things had turned out for him. She
hadn't really expected him to be here.

Looking up, she bit her lip. "Hello, Dylan. It's me. Mia.
Mia Larin."

The poleaxed look that crossed his face wasn't flattering. Only a blind woman could have missed the mix of
emotions that was a long way from "Great to see you." He
recovered quickly, though. "Good Lord. Mia Larin. What
brings you back to Silver Glen?"

It was a reasonable question. She hadn't lived here since
the year she and Dylan graduated from high school. He
had been eighteen and full of piss and vinegar. She had
been sixteen and scared of what lay ahead. She'd also been
a social misfit with an IQ near 170 and little else to com-
mend her. While she was in graduate school, her parents
had sold the family home and retired to the Gulf Coast,
thus severing her last connection to Silver Glen.

She shrugged, feeling her throat close up at the memories. "I don't really know. Nostalgia, I guess. How are
you doing?"

It was a stupid question. She could *see* how he was
doing. The boy with the skinny, rangy frame had filled
out, matured, taken a second helping of tall, dark and
gorgeous. His warm, whiskey-brown eyes locked on hers
and made her stomach do a free fall, even though she was
sitting down.

Broad shoulders and a headful of thick, golden-chestnut
hair, along with a hard, muscled body added up to a man
who oozed masculinity. She wondered if he was still as
much of a badass as he had been as a teenager. Back then
his aim in life seemed to be seeking out trouble.

He was the first boy she'd ever had as a friend, the only
boy who had ever kissed her, until she got out of college.

And here he was, looking too damned appealing for his own good.

Dylan grinned, the flash of his smile a blow to her already damaged heart. In an instant, she was back in school, heartsick with a desperate crush that was laced with the knowledge she had as much chance of ever becoming Dylan Kavanagh's girlfriend as she did of being voted Homecoming Queen.

He raised a hand, and at some unseen signal, the bartender brought him a club soda with lime. Dylan took a drink, set down his glass and flicked the end of her ponytail. "You've grown up."

The three laconic words held equal measures of surprise and male interest. Her stupid heart responded with adolescent pleasure despite the fact that she was now past thirty, held two doctoral degrees and, as of twelve weeks ago, had become a mother.

"So have you." Though it galled her to admit it, she couldn't hold his gaze. She was no longer the painfully shy girl she had been when he knew her before, but even the most confident of women would have to admit that Dylan Kavanagh was a bit overwhelming at close range.

He toyed with the straw in his glass, not bothering to disguise his curiosity as he looked down at Cora. The baby, bless her heart, was sleeping blissfully. It was only at two in the morning that she usually showed any aversion to slumber.

"So you have a child," he said.

"What tipped you off, smart guy?"

He winced.

Appalled, she realized that her careless comment must have sounded like a reference to the past. She'd tutored him because he had dyslexia. As a senior, Dylan had hated being forced to take help from a classmate, especially one who had skipped two grades and was only fifteen. The pride of a cocky teenage boy had taken a beating at having Mia witness his inability to read and master English textbooks and novels.

"That's not what I meant," she said quickly. "I'm sorry. I'm a little self-conscious about having a baby and not being married. My parents are adjusting, but they don't like it."

"So where's the kid's dad?" Dylan seemed to have forgiven Mia for her awkward comment. His eyes registered more than a passing interest in the answer to his question as he waited.

"I'm not really prepared to go into that."

The man on her right reared back in raucous laughter and jostled her roughly. Mia cuddled Cora more tightly, realizing that a bar was the last place in the world she should have brought her infant daughter.

Dylan must have come to the same conclusion, because he put a hand on her arm and smiled persuasively. "We can't talk here. Let's go upstairs and get comfortable. It used to be my bookkeeper's apartment, but she moved out last Tuesday."

Mia allowed him to help her to her feet. Grabbing the diaper bag she'd propped on the foot rail, she slung it over her shoulder. "That would be nice." For a woman with a genius IQ, she probably should have been able to come up with a better adjective. But this encounter seemed surreal. Her social skills were rusty at best. Given the fact that she hadn't slept a full night since Cora had been born, it was no wonder *nice* was the best she could do..

"Follow me." Dylan led her across the restaurant floor to a hallway at the back of the building. The steep, narrow staircase at the end was dimly lit.

He insisted on taking the diaper bag and would have taken Cora as well, but Mia clutched her tightly. "I can carry her." She trailed in his wake as they ascended, trying not to ogle his tight butt packaged nicely in well-washed jeans.

She knew the man in front of her was a millionaire several times over. Yet somehow, he had the knack of appearing to be just one of the guys. It was a talent she had envied in high school. Mia hadn't fit in with any crowd or clique. Shy and serious, she had been all but ostracized by her classmates who were two years or more ahead of her in adolescence.

On the landing, Dylan paused, giving her a chance to catch up. "The area to our left is storage. As I said, this apartment up here was my bookkeeper's. But she got engaged and moved across the country. You can imagine what a mess I've made of things. I need to hire somebody soon or I'll have the IRS on my back for not paying my quarterly taxes."

He opened the nearest door and ushered her inside. Mia looked around with interest. They stood in a good-size living area furnished with a sofa, loveseat and two chairs upholstered in a navy-and-taupe print. The neutral rug was clean but unexceptional. Faded patches on the walls indicated where pictures had hung. "How long was she with you?"

Dylan dropped the diaper bag on a chair. "Nearly since the beginning. Her first husband died and left her with almost nothing. So this job was a godsend both for her and for me. But a couple of months ago, she met a trucker downstairs, and the rest is history."

Mia sank onto the sofa with a sigh and laid Cora beside her. The baby didn't stir. "Life is full of surprises."

He sprawled in a chair at her elbow. "It sure as hell is. You remember my brother Liam?"

"Of course I do. He always scared me a little bit. So serious and intimidating."

"He's loosened up a lot since he met Zoe. She's his new

wife. You should meet her. The two of you would probably get along."

"Really? Why?"

Obviously his throwaway statement was meant to be
rhetorical, because he hesitated. "Oh, you know. Girl
stuff..."

Her face flushed. This was always her problem. She
had never mastered the art of careless chitchat. Fussing
with Cora's blanket for a moment gave her a chance to
look away. She should probably go. But she'd made such a
complete and total mess of her life, she was deeply grateful
to have an excuse to focus on someone other than herself
for a moment. Gathering her composure, she leaned back
and gave Dylan a pleasant smile. "Well, other than your
brother's marriage, what's been going on in Silver Glen
since I've been gone?"

Dylan propped an ankle on the other knee and tucked
his hands behind his head. "Have you had dinner?" It
wasn't an answer to Mia's question, but he was starving.

"No. Not really. But you don't have to feed me."

"It's on the house. For old time's sake." He pulled out
his cell phone and sent a text to the kitchen. "They'll bring
something up as soon as they can."

"Sounds good." Mia's smile was shy. He remembered
the slight duck of her head and the curve of soft pink lips
when something pleased her. Not that pleasing Mia had
been Dylan's forte. He'd resented like hell the fact that he
had to take help from a fifteen-year-old kid. And truth
be told, he had probably made Mia's life a misery more
often than not.

"Why did you do it?" he asked. The question tumbled
out. He hadn't even known he was going to ask it.

A slight frown creased her forehead. "Do what?"

"Tutor me." His face was somber.

"Wow, Dylan. It's taken you this long to ask that question?"

He shrugged, making her more aware than ever of the breadth of his shoulders. "I was busy before."

"You were, at that," she agreed. "Football, basketball, dating hot girls."

"You noticed?"

"I noticed everything," she said flatly. "I had the worst crush on you."

He blanched, remembering all his careless cruelties to her. Even though in private he'd been pathetically grateful when she helped him make sense of a Shakespeare play, in public he had shunned her…or made jokes about her. Even at the time, with all the cluelessness of an adolescent boy, he'd known he was hurting her.

But maintaining his image as a badass had been his one and only goal. While some of his classmates were getting scholarship offers from Duke or the University of North Carolina, Dylan had struggled to pretend he didn't care. College was stupid and unnecessary. He'd said it enough times that he almost believed it. But when he slunk off to community college and couldn't even make passing grades there, his humiliation was complete.

"I owe you about a million apologies," he said, his mouth twisting in a grimace of regret. "You tried so hard to help me."

"I might point out that you did pass senior English."

"True. And without cheating, if you remember."

"You wrote an essay about why Romeo and Juliet was such an unbelievable story."

"Well, it was," he protested. "What kind of idiot takes poison when he could have kidnapped the girl and run away to Vegas?"

Mia chuckled, the laughter erasing her air of exhaustion and making her look more like the girl he'd known in high school. "It wasn't your fault, Dylan. The problems you had. Someone should have diagnosed you in elementary school, and your educational career would have been entirely different."

"You can't blame them too much. I did a damned good job of pretending that I was lazy and unmotivated."

"You may have fooled a lot of people, but you never fooled me."

Two

Dylan's wry smile and self-deprecating assessment made Mia's heart hurt. Dyslexia was no minor roadblock. Mia knew that Dylan had scored above average on intelligence tests. When it came to creating ideas and working with people, he far outstripped her in ability. Dylan was smart and gifted. Unfortunately, his talents didn't align with the way traditional education evaluated achievement.

She circled back to his earlier question. "You asked me why I tutored you."

"Well, why did you?"

"I suppose it was for lots of reasons. For one thing, the teacher asked me to. And for another, I was no different than any other girl at Silver Glen High. I wanted to spend time with you."

He rubbed his jaw. "Is that all?"

"No." Time for brutal honesty. "I wanted you to succeed. And I thought I could help. No matter how hard you tried to pretend differently, I knew you hated feeling—"

"Stupid," he interjected with some heat. "The word you're looking for is *stupid*."

She stared at him, taken aback that his intelligence still seemed to be a sore spot for him. "Good grief, Dylan. You're a successful, respected businessman. You work for a living even though you don't have to. You've made the Silver Dollar Saloon into something special. Why does it matter *now* that you struggled in school? We're not kids anymore. You've more than proven your capabilities."

His jaw clenched, his eyes stormy, though somehow she knew his agitation was not directed at her. "And what about you, Mia? What do you do?"

"I'm a medical researcher. Over in the Raleigh/Durham area. My team has been working to prove that the standard series of childhood vaccines is safe for everyone."

"And I sell beer for a living."

"Don't be flip," she said, her temper starting to rise. "It's not a competition."

"Of course not. I was never competition for you. How many languages do you speak?"

His sarcasm nicked her in ways she couldn't explain. She hadn't asked to be smart. In fact, there had been many days in her life when she would have given almost anything to be the epitome of a dumb blonde joke. She glanced at Cora, who was still sleeping peacefully.

"I should go," she said quietly. "I didn't mean to stir up the past. It was nice seeing you again." A chill of disappointment clenched her heart and brought back unpleasant memories of being out of step with the world.

She and Dylan stood at the same moment.

His face registered consternation and shame. "Don't leave. I'm being an ass. It's not your fault you're a genius."

"I'm a woman," she said flatly. "And will it make you feel better to know that I've made an absolute mess of my life?" Her voice broke on the last word. Tears she had worked so hard to keep at bay for the past several hours burst forth in an unattractive sobbing mess.

Inside her chest, a great gaping hole filled with uncertainty and fear made it hard to breathe. She didn't feel smart at all. What she really felt was panicked and desperate.

She put her hands over her face, mortified that Dylan was here to witness her inevitable meltdown.

Without warning, she felt his warm hands on her shoulders. "Sit down, Mia. Everything's going to be all right."

"You don't know that," she said, sniffling and, as usual, without a tissue.

"Here. Take this." The pristine square of white cotton he pulled from his back pocket was still warm from his body. She blew her nose and wiped her eyes, feeling hollow and shaky.

Dylan tugged her down beside him on the sofa, both of them glancing at Cora automatically to make sure she was in no danger. The baby was oblivious. "Don't worry," she said, trying to laugh. "I'm not going to have a nervous breakdown."

He grinned, revealing the slightest hint of a dimple. "Why don't you tell me what's going on?"

"It's a long story."

"I've got all night."

The genuine concern in his eyes disarmed her, despite her embarrassment. It couldn't hurt to have an impartial opinion. She was at a crossroads, and perhaps she was too close to the situation and too sleep-deprived to make a rational decision.

"Okay," she said. "You asked for it."

"Start at the beginning." He stretched a muscular arm along the back of the sofa, making her uncomfortably aware of his masculine scent and closeness. His khaki slacks and navy knit polo shirt with the bar's name embroidered on the chest fit him in a way that emphasized everything about him that was male.

Her hands shook, so she clasped them in her lap. "After I turned twenty-nine, I realized that I wanted a baby. A cliché, I know, but my biological clock was ticking so loudly, I couldn't ignore it."

"Did the man in your life agree?"

"There was no man at that moment. Well, there was one. For about fifteen minutes. But we were a terrible match, and thankfully we both recognized it before we did anything irrevocable."

"So who did you have in mind for a daddy?"

"Nobody," she said simply. "I was well educated and financially secure. I decided that I could raise a child on my own." She couldn't fault the skepticism she saw on his face. In retrospect, she had been both naive and overly confident in her abilities.

"There's still the matter of sperm."

His droll comment made her cheeks heat again. "Well, of course, but I had that all figured out. As part of the scientific community in Raleigh, I possessed a working knowledge of what was going on in most of our experimental labs. And of course, fertility research was and still is a majorly funded arm of study."

"Still no sperm."

"I'm getting there. Once I found a doctor and a facility that I trusted, I had all the initial tests to see if I was healthy and ovulating well."

"And were you?"

"Definitely. So I knew the timing was right. Then all I had to do was visit a sperm bank and select the proper donor."

"Who, I'm assuming, would be a doctoral student with intellectual capabilities matching your own."

He was entirely serious.

She shook her head vehemently. "No. Not even close. I would never do that to a child of mine. I wanted a normal baby."

"Good Lord, Mia. You mean to tell me you deliberately tried to make little Cora less smart than her mother?" The baffled shock on his face gave her a moment's pause.

"I wouldn't say that." She heard the defensiveness in her words and winced inwardly. "But I selected a candidate who was a blue-collar worker with average intelligence."

"Why?"

"I wanted her to have a happy life."

Dylan honestly didn't know what to say. *I wanted her to have a happy life.* Those eight words, quietly spoken, told him more about Mia than if he'd had her résumé in front of him. For the first time, he understood that even if his school career had been painful and difficult, Mia's had also, but in an entirely different way.

The knock on the door saved him from having to respond to that last, heart-wrenching statement. Soon he and Mia were enjoying appetizers and burgers. Based on the drinks she had ordered downstairs, he avoided anything alcoholic and instead opted for Cokes to accompany their meal.

Mia ate like she hadn't eaten in a week. "This food is amazing," she said. "Thank you so much. I've been living off frozen dinners and frozen pizza for days. My mom helped out for the first week and a half, but the baby exhausted her, so I finally encouraged her to go home."

He lifted an eyebrow, helping himself to another handful of French fries. "You've left me hanging," he said. "Finish your story, please."

"I was hoping you'd lost interest. The whole sorry tale doesn't put me in a very good light."

When she wiped a dab of ketchup from her lower lip, to his surprise, he felt a little zing that was a lot like sexual interest. Squashing that thought, he leaned back in his chair. "I'm all ears."

Mia was slender and graceful. Though she wore neither makeup nor jewelry, she carried herself with an inherent femininity. Back in high school, he had kissed her once upon a time, more out of curiosity than anything else. The heat had surprised and alarmed him. He needed Mia's help with schoolwork. He couldn't afford to alienate her, just because his teenage libido was revving on all cylinders.

Now, thinking back to how he had perceived the fifteen-year-old Mia, he wondered what had attracted him. She'd been quiet and timid, although she *had* managed to stand up to him on more than one occasion when he tried to blow off a project or an assignment.

Her looks and figure had been nothing spectacular in the eyes of a teenage boy. Mia had been on the cusp of womanhood, with no breasts to speak of, and a body that was still girlish despite her maturity in other ways. Yet something about her had appealed to him. In all of their interactions, she had never once made fun of his ineptitude, nor had she patronized him.

Now, from the vantage point of adulthood, he marveled that she had put up with his arrogance and antagonism. Though eventually they had become friends, for weeks at the beginning of their relationship he had acted like a total jerk. And an ungrateful jerk at that.

He kept silent, counting on the fact that she would eventually talk to him if he didn't push.

Mia finished the last swallow of her drink, stacked her dishes neatly and curled her legs beneath her. "The thing is," she said, wrinkling her nose as if about to confess to a crime, "artificial insemination is expensive. I assumed, quite erroneously, that since I was young and healthy I would get pregnant the first time."

"But you didn't."

"No. And every month when I got my period, I cried."

"Why was it so important to you?"

She blinked, her expression one of shock, as though no one had ever dared ask her that question. "I wanted someone of my own to love. You may not remember, but my folks were older parents. They had me when my mom was forty-three. So though I love them very much, I understood why they wanted to retire and move south. Even when we lived in the same state, we didn't see that much of each other."

"Why not?"

She hesitated. "They were proud because I was smart, but they had no idea what to do with me. Once I was out on my own, the gulf widened. I'm sure part of it was my fault. I never quite understood how to talk to them about my work. And besides…"

"Go on."

"I found out when I was a teenager that my parents had never really wanted children. It was a Pandora's box kind of thing. I read one of my mom's journals. Turns out that when I was conceived, my mother was going through menopause and thought she couldn't get pregnant. So I was an unwelcome surprise in more ways than one. They did the best they could. I'm grateful for that."

Dylan thought of his big, close-knit, sometimes rowdy family. And of the way his mother cherished and coddled each of her sons though they were now grown men. They all had their moments of discord, of course. What family didn't? But he couldn't imagine a life where his brothers and his mom weren't an integral part of who he was. "I'm sorry," he said quietly. "That must have hurt."

Mia shrugged. "Anyway, you asked why the baby was so important. The truth is, I wanted someone to love who would love me back. I wanted a family of my own." She laid a hand gently on the baby's blanket. "It took eight tries, but when the doctor told me I was pregnant, it was the most wonderful day of my life."

Since Dylan had witnessed her tears not so long ago, he surmised that the euphoria hadn't lasted. "Was the pregnancy difficult?"

"Oh, no. Not at all."

"And did people ask questions?"

"My staff was actually fairly small. And we each worked on a particular aspect of the project. So we were more like professional acquaintances than the kind of deeper connections you sometimes make in an office environment. My friend Janette knew the truth. Frankly, she thought it was a bad idea all along...tried to talk me out of it more than once. But she was supportive once I actually became pregnant. She even went with me to childbirth classes and stayed with me at the hospital when Cora was born."

"So what went wrong? Why did you come back to Silver Glen and walk into my bar?"

She leaned her head against the back of the sofa, her gaze bleak. "A dreadful domino of events. My job paid well, and I had a healthy savings portfolio. But I drained all of it trying to get pregnant. Even that didn't seem *so* irresponsible, because I knew that I could live on a strict budget and build up my savings again. Only I hadn't counted on the fickle finger of fate."

"Meaning?"

"While I was on maternity leave, the funding for my research and my lab was eliminated. Big-time budget cuts. So now I had a brand-new baby and no job. And, as a wonderful dollop of icing on the cake, my roommate with whom I rented a condo decided to move in with her boyfriend."

He leaned forward and rested his hands on his knees, smiling at her with an abundance of sympathy. "That sucks."

She managed a somewhat teary chuckle. "I probably wouldn't be such a basket case if little Cora here slept at night. But no matter how many books I read and how many theories I try, all she wants to do is snooze during the day and play all night."

"I don't blame her. That's my M.O. sometimes."

His droll humor made her smile, when the last thing she felt like doing was smiling. She remembered that about him. Dylan was always the life of the party. He could rally a crowd around a cause, and best of all, he wasn't moody. Some guys like him, i.e. rich and handsome, were egotists. But Dylan was the opposite.

He'd spent his high school years trying to prove that he was one of the gang. No one special.

She felt embarrassed suddenly. He must think she was a total nutcase. It was time to go. But just as she was gathering herself to depart, little Cora stirred and cried out.

Dylan's face softened as he focused on the tiny hands that flailed above the edge of the blanket. "Somebody is about to get mad."

"I need to feed her."

"Do you have baby food with you? I can send one of the staff to the store to get some."

"Um…no…thanks. *I* need to feed her. You know… nurse her."

His neck turned red. She could swear his gaze brushed across her breasts before landing somewhere on the far wall. "Of course. No problem. There's a comfy chair in the bedroom. Will that work?"

"That would be perfect." She rummaged in the bag for a clean diaper and a pack of baby wipes, conscious that he noted her every move. "I won't be too long. But don't feel like you have to entertain me. It's been fun catching up. I'll leave when I'm done."

He stood when she did, watching intently as she scooped Cora into her arms and bounced her so the baby's displeasure didn't escalate into a full-blown crying fit. Fortunately, Cora settled down and even smiled.

"Don't be ridiculous," Dylan said. "I don't want you to rush off. In fact, I'd love to hold Cora for a little while when you're done. Would you mind?"

She gaped at him. Big, brawny Dylan Kavanagh wanted to hold a baby? The thought sent a warm curl of *something* humming in the pit of her stomach. What was it about men and babies that made women go all gooey inside? "Of course I don't mind. But don't you have things to do?"

He tucked his hands in his back pockets and shook his head, his face alight with mischief. "Are you kidding? Mia Larin has come back to town all grown up. This is the most interesting encounter I've had in a month. Go feed the little one. I'll be here when you get back."

Three

Dylan watched Mia walk into the bedroom and push the door closed, though the latch didn't click shut. His brain whirled with a dozen thoughts and emotions as he wondered what would have happened if he hadn't sat down beside her at the bar. Would Mia have taken the baby back out to the car and driven away?

The thought made him uneasy. Had she sought him out on purpose, or was their meeting an accident?

He paced the room, wondering how long it took a woman to nurse a baby. Thinking about Mia baring her breasts and feeding her child was not wise. He had the weirdest urge to go in there and watch. Such a normal, *human* activity shouldn't affect him so strongly. Maybe it was because in his memories Mia was little more than a young girl herself.

Women were always at a disadvantage when it came to child rearing. It was all well and good to say a mother could have everything—career and family life. But it required a hell of a lot of juggling and tag-team parenting to make it work. Dylan's mother, when widowed long ago with seven boys, had leaned on her eldest son, Liam, to help carry the load.

Mia had no one.

Dylan could have gone back downstairs for a few minutes. He could have turned on the television. He could have sat down and relaxed after a long day. But instead, he paced. Things he didn't even know he remembered came rushing back from his subconscious. The way young Mia had chewed on the ends of her erasers. The little huffing sound of exasperation she made when she thought Dylan wasn't trying hard enough. The small frown that appeared between her eyebrows when she concentrated.

Oddly enough, he had found the eraser thing endearing. It made her seem human. Most of the time Mia's grasp of the kind of books that befuddled Dylan either baffled him or angered him or embarrassed him. As an adult, he understood that his academic difficulties were the result of a very specific problem. But he still reacted to the memories with an inward wince that told him he had a chip on his shoulder, even now.

Without thinking about what he was doing, he worked his way toward the bedroom door. Because the door didn't latch and because it was old and not level, the crack between the door and the frame had gradually widened. Dylan stood mesmerized, seeing only a slice of the room beyond. But it was enough to witness the quiet radiance on Mia's face. The way she looked at her baby made his chest tighten.

He rested a hand on the doorframe, swallowing hard as he realized that one of Mia's breasts was bare. He couldn't really see all that much from his vantage point. Spying on her was unforgiveable. But he couldn't look away from the picture of mother and child. The entire world was made up of moments like these, day after day.

For Dylan, however, it was brand-new. Witnessing it wrenched something inside his chest. Seeing Liam with Zoe these past few months had made Dylan vulnerable somehow…as if he couldn't help but wonder whether he would ever want that kind of tie…that kind of bond.

As Mia buttoned her blouse, he retreated hurriedly. By

the time she walked into the living room, he was leafing through a magazine that had been left behind. He looked up and smiled. "Is her tummy full?"

"It is indeed. She's very happy at the moment if you were serious about holding her."

"Of course I was." As he took the baby from Mia, his hand brushed her chest inadvertently. He was a grown man. It shouldn't have embarrassed him. But all he could think about was the curve of Mia's breast as she offered it to this infant. He turned away so he could hide the fact that he was flustered. "She's beautiful."

"I think so, but I suppose I'm prejudiced."

In his peripheral vision he saw Mia sit down on the sofa again. He circled the room slowly, singing nonsense songs, crooning bits of nursery rhymes he remembered from his childhood. He could swear that Cora's big, dark eyes, so like her mother's, focused on his face.

Half turning, he spoke softly. "She's going to be a charmer. I think she's flirting with me." When there was no response from Mia, he looked over his shoulder. She was curled up on the sofa, her cheek pillowed on one hand. Apparently she had plopped down and simply gone to sleep. Instantly.

He shook his head at Cora. "You're going to have to give Mommy a break, little one. She's worn out."

Debating his options, he decided to sneak downstairs and let Mia rest. The town had declared all public buildings no-smoking zones last year, so there would be nothing to harm the baby. And besides, Mia had been the one to bring her child into the bar. Surely she wouldn't mind.

Mia awoke slowly, completely disoriented. Had Cora cried out? She listened for a moment, and then in a blinding rush of recollection she realized where she was. But as she sat up and glanced around, she noted that her daughter and Dylan were nowhere to be found.

Telling herself there was no need to panic, she scrubbed her hands over her face and tried to shake off the feeling of being drugged. The nap had helped, but it wasn't the same as a full night's sleep. She stood up and stretched.

Grabbing her things, she smoothed her shirt and her hair and walked downstairs. The bar was still noisy and busy. When she actually looked at her watch, she groaned. It was after midnight. She found Dylan seated in a booth playing patty-cake with her baby. Standing two deep at his elbow was a group of fawning women. Now *this* was the Dylan she remembered. She wasn't sure, however, that she appreciated his using her baby as entertainment for his admirers.

Behind the bar, the big man who had poured her drinks earlier sketched a wave as he continued serving customers. Good heavens, what must Dylan's employees think of Mia's presence? Of Cora's?

Screwing up her courage, she edged toward the booth. Though she was no longer a social disaster, approaching a cluster of strangers still wasn't easy for her. She cleared her throat to attract Dylan's attention. "I need to go," she said.

Dylan had the good sense to look abashed. "Sorry. I didn't see you standing there. Did you sleep well?"

The expression of every woman in earshot was the same. Shock. Dismay. Vested calculation.

Mia wanted to tell them not to worry, but it didn't seem the time. She held out her arms for Cora. "I'll take her. Thanks for dinner."

As Dylan wiggled his way out of the booth, his entourage melted away. He moved closer to Mia, forcing the two of them into an intimate circle. "Don't be in such a damned hurry."

She put her hands over Cora's ears, scowling. "Watch

your mouth. I'm surprised to see you looking so comfortable and domesticated with Cora. Or was that nothing but an act for your groupies?"

His eyebrows rose to his hairline, but still he didn't surrender the baby. "The little Mia I knew was never sarcastic."

"The little Mia you knew wouldn't say *boo* to a goose. I'm not a child anymore."

He stared at her. Hard. The way a man stares at a woman. "No, you definitely are not."

It appeared that the man flirted indiscriminately, because she knew for a fact that he had no interest in her. "Give me my child."

Holding Cora even more tightly, he nodded his head toward the back. "I've got a closet-size office back there. Give me fifteen minutes. Then if you want to go, I won't stop you."

She was confused and tired and more than a little depressed. But short of wrestling him to the ground and making a scene, it appeared she had no choice. "Fine. Fifteen minutes."

Dylan's office was a wreck. He must have been telling the truth about his bookkeeper, because there was easily a week's worth of receipts and purchase orders stacked haphazardly across the surface of the scarred oak table he used as a desk. Still holding Cora, he motioned Mia into one of two chairs in the small space. "I have a proposition for you."

"You must be hard up if you're propositioning a nursing mom with a bad haircut and legs that haven't been shaved in two weeks."

This time she definitely saw him wince. "You used to be a lot sweeter, Mia Larin."

"I'm a mom now. I can't be a pushover. Are you ever going to give her back to me?"

He kissed the top of Cora's downy head. "You forget that I have five brothers younger than me. I've changed more than my share of diapers over the years."

"But not recently."

"No. Not recently."

If he had an agenda for this awkward meeting, he was taking his good easy time getting to the point. "What do you want from me, Dylan?"

His smile could have charmed the bloomers off an old-maid schoolteacher. "I want to offer you a job."

"Doing what?"

He waved a hand at the mess. "Being my new book-keeper."

"That's absurd. I'm not an accountant."

He propped a hip against the table, forcing her to look at all the places his jeans were soft and worn. "You're a genius," he said, the words oddly inflected. "Keeping the books for the Silver Dollar Saloon isn't exactly rocket science."

"I don't need you to bail me out, Dylan. But thanks for the offer." Watching him absently stroke her daughter's hair undermined her hurry to leave. Dylan was big and strong and unabashedly masculine. But his hands held Cora gently.

"We'd be helping each other," he insisted. "The job comes with room and board. Or at least until you get tired of the food downstairs. I live five miles away, so you don't have to worry about me getting underfoot. There's an alarm system. You would be perfectly safe alone here when we're closed. I know the bar gets pretty noisy at times, but a fan or a sound machine would probably do the trick. The insulation between the floors is actually pretty good."

"Why are you doing this?"

"You need some time to regroup. I need a bookkeeper.

You won't have to worry about day care. Cora is welcome here always. And with a salary coming in—though I'm sure it's not even in the ballpark of what you were making in your field— you'll be comfortable and settled while you look for a new position."

It was a testament to her desperation that she considered it. Her résumé would have to be updated before she could job hunt. And the thought of spending more time with Cora was irresistible. Doing Dylan's books could be handled while Cora napped. But still she wasn't satisfied.

Shaking her head, she studied his face. "You can't tell me that you offer jobs to every hard-luck case who walks through the door. Why me? Why now?"

"I think you know why," he said quietly, meeting her gaze squarely. "I owe you more than I can ever repay. I'm sorry that I was a stupid teenage boy too proud to acknowledge what you were doing for me. But I'm saying it now. Thank you, Mia. For everything. The job is real. Please let me do this for you. It would mean a lot to me."

"You're serious? It was a long time ago, Dylan. And I liked tutoring you. You don't owe me anything."

"Then do it for Cora. Before you lost your job, you would have had to go back to work soon. Now you have a chance to spend several more weeks with her. Isn't that enough to make you say yes?"

Forty-five minutes later, Mia found herself checking into a hot, musty, generic motel room out at the interstate. Dylan had tried hard to get her to spend the night upstairs above the bar. But she needed some space and distance to weigh the pros and cons of his unexpected offer. He had the uncanny ability to make people see things his way. She wanted to be sure she was considering all the aspects of his proposal before she gave him an answer.

The pluses were obvious. Time with her daughter. An

immediate paycheck. No need to look for a new place to live when her lease ran out in a week. And it wasn't as if she had a lot of other appealing choices. She would get a job in the Raleigh/Durham area eventually, once she found another lab looking for her set of skills. If she were lucky, the employer might even offer on-site, discounted day care. She knew of several companies that did so. But tracking down such a position would take time—time when she wasn't bringing in money and didn't have a place to live.

Or if she agreed to work for Dylan, she would have a roof over her head, food to eat and more time with Cora while she looked for employment in her field. Only a fool would say no—right?

Then why was she hesitating?

It all came down to Dylan. It was one thing for a young girl to have a crush on a popular senior jock. That was practically a rite of passage. But as Dylan had pointed out, Mia was all grown up. And her reactions to the equally grown-up Dylan were alarming.

The times she had tried dating in her adult life had been either disastrous or disappointing. Until she walked through the doors of the Silver Dollar Saloon, she had honestly thought she didn't have much of an interest in sex or men. But coming face-to-face with Dylan exposed the lie she had told herself for years.

Dylan wasn't a high school crush. He was the boy, now the man, who had made her aware of her sexual self. His masculine strength and power made her feel intensely *female*. In every other area of her life, people looked at her as a *brain* first and foremost.

She did valuable work. She knew that. Her intelligence had led her to projects and challenges that were exciting and fulfilling. But sometimes it felt that she could have just as easily been a robot. No one cared that she had emotions or, heaven forbid, *needs*.

That wasn't *entirely* fair. Janette was a dear friend. And Janette was the one who'd introduced Mia to Howard, the botany professor who dated Mia for six months, courted her circumspectly and eventually shared her bed. Their relationship had been comfortable and undemanding, laden with pleasant conversation as well as shared interests and backgrounds.

But in the end, the absence of sparks between them meant a sad, inevitable breakup due to lack of sizzle.

With Dylan, there was plenty of sizzle—an entire forest fire of sizzle. Not necessarily on his part, but definitely on Mia's. All she had to do was look at him and she remembered exactly how she had felt as a girl of fifteen. Perhaps the tutoring had erased some boundaries between them. Or maybe because they had kept their relationship secret, it had felt safe to her. But whatever the reason, Dylan was the only male to make her feel this way.

Discovering that truth was disheartening. If she had let a teenage crush spoil her for other men, she was doomed to a single, celibate life. On the other hand, maybe she could make her obsession work *for* her, not against her. A hefty dose of exposure to the mature Dylan could prove to her that the boy she had idolized was just a guy like any other. She could flirt with him, maybe even sleep with him, and then go on her way.

She tucked Cora into the portable crib and sighed with relief when the baby actually curled into a ball and went still. Cora had fallen asleep on the ride over, but Mia had anticipated another long night of being up and down with her. Maybe Dylan had worn her out.

Showering and changing as quietly as she could, Mia crawled into bed and yawned. She had promised Dylan an answer tomorrow. He had given her both the bar's number and his cell-phone number. But now she had more to think about. Her limbs felt restless and her body heavy. If she stayed in Silver Glen for six weeks, or maybe eight, however long it took to find another position suited to her skills and experience, would that be long enough to get Dylan out of her system?

Merely the thought of it made her breath catch and her thighs clench.

Janette hailed from Silver Glen as well. Though she was older than Mia, their hometown connection was what led them to become friends in Raleigh. Janette kept up with several family members in Silver Glen, and it had been a source of hot gossip when Dylan's engagement to a young starlet ended abruptly a few years ago.

As far as Mia knew, Dylan had played the field since. If there was no one special in his life, she wouldn't have to feel guilty about using him for her own personal entertainment.

Maybe if she could work up the courage to let him know what she wanted, they could have a mutually satisfying sexual relationship, and then as soon as Mia got a job, she and Cora would move back to Raleigh.

Cora was sleeping, but Mia was not. Her pulse jumped and skittered. Her breath came in short bursts. The exhilaration she experienced was couched in incredulity and terror. What on God's green earth led her to think she could seduce any man, much less the gorgeous Dylan Kavanagh?

Before she could lose her nerve, she reached for her cell phone on the bedside table. Hands trembling, she sent a text. I'll do it. But only until I get a job in my field. Working for you will be strictly temporary. As she hit Send, she wondered whom she was trying to convince.

Ninety seconds passed before he responded. Had he been sleeping? Imagining him naked and warm beneath a thin sheet made her hot enough to toss back the covers.

A quiet ding signaled his answer.

Good. Need help moving?

No. Friends will help me pack or keep the baby. When should I come?

A week? Ten days? The sooner the better. I'm drowning in ledgers.

If you find somebody else in the meantime, let me know.

I don't want anybody else. I want you.

Four

As soon as Dylan hit Send, he groaned. That last text could be misconstrued. But surely the prim and proper Mia wouldn't read it that way. All he had in mind was repaying Mia for what she had done for him so long ago. Any man worth his salt knew that an honorable guy settled his debts.

He'd thought about Mia over the years, usually with guilt for the way he had treated her. Sure, they had ended up being friends before it was all over, but it had been a clandestine bond. He'd been too macho and too ashamed of his academic weaknesses to let anyone see that he actually liked and respected a mousy little fifteen-year-old.

Even if his bookkeeper hadn't quit, he would have found some way to help Mia. He had lots of friends in town. But serendipity meant that not only did he really need Mia's help, but he was able to provide a place for her and Cora to stay rent-free. This arrangement was going to go a long way toward easing his conscience.

He turned over in the bed and sprawled on his stomach, feeling sleep struggle to claim him. At times like this, he envied his brother Liam. What would it be like to have the woman you loved tucked up in bed beside you every night? Zoe's effervescence was the perfect foil for Liam's serious side.

Dylan had heard his brother laugh more in the past few months than he had since they were kids. Liam was happier, less stressed, infinitely mellower. Even when it came to Liam, Dylan had guilt. When their father disappeared two decades ago, Liam, a mere lad of sixteen, had manned up to help their mother run the Silver Beeches Lodge, the extremely high-end hotel that had built their family finances.

While the rest of them were exploring options and making mistakes and generally learning what life was all about, Liam had stepped forward in a course already mapped out. He claimed not to resent his lot. He'd told Dylan more than once that running the hotel with Maeve Kavanagh was something he enjoyed.

Even so, Dylan hoped that Zoe would help Liam take care of a few items on his bucket list. His older brother was a hell of a guy, and he deserved the best.

Dylan sighed deeply, his body boneless as it succumbed to sleep. He'd have to paint the apartment before Mia came, and rearrange furniture to make space for the baby bed… and maybe even…

Fortunately for Mia, she wasn't a pack rat. Most of her belongings consisted of books and bookcases, kitchen items and clothes. With Janette's help, she spent one weekend boxing up most of the contents of her condo and ferrying it a bit at a time to a storage unit. She paid for three months in advance, knowing that surely by that time she would be back on her feet.

She still had her suspicions that Dylan was inventing work for her. His need to say thank-you, or do penance, was not something she took seriously. Anything she had done for him in the past had been freely offered. But she wasn't going to turn down the chance to have a safety net while she looked for a new job and to spend time with Cora. Eight weeks…twelve at the most. That seemed reasonable.

Having a shot at becoming one of Dylan's *flings* was merely a bonus. He was a man. She was a woman. All she had to do was get him to concentrate less on her IQ and more on her curves.

Cora, bless her, had been in a sunny mood most of the time, snoozing in her crib until it had to be dismantled. Janette's boyfriend offered to pick up the small U-Haul trailer Mia had rented. He insisted on hooking it to her SUV and helping her load everything that was going to Silver Glen.

By the time Mia pulled away from her building, waving at Janette in the rearview mirror, she was exhausted, but the sense of turning a new page in her life was infinitely preferable to the miasma of panic and failure that had dogged her the last month. All of her misgivings had dissipated. Returning to Silver Glen was going to be wonderful.

Five hours later, she turned onto the street where the Silver Dollar was located and hit her brakes to avoid crashing into a fire engine. In front of her, two white-and-orange barricades made it clear that she had reached the end of the road.

She rolled down her window and leaned out to speak to a uniformed cop. "What's going on?" She couldn't see far enough ahead to tell what had caused the commotion.

The cop shrugged. "Fire at the Silver Dollar, but they've got it under control now."

All the breath left her lungs. "Dylan?"

Her pale-faced distress must have registered, because he backpedalled rapidly. "No one hurt, ma'am. It happened early this morning. The building was empty."

She leaned back in her seat and tried to catch her breath. "I'm supposed to meet someone there."

The officer glanced in the backseat where Cora was

sucking enthusiastically on a pacifier. "At the bar?" His skepticism made her feel unaccountably guilty.

"Mr. Kavanagh has hired me to be his new bookkeeper. I'm moving into the upstairs apartment."

The man shook his head, sympathy on his weathered face. "Not today, you're not. I hope you have a plan B. The second floor is a total loss."

Dylan leaned against a lamppost, grimly studying what was left of his saloon. Thankfully, the main floor had sustained mostly smoke and water damage. But it would be quite a while before the Silver Dollar could reopen for business. He would pay his staff full wages, of course. But that still left the problem of his newest employee. And her child.

As he pondered his next steps, someone tapped him on the arm. When he turned, Mia stood looking at him, Cora clutched to her chest. "What happened, Dylan?" Her eyes were round.

"My own damn fault, apparently. It's been hot as Hades this last week, so I left the window AC units in the apartment running on high all night. I didn't want you or the baby to be uncomfortable today while you were getting settled. From what the fire marshal tells me, it looks like one of them shorted out and started the fire."

Mia turned to stare at the building, her expression hard to read. The scene still crawled with firefighters and investigators. No one wanted to take a chance that nearby structures might get involved.

Her shoulders lifted and fell. "Well, I guess that's that."

"What do you mean?"

"It means Cora and I will be driving back to Raleigh."

He heard the resignation in her voice. "Don't be ridiculous. Nothing has changed except where you and Cora will be sleeping. My house is huge, with more than enough room for guests."

Her chin lifted. "I'm not a charity case. It's out of the question."

For a moment he saw a spark of the temper he hadn't known existed. Perhaps Mia wasn't so meek after all. "I hired you in good faith. I'll sue for breach of contract if you leave."

Her eyes narrowed. "Don't be absurd."

"The building may be a mess at the moment, but I still have a business to run on paper."

"I'll have to find a place to rent until the repairs are finished."

"First of all, rental property in Silver Glen is slim pickings. And even if you found something, they'd want you to sign a twelve-month lease. You and Cora won't be here that long."

"You have an answer for everything, don't you?"

He had ruffled her feathers for sure. "It won't be so bad, I swear. My place is plenty big. I won't bother you at all."

"And what if the baby bothers you? What if she cries in the middle of the night?"

He grinned, feeling his mood lift despite the day's events. "I think I can handle it. C'mon, Mia. Think outside the box. We were friends once upon a time."

"I've changed. I don't let people push me around anymore."

"From what I remember, that was never the case with us." He shrugged. "If anything, you were the one ordering me to do this and that."

"I wouldn't have had to get tough if you hadn't been so stubborn."

"I've changed," he said, echoing her assertion and giving her his most angelic smile.

"I'll have to see it to believe it."

"Then that settles it. Let me get my car and you can follow me home."

"I never agreed to this nonsensical plan."

"But you know you're going to in the end. From what I can tell, you're stuck with me for a few weeks. Chin up, Mia. It won't be so bad."

Mia knew Dylan Kavanagh was rich. Everybody knew it. But when you spent time with him, that knowledge tended to get shoved into the background. He had spent his life proving that he was just an ordinary guy. No flashy clothes. No Rolex watch on his wrist. No silver spoon.

The truth, however, was somewhat different. Mia had plenty of opportunity to chew on that fact as she followed Dylan's big, black pickup truck all the way outside of town and along a winding country road. When they turned off the main highway onto a narrow lane, weeping willows met overhead, creating a cool, green, foliage-lined tunnel that filtered sunlight in gentle rays.

Occasionally a pothole left over from the winter gave one of Mia's tires a jerk, but all in all, the road was in good repair. Cora slept through the trip, though soon she would be demanding to be fed. Thankfully, they rounded a bend in the road and Dylan's home came into view.

To call it a house would be like calling the Mona Lisa a finger painting. Dylan and his architect had created a magical fairy tale of a place. The structure, built of mountain stone, dark timbers and copper, nestled amidst the grove of hardwood trees as if it had been there forever. A small brook meandered across the front of the property. Someone had built a whimsical bridge over one section and a gazebo near another.

Flowers bloomed everywhere, not in any neat garden, but wild and free, as if they had claimed the space for their own. Mia rolled to a halt behind Dylan and turned off the car. She wanted to take in every wonderful detail, but Cora awoke as soon as the engine stopped.

Even now, Mia marveled that someone so small and perfect was hers to love. Except for getting her nights and days turned around, Cora was a very easy baby. She had already learned to smile and coo, and her pudgy arms and legs were the picture of health.

Try as she might, Mia couldn't see any evidence of traits from the anonymous man who had donated his sperm. Sometimes she felt guilty for robbing Cora of the chance to have a father, but other times she was simply happy to have a healthy child.

Dylan came back to help her with the diaper bag and the small suitcase that held immediate necessities. "You can have your pick of rooms," he said, ascending the wide stone staircase in step with her. "There are four bedrooms on the second story, but I'm sure you don't want to lug Cora up and down the stairs all the time. I think you'll like the guest suite on the main level. It has a small sitting room where you can put the baby bed, so you won't have to sleep in the same room with her."

As he opened the massive front door and ushered Mia inside, she almost gasped. The interior was straight out of an architectural magazine. Vaulted ceilings soared over the living area. Above them, a corridor with a fancy carved railing circled three sides. Doors opened off of it at regular intervals, presumably the bedrooms Dylan had mentioned.

On this level, however, the central open floor plan was flanked by wings to the left and right. "Kitchen, etcetera over there." Dylan pointed. "And in the opposite direction, two large suites."

Her cheeks heated. He was telling her that she and Cora would be staying in the wing that housed his quarters. She could ask for one of the rooms upstairs, but he was right.

Who wanted to carry a baby up and down the stairs for every nap and diaper change?

Cora began to whimper. Mia realized that feeding time couldn't be delayed much longer. Thankfully, Dylan was perceptive. He motioned toward the right side of the house. "If you go through the kitchen, you'll find a sunroom that has comfy chairs. It looks like she's getting hungry." He touched her head gently, stroking her silky hair. "She's been an angel, hasn't she?"

Mia nodded, feeling her breathing get jerky because he was so close. "It's actually easier to travel with her now than it will be in a few months. Once she's mobile, all bets are off."

His big body loomed over hers, his clothes smelling faintly of smoke, but not masking the aroma of shaving soap and warm male. Smiling, he cocked his head toward the opposite side of the house. "If you trust me to unload the trailer and set up the crib, I can get started on that while you're feeding her."

"I can't let you do all that," she protested weakly.

"Exactly how did you expect to hold an infant and unpack at the same time?" he asked.

"Quit being so damned logical." It had been a very stressful day, and it wasn't even dinnertime yet.

Dylan put an arm around her shoulders and steered her toward the kitchen. "It takes a village to raise a child—don't you know?" he said, grinning. "It wouldn't kill you to say 'Thank you, Dylan.'"

She sighed inwardly, feeling as if she were being railroaded, but not really having a choice at the moment. "Thank you, Dylan."

"That's better. Much better. Now go feed the kid before she gets any redder in the face. I'll handle all the rest."

Mia fell in love with the sunroom. It didn't really look like a Dylan room at all. At least not the Dylan she knew.

Cozy furniture covered in expensive chintz fabric beckoned a visitor to sit and fritter away a few hours. The windows were screened, so clearly when the temperatures allowed, they could be raised easily.

Bookcases lined the wall that bordered the hallway. Their presence gave her pause. Dylan had a long-standing battle with the written word, but maybe he had learned to enjoy some of volumes he had collected. In one corner of the room, a hammock suspended from a metal frame rocked slightly, as if propelled by an unseen hand. *Thou shalt not covet.* Mia remembered her mom's gentle admonition when she had wanted a shiny red bicycle like the one the girl next door owned.

Bicycles were one thing, but this room—oh, the temptation. Mia could see herself studying here, playing with Cora when she learned to crawl, perhaps knitting a sweater for someone she loved. In that instant, she realized that she had walked into danger.

Seeing Dylan every day in a business setting, even if it was a bar, would have been far less personal than staying in his house tucked away in the woods. Despite her silly fantasy of seducing him, she knew in her heart that the best course of action would be to keep her distance for however long she chose to stay in Silver Glen.

It was easy to imagine using him for a sexual fling, but she wasn't really that kind of woman. No matter how much she told herself she had come out of her shell, she wasn't in the category of females who took relationships in stride…who used sex as a game.

Case in point, her love life was so sterile, she'd chosen to conceive a baby with the help of an anonymous donor. That said louder than words she wasn't good at connecting with the opposite sex.

Sitting down and propping her feet on an ottoman, she settled Cora at her breast and gazed out over Dylan's backyard. It was a veritable Garden of Eden, filled with trees perfect for climbing. Why had he built such a house for himself? Did he plan to get married one day? Or had his aborted engagement soured him on the idea of wedded bliss?

It didn't really matter. The only thing Mia needed to know was that he was willing to play host to her and her baby until his building was repaired. At the rate of most home improvement projects, that could be well after Mia was gone.

Cora ate hungrily, her quiet slurping sounds making Mia smile. Even in the darkest moments when she had lost her job and her roommate had moved out and Cora had been wide-awake at three o'clock in the morning, Mia had not regretted getting pregnant, not at all. Being a mom was hard. But she had done a lot of difficult things in her life. Starting school at age four. Skipping two grades. Entering college at sixteen. Tutoring a moody boy with enough anger and testosterone to make a girl feel faint.

He had tried so hard to pretend that he didn't care. But Mia had known. Dylan hated feeling stupid. He resented needing her help as much as he'd been relieved to have it.

Maybe this arrangement would give him some kind of closure. Seeing Mia's predicament should reassure him that intelligence was no buffer against the difficulties of life. No matter his challenges as a youth, he had far surpassed what many people had thought him capable of accomplishing. Even without the backing of his wealthy family, Mia was convinced that Dylan would have been just as successful. It might have taken him longer, but he would have gotten there eventually.

He had drive and determination and the kind of creativity that saw ideas and possibilities. Mia envied his fearlessness. It had taken her years to escape the prison of feeling socially inept and painfully shy.

Cora pulled away and looked up at her with bright eyes. Carefully balancing the baby on her knees, Mia buttoned her shirt and wondered whether to stay put or to seek out her host. "We're in uncharted waters, my little beauty."

Cora gurgled what might have been agreement. Mia put the baby on her shoulder and patted her back until a definite burp emanated from the tiny body. "Let's go find Dylan."

Five

Dylan gave the bed a shake to make sure it was steady. No squeaks. No wobbles. He plopped the mattress into place and stepped back to admire his handiwork. Printed instructions were often useless to him. Fortunately, he had a knack for three-dimensional reasoning that allowed him to construct almost anything that required wood and screws and nails.

"Wow, that was fast."

He turned and saw Mia and Cora staring at him with identical wide-eyed expressions. "It's not too complicated. But I didn't know where you'd packed the crib sheet. I put your three suitcases in the next room. I'm assuming the boxes can wait until morning?" He glanced at his watch. "I hate to be a poor host, but the fire marshal called to say I can come downtown now and go inside to assess the damage. And I promised some friends of mine we'd play pool at a buddy's house tonight. I can cancel, though…."

Mia straightened her spine, her arms wrapped protectively around Cora. "We don't need you to look after us. We'll be fine. Go. Do whatever you have to do."

As he drove away from the house a few minutes later, he told himself that the weird feeling in the pit of his stomach wasn't disappointment. Of course Mia didn't need him. This whole setup was for *his* benefit…so he could assuage some lingering guilt from high school. He was giving her a place to stay, sure. But she would more than earn her keep when she combed through the mess that was his bookkeeping system.

Dylan had tried to make sense of the various computer files. But in the end, he'd been nothing but frustrated. He suspected that he'd done more harm than good when he'd tried to enter recent debits and credits. Though he had learned to read for pleasure, it was a slow process. Numbers were a nightmare.

When he pulled up in front of the bar, the fire marshal waved him forward. "The upstairs is not safe to access, but you're welcome to take anything you need from the main level."

Dylan wrinkled his nose at the acrid odor of burnt wood. "My insurance company is in Asheville. They're sending someone out tomorrow."

"The numbers will add up. You'd be amazed at how much it costs to recover from water damage alone, much less the smoke."

"Yeah. But I'm more worried about the time. I'd like to reopen in a month. You think that's possible?"

The other man shook his head. "I don't know, Mr. Kavanagh. Money can grease a lot of wheels. But it's still a cumbersome process. Be careful in there. The floors are slick."

Dylan walked through the door of the Silver Dollar and groaned inwardly. The place over which he had labored so hard and so long was a wreck. He didn't have to worry about vandals. There was nothing much left worth stealing at this point.

His main objective was to recover anything Mia might need from his office. The small space smelled as bad as the rest of the building, but it wasn't as wet. Fortunately, he had a remote server at home that served as a backup for all his work files. His computer now stood in a puddle of water, so he didn't have much faith that it would reboot.

He found a cardboard carton that was mostly intact and scooped all the papers off the top of his desk. They could be dried out, and if worst came to worst, he'd ask vendors to resend their invoices.

This wasn't how he had anticipated getting reacquainted with Mia. He wanted to give her the impression that he was a solid businessman with an enthusiastic clientele. Instead, he was left with a smelly, sodden mess.

All in all, it could have been worse. At least the outer structure was intact. Since there was no rain in the forecast, he loaded everything into the back of his truck. He definitely didn't want that smell in the cab.

Over beer and burgers, his friends grilled him about the fire. They were equal parts sympathetic to his predicament and bummed out that their favorite watering hole was closed down indefinitely. Dylan managed to change the subject eventually, uncomfortably aware that several of these men barely managed to make ends meet from paycheck to paycheck. He didn't want anyone feeling sorry for him when all he had to do was throw money at his problem, and eventually it would resolve itself.

If the men sitting around the table ever resented the fact that his bank account ran to seven figures, they never showed it. But he had to wonder if his connection to the Kavanagh fortune at times made them uncomfortable.

Shaking off the odd sense that he didn't belong, he finished off his drink and stood. "Who's gonna be first in line for an ass-kicking at eight ball?"

When Cora went down for an early-evening nap, Mia snooped unashamedly. She'd put the baby monitor beside Cora's bed and carried the receiver in her pocket. That left her free to roam Dylan's gorgeous house at will. She started with the upstairs bedrooms. They were immaculately decorated and looked ready to welcome guests at any moment.

Despite that, they had an air of emptiness about them. Exactly how often did Dylan actually have overnight company?

His kitchen was a dream, especially the fancy appliances. Mia knew how to nuke anything, but the largesse in Dylan's refrigerator made her stomach growl. He'd told her his housekeeper kept him well stocked with food, but that was somewhat of an understatement. Mia found a freezer full of packages labeled with names like chicken parmesan, vegetable soup, whole-wheat bread. Added to what was in the fridge itself, she surmised that Dylan could easily hole up here and not go hungry for a month or more.

Since he had enjoined her to make herself at home and help herself to anything she wanted for dinner, she wasted no time in picking out what looked to be an individual serving of chicken potpie. While it thawed in the microwave, she glanced at the monitor, making sure Cora was still asleep. The little girl was in her favorite position, with her butt lifted in the air and her knees pulled beneath her.

Shadows fell as Mia ended her meal. She would have to wake the baby up soon or Cora would never sleep tonight. Although Mia was not particularly anxious about staying alone, the house did seem bigger and emptier with dark on the way. She wondered how long Dylan would stay out.

None of her business, she reminded herself. If the original plan had worked out, she and Cora would be alone in the apartment over the bar. But at least the people and the noise would have kept her company until closing time.

Cora was in her usual sunny mood when Mia got her up. Somewhere in the car there was a plastic storage box with the baby's bathtub and other important items, but Mia decided to do without them tonight. She put Cora in the sink and managed to bathe her quickly before the odd circumstances could unsettle the infant.

Smelling like lotion and clean baby, Cora wriggled as her mother tucked her into pajamas. For an hour, they played on the king-size bed that was to be Mia's for the next several weeks. If Mia listened occasionally for the sound of a vehicle coming up the road, it was only because she was a little nervous about being so far out in the woods all alone.

It certainly wasn't because she was hoping to see Dylan again before she went to sleep.

Cora, for once, was cooperative when it came to bedtime. Her little eyelids drooped as Mia stood rocking her back and forth and singing one of the songs that was part of their bedtime ritual. When Mia laid Cora carefully in the bed, the baby wiggled for a moment and then curled her arms on either side of her head.

Turning out the light, Mia tiptoed backward out of the room and eased the door shut. Her heart jumped in her chest when she bumped into something big and warm. A hand came over her mouth, muffling her shriek.

"Easy, Mia. It's just me."

She struggled until he freed her. "You scared the heck out of me," she cried, glaring at Dylan as she tried to breathe normally.

"Sorry." He didn't seem overly penitent. "I thought you would hear me come in the front door, but you must have been busy with the baby. You want some ice cream?"

His prosaic question was at odds with the way his gaze roved over her body. She had changed into thin knit sleep pants and a spaghetti strap tank top. It was a perfectly respectable outfit for a hot summer night, even if it did reveal her nipples a tad too much.

"Ice cream would be nice," she said, crossing her arms over her chest. "Let me put a robe on."

His half smile made her knees quake. "Not on my account," he said. "I like you just the way you are. Follow me."

The house didn't seem nearly as big and threatening with the owner in residence. Mia sat down at the small table in the breakfast nook and watched as Dylan dished up enormous servings of praline pecan for each of them. Judging from the condition of his body, he clearly expended calories somehow, because there wasn't an ounce of fat on him anywhere.

He was lean and muscular. Physical power was on display, but restrained. Dylan was the kind of man a woman would want at her side if she were lost in the wilderness.

Joining her at the table, he offered her a bowl. "Dig in."

After four bites, she put down her spoon. "You're staring at me."

"Sorry." He leaned forward and wiped a smudge of caramel off her chin. "I'm still trying to match the grown-up Mia to my memories of a young girl."

His touch rattled her. "I'm surprised you remember anything at all about me. You were a senior, an exalted star, and I wasn't even in the same orbit."

"You were a senior, too," he pointed out, studying her as he licked his dessert off the back of his spoon.

She had never before seen anything sexy about eating ice cream, but Dylan was in a class by himself.

"I wasn't a *real* senior," she said, remembering the taunts and ostracism. The pecking order in high school was rigid and unbending. The fact that she was only fifteen years old and about to get her diploma was a sore spot for many of her classmates struggling to pass required courses.

"You had a hard time, didn't you?" In his eyes she saw dawning adult comprehension of what her life must have been like. "I'm sorry, Mia."

She shrugged. "I was used to it. And besides, I was neither the first nor the last high-school kid to be bullied. It could have been a lot worse. I always wondered if you had something to do with the fact that after Christmas, a lot of the kids suddenly changed toward me. They weren't exactly nice, but they weren't outright hostile anymore. Did you say something?"

"I might have. A bunch of us went on a ski trip over New Year's weekend. A couple of the jocks were talking about getting you in bed to prove that they could. I shut them down. That's all."

She paused, her spoon halfway to her mouth. "Why, Dylan Kavanagh…you were looking out for me." The knowledge gave her a warm fuzzy feeling.

His quick grin made him look more like the kid from high school. "Don't make me out to be a hero. I'm well aware that I gave you plenty of grief."

"And yet you kissed me once."

The words tumbled out of her mouth uncensored. She froze, aghast that she had dropped a conversational bomb.

Dylan was shocked that she had brought it up. And vaguely uncomfortable. He'd wondered if she even remembered the spring night right before they graduated.

"I never should have done that," he muttered, taking another bite of ice cream and hoping she didn't notice that his face had flushed. Even now, he could remember the taste of her lips.

But she had been fifteen, her sixteenth birthday still two months away, and he had been a man of eighteen by that time. His awkward embrace and quick, furtive kiss had felt both deliciously sweet and at the same time terribly wrong.

Mia set her spoon in her empty bowl and propped her

chin on her hand. "I always wondered why you kissed me. Was it a dare?"

"No. Hell, no." The idea was insulting. That would have made it even worse. "I had the urge, that's all. We'd been together all year, more hours than I cared to admit, and we were getting ready to graduate. Probably never going to see each other again, since you were headed off to school at some brainiac university."

"You can't tell me the Dylan Kavanagh I knew back then was sentimental. Try again."

"You were pretty in the moonlight," he said flatly. "I went to get something from the concession stand and there you were." They'd both, separately, been at Silver Glen's one and only drive-in theater. The place was in business even today. The owners were careful to keep it in good shape and to hire off-duty police officers for the premises so parents would still let their kids go there.

"You were with a date, weren't you?"

How could big dark eyes make him feel like such a heel? "Yes."

"So again...I have to ask. Why?"

"Damn it, Mia, I don't know." He stood and took his bowl to the sink, dropping it with a clatter. "You fascinated me. And intimidated me."

Her jaw dropped. "That's the most outrageous thing I've ever heard you say. You hated me for a long time. And after that you barely tolerated me."

"Not true." He leaned against the counter, his hands propped behind him on the sink. "I never hated you. It may have seemed that way in the beginning, but it was really myself I hated. You just caught the fallout. I may have acted like the biggest horse's ass ever, but I thought you were sweet and impossibly complicated."

She looked at him as if he had grown horns and a tail.

"Why won't you tell me the real reason you kissed me, Dylan?"

Fed up with her stubbornness and her utter lack of faith in her appeal, he strode to the table and grabbed her wrist, pulling her to her feet. "I kissed you because you made me hard and I dreamed about you most nights." Without thinking about the ramifications or the consequences, he lowered his head, muttering softly as he brought his lips close to hers. "You were an angel to me, the one and only person who could rescue me from the mess that was my life."

He came so close to kissing her, he could taste it. But Mia was rigid in his embrace. For about thirty seconds. Then something unexpected struck him in the chest and spread throughout his body. It was a feeling like being caught in a summer rain, drenched to the skin and laughing because it felt so good.

She hugged him. Her technique was awkward and tentative. The very lack of confidence in the way she responded stole beneath his defenses and swamped him with tenderness. She was not a young girl anymore. She was a grown woman with a soft body and full breasts and curvy hips that begged for a man's touch.

Much longer, and he'd be tempted to take her standing up. *Bad idea, Dylan.* He backed away reluctantly, breaking the physical connection though he couldn't deny a less tangible link that bound them together.

Mia stared up at him with an expression that was impossible to define. "You almost kissed me," she said.

He shrugged. "I thought better of it. You didn't believe me about that night at the drive-in, but it's true. I had a little bit of a forbidden crush on you back then."

"Forbidden?"

"You were too young, even if we *were* in the same grade. I may have been a hormonal teenage boy, but I knew you were off-limits."

"I was headed to college, same as you."

"Didn't matter. You were a kid, a very pretty, not-old-enough-to-be-legal kid."

"Am I supposed to be grateful that you kept your hands to yourself?"

He might not be the smartest man in the world, but he knew a pissed-off woman when he heard one. "What do you want from me, Mia?"

She was silent for so long, he began to sweat. And when she spoke she didn't really answer his question. "If we're being honest here, I suppose I should tell you that I didn't happen upon the Silver Dollar by chance."

His eyebrows went up. "You didn't?"

"No. I wanted to see you, and it wasn't hard to find out that you owned the saloon."

"You couldn't have known about the job, so why did you come?"

Mia sat back down, resting her elbows on the table and putting her face in her hands before she looked up at him with a crooked smile. "I've screwed up just about every aspect of my life. At the moment, I'm a homeless single mom with a helpless baby and limited funds. I thought it might make me feel better if I could be sure that *you* were doing well…that the tutoring I did in high school meant something. So I came back to Silver Glen for a visit."

"How did you know I would sit down at the bar and speak to you?"

"I didn't. But it wouldn't have mattered if we never came face-to-face. I could see right in front of me what you had created. A thriving business. People eating, drinking, having fun. Camaraderie. You're a success, Dylan. And that makes me feel good."

Six

Mia almost regretted her honesty. Dylan's visible discomfort was not the reaction she had expected. But he responded gruffly, "I'm glad."

"Don't get me wrong," she said quickly. "I'm not taking credit for your success. That's all you. But in high school you were at a critical juncture, and I like to think I helped…at least a little."

"Of course you did." He glanced at the clock on the wall. "If you have everything you need, I think I'll turn in. Whenever the baby naps tomorrow, you and I can go over the books, and hopefully you can get started when time permits."

The switch from personal to business gave her mental whiplash. Had Dylan been offended by what she said? Perhaps he thought she was presumptuous to pat herself on the back. Maybe the feeling she was trying to express had come out all wrong. "Dylan, I didn't mean that you couldn't have done it without me. That's not what I was saying."

He shoved his hands in his pockets, the line and angles of his face set in stone. "But it's true, isn't it? Without your help, I would have flunked out of high school. And when I dropped out of college, if my family hadn't had money I would have ended up flipping burgers at a fast-food place."

"That's crazy, I—"

He strode out of the room so quickly she was caught off guard. Running to catch up, she followed him across the huge, open living area. Just before he reached the wing where their bedrooms were located, she grabbed his sleeve. "Listen to me, Dylan. Your money isn't what made the saloon a success. It's you. The way you draw people together. Everybody loves hanging out at the Silver Dollar because you've made it comfortable and fun. Do you know how much I wish I had your gift for reaching people?"

He stopped. Not much choice, really, with her hanging on to his arm. But his face softened. "Still trying to save me from myself, Mia?"

"You don't need saving," she insisted. "But that chip on your shoulder must be getting hard to carry."

He ignored her deliberate provocation. "I'm meeting with the insurance adjustor at ten tomorrow. I should be back sometime after lunch. We can work on the bookkeeping stuff then. My housekeeper will be here in the morning. Please make yourself at home."

Before she could respond, he disappeared into his suite of rooms and closed the door firmly behind him.

Mia stood, nonplussed, and felt a rush of mortification. She shouldn't have brought up the past. Clearly it was still a sore spot. But it baffled her that no one else saw this side of Dylan. At the saloon, the customers related to him like he was a rock star, the women giggly and starry-eyed and the men standing a little straighter and pulling in their beer guts in an attempt to emulate the man whom everyone admired.

Dylan, by every definition, was a success in life, both professionally and personally. Despite his aborted engagement, he had surrounded himself with a wide circle of family and friends. Someday there might be a woman lucky enough and smart enough to snag him for a husband.

Turning and tiptoeing into her suite so as not to wake

the baby, Mia crawled into bed and turned out the light. In the dark, and in a strange place, she heard all sorts of pops and creaks as the house settled for the night. To take her mind off the unfamiliar noises, she imagined what Dylan might be doing. Perhaps he had showered and walked nude back into his bedroom. It was safe to imagine that a man like him slept in the buff. Just thinking about it made Mia shiver.

Sex with the professor had been unexceptional. Unlike Indiana Jones, Mia's short-lived lover had a body almost as soft as a woman's. The most physical thing he ever did was lift his arm as he wrote on the dry-erase board. Surely she wasn't so shallow that she had to have rock-hard abs and spectacularly defined muscles to get turned on.

A more likely and more palatable explanation was the fact that Dylan had stolen a piece of her heart when she was fifteen, and she had never gotten it back. She was an adult woman now. With needs. Needs that went beyond the necessity of finding a job or a place to live.

Sometimes at night, she lay in bed imagining what it would be like if she had a husband tucked in beside her, a soul mate to share the ups and downs of being a parent. It wasn't that she was afraid to work hard. She would do anything to ensure Cora's happiness and well-being. But even so, single parenting was lonely.

She didn't regret getting pregnant. Cora was a gift unlike any she had ever received in her life. Perhaps she was overthinking her decision. In the end, it didn't really matter if she had chosen a less-than-perfect route to motherhood. The deed was done. She had a baby. And the two of them were a family.

Moments later, hovering on the edge of sleep, deliciously drowsy and comfortable in Dylan's luxurious guest bed, Mia groaned when she heard the unmistakable sound of her daughter's cry.

Dragging herself upright on the side of the bed, she scraped her hands through her hair and rubbed her temples. Judging by the experience of past nights, she had about sixty seconds to pacify her baby before Cora launched into full-scale squalling. With a deep breath and a prayer for patience, she headed for the adjoining room, wondering if she would ever again get a full night's sleep.

Dylan heard Cora cry out. His first instinct was to get up and go see if he could help. But that seemed uncomfortably intimate in light of the fact that he and Mia had barely reconnected after not seeing each other for a dozen years. He had certainly never anticipated having her live in his house.

The truth was, he could more than afford to put her up at a hotel. Hell, his family owned the swank, exclusive Silver Beeches Lodge on top of the mountain. The hotel was no place for a baby, though. Not only might the other guests complain, but Mia and Cora needed privacy and space to be comfortable. He had more than enough room. One slip of a woman and her tiny infant were hardly likely to cramp his style, and besides, part of him wanted them close by.

He turned over in bed and lay on his stomach, his face buried in one arm. The air-conditioning was set at the usual temp, but he felt hot and restless. It had been too long since he'd slept with a woman. Seeing his brother's happiness made him jealous.

There…he'd admitted it. Which made him a pathetic lowlife. Knowing that his own engagement had crashed and burned when the woman he'd loved decided Hollywood had more to offer than Dylan Kavanagh had been a blow to his heart and his ego. He didn't begrudge Liam his happiness. Not at all. His older brother deserved every ounce of joy he'd found in the exuberant Zoe.

But Dylan's failure in the relationship department made him wonder if his judgment about women was as screwed up as his perception of numbers and letters.

Self-pity was a disgusting emotion. Normally, he spent little time bemoaning the defection of his fiancée, or even the fact that his reading comprehension sucked even now. But getting to know Mia again, on top of seeing the business he'd worked so hard to establish going up in smoke, had rattled him.

Tomorrow morning he'd get his head on straight. Tomorrow morning he'd make a fresh start in more ways than one.

In the meantime, surely it wasn't hurting anyone if he imagined what Mia Larin looked like all grown up. And naked.

When light filtered into Mia's room, she wanted to pull the covers over her head and pretend that it was still the dead of night. Cora had played on Mia's bed, cooing and clutching a rattle, until almost one in the morning when she finally wore herself out and fell asleep. Mia had laid her daughter gently in her crib, returned to her own room and been comatose almost instantly. The baby awakened at five for her usual feeding, but thankfully, had gone right back to sleep.

Mia felt sluggish and hungover, which really wasn't fair since she hadn't consumed so much as half a glass of wine since the first day she decided to get pregnant. Before launching on her solo adventure, she had read book after book about nutrition, ovulation, maternal health and mental preparation. Given the repeated disappointments she had weathered as the months passed, there had been more than one occasion when a good, stiff drink might have helped.

Rolling onto her side, she glanced at the clock. The

thought of another hour's sleep sounded like heaven, but her stomach rumbled, and she knew that once Cora was up, Mia's morning meal would consist of little more than a banana eaten standing up and a cup of coffee.

Ever so quietly, she dressed in jeans and a yellow cotton shirt that buttoned up the front. Maybe the cheery color would help cut through the fog of sleep deprivation.

Though she had never exactly been a fashion icon, her wardrobe lately tended more toward practical than stylish. Though she would have liked to appear trendy and put together for Dylan's benefit, it probably wasn't going to happen. Lately, more often than not, she noticed halfway through the day that Cora had spit up on her shoulder. Not exactly the way to entice a man.

With the baby monitor tucked in her pocket, Mia crossed the living room in her bare feet, making a beeline for the kitchen and the smell of coffee. Though Dylan had warned her his housekeeper would be in residence this morning, it was still somewhat of a shock to come face-to-face with an angular woman whose short-cropped gray hair—along with a black uniform—gave her a stern look. Mia judged her age to be between sixty-five and seventy.

"Oh," Mia said, pulling up short. "I'm Mia Larin. And you must be Dylan's housekeeper."

When the woman smiled, her entire demeanor transformed. "That's me," she said. "My name's Gertie. What can I get you for breakfast, dear?" Without asking, she poured a cup of coffee and pressed it into Mia's hand, pointing out the sugar and creamer on the table.

Mia shook her head. "Please don't think you have to wait on me. I'm here to work for Dylan. In fact, I was supposed to be living above the bar, but, well…you know what happened."

Gertie grimaced. "A damn shame. But Dylan will put it to rights. That boy never loses sight of a goal. And by the way, my job is to take care of Mr. Kavanagh and his guests. He specifically asked me this morning to make sure you and the baby were settled in. So no back talk from you, young lady." Her smile indicated that she was joking, but Mia had a feeling that crossing Gertie wouldn't be a good idea.

"Well, in that case, I'd love some toast and one of those grapefruits over there."

Gertie hunched her shoulders and scowled. "You nursing?"

It was a rather personal question from someone she had just met, but Mia answered anyway. "Yes, ma'am." She'd been brought up to respect her elders. Despite Gertie's position as housekeeper, Mia felt deference was in order.

"Then you need more food than that. You like your eggs scrambled?" At Mia's nod, Gertie turned toward the refrigerator. "Newspaper's on the counter. I know you young people get the headlines on your fancy phones or whatever, but in my opinion, nothing gets the day off to a good start like reading the comics and the obituaries over a decent cup of coffee."

Mia, somewhat chastened, picked up the copy of the *Asheville Citizen-Times.* "Dylan subscribes to this?"

Gertie snorted. "No. I bring my copy from home. But I've caught him checking his stocks a time or two."

"Have you worked for him very long?"

"Ever since he built this house. So, I suppose we're closing in on three years or so."

That answered the question of whether or not Dylan had put down roots when he fell in love. The engagement had been longer ago than that, so he must have broken ground for this amazing house simply because he wanted a place of his own.

Mia pretended an interest in the paper, but she was more enthralled in watching Gertie. The older woman moved about the kitchen with an economy Mia admired. Mia rarely cooked, and when she did, the results were never the same. She knew how to read a formula and how to follow rules. But somehow, her culinary efforts always fell short. Perhaps she could pick up a few tips while she was here.

In no time, Gertie set a plate of eggs, sausage and biscuits in front of Mia, flanked by a small bowl holding a perfectly sliced and sectioned grapefruit half. "Thank you," Mia said. "This looks delicious."

"It is." Gertie's grin was smug. "Mr. Dylan likes a clean house, but he didn't hire me 'cause I know how to vacuum. That boy loves his food."

"You'd never know it to look at him." Mia's face flamed, realizing that it probably wasn't good form to exhibit such oblique though obvious appreciation of her landlord's physical attributes.

Gertie merely chuckled. "He burns it off. Never sits still that I can tell. How do you two know each other?'

"We were in school together."

"Ah." Gertie washed the iron skillet she'd used to fix Mia's eggs and dried it with a paper towel. "Mr. Dylan told me you're going to be doing the books for him. I want you to know that I'd consider it an honor to take care of the baby whenever you ask."

Mia gaped. "Well, uh…"

"Oh, you can trust me, honey. I've got five kids of my own and twelve grandchildren. Don't get to see them as much as I'd like. They're spread all over the country. But I'm good with babies."

"That's a lovely offer," Mia said faintly, feeling a bit overwhelmed. "I'm sure it will take me a few days to get into the swing of things, but I'll keep that in mind."

"I'd do anything for Mr. Dylan."

There was a certain level of fervor in the terse statement that begged for a question. "Because he pays well?"

"No." Gertie paused. "Well, yes, he does. But that's not what I meant. Mr. Dylan helped me out of a tight spot once, and I owe him."

Mia wasn't nosy as a rule. And she certainly wasn't assertive in situations like this. But Gertie seemed primed to share information. "How so?"

The housekeeper poured herself a cup of coffee, leaned against the counter and took a sip. Black. No sugar. "One of my grandsons came to live with me three summers ago. He'd been raisin' hell back home and his momma and daddy thought a change of scenery would do him good. But the little weasel brought drugs with him here to Silver Glen and tried to sell them. Sheriff caught him and tossed him in jail. I had to bail him out."

"So Dylan loaned you the money?"

"I had the money. It wasn't that. But I'm an old woman. A fifteen-year-old boy with an attitude won't take advice, even from me. Dylan hauled his butt out of jail and gave him a tongue-lashing for upsetting his grandmother. The boy had a choice between doing jail time, going home to his momma and daddy or working for Dylan all summer."

"I'm assuming he chose Dylan?"

"Sure did. In ten weeks, Mr. Dylan talked more sense into that hardheaded rascal than the rest of us put together. The kid looked up to him, and the lectures came easier from his mentor than from me or his parents. My grandson is in college now. Making straight As. And he hasn't touched drugs since he left Silver Glen. Mr. Dylan did that."

Mia ate her breakfast in silence, her respect for Dylan growing. Perhaps because he'd been such a hell-raiser himself, he understood the mind-set of a rebellious teenage boy. Not that Dylan had ever dabbled in drugs. He'd been a sports fiend, determined to keep his body in top physical shape. But he had definitely taken pride in flouting authority.

It didn't take a psychologist to see that Dylan had been compensating for his struggles in the classroom. It was no help that his older brother, Liam, had breezed through high school and gone on past college to get an advanced degree.

Sibling rivalry at that age was tough. Dylan must have felt the sting of not measuring up. So to prove he didn't care, he'd pulled stunts like kidnapping Mr. Everson's prize bull and tying it to the flagpole in the center of town. Dumping a case of red food coloring and a gallon of detergent into the fountain in front of the bank. Snitching the principal's ugly burgundy blazer and literally running it up the flagpole.

No one was ever harmed by Dylan's pranks. And he was usually the one who had to pay the price for cleaning up his messes. But his antics had worked. In Silver Glen High School, by the time Dylan reached his senior year, he was the most popular guy around, hands down. Mia had been an invisible nobody.

She finished the last bite of her lighter-than-air biscuit and pushed back from the table. "That was wonderful, Gertie. Thank you so much."

"Glad you enjoyed it. Lunch will be ready at twelve-thirty, as long as Mr. Dylan makes it back from town. Anytime you need washing done for you or the baby, just drop it on the floor in the laundry room."

"Oh, but I—"

Gertie held up a hand. "It's my job. *Your* job is to look after the baby and the books. Don't be tryin' to wash dishes or mess around in my kitchen. This is my turf. And I'm going to make your life easier, because that's what Mr. Dylan wants."

Seven

Dylan had a good news/bad news kind of morning. On the upside, he had very good insurance. The financial hit wasn't going to be too bad at all. But in the negative column was the fact that the contractor he wanted to do the renovation couldn't start for three weeks. In other words, hurry up and wait.

He swallowed his impatience as best he could. Sooner or later the bar would reopen, and he was confident that his regulars would return. Nothing could be done about the lost business in the meantime.

When he was satisfied that he had taken care of the essential details to get the ball rolling with the adjustor and the repair work, he jumped in his truck and headed for home. Knowing that Mia and Cora would be there when he arrived was another item for the plus column.

He found his houseguests in the sunroom. Pausing in the doorway, he absorbed the picture they made. Mia was down on the carpet, stretched out on her side. Where her yellow top buttoned near her waist, one side of the fabric gaped, giving him a tantalizing glimpse of pale white skin. Cora lay on a fuzzy pink blanket, kicking her legs and rolling from side to side as Mia laughed softly. "It won't be long, sweet pea."

"Won't be long until what?" Dylan strolled into the

room and sprawled into his favorite recliner that just happened to be at Mia's elbow.

She sat up and straightened her clothing, her cheeks flushed, either from playing with her daughter or because seeing Dylan flustered her. "Until she rolls over completely. The doctor says Cora's at the top of the charts physically."

"You may have an athlete on your hands."

Mia shook her head. "Not if she has my genes. I was lucky that my high-school gym classes were pass/fail, or my grade point average would have suffered. I've been known to trip over my own feet."

"That's only because your super impressive brain is tied up with loftier matters."

She gazed at him askance. "Are you making fun of me, Kavanagh?"

He reached down and tugged her ponytail. "Maybe. What are you going to do about it? I'm bigger and faster than you."

She scooped Cora into her lap and nuzzled her head. "I like the grown-up Dylan."

Her non sequitur caught him off guard. "What does that mean?" It sounded like a compliment, which made him suspicious. The Mia he had once known would never have been confident enough to flirt with a guy, even one she felt comfortable around.

"It means that I'm impressed with the man you've become. You're not angry anymore. And not out to prove anything, at least I don't think so. Some people would have been apoplectic after the fire yesterday, but you've handled it all so calmly."

The praise made him oddly uncomfortable. "Believe me, Mia, I'm nothing special. I have the luxury of a safety net. Not everyone is so lucky. It's not like I'm going to be destitute and on the street if the Silver Dollar goes belly-up."

She frowned. "Do you think it will?"

"I hope not. The guy I trust to do the restoration can't get to me until three weeks from now. Which means a long wait until I can reopen. But I'm pretty sure my regulars will come back."

"I can't imagine that they wouldn't." She glanced at her watch. "We'd better head for the kitchen. I don't want to get my knuckles rapped with a ruler if we're late for lunch. I think I'm scared of Gertie."

"Her bark is worse than her bite." He extended a hand and helped Mia to her feet. Cora yawned hugely, making him laugh. "Maybe I'm prejudiced, but she's really cute. Did she sleep okay last night?" He had heard her only that one time, but he didn't know how long the baby had stayed awake.

"So-so."

"Do you mind if I carry her?"

Mia surrendered the baby without comment, walking ahead of him as they followed their noses to the appetizing aromas of Gertie's handiwork. Dylan enjoyed the feel of the infant in his arms. The smell of baby shampoo brought back good memories from his childhood. Cora was still young enough that having a stranger hold her wasn't alarming.

That first evening at the Silver Dollar, she had gone to him without protest, her big brown eyes and pink dimpled cheeks the epitome of a happy baby. Dylan wondered which, if any, of her anonymous male parent's traits she had inherited. Dylan wasn't sure where he stood on the whole nature/nurture thing. But his gut told him that what mattered most was the love a child received *after* birth.

In the kitchen, Gertie bustled about, shooing them to

seats at the table and pouring iced tea and lemonade to go along with the home cooked vegetables.

Mia's face lit up. "Food, real food. I've about had my fill of microwave dinners."

Dylan sat down with Cora in his lap, scooting his silverware out of the way when the baby predictably reached for a fork. "You won't go hungry while you're under this roof. Gertie is so good she could be on one of those reality cooking shows."

Gertie turned bright red. "Oh, hush, Dylan. You're exaggerating."

At that very moment, Mia realized that the housekeeper loved her boss like a son. It was cute actually. The woman obviously doted on Dylan, and he treated her with a mixture of respect and affection that was very sweet to watch. He would probably hate knowing Mia thought anything about him was sweet. He might not *need* to prove he was a bad boy anymore, but there was nothing overtly soft about him.

He exuded masculinity effortlessly. It was in the way he walked and in the breadth of his shoulders and in the low rumble of his laughter. This Dylan might be older and more sophisticated than the boy she had known in school, but beneath the skin he was still a rough-and-tumble guy.

With Dylan behind the bar at the Silver Dollar, there would be no need for a bouncer. He could probably corral a rowdy drunk with one sharp frown and a quick trip through the front door. Dylan had never initiated fights as a teenager, at least not that Mia remembered. But there was no doubt in her mind that he possessed the physical strength and agility to handle himself in any situation.

Back in high school, he had been on the wrestling squad for a little while. But though he was very good at the sport, he hadn't seemed to enjoy it the way he did football and baseball. Dylan liked being part of a team and thrived on the camaraderie of the locker room. His leadership skills were apparent even then.

As Gertie refilled Mia's glass, Mia wondered if the other two had noticed her silence. She had "checked out" for a few minutes thinking about Dylan. Somehow, he managed to clear his plate and have second helpings while still holding Cora in the crook of his left arm. The baby had actually fallen asleep.

Gertie cleared away the dishes and stopped at Dylan's elbow. "I know you two have business to discuss. Miss Mia, what if I take the baby for a walk in the backyard? I promise I'll keep her in the shade."

Dylan looked at Mia inquiringly. "It's up to you."

Mia nodded. "Of course. If you don't mind. And please call me Mia."

Gertie seemed pleased. Dylan handed Cora over to her so carefully that the baby never stirred. Mia realized ruefully that being spoiled was dangerously addictive. Suddenly, she had a beautiful, albeit temporary, home, and on top of that no need to cook or clean. She even had a built-in babysitter when needed. The change from desperate exhaustion to a return of her usual energy told her how much she had been struggling.

Once it was just the two of them in the kitchen, Mia cocked her head and smiled at Dylan. "You're a natural with kids. Do you think you'll want a big family someday? Another limb on the Kavanagh family tree?"

His face darkened and he got up from the table, turning his back on her as he poured himself a cup of coffee. "I don't plan to have children."

The words were curt. His tone of voice said *not up for discussion*. Mia, however, was so shocked she didn't pause to consider dropping the subject. "Why not?"

The glance he shot her over his shoulder was stormy.

"Because I might have a kid just like me. And I wouldn't wish that on anybody. No kid deserves to feel stupid."

The vehemence in his voice stunned her. "Is that why your engagement broke up? She wanted kids and you didn't?"

He faced her now, nursing the mug in his big hands. His face was wiped clean of expression, but there was turmoil in his gaze. "Having kids never even came up. We didn't get that far."

"Sorry," she muttered. Seeing the way he interacted with Cora told her that he would be a wonderful father.

He shrugged. "Anyone in town could fill you in on every titillating detail of my engagement and its ignominious end."

"Forget it. I shouldn't have asked. Why don't we get started looking at the saloon books?"

"Not yet. Obviously you're interested. And I've got nothing to hide. I fell for a cute blonde with a bubbly personality that nicely disguised a streak of ambition a mile wide."

"There's nothing wrong with having ambition."

"True. But it's not like I was planning to keep her barefoot and pregnant. The thing is, I was embarrassingly infatuated with her. Bought her a flashy engagement ring. Showered her with gifts. Maybe dating a movie star fed my ego, who knows?"

"I'm sure it was more than that."

"I never have been able to decide if it was my heart or my pride that took a hit. Doesn't really matter, though. She was here for three months filming a movie. When it was over, she had convinced herself that she loved the pace of life in Silver Glen, the sense of community and me."

"But she didn't."

"Let's just say that when her favorite director called

with an offer for the role of a lifetime, she hit the road so fast I never saw it coming."

"Surely you could have worked something out."

"She didn't want to. And in the end, that was probably for the best, because I belong in Silver Glen and she doesn't. She gave the ring back, kissed me with a tearful apology and left."

"I'm sorry, Dylan. That must have been a wretched time for you."

"It's worse in a small town. No place to hide."

His crooked smile tugged at her heartstrings. Mia couldn't imagine walking away from Dylan Kavanagh if he were in love with her. Clearly, the actress wanted success more than she wanted love. Or maybe she realized that whatever she and Dylan shared wasn't love at all.

"I hope I didn't bring back bad memories," she said.

It surprised Mia a little bit that she still felt so comfortable around him. Much like catching up with a cousin you hadn't seen in years, she and Dylan seemed to have picked up where they left off. But that analogy went only so far. There was nothing familial about her reaction to him.

"We all learn from our mistakes. Mine was a big one, but I've moved on." He took a cautious sip of coffee. "What about you? Is there a romantic debacle in your past?"

She sat back in her chair, enjoying the picture he made. Despite the fact that he leaned against the counter by the kitchen sink, there was nothing domesticated about him. He was a natural with children, but he didn't want any of his own. The knowledge made Mia sad.

The Kavanaghs had always seemed like a fairy-tale family to her. Despite the tragedy of losing Reggie Kavanagh, their close-knit relationships as they pulled together after his death fascinated an only child. As adults, the siblings probably had busy lives and didn't see each other as often as they liked. Maybe there were even sibling rivalries that carried over into adulthood. But despite any possible tensions, Mia envied them.

"I wouldn't call it a debacle," she said. "I dated a professor for a while. We had a lot in common, but not much sizzle."

One corner of Dylan's mouth lifted in a sexy grin. "Why, Mia. I didn't even realize you knew what sizzle was."

"I'm neither a prude nor an innocent. Though I will concede that my sexual experience compared to yours is probably the equivalent of comparing miniature golf to a professional game."

"Balls? Really? That's the metaphor you're going with?"

His wicked teasing shouldn't have rattled her. But he'd always had the ability to throw her off-kilter. "Behave," she muttered. "If you know how." She stood and faced him. "Shouldn't we get down to business?"

Dylan was somewhat perturbed that everything Mia said sounded sexual to him. She wasn't doing it on purpose. At least he didn't think so. Maybe having a woman sleeping in his house was not such a good idea. Too intimate. Too accessible. Too everything.

"The office is this way," he said gruffly.

Fortunately she followed him down the hall without comment. Dylan's home office opened off the corridor opposite the sunroom. He didn't spend much time there. It was mostly a repository for business paperwork, because at the saloon his walled "cubicle," as he liked to call it, was much too small to house file cabinets. This room had windows that let in the summer sun, and thick navy carpet that made a man want to go barefoot.

Today, however, he was the boss showing a new employee the ropes. As he glanced around the room, he felt his neck flush. The place was a wreck. He hadn't realized how bad it looked. Picking up a stack of *Sports Illustrated* magazines, he shoved several bunches of mail on top of them, attempting to clear a spot where Mia could work.

"Sorry," he said. He hadn't realized what a mess the room had become. "It's usually just me in here, so I don't bother much with cleaning."

Mia looked around with interest. "Don't worry about it. I'm sure you're always busy down at the bar. But I'd be happy to take a shot at organizing things a bit…if you trust me."

"Of course I trust you." He picked up a flat package that he had already opened with a knife and handed it to her. "I bought this to get you started."

Mia opened the carton and stared. "You got me a laptop?"

"It's top-of-the-line. And I had the guy at the computer store move all the files from the desktop at the Silver Dollar onto this baby. Fortunately, I had already dealt with that last week, because I think the old computer sustained some water damage."

Mia looked at the slim piece of technology with appreciation. "I've always wanted one so thin and light. Not that this one is mine, but it will be fun to use."

He pulled out the leather desk chair. "Sit down. Fire it up."

While he plugged in the power cord in case the unit wasn't fully charged, Mia opened the new toy and turned it on. When he stood from his crouched position on the floor beside her chair, her fingers were flying over the keys. "It's so fast," she said, her voice laden with excitement.

Rolling his eyes, he wondered if she had forgotten his presence. Testing a theory, he leaned forward and rested his forearms on the back of the chair. Now his head was close to hers, close enough that he could have kissed her cheek if he had been so inclined. He hadn't really *stopped* thinking about kissing her since last night.

She smelled good. The temptation was almost irresistible. But she was a guest in his home. His gut-deep need to nibble the curve of her ear was inappropriate. He did touch her hair, but so softly that he was sure she wouldn't notice.

Mia never flinched. "Where are the bookkeeping files?" she asked.

"Everything you need is right here." He reached around her and pointed to a tab. The faint, pleasing scent of her perfume teased his nose. Her hair, tucked up in a ponytail again, was silky and thick—the color of rich chocolate. The urge to press his lips to the nape of her neck almost shredded his resolve.

When her hands went perfectly still on the keyboard, he knew she had finally realized that he was practically embracing her. "Dylan?"

She turned her head and looked up at him. Without analyzing it, he brushed the pad of his thumb across her soft cheek. "What?"

Mia's small white teeth worried her lower lip. "I wondered when I accepted this job if we might become lovers."

He jerked upright so fast he practically cracked his spine. It was one thing for him to try and rattle the sweetly serious girl he had known in high school. Apparently this new Mia was bolder. And apparently he wasn't as slick an operator as he thought, because the light of interest in her eyes threatened to knock him on his ass.

How had he lost control of the situation so quickly?

"That's not funny," he said. "Open one of those files and let me show you how things work."

She swiveled her chair until she faced him. Her lips twitched. "I'd like that. A lot."

"Stop it," he demanded.

"Stop what?"

"Acting like you want me to seduce you."

"I don't," she said simply, her hands now tucked primly in her lap. "I'm more interested in seducing *you*."

Maybe he had stepped through some kind of time warp into a parallel universe. It was the only explanation for this surreal conversation. He ran a hand across the back of his neck. "Are you trying to get back at me for being such a jerk in high school? Is that the reason for this charade?" She couldn't be serious.

Mia smiled sweetly. "You seem upset."

"I'm not upset, I'm just…" He trailed off, not quite able to articulate his feelings. It certainly wasn't unusual for a woman to come on to him. But Mia? Even in the midst of his consternation, his libido was at work, urging him to stop rationalizing and take advantage of the situation. "Maybe you're suffering from stress," he said desperately, reaching for any feasible explanation for her attitude. "Perhaps you should go lie down."

"Is that an invitation, Dylan?"

Eight

Mia wanted to laugh out loud at Dylan's hunted expression. He was the one who had touched her, not vice versa, but clearly he hadn't expected her reaction. Truthfully she was surprised at herself. When had she decided to reach for what she wanted? Both literally and metaphorically?

Perhaps trying so hard to get pregnant and finally succeeding had given her the confidence to face her fears. She had never had any trouble with academic challenges, but steering her personal life in a positive direction? That was a bigger hurdle to jump.

"Oh, forget it, Dylan," she said, keeping her tone light and teasing. "You're looking at me like I sprouted two heads. Your virtue is safe. Go away and let me get started on this."

The naked relief on his face was comical. "That's a good idea," he said heartily. "Having me here will be an interruption. That's my old bookkeeper's cell number there on the bulletin board. She said for you to call her anytime if you have questions."

The next thing Mia knew, she was alone in Dylan's office. His defection disappointed her. But she knew he was interested. The signs were all there. That *almost* kiss when they'd shared ice cream. His soft touch on her hair when he thought she didn't notice. He kept reaching out to her. She would give him time to get used to the idea.

Glancing at her watch, she realized that Cora would be ready to eat soon. Still, there was enough time to comb through the Silver Dollar's accounts-payable and accounts-receivable files. As she delved into her task, she saw that the computer program was straightforward. Her math skills were almost as strong as her language skills, so she soon felt confident that she could help Dylan.

That he would be helping her as well was a given.

By the time she shut everything down and went in search of her baby, Dylan was nowhere to be found. Gertie was sitting in the living room bouncing Cora on her knee. The baby was happy, but when she saw her mother, Cora wanted her.

Gertie handed Cora over with a smile. "Cute kid. Looks like you."

"Thank you for looking after her."

"Glad to do it."

"Is Dylan still around?"

"Nope. He lit out of here like a crazy man, mumbling something about a meeting in town. But it was the first I heard of it."

Mia grimaced inwardly. "I'm sure the fire has created a host of problems for him. Once I get the baby down for her afternoon nap, I plan to spend a couple of hours in the office seeing what things are urgent and which ones can wait. You don't have to cook for me if Dylan will be out. I'll be fine with a sandwich."

Gertie bristled. "Nonsense. You and the baby are my responsibility. That's what Dylan wants."

Dylan drove around town aimlessly. He couldn't go to work and he couldn't go home. That was a hell of a thing for a man to admit. Now that Pandora's box had been opened, all he could think about was what it would be like to have Mia Larin in his bed.

His fingers gripped the steering wheel as he broke out in a cold sweat. No good deed went unpunished. All he had wanted to do was give her—temporarily— a job and a place to live. To express his appreciation for what she had done for him in high school.

That was a noble goal. Right? So why was he hiding out? He was a man, damn it. Mia was a little mouse of a woman.

Except that she wasn't. Even as he said the words out loud, he knew they weren't true. Maybe Mia had been bashful and socially backward at fifteen, but definitely not now. She was a grown woman with goals and dreams. She'd wanted a baby, and she'd made it happen.

Was she serious about wanting Dylan?

Even as his body tightened at the thought, he acknowledged that it was a bad idea all the way around. Not on a physical level. Hell, he'd been on board with that since the moment he realized the grown-up Mia was a sensual, alluring woman.

But Mia didn't belong in Silver Glen, and he didn't want a woman getting close enough to him again to make him do something stupid. It didn't help that Mia had a beautiful little baby. The two of them together were a temptation he didn't need.

The idea of family and hearth and home had become more appealing to him in recent months. After his broken engagement, he had closed himself off emotionally. Aside from work, he was interested only in fun and games… having a good time. But after Liam and Zoe's wedding, some of the ice around Dylan's heart began to thaw.

Now he had brought two females into his home. Females who brightened up the place and gave it new life. So the temptation returned.

When his relationship with Tara ended, it had been tough. But there were no children involved. That experience had taught him a bitter truth. Either he picked the wrong women, or he himself wasn't very good in the relationship department.

Regardless, he was skittish about getting serious again. Especially with a woman who was already a parent. Dylan liked kids. No question there. But he doubted his ability to be the kind of parent who could nurture and care for a child of his own.

The only example he'd had growing up was Reggie, his feckless father. Dylan's dad was a Peter Pan at heart, always chasing the next crazy idea, leaving it to Maeve to do the lion's share of guiding seven boys. Dylan suspected he had inherited some of his dad's lack of focus. He'd be damned if he would ruin some kid's life.

Dylan had to keep reminding himself that Mia was passing through. Like his ex-fiancée, Mia would not be sticking around when the right job offer came along. Even if she *was* attracted to him, it was up to Dylan to be strong for both of them. Mia's defenses were down. She'd been through a grueling few weeks. An honorable man would not take advantage of that weakness. No matter how very badly he wanted to.

By the time he returned home in the late afternoon, he was certain he had a handle on the Mia situation. What he hadn't counted on was finding his mother, Maeve, sitting on his sofa conversing with his new houseguest. It wasn't entirely unheard of for his mom to drop by, but she usually called first. Maybe the gossipy grapevine had alerted her to Mia's presence. Maeve had been doing her best to play matchmaker for Dylan since the Tara incident.

Every one of his bachelor survival skills kicked into gear. "Hello, Mom. What brings you here?"

Maeve Kavanagh was an attractive woman in her early sixties. Her auburn hair with touches of gray, habitually kept in a bun, gave her an air of authority, but there was nothing matronly about her. Along with Liam, Maeve ran the Silver Beeches Lodge.

Dylan tossed his keys in a disk on the credenza by the front door and took a seat across from the two women. His mother cuddled Cora, a look of absolute joy on her face as she played with the baby.

Mia shot him a look that could have meant anything. "Your mother was worried about you. Because of the fire."

"I'm fine, Mom. But I appreciate your stopping by. Mia is staying with me for a bit. I guess you've already introduced yourselves by now. Do you remember her at all?"

Maeve tore her attention away from the infant long enough to frown at her son. "Of course I do. I thanked God for her every minute of your senior year. You were so busy being a rebellious adolescent that I couldn't get through to you, so I looked on Mia's assistance as a miracle."

Mia frowned. "It hadn't been that long since Dylan lost his dad. I think his behavior was understandable."

Dylan squirmed when his mother raised an eyebrow. He didn't need Mia defending him. Especially not to the parent who remembered all too well the many ways that he'd once tried to ruin his life. He stood, not caring if he was being rude. "I'll walk you out to the car, Mom."

Maeve grinned at Mia. "I believe that's 'Here's your hat, what's your hurry.' But since I do have a million things waiting to be accomplished, I'll go. It was lovely to see you again, Mia. I hope you'll join me for dinner at the Lodge one evening soon."

"Thank you, Ms. Kavanagh. I'd like that."

"As long as you bring the baby and call me Maeve."

Dylan escorted his mother out of the house, well aware he was about to get the third degree. What he hadn't expected was the way his parent looked at him with calculation in her eyes.

Opening her car door, but not getting in, she rested her arm on the frame. "Tell me the truth, Dylan. Is that baby yours?"

Startled shock tensed every one of his muscles. "Good God, Mother, no. I haven't seen the woman since high school."

"And yet she's tucked up nice and cozy in your house."

If anyone else, including his brothers, had subjected him to this line of questioning, he'd have told them to mind their own damn business. Unfortunately, that wasn't an option with his mother.

"Mia lost her job. I needed a bookkeeper. It's temporary. The plan was for her to live in the apartment over the saloon. Obviously, that's not an option right now."

Maeve's expression didn't change. "I don't want to see you get hurt. I don't want anyone taking advantage of your kind heart. You have this wonderful capacity for helping people, but it doesn't always serve you well in the end."

He stared down at the driveway, kicking a pebble with enough force to express his frustration. "You're talking about my ex-fiancée."

"Tara, the tramp, we call her. She used you, Dylan. It fed her ego to have a handsome hulk of a young man—a wealthy one at that—squiring her around town. I know the shape you were in when she left. You care, Dylan. Sometimes too much. Because people are not always what they seem."

"Mia's not like that. And the situations are totally different."

"I saw the way she looked at you when you walked into the room a moment ago."

He would have liked to argue the point, but given the surprising turn of events in his office earlier, he couldn't. "You have nothing to worry about. Mia's time here is very short. A woman with her qualifications and capabilities will have another job in no time."

"Bring her to dinner at the hotel. Zoe has been dying to cook for us in their suite."

Dylan's brother and his new wife lived on the top floor of the Silver Beeches Lodge, but they already had plans underway to build an incredible house. "I think being included in a family dinner would make Mia uncomfortable."

"Nonsense. I already invited her."

"She's nursing. I doubt she'd want to leave the baby for that long."

"Bring the baby with you. Maybe little Cora will give Liam and Zoe ideas. I'd like to be a nana before I have one foot in the grave."

"You never give up, do you?" He smiled, acknowledging the love and affection he felt for his mother. She had been widowed very young and yet managed to raise seven rambunctious boys and keep the family fortunes afloat. "I love you, Mom."

He kissed her cheek and tucked her into the car.

She stuck her arm out the window and waved a finger at him. "I'll check with Liam and Zoe and see what night works for them. No excuses."

Without answering, he watched her drive away. Hearing someone who cared so much about him put into words some of what he had been thinking sobered him. Was he susceptible to Mia simply because of auld lang syne and propinquity?

When he went back inside the house, he stopped to speak to the woman who had occupied his thoughts for most of the day. "Mia."

She looked up at him and smiled. "Your mother is sweet."

Dylan thought about that for a minute. Maeve had been

called headstrong and caring, but sweet? He squelched the instinct to plop down beside Mia and play with the baby, reminding himself of his recent resolve to keep them at a distance.

"I have several calls to make this evening, so I'm going to have dinner in my suite. You and Cora are welcome to make yourself at home anywhere in the house. I'll talk to you tomorrow."

I'll talk to you tomorrow.
But he didn't.
Mia was first surprised, then angry, then sad when she realized Dylan was making a concerted effort to be invisible. For five straight days, she never saw him nor heard from him. Gertie said he was hard at work tearing out the insides of the bar so that when the contractor was ready, the work could begin at once. None of which explained why a man with Dylan's fortune hadn't hired a crew to take over the dirty, smelly work. At night she caught sounds that might be him moving around in his room, but he came and went like a ghost.

It didn't take a genius to understand that Dylan was not going to follow up on her blatant invitation. Something inside Mia shriveled and died with the knowledge that for once in her life she had made the first move with a man, and now he was avoiding her as if afraid she might somehow jump him in his sleep. *Embarrassed* didn't begin to describe how she felt.

When she had been in residence almost a week, it became clear that she needed to be proactive about finding a *real* job. Living in Dylan's house was an untenable situation. The man was literally skulking around like a phantom because she had told him she wanted him.

Besides that, she needed to get back to work. As much as she adored Cora—and as lovely as it was to be waited on hand and foot—her brain needed the challenges it was accustomed to handling. The work she did was important. Her skills were a rare gift, one she could not in all good conscience fritter away.

One morning when Cora napped and after the records for the bar were in good shape, Mia used the laptop to write a new résumé. She'd been in her last job a very long time, so it wasn't hard to piece together her employment history.

Dylan had dangled the prospect of spending more time with Cora as an incentive for Mia to take the flexible bookkeeping job. But no matter how much she cherished being with her child all day, it was equally necessary to set a good example for her daughter. Mia's career was important. It changed lives. The work she was trained to do, the work she enjoyed, was more than a means of income. It was what she was good at…what she contributed to the world at large.

Once the résumé was polished, she compiled a list of all the influential contacts she knew in her field and emailed them her portfolio. After she clicked the send button, she felt her heart sink. She wished she had time to follow up on her attraction to Dylan. But if he was not interested, then the sooner she left, the better. Besides, getting involved with him would only lead to heartbreak. Dylan belonged in Silver Glen. Sadly, there was nothing here for Mia.

That night, Cora did not sleep well at all. She was restless and cranky, perhaps picking up on her mother's unsettled feelings. At two in the morning, Mia wandered to the other side of the house to get a glass of milk. Cora whimpered and squirmed in her arms, her little face red and blotchy from crying.

Mia knew how she felt. For two cents, she would plop down on the floor and bawl herself.

Instead of reaching for the light switch—because she definitely wanted Cora to know it was not morning—she tiptoed carefully across the kitchen, hoping to avoid a stubbed toe. But when she did run into something, it was big and warm and solid. Her muffled shriek came seconds before the realization that Dylan held her by the arms.

Her pulse racing like a train bound for the station, she wriggled free. "You've got to stop doing that. My heart can't take it." The complaint didn't hold much heat, since she was whispering.

He ran a hand over Cora's downy head. "You think she's getting a tooth?"

Mia yawned, not even protesting when Dylan reached for Cora. "It's a little too soon for that. Maybe I'm being punished for something."

"You want some company while she's awake?" His question was quiet, but it seemed significant somehow.

"I haven't seen you for days."

"Did you miss me?" Even in the gloom she could see the flash of white teeth.

"Barely noticed you were gone," she lied. "And yes…if you have insomnia, I'd love to have an adult to converse with. My repertoire of baby talk is all panned out."

Dylan brushed past her. "Follow me."

In the living room, he flipped on the gas logs, even though it was the height of summer. The dancing flames cast a rosy glow of illumination that was gentle enough not to stimulate Cora.

Mia collapsed onto the sofa, so tired she could barely sit up straight. "I can hold her," she said.

"Relax, Mia. I've got this."

As she watched through heavy-lidded eyes, Dylan walked Cora around the room, singing to her in a voice that was pleasant but definitely off-key. His husky serenade seeped into Mia's bones and muscles, relaxing them until she slid further down into the cushions.

Only then did it dawn on her that he was naked from the waist up. In the illumination from the fire, she could see the beautiful delineation of his muscles. He looked powerfully masculine, and—in spite of the baby cradled in his arms—untamed, pagan. His drawstring pajama pants, navy with a yellow stripe, were most likely a concession to his houseguests.

Cora quieted finally, lashes settling on rounded cheeks. Mia knew she should get up and take the baby, but she couldn't seem to move....

Dylan cuddled Cora. Sweet, snuggly, pudgy Cora. She rested against his chest trustingly, a little streak of drool wetting his skin. He loved babies, always had. They smelled like home and happiness and love. An infant's smile was the greatest promise that the world would go on, no matter how much the grown-ups mucked around with it. When he was sure she was out for the count, he laid her in the crib, crossing his fingers that she would stay asleep.

When she didn't stir after a full minute, he was fairly certain she was down for the night. Returning to the living room, he found Mia fast asleep, as well. She had tugged an afghan from the back of the sofa. All he could see of her was the top of her head. Smiling wryly, he bent and scooped her into his arms.

If Cora reminded him of peace and security, Mia's warm body had just the opposite effect. The weight of her in his arms gave him a jolt of excitement and possessive hunger. Holding her, he wanted to believe that it was possible to keep her here. Silver Glen was his home. If he tried hard enough, he could envision Mia returning to her roots as well.

Although he had worked hard to create himself in the

image of a carefree, never-serious party guy, he knew in his heart that the fabric of life was more than that. It was woven of simple pleasures like holding a quiet, complicated, soft-skinned woman in your arms and wondering what it would be like to kiss her.

From happier days of his childhood, he remembered his family sitting around the table playing board games and laughing, always laughing. After Reggie's death, much of the laughter had stopped. Perhaps that was why Dylan had tried so hard to be the life of the party. He remembered those good times and yearned to recreate them.

Mia reminded him anew of what he was missing. She spoke to him at a visceral level, underscoring the value of things like hard work and loyalty and selfless giving. Seeing her with Cora made him want to be a better man.

Mia's room was semidark. She had left a light on in the bathroom with the door cracked, so Dylan was able to carry her easily without crashing into furniture. With one hand he straightened the tousled sheets and spread. The state of her bed told him more than words about her interrupted night.

When he folded back the covers and laid her gently on the mattress, she stirred, her eyes opening slowly. "Cora?" She sat up on her elbows.

Dylan smoothed the hair from her face. "She's asleep. In her bed."

"Oh. I'm sorry."

"Nothing to be sorry about. There's no reason not to ask for help, Mia. As long as you're here."

"I'm making you uncomfortable. Your family has questions. And you want to draw a line in the sand between business and personal. I'll go as soon as I can find somewhere else to live."

Nothing she said was untrue. But it wasn't the whole truth. "What makes me uncomfortable," he said slowly, "is that I want you and I'm not sure if I should."

Nine

He hadn't meant to be quite so honest.

Mia's nose wrinkled. "Ouch. Am I that much of a liability?" Though she said it jokingly, he fancied that in her eyes he saw vulnerability and hurt. But that might have been a trick of light and shadow.

He sat down beside her on the bed. "You don't belong in Silver Glen, Mia." The truth might hurt, but it was better that they each acknowledge the reality of their situation. "Your intellectual gifts can make a difference in the world. For now, you've had a hiccup. You need time to regroup. That's understandable. And I'm happy I can help. I owe you that. But we can't forget that your stay here is temporary. I've already had one relationship with a woman who was just passing through. It was a messy, public breakup. No one gets privacy in a small town. I'd rather not repeat the experience."

"That's quite a speech. Would you care to cut to the bottom line and tell me what the heck you're saying?"

"I'm saying that I want you."

He stroked her arm as he said the words, completely aware that Mia was unlike anyone he had cared about before. Beneath the very real sexual hunger he felt for her was a vein of something he couldn't pin down…tenderness maybe, but more than that. She was a part of his past, a very significant part. She had helped shape him into the man he had become.

After his blunt statement, she sat straight up, crossing her legs pretzel style and staring at him. "You may be disappointed. I'm not very good at it. Sex, I mean."

Humor slipped in unannounced, lightening the mood. "In this particular situation, I think it's safe to assume that I won't have any complaints. Not that I'm bragging, but you probably were with the wrong men before."

"Man. Only one."

"Ah, yes. The professor. I may not have his brains, but I've researched the hell out of this particular topic." Perhaps he shouldn't have alluded to other women, even obliquely. Mia was acquainted with his past exploits, but she flinched when he mentioned them.

"Are you sure, Dylan?"

Again that heartbreaking vulnerability. "We were friends once. I hope we still are. But the connection I feel to you, to the grown-up Mia, is brand-new. I'd like to see where it goes."

Only a prospective lover with Mia's IQ could induce Dylan to use such an academic approach to sex. Ordinarily, a couple of drinks, soft lighting and a willing woman took care of any negotiations in that arena. But for whatever reason, it seemed important to him that she knew he had thought about this. That he wasn't being ruled by his baser instincts.

On the other hand, his carefully worded analysis of the spark between them didn't seem to be making her very happy. Hell, why was he second-guessing everything?

Carefully, giving her one last moment to change her mind, he slid both hands beneath her sleep-ruffled hair and cupped her neck. His head lowered. Women normally closed their eyes at this point. Mia didn't. She watched him with fascination in her dark-eyed gaze.

He hesitated. "You make me a little nuts," he confessed.

"Why?" This close he could see how thick her lashes were.

"I sometimes feel like you're studying me."

"Why on earth would I do that?" Sexual anticipation was replaced by frustration on her face and in her voice.

"You're the only genius I've ever met. I don't know what goes on inside your head." Why he was baring his soul like this, he hadn't a clue. But it obviously was the wrong tack to take with Mia.

Her chin wobbled. "I'm no different than any other woman, Dylan. Same body parts, same emotions, same wants and needs. I hate it when you say things like that."

"I'm sorry." And he was.

"Forget all that other stuff. Pretend you picked me up at a bar. Not the Silver Dollar. Someplace else. We met and flirted and all we could think about was jumping each other's bones."

In that moment, he understood what she wanted. Mia needed to feel like an ordinary woman. She wasn't ordinary. Far from it. But he was hurting her by hiding the depth of his hunger, when all he had ever wanted to do was protect her.

Deliberately, he reached for the hem of her tank top and peeled it upward, forcing her to raise her arms as he lifted it over her head. His sharp, audible intake of breath was loud in the hushed silence of her room. "God, you're beautiful," he muttered. White-skinned and pleasingly curved, she was a sculptor's dream. But unlike marble, she was real and soft and warm. Locking his gaze with hers, he cupped her breasts with his hands, testing their weight and fullness.

This time Mia closed her eyes.

He took that as a positive sign. Suddenly, he felt like a kid in a candy shop, not sure what he wanted first. A linear approach seemed feasible. He started with her delicate eyelids, drifted down her perfect nose, and settled his lips over hers. The contact rocked him on his ass. Nuclear fission couldn't have been any hotter.

Even as his hands kneaded her flesh and teased her nipples, his mouth ravaged hers. Tongues tangling. Breath laboring. She was as eager as he was, her slim arms going around his neck and tightening as he deepened the kiss. It wasn't what he expected at all.

He had thought Mia might be tentative or clumsy or awkward. Instead, he—Dylan—felt completely out of his depth. She was intensely female despite the fact that she did little to enhance her looks with the usual feminine paints and potions. He had barely touched her, and already he was hard enough to make his position on the bed uncomfortable.

"Mia?" he asked hoarsely, not really sure what he wanted her to say or do.

"Take off your clothes, Dylan. Come to bed with me."

Mia couldn't believe it was really happening. All the fantasies about Dylan she had entertained over the years were pale imitations of the real thing. His skin was hot beneath her touch, though the room was plenty cool. The muscles that rippled in his arms and torso were strong and defined. She stroked him with giddy delight. He was hers. Maybe only for tonight. But he was hers.

Her confidence wavered when she saw him fully nude. Standing beside the bed, arms crossed, shoulders squared, he projected determination and an unmistakable intent to have his way. His erection bobbed high and strong against his flat, corded abdomen.

She swallowed against the sudden lump in her throat. "You're a very striking man," she said quietly.

He tugged her toward the edge of the bed and dragged

her sleep pants down her legs, along with her undies. She was a grown woman. Not without experience. But allowing Dylan to look his fill of her naked body required a surprising amount of courage. Her belly was no longer as flat as it once was, and she had a couple of stretch marks.

In her imagination, this was the moment when he joined her beneath the covers. The reassuringly *covering* covers. But he took her off guard again. Gently, he took both of her hands in his, gripped them, and pulled her to her feet. She was not a noticeably short woman. But toe-to-toe with Dylan she felt small and defenseless.

His devilish grin warmed the cold places in her body. "Touch me, Mia. Please."

It reassured her to realize that his need was every bit as great as hers. She went up on tiptoe and kissed his mouth, lingering to slide her tongue between his teeth, relishing the response that quaked through his frame. Against her belly, his eager flesh twitched. She clasped him in one hand, squeezing gently. His clenched jaw and damp forehead revealed the extent of her power. Power she had never claimed before.

Tilting back her head, she searched his gaze. "Is that what you meant?"

"Damn, woman. I thought you said you weren't good at this."

She rested her cheek against his chest, feeling the steady thump of his heart. When her arms clasped his waist and his circled hers, she felt as if something precious had been born. "These are just the preliminaries," she whispered. "Don't get too excited, Dylan. I may not measure up in the main event."

She'd spent most of her life being judged on her abilities. Here, now, on the verge of having sex with the man of her dreams, it had never mattered more that she did and said the right things. It would be crushing if Dylan found her naiveté boring or, even worse, amusing.

But he totally disarmed her by laughing. "Good Lord, Mia. It isn't an exam. And besides, I'm supposed to be the one pleasing *you* tonight, not the other way around. You'll get your turn. Relax, sweetheart."

He scooped her into his arms and sprawled on the bed with her, his big, hairy legs tangling with her smaller, paler ones. Though he kept most of his weight on his hands, she shivered at the delicious feel of his tough, honed body pressing hers into the mattress. Such a primitive response. But entirely inescapable.

Scraping her thumbnail along his chin, she smiled. "I like you all rough and scraggly."

Nuzzling her neck, he chuckled. "You may sing another tune when you wake up in the morning wearing my marks. If I'd known this was a possibility, I'd have shaved for you."

She cocked her head, staring up at him. "Do things usually start off this slowly? Not that I'm complaining."

"Well, Miss Impatient, do you have condoms?"

"Um, no…" She flushed from her throat to her hairline. Just when she thought she was giving a great performance as a woman of the world having casual sex with a hot, hungry guy, she betrayed her true colors.

Though a pained look crossed his face, he spoke gently. "I'll go get some." Climbing off the bed, he towered over her. "You won't change your mind?"

She pulled the sheet over her nudity, not quite as nonchalant as she hoped to be in this situation. "I won't change my mind."

Dylan must have dabbled in time travel, because he made it to his bedroom and back to hers in a nanosecond.

After dropping a handful of packets on the bedside table, he held one out to her. "You want to do the honors?"

"No. Thank you." To be honest, she wasn't at all sure that little piece of latex was going to fit over and around Dylan's aroused shaft.

Nevertheless, he rolled it on with an economy of motion she admired and then climbed back in bed. "Move over, woman."

"Your feet are freezing," she exclaimed.

"Then warm me up."

After that, any conversation gave way to sheer physical sensation. Despite his chilled feet, the rest of Dylan's body radiated heat. He settled between her thighs with a groan that sounded as if he had waited a hundred years to find that exact spot. She wrapped her legs around his waist, lifting her hips to urge him on.

And yet still, he didn't join their bodies. His erection, hot and firm, rubbed lazily against the cleft between her legs. Zings of sensation flooded her pelvis with restless pleasure. She had known that sex with Dylan would be incredible. Sheer physical delight. What she hadn't expected was the rush of emotion. Tears stung her eyes, though she wouldn't let them fall for fear he would misunderstand.

He was so dear, so special, so deserving of a woman's love. It was incomprehensible to her that his fiancée had walked away from him. Perhaps one day the woman would realize what she had lost. Or perhaps she and Dylan were never really right for each other at all.

The girl Mia had been in high school still lived somewhere deep inside the adult Mia. That shy, backward teenager who had adored the angry, sullen Dylan now wanted the stronger, happier Dylan with equal measure. He'd thrown up barriers between them already. Telling her she didn't belong. Making his learning challenges and her intellectual capabilities some kind of überforbidden matchup.

They weren't the Montagues and Capulets.

When he braced himself on one hand and stroked his fingers over her lower lip, she tasted him involuntarily, her tongue wetting the pad of his thumb. He shuddered. She bit the same spot with a sharp nip.

Clearly Dylan had himself on a tight leash. She was well aware that he was holding back. But she didn't want his gentleness, at least not right now. Hunger rose like an irrepressible tide, making her reckless.

"I won't break," she muttered. "I want you in me, over me, on me."

His pupils expanded as hot color flushed his cheekbones. He dropped his forehead to hers. "You've got it, Mia." The words were guttural, a hoarse accompaniment to the forceful thrust of his hips that buried him deep inside her.

She was fairly certain they both gasped in unison, but with the sound of her heartbeat loud in her ears, she couldn't be sure.

Mia had the ability to convert complicated numerical equations into their metric equivalents without using a calculator. Her papers had been published in academic journals and had even been presented at international conferences. Abstract ideas and three-dimensional thinking were her bread and butter.

But what she couldn't fathom was how one man, *this* one man, could reduce her from a practical, down-to-earth scientist and mom to a shivering mass of nerves and need. She swallowed hard and tried to force words from a dry throat. "That's more like it."

Dylan nibbled her collarbone, his lower body momentarily still. His pause gave her a chance to absorb the effects of his possession. Pleasantly stretched and undeniably filled, her sex welcomed him enthusiastically, little muscle flutters massaging his length.

The hair on his chest tickled her breasts. She liked the sensation. Their coupling had an earthy, elemental rightness to it that she and the professor had never quite attained. This breathless moment seemed preordained, as if long ago, Dylan and Mia's teenage friendship prepared the ground for what was to come.

He moved his hips without warning, gaining another half inch of penetration. "You're tight," he groaned. "I don't want this to end."

"You've barely started yet," she pointed out, a little miffed that her charms weren't sufficient enough to drive him insane with lust.

Dylan didn't answer with words. Instead, he began moving slowly, drawing a tremulous cry from her parched throat. Beneath her, his expensive sheets were cool and smooth against her heated flesh. Above her, his big, hard body enveloped her in a stimulating mélange of sight and sound and touch. The room smelled of warm skin and hot sex.

"Open your mouth, baby."

When she obeyed, the thrust of his tongue mimicked the movements of his hips. The dual possession melted her, incinerated her. Feverish and desperate, she raked his shoulders with her fingernails, barely conscious that she did so. "Please," she whispered. "Please."

Impossible pleasure beckoned, her orgasm building with the heat of a thousand suns, barely contained. Dylan took her again and again, his movements bold, giving no quarter. She would be sore tomorrow. That fleeting thought escaped from some last coherent corner of her brain.

"Come for me, Mia," he rasped, the words barely audible.

And she did....

Dylan held her as she writhed and cried out. He ground the base of his erection against her mound, sending her up yet again. Feeling her climax, watching the sharp jolt of completion paint her face with rosy color, sent exultation fizzing in his veins, despite the fact that he had thus far denied himself release.

Holding back was next to impossible, but he wanted to enjoy her pleasure. When she was sated and still, her eyes closed, he withdrew and leaned down to whisper in her ear. "You screamed my name," he said smugly.

Mia opened one eyelid. "Did not."

"Did, too."

Playing with her was fun. But fun was not even on the scale of what he needed now. "I'll let you sleep soon," he promised, not at all sure he wasn't lying. He rolled to his back, taking her limp body with him. Arranging her like a sleepy rag doll with her legs straddling his hips, he lifted her gently, positioned the head of his erection at her entrance and pushed.

Mia's lips parted, an arrested expression on her face. "Oh," she breathed, her hands settling on his shoulders.

Oh, indeed. The new angle put increasing pressure on his hypersensitive sex. Straining to give her as much as she could take, he flexed his hips and drove upward, shaking the bed with the force of his rhythmic movements. Mia's hair fell around her face. Her breasts swung enticingly above him.

Rearing up, he captured one nipple with his teeth and sucked it into his mouth. Mia moaned. He felt the clasp of her inner flesh tighten around him. The visual stimulation and the feel of her in his arms snapped the last of his control. He rolled the two of them again, needing the mattress to brace against as he lunged wildly toward the finish.

Holy hell. Sharp yellow lights obscured his vision. Uncontrollable trembling sapped his muscles of their strength. Lightning struck his groin with paralyzing heat, and he slammed into the end with a shout.

Ten

Dylan lay stunned on top of Mia, barely able to breathe. What in the hell had happened to him? Instinctively, he gathered his defenses, unwilling to let her see that their lovemaking was anything out of the ordinary. Already, Mia knew far too much about his psyche for him to feel completely at ease with her. A man liked to hide his weaknesses.

It remained to be seen, however, if the last hour was a weakness or a catastrophic shift in the continental plates.

When he thought he could force his muscles to move, he lifted away from her, stumbled to his feet and went into the bathroom to take care of the condom and splash water on his face. In the mirror his eyes were overbright, feverish. He ran both hands through his hair, raking his fingers across his scalp.

When he returned to the bedroom, braced for the inevitable postcoital conversation, Mia was sound asleep. She lay on her back where he had abandoned her, arms outflung, hair mussed, her body bare as the day she was born. He couldn't decide if relief or disappointment held the upper hand. Looking at her made his chest hurt and his head throb.

What had he done?

The clock ticked away the minutes before dawn. Mia needed her sleep. Even if he was already partially erect and wanted her again with an alarming desperation, it would be cruel to wake her. Cora was a lively handful. A rested Mia would be better able to handle her daughter's demands.

Quietly picking up his scattered pieces of clothing, he bundled them into his arms and lingered by the bed. Mia and his ex-fiancée, Tara, were as different as two women could be—in looks, in temperament, in every way. What did it say about him that he had so quickly recovered from a broken heart? Had Tara's defection been more a blow to his pride?

In all honesty, the sex with Tara had been fun. And she had been fun. Always urging him on to the next wild adventure. In retrospect, it was kind of ironic. Tara was a female version of himself, or at least the self he had been in high school and later as a young adult.

Maybe that had been the attraction. He understood her.

Mia, on the other hand, was a complete mystery. Even given her history of crippling shyness, it was hard to imagine that no man had managed to put a ring on her finger. She was warm and funny and loyal and brave. That she had resorted to a sperm donor to become pregnant baffled him.

Such an action pointed to the fact that she didn't want any messy involvement with a man who might make demands. Had she never been in love? Ever?

Now that he thought about it, he surely hadn't. The relationship with Tara had been two parts lust and one part male hubris. Dating a beautiful actress made him feel like a million bucks. He could be excused for believing their short-lived engagement was the real thing, because he'd been thinking with his male anatomy and not his brain.

He liked to imagine that in the intervening years he had matured. At least he'd been smart enough not to get entwined in any further unsuitable relationships. His dating nowadays was light and fun. No commitment, no complications.

Up until tonight.

He backed away from the bed a step at a time, his feet silent on the plush carpet. When he reached the door, he opened it quietly. Mia slept so deeply, she never even stirred.

The bed and the woman were inviting. All he had to do was lift the covers and take her in his arms. His hands tingled as he imagined the feel of her skin. Warm. Incredibly soft.

Damn. He had a sick feeling that he had let the genie out of the bottle. What was he going to do about Mia and Cora now?

Mia rolled over and glanced at her phone to see what time it was. Weak, early-morning sunlight filtered into the room through a crack in the heavy brocade drapes that matched the moss-green color palette of the room. Her breasts ached, heavy with milk. Cora would be awake any moment now. On the monitor, the grainy picture of Mia's daughter showed a reassuring image of the infant sleeping peacefully.

Concentrating on the baby wasn't working. Movielike flashes spun through Mia's head. Arousing, incredible memories. She needed to believe that the stimulating pictures were nothing more than a surreal dream. But the fragrance of a man's skin lingered on her sheets.

Even as her legs moved restlessly, her heart and soul ached with the breath-stealing certainty that she and Dylan had been lovers last night. In the wee hours when rational thought was easily subverted by yearning and need. During the drowsy moments when phantoms seemed real and the concrete world faded into shadows.

The emptiness of the bed mocked her. If the dreams were real, where was Dylan? Why wasn't he curled up with her beneath the sumptuous covers, his body warm and hard and ready for a morning tête-à-tête?

Shaking all over, she fled to the bathroom, taking the baby monitor with her. If she were lucky, she would have time for a quick shower before Cora demanded her breakfast. Beneath the hot, pelting spray, Mia soaped herself furiously, trying to erase the feel of Dylan's touch.

His absence spoke volumes. Even in the beginning, he had expressed his doubts. Perhaps he had been looking to her to put a stop to the madness that had caught them up in the middle of the night.

Mia hadn't been interested in making rational, grown-up decisions. Dylan had stood before her, wanting her. So she took without asking, without considering Cora, without deciding if her selfish behavior had consequences. What did Dylan think of her? Why wasn't he here?

Closing her heart to the pain she didn't want to face, she returned to the bedroom to dress. By the time she had finished, Cora was stirring. As she went to scoop up her daughter and change her diaper, Mia reminded herself how lucky she was. Cora was the sunshine in her life. The one true lodestar that kept her focused and reminded her that a mother's job was to be selfless…to put her child's well-being ahead of her own.

Mia was in Silver Glen so Cora would have a roof overhead while her mother found a job. Touching base with Dylan had accomplished that. He needed Mia's help, and she heeded his. But their bargain had a definite timeline. A beginning and an end.

As she sat in the rocking chair nursing her daughter, the familiarity of the routine brought some peace to her heart. Dylan wasn't hers. She'd known that at fifteen and she knew it now. Her only mistake had been thinking sex with him would end the wondering and the wanting.

Well, now she knew. Sex with Dylan was deserving of

all the superlatives she could summon. But she wouldn't embarrass him by letting him think she was expecting more. Neither more intimacy nor more attention. She was living in his house because of a fluke. It would be wrong to put him in an awkward position by burdening him with her feelings.

When Cora was finished, Mia dressed her in a teal-and-yellow sundress. Mia's stomach was growling so loudly she knew it was impractical to put off breakfast any longer. As she suspected, when she and Cora entered the kitchen, there was no sign of Dylan. Only Gertie…frying bacon.

The older woman turned and smiled. "There you two are. I had a feeling someone kept you up during the night, Mia."

Mia felt her cheeks redden and hoped the housekeeper didn't notice. "Yes, as usual. I came in here for a glass of milk, but thankfully Cora finally settled down and slept until morning."

Without asking, Gertie waved Mia to a seat and put a bowl of fresh strawberries and blueberries in front of her. "I've got some cinnamon muffins coming out of the oven in about a minute. Eat up."

"Did Dylan have an early appointment?"

"Not to my knowledge. He left about thirty minutes ago to head down to the Silver Dollar. Why? Did you need to speak to him?"

"I did have a few questions about the books. But it can wait."

Mia had barely finished her meal when the landline phone rang. Gertie answered it and then held out the cordless receiver to Mia. "It's for you. Ms. Kavanagh."

Gertie swooped in and scooped Cora from Mia's lap. Mia answered reluctantly. "Hello?"

"Good morning, Mia. This is Maeve. Zoe and I have put our heads together, and we would like for you and Dylan to come to dinner tonight up at the lodge. Zoe wants to cook for us. We have several portable cribs here for the hotel guests. We can set one up in Zoe and Liam's bedroom, so you can put Cora to sleep and not have to rush off."

"But, Ms. Kavanagh, I have no idea if Dylan is available."

"Call me Maeve. Please. I've already talked to him this morning. He said it was up to you."

Mia was stuck. Social convention dictated that she accept the invitation, but she could think of nothing more awkward than sitting across the dinner table from the mother of the man with whom she'd been naked the night before. Since she didn't have a valid reason to decline, however, she was forced to agree. "Well, yes, then. That would be lovely. And thank you for making arrangements for Cora. Since I'm nursing, I don't want to be away from her for too long."

"I understand completely. We'll look forward to seeing the three of you around six-thirty. Oh, and Mia?"

"Yes?"

"Would it be a problem to dress for dinner? Zoe has worked hard on this meal, and I thought it would be fun to celebrate."

"Not a problem at all. See you soon."

Mia hung up the phone wondering ruefully when she had become such a good liar. Dress for dinner? Good grief. She had brought all of her clothes with her to Silver Glen except for winter things that were in storage, but she had no idea if she could find anything suitable, since most of the cartons were still out in the garage.

When she asked Gertie to help with the baby so Mia could rummage in her boxes, Gertie offered a solution. "After the baby's next feeding, why don't you put her down for a nap and let me keep an eye on her? You could go into town and visit that cute little shop called Silver Linings.

They have beautiful things for women your age. I'm sure you can find what you want."

"I hate to take up your time, Gertie."

The woman, still holding Cora, waved a hand dismissively. "If I have to choose between babysitting or doing the laundry, it's no competition. Go. Have a few hours to yourself. All new moms need that. I swear I'll take good care of her."

"I know you will."

Mia's other problem wasn't so easily solved. It seemed self-indulgent in the extreme to buy a new dress for herself when her finances were so tight. On the other hand, wearing the appropriate feminine armor for the night to come would go a long way toward helping her face Dylan.

She needed something that would make it clear, without words, that she knew the score and was confident in her own skin. A sexy frock that would knock his socks off and at the same time convince him she had no designs on his bachelorhood.

By the time Cora fell asleep right after lunch, Mia was itching to get out of the house. She hadn't realized how much she had been *chained* to Cora's side until she had the opportunity to be out and about without a diaper bag or a stroller. Not that she was unhappy with her new role. She loved being Cora's mom. Every minute of it.

Still, the prospect of stealing away for a couple of carefree hours held definite appeal.

Gertie's directions were spot on. Silver Linings had not been around when Mia was a girl. The trendy shop occupied the ground floor of a historic building adjacent to the bank. When Mia parked and got out to glance in the storefront windows, a little flutter of excitement skittered down her spine. There, on a mannequin, was the exact dress she'd imagined.

Nursing moms were often limited in their choice of

clothing due to necessity, but this dress opened down the front. Without wasting further time, she went inside to try it on.

The salesclerk was a young woman several years younger than Mia. "I'm Dottie. May I help you find something?" she asked politely. Her nose was pierced and she had a tattoo down her left forearm. In high school, this was the sort of person who'd looked down at Mia and made fun of her. But Mia was an adult now and no longer cowed by the idea of someone judging her. It had been a long road, but she was happy with who she was.

"The red dress in the window? May I try it on? I became a mom not that long ago, and my wardrobe is in need of help." Fortunately, the store had her size. Otherwise she would have had to swallow her disappointment and choose something else. Though she took three additional dresses into the changing room, she had her heart set on the sexy one from the window display.

Stripping down to her bra and panties, she stepped into the sleeveless, cocktail-length dress. It was not at all conventional. The fabric was a heavy watered silk. The design featured a nipped-in waist and a skirt that flared slightly in a bell shape. The back was scooped out, but the front dipped into a low V topped with a single pea-size clear crystal that served as the zipper pull.

Even before she zipped up the dress, Mia knew her bra would have to go. Unfastening the undergarment and dropping it onto a stool, she stared at her bare breasts in the mirror, reminded of the hungry way Dylan had gazed at her. And then touched her....

Her nipples ached as they furled tightly. She would have liked to blame the telling response on the air-conditioning, but the small space was actually quite warm.

As Mia struggled to close the bodice, the saleslady

spoke from just outside the door. "How are you doing in there?"

Mia grimaced at her reflection. "This is the same size I always wear, but…"

The clerk's voice was sympathetic. "Don't worry if you still have a few pounds of baby weight to lose. It will come off in no time. Do you need me to bring you another size?"

"It's not that. Look at me." She opened the door. "Tell me what you think."

The young woman's eyes widened and she grinned. "Ah. Now I get it. You've got nursing boobs. I say enjoy them while they last. Same thing happened to me when my son was born. My husband loved it."

Mia's cheeks warmed. The woman in the mirror had Mia's face and hair, but beyond that she seemed like a stranger. The bombshell image made her uncomfortable. She'd spent most of her life trying to blend into the woodwork. This dress made a statement, even more so because of her breasts. "You don't think there's too much…"

"Cleavage?"

"Yes."

"Not at all. You're probably not used to showing off your body. I see it all the time. Just because you've got a kid doesn't mean you have to wear a shroud. You've got a kickin' figure. And if I'm not mistaken, you're hoping to catch someone's eye with this—right?"

"It's a small dinner party."

"You didn't answer my question. Which is as good as a yes. Buy the dress. You know you want to." She glanced at the three hanging on a hook at Mia's shoulder. Turning up her nose, she shook her head. "Those other ones are fine if you're presenting an award to the parent-teacher association or visiting your grandma's church. But if you want to say, 'I'm available,' then the red is your best bet."

Mia swallowed her misgivings. "I'll take it."

Three hours later she had a mild panic attack. If it had been feasible, she would have ripped open every one of her moving boxes until she found a nice, safe, boring outfit to wear tonight. But it was about a thousand degrees out in the hot, muggy garage, and besides, Dylan was going to be ready to leave in less than half an hour.

She still hadn't seen or heard from him today. Not so much as a peep, other than a terse text indicating their time of departure. Clearly, he had chatted with his mother and knew the plan.

Once more, Mia looked in the ornate, full-length mirror. Her strappy black sandals were not new, but they were comfy and flattering. She had left her hair loose and wavy on her shoulders. For once, the style was cooperating, though all bets were off when she had to step outside into the heat and humidity.

But between her head and her toes, there was a revolution going on. Somehow, the new dress looked even more outrageous than it had in the store dressing room. The fit was perfect at the waist. The hemline was elegant, flattering her legs. But the top? Holy cow. She looked like a Victoria's Secret model. Breasts that had never been more than a B cup now thrust up and out in all their rounded glory.

How had she not noticed before? On maternity leave, her clothing of choice had been T-shirts, nursing bras and sweatpants. Her biggest goal during the first six weeks had been not to burst into tears more than once a day. With her hormones all over the map, she had felt frumpy, overwhelmed and inexperienced.

Noticing that her breasts had morphed from barely there to bountiful hadn't been on her radar.

Tucking her hair behind her ear, she made one last pirouette and put a hand to her fluttery stomach. For better or for worse, it was showtime.

Eleven

Dylan ran a finger inside his collar, trying to loosen his tie without removing it and starting all over again. What had his mother and Zoe been thinking? He hated wearing a tux. The more formal dress reminded him that he was a Kavanagh and thus on display to the community all the time. Dylan didn't want to be *anyone's* role model.

He much preferred the comfort of his jeans and cowboy boots. In his role at the Silver Dollar, he could pretend he was like all the rest of the working stiffs. But tonight, dressed in an expensive European-made jacket and trousers that he wore as seldom as possible, he felt as if he were playing a part. Liam wore dress clothes effortlessly. In fact, Dylan sometimes wondered if his older brother had his boxers starched and pressed.

It was no picnic following along in school behind the sibling who excelled at everything. Liam's academic awards and accolades had taken over his bedroom bookshelves by the time he was sixteen, along with an equal number of sporting trophies.

Dylan had his own ribbons and medals and letterman jackets, but he would have traded it all for just one visible, pen-on-paper acknowledgement that he had a decent brain.

Shaking off the stupid childhood trauma of never measuring up, he pulled the car around front, turned on the AC and moved Cora's infant seat from Mia's vehicle to his. Since they were both going to be dressed to the nines, he wanted to pamper his date in something other than his utilitarian, though expensive, pickup truck. The late model Mercedes had been a gift from his mother, a reminder that he was one of the family no matter how hard he tried to pretend otherwise.

The Kavanagh wealth made him uncomfortable. Especially since he was the only one in the family with no discernible talent or passion. He didn't *excel* at anything.

As he walked back through the front door into the house, he stopped dead in his tracks. Mia had just stepped into the living room. When she saw him, she halted as well. "Hello, Dylan." Her voice was polite…cool…no inflection at all.

Despite her somewhat chilly greeting, his temperature shot through the roof and his mouth dried like a snowflake in Death Valley. The woman standing in front of him was no longer merely an attractive female with whom he'd had sex. She was a goddess…or an angel. He couldn't decide which. Dark, shiny hair tumbled artfully onto white shoulders. Deft, completely natural-looking makeup accentuated her eyes, making them bittersweet chocolate instead of the lighter, milkier variety.

Dangling earrings fabricated of some clear, faceted material caught the light, drawing attention to her swanlike neck. Her lips were red. Sin-red. A shade to match her dress and make a man shudder with desire.

But it was the single glittery bead at the top of her bodice that caught his attention. The small piece of glass was attached to a zipper that ran the entire length of the dress. All a man would have to do is tug gently, but inexorably, and in seconds the woman would be naked.

He cleared his throat. "You look very nice."

A small frown creased the space between her eyebrows. "So do you."

Gertie, toting the baby on her hip, came in from the kitchen at that moment, rescuing Dylan and Mia from their awkward conversation. She whistled. "Lord, have mercy. You two clean up real nice. See, Cora. Look how pretty your mama is. And my boy, Dylan. Why, if I was forty years younger, I'd take a run at him myself."

Dylan kissed Gertie's cheek and the top of Cora's head. "You're good for my ego, but don't go overboard. You know you'll always be my favorite." He took the baby, who immediately tried to grab for his bow tie. "You ready, Mia?"

She nodded. "Yes."

Her stilted response pretty much set the tone for their drive up the mountain. The Silver Beeches Lodge, constructed after the Second World War, was an elegant and outrageously expensive hotel that catered to high-end clients who demanded privacy and discretion. From the silver screen to politics, the majority of guests had money and wielded power.

As they drove up onto a sweeping flagstone apron, Dylan shot a sideways glance at his passenger. She sat primly, knees pressed together, hands clasped on the small black clutch purse in her lap. Cora had babbled happily during the short trip, diverted by the sights and sounds outside the car.

As the valet approached, Dylan drummed his fingers on the steering wheel. "Shouldn't we get our stories straight?" he asked.

For the first time, Mia looked straight at him, her gaze stormy. "I don't think we have a story. So no problem."

"You're mad because I wasn't there when you woke up." He still felt bad about that. But he'd had to get out of the house, had needed physical distance to clear his head and analyze what had happened to him when he made love to Mia. If he'd had his way, he would have avoided her even

longer, but tonight's dinner was in the nature of a command performance.

Mia's eyes narrowed. "I'm not mad. Not at all. Sleep is
far sweeter than anything else I could be doing these days."

Wow. Direct hit. She'd just relegated mind-blowing sex
to a spot somewhere below snoozing. Fair enough. If that's
how she wanted to play it… Opening his car door with
a jerk that nearly twisted it off the hinges, he went to the
back and talked to Cora while he released her from her
seat. The baby's smile took the sharp edges off his anger.

In his peripheral vision, he saw Mia get out of the car
and smooth her skirt. Five men stood on the steps of the
hotel, some guests, some employees. Five sets of eyes
locked on Mia and stared. He couldn't blame them. She
radiated sexuality. Her lush breasts were evidence of the
elemental, primitive truth that mankind needed a fertile
woman for the continuation of the species.

Except for the occasional moment of temptation, Dylan
had little interest in fathering children. But Neanderthal or
not, he understood the urge to mate. Only in his case, the
urge was surprisingly more than physical. He was proud
of Mia, not for her breasts or her killer legs, but for her
incredible brain that had so much to offer society. And for
other equally important things like her care with Cora, and
her gentle acceptance of a high-school boy who had done
his best to alienate her.

Even if she *was* pissed at him, he was glad they were
friends. Although after last night, the *friend* word could be
called into question. She certainly deserved to be angry.
Walking out on her after sex had been unconscionable,
despite the fact he *had* needed to retreat and figure out
what was going on inside his head.

In spite of all his reservations, he liked the family tableau they made. Mia insisted on taking the baby as they
ascended the shallow steps. "I'll carry her."

He surrendered without protest, guessing that the baby acted as a sort of shield. It had to be intimidating for Mia to walk into the Silver Beeches knowing that she was going to be sharing dinner with Maeve Kavanagh. His mother came by her reputation honestly. She was kind and fair, but he'd seen big strong men quake in their boots when she was displeased about something.

"Liam and Zoe have an apartment on the top floor," he said. The elevator ride was silent, save for Cora's little baby sounds. She enjoyed playing with her reflection in the mirror. Fortunately, she was too young to comprehend that the adults momentarily caged in the small space were not speaking. Or to notice that their body language was hostile.

When they exited the elevator, Dylan took Mia's elbow and steered her to the right. Liam answered the doorbell on the first ring. The eldest Kavanagh son greeted them warmly. "Zoe's been on pins and needles. It's about time you got here."

Dylan curled an arm around Mia's waist, surprising her. "This is Mia. Mia, Liam."

Liam shook Mia's hand, but his attention was on Cora. "May I?" he asked. At Mia's bemused nod, he reached for the baby and called out over his shoulder. "Zoe. Come see what I found, my love."

Zoe Kavanagh was bright and beautiful and artlessly charming. The gold lace camisole and flirty skirt she wore along with gold, high-heeled pumps suited her airy personality. Even without the bright clothing, she would have lit up the room. Mia envied her easy social skills. The slender blonde rarely sat still, scooting back and forth from the kitchen to grab something or the other. "It's almost ready," she said.

Liam's smile as he watched his wife was telling. He

was deeply in love and not afraid to show it. "My Zoe insists on cooking for me even though we have a five-star chef presiding over the restaurant downstairs. But I have to admit she's a natural. I'm sure I've gained five pounds or more since we got married."

Given that Liam was as lean and toned and muscular as his brother, Mia wondered if he were joking. She had refused a glass of wine and was sipping tonic water when the door of the apartment burst open after a brief knock and Maeve Kavanagh sailed into the room followed by a handsome man who bore a striking resemblance to the two male Kavanaghs already present.

"Look who I brought with me," Maeve beamed. "I convinced Aidan to fly down for the evening." Maeve's plum Jackie-O sheath was accessorized with a matching short-sleeved jacket.

After a flurry of introductions all around, and lots of hugging, Mia found herself shaking hands with Aidan, who was as tall as his brothers, but even more suave and polished than Liam. "I feel like I'm intruding," she said, shooting a sharp, disapproving glance at Dylan.

Aidan kissed the back of her hand with a gesture that seemed completely natural. "Not at all. I'm the party crasher. I live in New York, but you'll find me here in Silver Glen frequently. Despite being a city dweller now, I can't resist the lure of home. I was hoping the whole gang would show up here tonight."

Zoe wrinkled her nose. "Conor, Patrick, Gavin and James all *claimed* to be otherwise occupied."

Liam put an arm around his wife's waist. "It's hard to corral everyone on short notice. But we'll try again soon."

Maeve threw up her hands and made a beeline for Mia. "There's that precious baby."

Dylan and Liam snickered. "You know that's the only reason she came," Dylan said in a stage whisper.

As Maeve took Cora from Mia's arms, Zoe paused long enough to put her hands on her hips and pout. "Hey, I think I've been insulted."

Liam gave his wife a long, enthusiastic kiss that soothed her ruffled feathers. When they came up for air, his throat was flushed and his eyes glittered. "I'm sure she'll be just as excited, my love, when and if you give her a grand-child."

Mia was the only one standing close enough to hear his muttered comment. And she was sure it wasn't for pub-lic consumption. Zoe's cheeks turned a delightful shade of pink and her smile softened before she escaped to the kitchen.

Amidst conversation and laughter, the finishing touches were added to the table. Mia helped, since her child had been kidnapped by the force of Maeve's personality and seemed quite happy. Just before they sat down, a second knock sounded at the door.

"I'll get it," Maeve said, the baby comfortably settled on her hip. "I asked one of our summer employees to come up and entertain Cora in Liam and Zoe's den. Paula is a senior at the University of North Carolina, majoring in child development. I hope you don't mind, Mia."

What could she say? "Of course not. It will be nice to enjoy an uninterrupted meal." Honestly, she was being spoiled. After all the help from Gertie and Dylan's family, it might be a challenge to manage on her own.

Dylan came close enough to whisper in her ear. "I'll apologize in advance for anything my mother says or does to upset you."

Mia shook her head briefly. "It's fine." She was still try-ing to get accustomed to Dylan's magnificence in formal attire. The snowy white shirt brought out his tan, and the traditional black tux fit his body as if it had been made for him. It probably had.

She liked the casual Dylan very much. But this sophisticated Dylan made her shiver.

As the adults seated themselves at the table, Zoe brought out the last dish and joined them. "We won't stand on ceremony," she said. "Pass the food and help yourself."

Amidst the clatter of silverware and china and crystal, Mia absorbed the atmosphere and studied the Kavanagh family. Zoe seemed a natural part of the bunch, even though she and Liam hadn't been married all that long. She laughed and shared anecdotes and teased her husband. Liam and Dylan and Aidan bickered amiably, as siblings did, covering every subject from sports to movies to politics. Maeve had strong opinions and wasn't afraid to express them.

Only Mia was silent. She wasn't *afraid* to speak. But the conversational dynamic was such that she found it difficult to get a word in edgewise. During a momentary lull in the rapid-fire back-and-forth chatter, Maeve launched her first volley, taking Mia completely off guard.

The older woman took a sip of wine, set down her glass and pinned Mia with a deceptively gentle stare. "So tell me, Mia," she said. "Is the baby's father in the picture?"

Mia choked on a piece of walnut in her salad and Dylan had to pat her on the back. Hard.

He glared at his mother. "I thought you were the woman who hated gossip."

Maeve didn't look the least bit repentant. "I do. Which is why I'm going directly to the source. But Mia can tell me to mind my own business if she wants to." She smiled at Mia. "You can, my dear, honestly."

Mia felt her face and neck turning red as the eyes of her dinner companions fixed on her with varying degrees of sympathy. "It's no secret," she said. "I was ready to have a baby, and since there was no man in my life, I chose to use a sperm donor."

Silence fell.

"I see." Maeve's perplexed expression held a hint of disapproval.

Mia was used to that by now. If she had decided as a single person to adopt an infant, no one would have batted an eye, but somehow, the path she had chosen was far less acceptable. Perhaps it was the clinical nature of the process. Or the lack of loving conception.

Zoe broke the uncomfortable impasse. "So, Mia. How did you and Dylan meet?"

Again, Mia was taken aback. She had assumed someone would have filled Zoe in before Mia and Dylan arrived, but maybe this was supposed to be a secret. Liam had been away at college when Dylan was a senior, so he and Mia had never met. But surely the family had realized Dylan was getting tutoring help. Aidan had been a sophomore or junior at the time.

Mia opened her mouth to speak, but before she could explain, Maeve rushed into the breach, addressing her daughter-in-law. "Dylan and Mia knew each other back in high school. They reconnected recently."

Zoe nodded, satisfied with that explanation. "And what do you do for a living, Mia?" she asked.

"I'm a medical researcher. But the funding for my lab and my program was cut off recently. I came back to Silver Glen for a visit and ran into Dylan at the Silver Dollar."

Dylan picked up the tale. "My bookkeeper quit, so Mia is helping me out temporarily since she's between jobs."

Zoe's eyebrows went up. "You must be very smart," she said, studying Mia's face as if she could see IQ points written there.

"Off-the-charts smart," Dylan said, his smile rueful. "I'm lucky she was available to help me out."

Mia was desperate to change the subject. As Zoe stood and began to clear the dessert plates, Mia leaped to her feet as well. "Let me help," she said. "Please. The dinner was amazing."

In the kitchen Zoe began rinsing china. "Liam tells me to let the housekeeper take care of this in the morning, but I can't stand a messy kitchen." She handed Mia a plate to put in the dishwasher. "What about you? Do you like to cook?"

"I don't really have much opportunity. I worked all the time before Cora was born, and now I'm still learning how to care for an infant. There don't seem to be enough hours in the day."

Zoe nodded, her expression thoughtful. "The Kavanaghs can be a bit overwhelming, especially when the whole clan gets together. You and I should stick together."

"I think you have the wrong idea. I work for Dylan."

"Maeve told me you're living with him."

"Only because the building burned. I was supposed to be staying in the apartment upstairs above the Silver Dollar."

Zoe rolled her eyes. "Men don't take women into their homes without some kind of ulterior motive."

He feels like he owes me something for the past.

But Mia couldn't say that. Not when Dylan's brother and sister-in-law apparently did not know how severely Dylan had struggled in high school. "Dylan is a kind man. He told me that rental property is hard to find in Silver Glen. If it had been just me, I'm sure he would have let me fend for myself. But he has a soft spot for Cora. That's probably why he suggested that she and I move in."

Zoe dried her hands on a towel and turned on the dishwasher. "Is the baby his?"

Because the other woman's back was turned, Mia couldn't see her face. "No. Of course not."

Mia's hostess faced her with a look in her eyes that told Mia she was not easily duped. "You might have concocted that story to give yourself time to figure out what to do. Not that I would blame you. The Kavanaghs would go nuts if they thought Cora was the first of the next generation. I should know. The hints have been flying thick and fast for me to get pregnant."

"Well, she's not," Mia said, the words flat. "Maybe I was naive to do what I did, but I adore Cora and I wouldn't change a thing. I know the father was healthy and normal in every way. That's enough for me."

"I didn't mean to make you angry." Zoe's big blue eyes shimmered with emotion.

Mia swallowed her pique. "I'm not angry. More defensive, I guess. I never expected people to react so strongly, my parents included."

"Do they live close by?"

"No. They're in Florida. My mom came up for the first ten days to help. She loves the baby, of course, but I could tell from the first moment I told them I was pregnant that they thought I needed a flesh-and-blood man and not an anonymous donor."

"Dylan's a man." Zoe's sly smile was not at all hard to decipher.

"Dylan and I are *not* an item."

"I watched the way he watches you. He's possessive. Though I suppose he might not even realize he feels that way. Men can be clueless about these things."

"You're way off base, Zoe. His broken engagement burned him. He's not interested in marriage or fatherhood or any commitment at all, for that matter. If you're planning on matchmaking, you should know that he and I are not a couple. Period."

Twelve

He and I are not a couple. Period.

Dylan winced, pausing just outside the kitchen door. He'd caught only the tail end of Mia's statement, but it was enough to understand the gist of her conversation with Zoe. Apparently, Dylan's sister-in-law had been understandably curious about Mia's relationship with Dylan, and Mia had set her straight.

Dylan should be elated that Mia knew the score. No need for an embarrassing face-to-face where he had to explain that he had no plans to settle down, much less with a ready-made family.

In that case, why did he feel like he'd been punched in the stomach? Striding into the kitchen, he faced the two women whose faces held identical guilty looks. "Paula says Cora is getting fussy. They're waiting for you in Zoe and Liam's bedroom. Isn't it time to feed her and put her down?" He addressed his comments to Mia impassively.

Mia, clad in the ruby dress that made her look more like a Russian princess than a new mom, glanced at the clock on the wall. "Oh, gosh, yes. Zoe and I were having so much fun getting to know each other I lost track of time."

"I'll bet you were." He wanted Mia to squirm a little, wondering whether or not he had heard what she said.

Zoe piped up, her expression beseeching. "Would you

like me to sit with you while you feed her? I assume you're nursing?"

Dylan kissed his sister-in-law's cheek. It wasn't her fault that things were weird. "I'll sit with her, Zoe. But thanks for offering. Go snuggle up with your husband on the sofa. He's looking neglected."

They exited the kitchen as a trio. Zoe headed for the living room, and Dylan and Mia searched out the master suite. As promised, the crib was set up and ready. Two comfy armchairs by the window, each with matching ottomans, offered an ideal spot for Zoe to feed Cora.

The young college student handed Cora over with a smile. "Your baby is adorable, and so even-tempered. Thank you for giving me the opportunity to play with her. The diaper bag is there on the bed. If you need babysitting help any other time this summer, please feel free to call me. Mrs. Kavanagh has my contact info."

Mia smiled. "Thank you, Paula. I'll keep that in mind."

When the door closed, Dylan rummaged in Cora's tote for pajamas, diapers, wipes and a changing pad to protect the bedspread. "There you go," he said, determined not to give Mia a chance to kick him out. "All set."

Mia clutched the baby. "Why are you in here? This is pretty much a solo operation."

He shrugged. "Give me the kid. Go sit in the chair and I'll bring her to you." It was a matter of minutes to change the diaper and tuck Cora into soft pajamas that snapped up the front. In his peripheral vision, he was aware that Mia had cooperated with his instructions. He was under no illusions. If she told him to leave, he would have to obey her wishes. But he was counting on the fact that she would let him stay.

When he turned and walked toward the window and the woman who stared at him with big, dark eyes, he felt something shift inside him. The setting lent a certain note of intimacy, but it was more than that.

Mia took Cora from him, her gaze unreadable. "Will you turn your back, please?"

He crouched beside her. "I'd rather not. I've seen all there is of you to see, Mia. Remember? Last night?" Slowly, giving her time to protest, he caught the crystal at the center of her bodice and began to pull.

She slapped at his hand, her cheeks hot with what appeared to be mortification. "Don't be ridiculous, Dylan. There's nothing remotely sexy about what I'm getting ready to do."

Surprisingly, a lump in his throat made it hard to speak. "That's where you're wrong." Locking her gaze with his, never looking down, he opened the zipper, hearing the soft rasp as the sides of the dress parted. In Mia's eyes he saw confusion and vulnerability and something else. Desire.

The desire was a welcome sight, because he had been wondering if it was wrong to be turned on by the prospect of Mia offering her breast to a hungry child. At last, the zipper reached the end of its track. Unable to resist any longer, he stared at the bountiful sight that was Mia's bosom. A single drop of pale milk clung to one nipple. He caught it on his finger and tasted it. "Lucky baby," he said. The words were hoarse.

Mia's lower lip trembled. What was she thinking as she stared at him so intently? As he watched, she tucked the infant in her arm and let Cora nuzzle until she found her goal and latched on. As the child sucked at her mother's breast, Dylan felt an answering pull in his groin. He shifted the second chair closer and sat down, wrapped in some mystical moment that shut out the world and enclosed Mia, Cora and him in perfect intimacy.

Mia kept her eyes downcast, her free hand coming up now and again to stroke Cora's small, perfect head. When it was time, she switched the baby to the opposite breast. Without asking, Dylan reached in his back pocket and extracted a handkerchief. Leaning forward, he carefully dried Mia's skin where the baby had eaten so enthusiastically.

He didn't linger, nor did he do anything else that might be construed as sexual. The quiet tableau was almost sacred to him. This ancient, elemental, perfectly *right* moment where life, *literally* life, was offered to the helpless in an act of love.

When Cora's long eyelashes settled on rounded cheeks, Mia pulled her away from the breast and handed her to Dylan. "Hold her please."

As he watched in silence, Mia removed the last of the sticky milk and refastened her gown. When she was fully clothed once more, she held out her arms. "I'll put her in the bed."

"Let me." He deposited Cora in the crib, smiling when she never even moved. Poor babe was tired out from an evening of fun and attention. He turned to face Mia. "Thank you."

She was still seated, her fingers moving restlessly on the arms of the chair. "For what?"

"For letting me be here. For sharing Cora. For trusting me." He pulled her to her feet. "I'm sorry I didn't stay last night."

Mia had kicked off her shoes before she fed the baby, and now, standing in front of him, she seemed fragile and helpless. Even though Dylan liked the role of protector, he knew Mia didn't need him. Not really. She was strong and smart and well able to care for herself and her offspring.

She pulled away from his grasp, her expression guarded. "Why didn't you stay?"

"Lots of reasons." *I was getting in too deep. You'll be*

gone soon. "I knew you needed your rest to take care of Cora."

"A weak excuse at best. I'd have thought a man with your experience would have come up with a better line than that."

Ouch. Not helpless at all. "It's the truth."

She crossed her arms, perhaps unaware that the action threatened to topple her breasts from their crimson cage. "Let's get something straight, Dylan. I appreciate your helping me out in a bad situation. But I'm not going to get any crazy ideas. You've told me I don't belong in Silver Glen, and you're right. I'm not stupid enough to think that you and I are in some kind of relationship. So relax."

"Impossible," he muttered. "When I'm in the same room with you, relaxing is the last thing on my mind." He toyed with the seemingly innocuous crystal zipper pull. There was something intrinsically sexual about the damn thing. Gently, he lowered it two inches. Mia's sharply indrawn breath told him volumes. The curves of her pale breasts beckoned a man to touch, to worship.

When she didn't protest, he tugged again, this time uncovering her to the navel. "Lord, Mia," he said as his hand trembled. "You have the most incredible body. I can't stop thinking about last night."

Her head dropped backward. Her eyes closed as he traced the faint, silvery lines that marked places where her body had readied itself to give life. Slowly, he pushed the dress down her arms until it hung from her hips. Now she was naked from the waist up, a lush, erotic invitation. He gathered her close and held her, stroking her bare back.

They were standing in his brother's bedroom. Behind them a baby lay sleeping. Close by, a dinner party awaited their return. He shook with the urge to lift her against the wall and fill her. His erection was full and ready. Desire was a writhing, clawing beast inside him. He could lock the door. Pretend that Mia was still nursing Cora.

It was a measure of his desperation that he seriously considered it.

Instead, he released her and did the only thing left to him. Fisting one hand in her hair at the back of her head and using the other to tip up her chin, he kissed her roughly, forcefully. "Tonight, Mia. I want you again. And this time I won't leave." He wouldn't be able to, not again. He didn't have the will to walk away from something so perfect, even if the outcome would never fall in his favor.

Her arms twined around his neck. "Yes." The single word was a barely audible whisper.

He knew on some hazy, faraway level that they were crushing her dress. Imagining what she would look like if he helped her step out of it only made the ache in his gut worse.

Her lips were soft beneath his, unbearably sweet. For a split second he flashed back to that stolen kiss in high school, the one that had confused him and made him ashamed. Even then, there had been something about Mia that drew him. Some essential goodness that he sensed he lacked. As a seventeen-year-old, he'd known it, and he knew it now.

He didn't deserve a woman like this. He was selfish and focused on the here and now. Mia had a child to consider. She contributed to the greater good with her work. Frivolity wasn't in her repertoire. But perhaps in the short time she was with him he could teach her the benefits of being naughty once in a while.

When her small hands tugged at his shirttails and slipped beneath to settle on the bare skin at his waist, he flinched. He'd kept a tight rein on his libido this far, but feeling her fingers on him made his vision go fuzzy. "We have to stop," he said gruffly, cursing the situation and the lousy timing that ensured, at a minimum, a miserable hour ahead.

Mia moved her hands, now pushing against his chest. When she was free, she tugged at her dress, pink-cheeked.

At that very moment, a quiet knock sounded at the door and Liam's voice came softly. "Dessert and coffee on the table. You guys ready?"

Dylan brushed the hair from Mia's flushed cheeks. "On our way," he said. Carefully, he raised the zipper of her dress all the way to the top and smoothed her skirt with two hands. "You okay?" he asked, gazing at her intently. He couldn't read the secrets hidden in her eyes.

She nodded. "Let's go. They're waiting."

He allowed her to pass him, but at the last moment snagged her wrist and reeled her in for one last quick kiss. Thank God she was wearing smudge-proof lipstick. "I'm glad you came back to Silver Glen," he said, resting his forehead against hers.

"Me, too." She touched his cheek with a fleeting caress that made him shiver. "Me, too."

Mia had never been in such a situation. Dylan ushered her to the dining room, his hand at the small of her back. She felt exposed and embarrassed, but at the heart of it, disappointed that she and Dylan were not alone.

Zoe had made an angel food cake from scratch and topped it with a fresh strawberry compote. "Is Cora asleep?" she asked.

The question was innocent, but Mia blushed anyway, as if the three adults at the table knew exactly what she and Dylan had been up to. "She went down without a peep," Mia said, sitting down as Dylan took the chair to her right. "*Getting* her to sleep is never a problem. It's the two a.m. playtime that's killing me."

Maeve sat at the head of the table, Aidan at the foot.

The two couples occupied either side. Mia liked Maeve, though the woman's personality was one part steamroller and one part matriarch.

The older woman waved a hand. "Hang in there, my dear. I went through that with at least three of my boys. It will pass. In my experience, parenthood is an endurance test, a marathon where the stubborn win out in the end."

Mia laughed. "I hope you're right. But at this point, my chances of *winning* are no more than fifty-fifty at best."

Dylan interrupted. "Don't let Mia fool you. She's doing a wonderful job as a mother." He poured himself a cup of black coffee from a fancy silver pot. "Cora clearly is thriving."

Maeve focused her gaze on Mia. "So what will you do with Cora when you get a new job?"

There was no mistaking the note of disapproval. Mia felt her defenses go up, but tried to answer calmly. "I'll find a reputable day care, of course. There are quite a few good ones in the Raleigh/Durham area."

"Have you considered taking a leave? I know how hard it is to deal with an infant and be productive during the day."

It was Zoe's turn to jump into the conversation. Apparently she wasn't scared of her mother-in-law. "That's not always feasible, Maeve. Most women have to work outside the home. Particularly single moms. Not everyone has a fortune like the Kavanaghs. And besides, from what Liam has told me, Mia's work has far-reaching applications."

Mia gave Zoe a grateful smile. "I hope to find a balance that works for Cora and me. As much as I love my baby, my career is also important. I find it challenging and fulfilling. Ultimately, I think Cora will benefit from having a mother who uses her abilities and contributes to society. But I know that life is never perfect."

She saw the three brothers glance at each other. The

Kavanaghs had certainly known their share of heartache over the years. Losing a parent was never easy, and Reggie Kavanagh's body had never been recovered. Maeve had stepped into the breach, giving her boys all the love and support they needed to become successful adults. Perhaps she thought Mia was selfish to get pregnant as a single woman, because Maeve knew exactly how difficult it had been to be both mother *and* father. Mia wondered how the other brothers had fared in the absence of a male parent.

Dylan put an end to the awkward conversation. "I think Mia and I will call it a night. Zoe, the meal was fantastic. Feel free to try your culinary skills on me anytime."

Liam gave him a mock glare. "Quit flirting with my wife."

Dylan raised an innocent eyebrow. "Who, me?" As the group stood, he kissed Zoe on the cheek. "My brother is a Neanderthal. It's perfectly acceptable for men and women to be friends."

Zoe pinched his cheek. "You are such a rascal. Behave yourself and take Mia and little Cora home. I promise to feed you another day."

When Mia excused herself to put the baby in the infant carrier, she could hear the five Kavanaghs talking animatedly. Clearly they enjoyed spending time together. It made her realize that she wanted more children, at least one more. Cora would need a sibling, someone to have her back when life was hard. But in some corner of her heart, Mia knew that Cora needed a daddy as well. In all the struggle of trying to get pregnant, it had honestly not seemed like that big a deal.

Now, however, the truth stared her in the face. Seeing Dylan with Cora was an inescapable revelation. As she grew, Cora would want a father. And at some point, she would ask questions.

On a more practical note, having so much help with

Cora in recent days showed Mia that she was missing out
on many things by trying to do it all herself. For a woman
who was supposedly a genius, she had been woefully un-
prepared for the consequences of her actions.

As she gathered up her purse and the baby's accou-
trements, Dylan came to help her carry Cora. They said
their goodbyes and finally escaped into the hallway. Mia
wondered if Maeve and Aidan were lingering with Liam
and Zoe to discuss what was going on in Dylan's life and
whether or not Mia was taking advantage of him.

In the elevator, Dylan was suspiciously quiet. Cora had
stayed asleep through all the noisy goodbyes. Mia stared
down at her skirt, trying not to remember how the fabric
had pooled around her hips when Dylan half undressed
her. She couldn't figure him out. At times he seemed intent on seducing her into his bed, and at others he kept his
distance…almost as if Mia was a threat to him.

She wanted to talk to him during the ride home, but
maybe there was nothing to say. He was a Kavanagh and
she was a new mom with a baby and no real job at the moment. They had a tenuous connection at best, even though
they had added a sexual component to their relationship.

Men liked sex. Men, as a rule, took sex when it was
offered. What they did not do was give up their bachelor
status without a fight.

Fortunately for Dylan, Mia had no intention of fighting. If she ever did get married, she wanted a man who
wanted her. Completely. Brains and all. Dylan still wasn't
comfortable with Mia knowing about his past struggles.
If Mia's hunch was correct, no one in his family knew
except for Maeve.

She wanted to whack him over the head and get him
to admit that he was a smart man in all the ways that
counted. But she had a feeling he wouldn't listen. Dylan
was stubborn.

Her brain ran in circles searching for solutions. She couldn't turn her back on a lifetime of study and work that was significant and valuable. That would be selfish and irresponsible. But every day the prospect of staying in Silver Glen with Dylan held more and more allure.

As they neared the turn to his property, she took a deep breath, mentally gearing up for the evening ahead. In Liam and Zoe's bedroom, she and Dylan had seemed in perfect accord. But what would happen now?

Gertie had left lights on to welcome them home. For Mia, the sight of Dylan's beautiful house elicited much more than gratitude for the roof over her head. She loved the way he had made his place seem like part of the countryside. Privacy and seclusion created peace and a feeling of home in the deepest sense of the word.

For one fleeting second, she allowed herself to acknowledge the truth. She had feelings for Dylan Kavanagh. Messy, wonderful emotions that couldn't be organized in spreadsheets or analyzed by computer programs. Exhilaration and panic duked it out in her stomach.

Dylan had made Mia comfortable and welcome in his home. He had been charming and gentle with Cora. He had even tried to protect Mia from his desire for her, though that hadn't lasted long.

But what if she admitted she was equally hungry? Would it make a difference if she told him what she wanted? Was there a chance Dylan might want something more, as well?

She was in trouble either way. If his answer was no, she faced humiliation and hurt. But if his answer was yes, she faced another set of problems. Could she give up her career and be content as a wife and mother? No matter how wonderful living in Silver Glen might be, it would mean relinquishing an entire part of the life that had defined her since she'd become an adult.

All of her life she had dealt with difficult challenges. But this situation she *now* faced would require hard choices. If she took the wrong path, the consequences for her and for Cora could be devastating.

Thirteen

Dylan scooped the infant seat out of the car and followed
Mia up the stairs. Unlocking the front door while juggling
a baby was a skill he hadn't known he possessed, but
something about it was satisfying. Cora was so innocent,
so perfect. It made him feel good to know that in some
small way, he was helping protect her.

In deference to the sleeping child, they made their way
across the living room without turning on additional lights.
Mia had been remarkably quiet on the way home. He wondered if his mother's veiled criticisms had pissed her off.
She'd be justified.

After they put Cora down and closed the door, he took
Mia's hand. "Let's have some coffee and sit in front of
the fire."

"It's late."

He lifted her fingers to his lips and kissed them. "Are
you going to turn into a pumpkin?" She had already kicked
off her shoes. The disparity in their heights emphasized
the contrast of male to female.

Mia shrugged, her expression difficult to decipher. "I'll
change and meet you in the kitchen."

"Don't," he said gruffly. "Don't change. Please. I have
a few fantasies about this dress."

That brought a smile to her face. "It *is* a nice dress,"
she said, the words demure.

"Very user-friendly." He cupped a hand behind her neck and massaged the spot beneath her ear. "Maybe we don't need coffee." He'd never brought a lover to this house. Perhaps his social skills were rusty. Or maybe he was simply losing control.

Mia strained on her tiptoes to kiss him, her lips warm and eager against his. "I'm not at all thirsty," she said. "Maybe we should go to bed and get some rest."

"Rest?" He was befuddled by her scent and by the feel of silk beneath his fingertips. Silk fabric. Silky-skinned woman.

She drew him toward her bedroom. "We *will* rest. Afterward."

It boded well for him that Mia made no pretense of resistance. He liked not having to guess whether or not she wanted him. No mixed messages. No hidden agendas. Just a man and a woman sharing pleasure.

For a moment, he wanted to take her to *his* suite…to play sexy games on his turf. But there was Cora to consider, and besides, perhaps he would regret making erotic memories in his bed when Mia was gone.

Thinking about her departure gave him an uneasy feeling. So he shut down that particular train of thought and focused on the temptress in the red dress.

Once the bedroom door closed, Mia stepped away from him and seemed to lose her courage. She fidgeted.

He put his arm around her waist and walked her to the bed. Sitting on the edge of the mattress, he positioned her in front of him, still standing. "You are a beautiful woman, Mia Larin, but in this dress… Lord, have mercy. It's a good thing my heart's in good shape."

Her tense posture relaxed. "You're really good at that."

"At what?"

"Making a woman feel special."

"You *are* special," he insisted. There was doubt in her

eyes, so he set out to make a believer out of her. Tracing the edge of her bodice with a fingertip, he grinned when gooseflesh erupted on her bare arms. "Do I make you nervous, Mia?"

"A little." Her arms hung at her sides, but her fingers curled, indicating that she was not completely at ease.

"I'm the most amiable guy on the planet. No one is scared of me."

At last she moved. Running her thumb across his bottom lip, she knocked the breath out of him with her tender caress. "I don't have a great deal of experience with men, but you're different."

He didn't know whether to be pleased or annoyed. "That doesn't sound entirely like a compliment."

Her skin was pale in the dimly lit room, her dark-eyed gaze impossible to decipher. "I don't want to fall for a guy who has *carefree bachelor* tattooed across his libido." She ruffled his hair. "You make a woman want things you're not willing to give."

He felt a twinge of guilt. Mia wasn't wrong. "We never had any idea that this was anything more than fun."

"I know."

"And besides," he said, feeling defensive, "there's nothing for you here in Silver Glen. You know that."

"There's you." The absolute conviction in those two words rocked him on his heels.

His heart twisted…hard. She was making herself completely vulnerable to him, but he couldn't reciprocate. "I'm not anyone's prize. Trust me. If you want fun and games, I'm your man. But don't expect more from me than I can give, Mia. I thought you'd learned that lesson a long time ago."

Nothing on her face indicated that his blunt refusal of her unspoken request had hurt her. But she took a ragged little breath that could have meant anything. "You're honest. I'll give you that. I won't embarrass you anymore. Make love to me, Dylan."

He felt a lick of relief that she had dropped the subject, but at the same time a raw feeling he was closing a door that might never reopen. "I can do that." The words were forced from a tight throat.

That damned crystal beckoned him irresistibly. He toyed with it, the backs of his fingers stroking her cleavage. "I feel like it's Christmas morning and Santa brought me a special package wrapped in red."

The anticipation was almost more than he could take. But he wanted to draw out the pleasure until they were both drunk with it.

When he tugged at the faux jewel, the zipper gave easily. Too easily. He forced himself to stop at two inches.

Mia's eyes closed, her chest rising and falling with rapid breaths. "I swear I would have pegged you as one of those guys who rips off the paper to see what's inside."

He spanned her hips with his hands trying to decide if she was wearing panties. Surely so. His Mia was shy... though present evidence didn't support such a hypothesis.

"I am," he admitted. "But sometimes patience is a virtue."

"Not at the moment," she muttered.

He played with the clear stone again. Such a simple thing to torment a man—but oh-so-effective. Any other day, if he and Mia had shared more than a single encounter prior to tonight, he might have submitted to his caveman instincts and yanked the sparkly pull as far down as it would go in one rash movement. Even thinking about it gave him chills.

But he needed to work up to that. By her own admission, Mia was not widely experienced in the erotic arts. He didn't want to scare her by coming on too strong.

The zipper conceded another four inches. Now the dress

was in danger of falling. It clung to Mia's breasts tantalizingly, held there by nothing more than a whisper.

When he teased her tummy with a fingertip, he evoked a surprisingly strong reaction. Mia grabbed the top of her dress and held it close, her hand batting his away. "Stop that," she hissed. "I'm ticklish."

"I'll keep it in mind." Allowing her the pretense of holding him at bay, he took the zipper to its final destination. "Move your hands, Mia."

When she shook her head, a lock of dark, wavy hair fell over her almost bare shoulder. "You're still dressed," she protested.

"My turn will come." He grasped both of her wrists in one of his hands and held them away from her body. Gently, awkwardly—since he had only one hand to work with—he peeled the dress down her arms. Clearly, he hadn't thought this through, because Mia's bound wrists halted his progress. "Well, damn."

She had the audacity to laugh. "Now what? Maybe you're not as smooth an operator as I thought."

"You have a sassy mouth for someone who's supposed to be shy."

"I've changed, Dylan."

"I noticed."

The act of trapping her delicate wrists with one of his big hands had aroused him even more if that were possible. But his ultimate goal meant he had to release her in the short-term. Before she could grab the dress again, he took handfuls of the skirt and pulled. In a split second she was naked. Or almost. The tiniest pair of red undies covered only the essentials.

Mia took the poleaxed expression on Dylan's face as a good sign. "Are you window shopping?" she asked politely. He sat frozen, his gaze fixed on her underwear. The intensity of his gaze made her damp in a very intimate spot. Surely he couldn't tell.

Dylan cleared his throat. "Let's not ruin the dress."

He held her hand gallantly as she stepped out of it and tossed it toward a chair, not bothering to see if it landed properly. At the moment she was more interested in breaking Dylan free of his trance. Since he appeared to be stunned, she sat down beside him. "You've seen me naked before," she teased.

"Only once." He ran a hand from the middle of her thigh to her knee. His darker skin against hers made her shiver.

"I don't mean to criticize," she said, resting her head against his shoulder, "but there's a good chance Cora will be waking up soon. Do you mind if we speed this up?" She reached over and began unbuttoning his shirt with her right hand. Truthfully, she wouldn't mind if he made love to her with his tux on. Dylan was a younger, more handsome James Bond.

Or maybe she was a tad prejudiced.

Finally, he snapped out of it. His hand covered hers. "Stretch out on the bed, Mia."

It was an order. She took it as such, feeling ridiculously turned on by his air of authority. As she scooted toward the headboard, trying to act as if being mostly naked in front of a handsome man was the norm for her, Dylan stood with his hands on his hips and tracked her every move.

When she was settled, he tugged at his bowtie, beginning an unapologetic striptease entirely for her benefit. At least she assumed that was his intention. Maybe he just didn't like being rushed.

First he toed off his shoes and stripped off his socks. His trousers were next. The black silk boxers he wore did little to disguise his masculinity. His thrusting erection pushed out the fabric. His excitement was evident in the small wet spot near his waist.

He left the underwear in place and reached for the studs on his shirt. Instead of scattering them across the rug, he removed each one with painstaking slowness and dropped them into a glass dish on the dresser.

"Take the shirt off," she pleaded. If Cora woke up at this exact moment, Mia would die of frustration.

Dylan complied in silence, his eyes flashing, his face flushed.

When he was down to his one last item of clothing, she held out her hand. "Hurry. I can't wait anymore."

At last he showed some evidence of the impatience she was experiencing. He strode to the bed and came down beside her on one knee. "It was worth the trouble tonight of getting into a tux for the chance to see you in that dress. But without it, I think you're even more beautiful."

Before she could respond, he gathered her into his arms and rolled with her. Now she was on top with his silky drawers massaging her female bits. Shivers of anticipation raced up and down her spine. She rested her hands on his hard chest. Tonight he had looked every inch the wealthy, sophisticated Kavanagh.

Yet here, in the intimacy of her room and her bed, Dylan's true essence shone through. He could play the part of a civilized man about town when required. But the real Dylan, the bad boy she had met in high school, was this wild-eyed, feral male. Undomesticated. Determined to get what he wanted, no matter the cost.

She wasn't resisting. Why would she? Leaning down, supporting herself with one palm braced on his warm shoulder, she traced his jawline with her fingers, feeling the late-day stubble. "Your family loves you very much," she said. "And Liam and Aidan trust your opinions. I watched them tonight. They respect and admire you."

His smile was lopsided. "Not that I mind being buttered up, but what's your point?"

She felt his hands caress her butt. Did she really want to carry on a rational conversation at this particular juncture? "Never mind," she muttered. "It will keep." She wriggled her bottom, making Dylan groan.

Without second-guessing herself, she slid down in the bed and settled between his thighs. Licking gently, she dampened the silk that covered his sac. Dylan's back arched off the bed.

Panting, he fisted his hands in her hair. "I have a condom in my billfold," he croaked.

"You won't be needing that just yet."

Dylan's ragged curse ended in a moan as she gently bit his shaft through his boxers. She loved feeling him like this. His fiancée must have been insane to walk away from a man like Dylan.

It was clear his patience was at an end when he put his hands under her arms and dragged her upward for a hot, punishing kiss. "You're a heartless tease," he accused.

"All the better to seduce you, my dear."

He went still. "Is that who I am? A notch on your bedpost?"

"What does that mean?" Irritated, she pulled away.

He lay there like a great cat, his tawny skin radiating heat as he stared at her with an unreadable gaze. "You move in academic circles with men whose intellects are equal to yours. Is what we're doing here your walk on the wild side?"

She scowled, the impulse to slap him almost winning. "That's insulting to both of us. I thought we were having fun. Clearly I was wrong." Furious, she scrambled away from him, intent on fleeing.

But Dylan had other ideas. One strong hand grasped her ankle and pulled her back. He sat up, gripping her shoulders and shaking her gently. "I needed to know the truth, Mia."

Tears stung her eyes, but she blinked them back. "Why?"

His jaw worked. "I've been used before. I didn't particularly enjoy it."

"Well, I *am* using you," she cried. "Though maybe not in the way you're thinking. You're housing and feeding my daughter and me. You're paying me to do a job that any one of a dozen people in Silver Glen could have handled easily. So what does that make *me?* I've hit rock bottom. If I wanted to make love to you, it sure as hell had nothing to do with scoring some imaginary coup."

Their faces were mere inches apart, his breath warm on her cheek. She could see his long, thick lashes and the way they framed his beautiful, intense eyes.

He kissed her lazily. "Fair enough. I should have known you couldn't resist my animal magnetism."

Resting her forearms on his shoulders, she linked her hands behind his neck and played with his hair. "Modesty isn't one of your strong suits, is it?"

"I'm cursed with being irresistible to women."

His tongue-in-cheek humor restored her equilibrium. "Thank God you have me to take you down a peg or two. Otherwise, your head would be too big to get through the door."

"Hold that thought."

He rolled away long enough to get rid of his boxers and to grab protection. Though the banter was lighthearted, his expression was anything but. Standing beside the bed, he rolled latex over his straining shaft.

When he returned, settling on his knees in front of her, it was clear that the time for talking was past. He touched her intimately, checking her readiness. She was mortifyingly wet. Wanting Dylan was a living, breathing ache.

She rested her forehead against his shoulder. "I need you," she whispered.

Lowering her carefully onto her back, he moved over

her with purpose, fitting the head of his erection to her center and pushing with a firm thrust. She inhaled sharply, her mind spinning in a dozen directions.

The confidence of his possession was warranted. His knowledge of a woman's body guaranteed satisfaction. Mia realized he was bringing her to the brink in record time. She savored the physical connection, convinced that Dylan was the only man who ever had or ever would be able to touch her so deeply, so well.

The room was quiet, save for the sounds of his exertion. Whatever veneer of polish he had donned for the evening with his family was stripped away, incinerated in the heat of their coupling. She wrapped her legs around his waist. "Don't stop," she begged, spiraling upward toward an invisible peak.

"Never."

It was a futile request and an unrealistic answer. The force of their need reduced them to the most basic human level. She bit his neck, marking him as hers. His skin was damp with sweat. Her mouth was dry.

Suddenly, he cried out, his big body shuddering atop hers. What sent her over the edge was the realization that for this one moment in time, Dylan wanted her and needed her.

For now, it was enough.

Fourteen

Sometime in the wee hours of the morning, a sound woke Dylan. He lay still for a moment, processing the fact that he was not in his own bed. Then everything came rushing back. His sex stirred reflexively, stimulated by the memories.

The sound came again. He reared up on one elbow long enough to observe the monitor. Cora was stirring.

Stealthily, he slid out of bed, anxious to catch the baby before she awakened Mia.

Cora gave him an adorable toothless smile when he bent over her crib. "Hey, sweet cheeks." The way she looked at him made it clear that she already recognized the man in the house. When he picked her up and snuggled her, the baby smell entranced him. He realized in an instant that he had fallen in love with Cora. The sensation that gripped his chest was a simple, entirely natural emotion, but a profound one.

As he changed her diaper, she kicked her feet and cooed. Blowing a raspberry on her chubby tummy, he felt his heart turn over. She was so sweet and perfect. And she deserved a father.

The knowledge made him uncomfortable. He knew his limitations. What would it be like if he ever had a child of his own, and Dylan were unable to help with homework? Or even worse, what if the kid took after him?

Cora would be smart. He knew it. But Cora and Mia were a package. If he couldn't keep Mia, the baby wasn't his either. Wrapping the infant in a thin cotton blanket against the chill of the air-conditioning, he carried her into the bedroom and sat down on Mia's side of the bed. Touching her hip through the covers, he shook he gently. "Someone wants her mama," he said quietly.

Mia sat up, shoving the hair from her face. She was nude. The realization seemed to take her by surprise, because she flushed and scrambled for the safety of the bathroom.

Dylan kissed the baby's cheek. "Don't worry. She'll be back."

When Mia returned moments later, she was covered neck to toe in a thin black robe made of a soft knit that clung to her body. With her hair tumbled down around her shoulders, she looked like a sexually sated woman. She settled herself back in bed without looking at Dylan and reached for the baby. "You should have woken me up. Cora isn't your responsibility."

He stood for a moment, watching as the baby rooted for a nipple. "I love your daughter," he said flatly. "Nothing about caring for her is a chore."

Pissed for no good reason, he returned to his side of the bed and climbed under the covers, sprawling on his back. With one arm flung across his face, he listened to Cora's enthusiastic nursing. Occasionally, Mia murmured to her daughter. Although the tenor of the words was soft and affectionate, he couldn't actually make out what Mia said.

He was almost asleep when she addressed *him*.

Perhaps Cora was nodding off already, because Mia's words were a whisper. "When Cora gets in school, will you think less of her if she has learning difficulties?"

The out-of-nowhere question jerked him from the edge of slumber. "Of course not."

"So you won't think she's stupid or slow?"

Suddenly, he saw where this was going. "No," he said. "I won't."

He didn't need any further explanation to get what Mia was trying to tell him. He had worn the hair shirt of his academic failures stubbornly, unable to see past his youthful struggles. The truth was, he wasn't that high-school boy anymore. Sure, he still had trouble with numbers and letters, and he always would. But what did that matter?

Suddenly, the ridiculous irony of their situation slapped him in the face. Mia had used an "average" sperm donor so she wouldn't have a child as smart as she was. Dylan was unwilling to father a child who might struggle in school as he had. Unwittingly, he and Mia were trying to play God.

Neither of them had asked to be born with a high IQ or a reading disorder. They had both played the hands they'd been dealt. It was long past time to move on.

He'd used his frustrating studies as a yardstick to measure his success, but Mia was right. He had a lot to be proud of. The Silver Dollar drew customers from miles around and was a stopping-off point for those who wanted to explore the town. His family was close and supportive. He had a wide circle of friends and a house he'd designed from the ground up, a place of respite and peace at the end of the day.

Everything a man could want or need was his. Except for a wife. And a baby. Mia and Cora fit the bill more perfectly than any two people he could have conjured up in his imagination. There were obstacles. He'd be the first to admit it. But he loved Mia. Her job and her talent had kept him from admitting it. Now he acknowledged the truth.

He had believed he wasn't good enough for her. But maybe love was the one ability that trumped all the rest. He could offer Mia things she had never found with other men. And by God, he was going to make her believe it. The joyous possibilities swelled in his chest, though he tempered his enthusiasm, unwilling to tip his hand too soon.

His heart thudded in his chest. Was he really contemplating such an enormous change in his life?

As Mia shifted Cora to her other breast with a smile for her infant daughter, he knew that his answer was yes. Mia brought something unique to his home and to his life. Excitement, yes. But also a deep sense of satisfaction. When he was with her, he felt at peace. Which was odd, because until Mia and Cora arrived in Silver Glen, Dylan would have sworn that his life was perfect as it was.

Imagining his house without them, even after such a short time, was unthinkable. Here in Mia's bed, he realized that what he had shared with his ex-fiancée had been ephemeral at best. It was the difference between a flesh-and-blood woman and a hologram. Tara had been a chameleon, playing a part even when the cameras weren't rolling.

Mia was exactly the opposite. She was real and grounded and complete. Even with his eyes closed, he knew the moment when she got up to carry Cora back to her crib. Moments later the covers rustled as she climbed back in bed, this time staying far to her side of the mattress.

Despite the late hour and their need for sleep, a stronger need drove him. In the dark he donned a condom and then took her arm and urged her closer, meeting her in the middle of the bed. Mia came willingly. She was naked again—soft and warm and so intensely feminine in his arms. He was beginning to learn the touches that pleased her, the little catches of breath that told him he had found a sensitive spot.

Though his hunger for her was as fierce as it had been in the beginning, he didn't mount her at first. Instead, he reveled in the feel of her body pressed against him. Her legs tangled with his. Her hands pulled his head down for a kiss that was equal parts passion and play.

"You amaze me," he muttered.

"It's the testosterone talking." She slid her fingers into his hair, making him shiver. "I'm a rookie. Maybe it's beginner's luck."

Though she turned his rough praise into a joke, he had never been more serious. Parting her thighs with his hand, he moved between her legs and entered her slowly. Someone sighed. Maybe her. Maybe him. This time, there was no rush.

In the darkness, he could pretend this was all that mattered. This heady rush of physical bliss. This feeling that he was in control of his domain. That all was right with the world.

Mia came before he did, her orgasm a gentle rolling wave. He picked up the pace of his thrusts and followed her, welcoming the now familiar physical release that racked him and turned him inside out.

In the aftermath, he heard her breathing settle into an even cadence. In moments she would be asleep.

"Mia." He whispered near her ear, his lips brushing her temple.

"Hmm?" She was tucked into his embrace with her bottom nestled against his groin. It was time to yield to slumber, not to talk, but this couldn't wait.

"When the apartment over the Silver Dollar has been repaired, I don't want you and Cora to move. I want you to stay here."

He couldn't miss the way her body stiffened.

"Why?" she asked.

Because I like having you under my roof and in my bed.

That kind of declaration was a lot to throw at a woman in the middle of the night, so he backpedaled. "I think it would be better for Cora to have some continuity. She's already moved once, and she seems to like it here. Besides, I have a yard for her to play in."

"She's only three months old, Dylan. We'll leave Silver Glen before she even starts walking."

"I care about you," he said baldly, his hands shaking. "And about Cora. My house is still a healthier atmosphere for a baby than a cramped apartment over a bar. Promise me you'll think about it."

Her head pillowed on his arm, she yawned. "I care about you, too, Dylan. So I'll consider it. I promise. Go to sleep now. We can talk about this tomorrow."

When Mia woke up the next morning, Dylan was gone. Again. But this time, she knew he had spent the night in her bed. Shortly before dawn, he'd made love to her one last time.

It was anybody's guess as to where he was at the moment.

After pulling on clean undies and her robe, she went to fetch Cora, her limbs protesting every step. Much of her body was pleasantly sore, but any discomfort she experienced was offset by an almost palpable sense of well-being. She felt satiated and smug.

Dylan had told her he cared about her. It was a lot from a man who guarded himself so carefully. And she had been brave enough to reciprocate without worrying about getting hurt.

Cora was not a great conversationalist, but Mia engaged her anyway. "Dylan wants us to stay, little one. He loves you and he likes me. So we're going to enjoy the moment. Okay with you?" She took the baby's chortle as a sign of agreement.

Glancing at her watch, she decided to prevail on Gertie's good nature once again. She found the older woman occupying her customary morning post, frying bacon and scrambling eggs. "Good morning, Gertie."

"I suppose it is," Gertie said with a grin. "Did the baby sleep?"

"She did. One brief feeding in the middle of the night, but that was it, thank goodness."

The housekeeper set a plate on the table and motioned to Mia. "Eat it while it's hot." Mia, with the baby on her lap, wolfed down a double serving of both bacon *and* eggs and topped it off with one of Gertie's homemade biscuits and jam. It was embarrassing how hungry she was. Normally a cup of yogurt and some coffee would see her through the morning, but after last night's sexual excess, she was starving.

When Gertie finished up the last of the bacon and set it on a paper towel to drain, Mia suddenly realized that Dylan might not have eaten yet. Casually, she took a sip of her orange juice and fished for information. "Did Dylan head into town already?"

Gertie shook her head. "Nope. He's out back getting the boys started."

"The boys?"

"He gives jobs to boys in the foster-care system. Mostly yard work and the like. And he tells them if he ever catches them spending their paychecks on drugs, he'll tear them limb from limb."

"And they believe him?"

"Oh, yes. Mr. Dylan can be fierce when he needs to be. Everyone sees him as this laid-back, good-natured fellow, but he's got strong opinions and strong beliefs about right and wrong. Look how he brought you and the baby here to his house. He could have settled you in a motel room somewhere, but that wouldn't have been right. That boy's moral compass points due north. I know his mama raised her sons to be responsible, but Dylan takes it a step farther. He's a gentleman and a provider. He'll always look out for the weak and the helpless and the ones who've been given hard knocks."

As Mia finished her breakfast, she felt some of her euphoria winnow away. In the middle of the night when Dylan had asked her to stay longer than originally planned, her heart had flipped in her chest. Mentally, she had heard the word *care* as *love*. Dylan wanted to get closer to her. He wanted to pursue their burgeoning relationship, sexually and otherwise.

Now, in the cold light of day, and with Gertie's passionate analysis of Dylan's personality, it seemed more than likely that Dylan's invitation had been the result of altruism. Her mood deflated like a cheap balloon. She gave herself a mental pep talk. Nothing had changed. Cora and Mia still had a home. Mia had a job.

Best of all, Mia was sharing Dylan's bed for the moment. She had never expected more than that. So why was she now feeling disappointed and low?

Wiping her mouth with an elegant cloth napkin, she gave Gertie a beseeching smile. "Would you mind playing with her for twenty minutes while I grab a quick shower?"

"You know the answer to that." Gertie took the baby with alacrity. "Go do what you need to do. Me and this little lady will entertain each other."

Mia crossed the house toward the wing that housed her suite and Dylan's. As she passed his doorway, an unwelcome thought occurred. When Gertie went to tidy her boss's room and make his bed, she would see that the bed hadn't been slept in. The woman was smart enough to put two and two together. Surely she would guess that Dylan had been in another bed. Very close by.

Stealthily, Mia opened Dylan's door. She had never been inside. The furnishings and decor were equally as luxurious as hers, but the colors were more masculine.

Lots of navy and burgundy. Rapidly, she went to the huge bed and threw back the covers, twisting them until they looked like the remnants of a good night's sleep.

One by one, she plumped the pillows. She even knocked one onto the floor for good measure. Satisfied that she had done her best, she turned to leave and ran smack into the bed's owner.

"Dylan," she squeaked, feeling as guilty as if he had caught her raiding his safe.

The flash of white teeth in his broad grin added further color to her hot cheeks. "Whatcha doin', little Mia?" He crossed his arms over his chest. Since he was blocking her only exit, his stance surely wasn't coincidental.

"I, uh…" Well, shoot, she might as well fess up. "I didn't want Gertie to know you hadn't slept in your bed."

His lips twitched, but he didn't laugh. "I'm a grown man," he said, his voice deceptively mild considering the predatory gleam in his eyes. "Gertie doesn't weigh in on my sleep habits."

Before she could defend herself with additional rational explanations, Dylan reached out and stripped her out of the thin robe she wore.

She shrieked and batted at his hands. "Are you nuts? We're not alone."

With a calm she couldn't emulate, he turned and locked his door. "Gertie took the baby for a walk. I want you again, Mia."

The even tenor of his words didn't match the hot, intent gaze that took in every inch of her body. She didn't know why she was embarrassed. He had seen it all last night. Had touched it and kissed it and…

He cut short her mental gyrations by scooping her into his arms. But he didn't walk toward the bed. Instead, he pushed her against the nearest wall. Her legs went around his waist automatically. "Dylan, we can't." It was a weak protest at best, and he took it as such.

"A quickie, Mia. You've heard the term, I'm sure." Without letting her fall, he unbuckled his belt, unzipped his pants and freed his stiff erection. After one-handedly rolling on a condom, he bit her earlobe. "Hang on, honey. This is going to be hard and fast."

Before she could utter a word, he reached between her legs, thrust aside the thin cotton crotch of her undies and pushed inside her, all the way to the hilt.

Beyond the window, Mia could hear the voices of the young men working in the yard. Birds sang. A lawnmower roared. But in Dylan's beautifully appointed bedroom, there was no talking. He took her roughly, urgently, as if it had been months instead of hours since they had mated. His breath smelled of coffee. He tasted like bacon and orange marmalade. His big, tough body held her aloft easily.

She hadn't been prepared for this. No foreplay. No wooing. Which made it all the more mortifying when she climaxed wildly, even before Dylan had finished. The culmination of her pleasure galvanized him. Ramming into her with low groans, he jerked and cursed when his own release found him moments later.

Mia knew her bottom would be sore tomorrow from being pummeled against the wall. But she couldn't seem to care. The novelty of having a man go insane with lust in her presence was a powerful analgesic.

Dylan cleared his throat. "Should I apologize?" he asked, the words rueful.

She pressed her hand over his wildly beating heart. "I don't know. Maybe you should do it again so I can be sure."

Fifteen

Dylan was in over his head. In high school, as a popular kid with lots of money, getting girls had never been a problem. Fortunately, he'd had the good sense to use appropriate protection. But teenage sex and sex in his early twenties had been more about physical release than about bonding with any particular female.

He considered himself a generous lover. None of his partners had ever complained, not even Tara, who had appeared to enjoy his bed but not enough to stay. By the time he met her, he'd been old enough to actually consider settling down. She had flattered his ego. And he had been suckered into the fantasy.

But he had been naive. Fortunately, his broken engagement no longer gave him sleepless nights. He'd made a mistake. And he was lucky it hadn't taken him as far as the altar. Tara was firmly in the past.

Mia, on the other hand, managed to combine the past and the present in one confusing amalgam of nostalgia and sexual hunger.

Instead of releasing her, he carried her to his bathroom, knowing she would want to freshen up before she sneaked across the hall to the safety of her own bedroom. When he set her on her feet, he managed a smile, even though he was in no way sanguine about had just happened.

To be honest, he was pretty much a vanilla guy when

it came to sex. He liked sex. A lot. And often was always better than not at all. But Mia had done something to him. She'd made him feel a gnawing hunger that was not exactly comfortable. In fact, his response to her was pretty damned alarming. How could a meek, quiet, unassuming female turn him inside out and make him doubt everything he'd ever known about himself?

"Mia," he said, unable to keep quiet. "Are you going to stay? For now?"

At the moment, she clutched her robe to her chest with white-knuckled fingers. What she didn't know was that in the mirror he could see the outline of her cute heart-shaped butt through the thin fabric. Clenching his fists to keep from reaching for her again, he leaned against the doorframe. "I'd like an answer please."

When she smiled at him, his legs went weak. "Yes, Dylan. For now."

He cleared his throat, concealing the rush of jubilation evoked by her quiet agreement. "Good." He paused. "It's a gorgeous day outside. What if we get Gertie to fix us a picnic?"

"Cora, too?"

"Of course. She's part of the package."

"That would be nice."

Mia's eyes were huge. He noticed her gaze drop briefly to his pants where his fly was still open. Calmly, he tucked in his shirt, adjusted the rest of his clothing and hoped she didn't notice that he was still semierect.

"I'll go talk to her now," he said. "Let me know when you're ready."

"But we just ate breakfast."

"I'll throw in a tour of the house before we go. And there are things in the woods I want you to see."

"Sounds like the script for a horror movie."

He laughed out loud. Considering that he had to spend

the better part of the next three days dealing with construction headaches down at the Silver Dollar, he knew he deserved this outing. Mia's company was icing on the cake and then some.

Mia was grateful when Dylan disappeared. After one disbelieving look in the mirror, she straightened her hair, carefully fastened the sash of her robe and then returned to her own room to shower and dress. Since Dylan had given her a heads-up, she packed a diaper bag for Cora, and then chose for herself an outfit that was comfortable and suited to the outdoors.

The amber knit top and faded jeans were around-the-house clothing, but after she put her hair in a ponytail and slicked some lip gloss across her mouth, she didn't look half bad. Her canvas espadrilles were made more for style than for walking in the great outdoors, but they would do.

By the time she made it back to the kitchen, her twenty minutes had mushroomed to thirty-five. Since she couldn't explain why she was late, she decided it was better not to say anything at all.

Gertie and Cora were just coming in the back door when Mia found them. The baby threw out her arms when she saw her mama.

Mia took her, holding her tight. It never ceased to amaze her that her love for this little girl grew every day. "Come here, angel. Were you good for Miss Gertie?"

"Best baby I ever saw. Mr. Dylan asked me to put together a picnic. Any special requests?"

Mia shook her head. "Everything you make is wonderful. I've been avoiding spicy food since I'm nursing, but other than that, the menu is wide-open as far as I'm concerned."

Dylan joined them, his presence making the large

kitchen seem to shrink. "While Gertie is organizing our picnic, why don't I show you the upstairs?"

She didn't confess that she had already snooped. "Sounds good to me."

The guest rooms on the second floor were exquisite. "I had help with the furnishings and decor," Dylan confessed.

Each one was different and beautiful in its own way. "You must enjoy having company," she said.

"I do. Several of the guys I went to high school with have moved away. It's fun to host them and their families when they come back for visits to Silver Glen."

"And single women?" Mia gave him a wry look, knowing the answer to that one.

But Dylan surprised her. "If you mean girlfriends, the answer is no. I've never had a lover here."

"Not even Tara?" She raised an eyebrow.

"I lived in a condo in town when I was engaged to Tara. It was after we broke up that I built this place. It's my personal space. My retreat, I guess you'd call it."

"And yet you brought Cora and me here."

He shrugged. "No choice really."

"There's always a choice in life. You could have put us up in a hotel. Why didn't you?"

"I owed you something. For the past. And besides, Cora wormed her way into my heart."

"And me?"

His gaze settled on her mouth, hungry...wanting. "Let's just say that what I feel for you now is a wee bit different than it was in high school. C'mon," he said, taking her arm. His fingers were warm against her skin. She was so attuned to his touch that she felt little sizzles and sparks fizz through her bloodstream. It was impossible to be so close to him and not remember other things. More private things.

He led her to a door at the end of the hall.

"Another bedroom?" she asked.

"Nope. This is the attic access. Let me carry Cora. The steps are steep."

She trusted him implicitly with her daughter. And she was glad he had offered his help. The stairs were indeed slanted sharply upward.

When they reached the top, Dylan flipped a light switch. The cavernous, unfinished space smelled of wood shavings and dust. Cobwebs caught the light. "I'm not sure what we're looking at," she said. If this were a romantic tryst, he wouldn't have brought a baby along.

Handing Cora back to her, he cranked a large handle. Gradually, a section of the roof began to open. Now, with the sunlight pouring in, she saw a large telescope against the far wall. "It's a makeshift observatory," he said, clearly enthused about his revelation. "I come up here on clear nights and look at the stars. That's why I bought this property. We're far enough away from town to escape the light pollution."

"Where did you get the telescope? And how did you learn to use it?"

"I took a class online. Ordered the parts. Put it together."

"Dylan." The exasperation in her voice got through to him.

"What?" He seemed genuinely perplexed.

"I don't want to hear another damn word about how smart I am or how dumb you are. Are we clear?"

Dylan shrugged, grinning. "Yes, ma'am."

Poor Cora seemed baffled by her mother's rant.

Mia felt better for having that off her chest, but she realized that yelling at the man she was falling for probably wasn't the smartest tack to take.

Before she could apologize for her vehemence, an unexpected crack of thunder made all three of them jump.

A large summer storm cloud had come out of nowhere, it seemed, and suddenly the sky above was gray and roiling. The wind picked up, and they felt the first drops of rain.

Dylan manned the crank with all his might, closing the gap just in time to prevent the attic from being soaked. It was quieter suddenly, and awkward.

He put his hands in his back pockets. She saw his chest rise and fall. Sometimes she forgot how handsome he was. Looking at him now, she tried to see him through a stranger's eyes. Some people would write him off as a simple guy with a gift for gab and a charming smile. But there was so much more to Dylan. In that instant, she knew that her feelings were far more involved than was wise. She wished she knew what he was thinking. "I guess that's it for our picnic," she said.

"We could have it in the living room in front of the fireplace. I'm sure Gertie can rustle up an old blanket for us. Cora would like that, wouldn't she?"

"Of course."

Dylan busied himself carrying things from the kitchen to the living room, but he reeled mentally. Mia had read him the riot act upstairs in the attic. And she seemed so adamant that she was right. Had he really been so clueless about his own abilities? Had he allowed an unspoken competition with his older brother to make him feel inadequate?

As he settled onto the quilt with Mia and Cora, he had to smile. Awash in contentment, he listened as the storm raged in full fury. Rain lashed the windows in wind-driven sheets. Gertie, watching the radar, had decided to make a run for home half an hour ago, hoping to miss the worst of the weather. She didn't live far. Dylan was sure she had made it without much trouble, but he sent a text just in case and was reassured when she replied that she was home safe and sound.

Mia had said very little during their informal meal. In fact, she had addressed most of her attention toward Cora. Unfortunately for Mia, the baby was fast succumbing to sleep. Dylan, without asking, tucked sofa pillows around her so she wouldn't roll into anything hurtful as she slept.

When he was done, he crouched beside Mia and stroked her cheek. "Has the cat got your tongue?"

Her abashed look was adorable. "I shrieked at you like a fish wife," she said, her expression remorseful. "I'm sorry."

He drew her down onto the quilt, leaning against the low wall in front of the hearth and putting her head in his lap. "I'm actually flattered. And I'll concede, you may have a point."

After that, they were quiet, content to listen to the storm outside and the crackle of the fire close by. He combed his fingers through her hair, wondering if he would always remember this day as a turning point in his life. He knew what he wanted now. Mia. For always. And Cora. And maybe—when he'd had time to get used to the idea—a second kid.

There was still the matter of Mia's work. To be honest, he couldn't imagine ever leaving Silver Glen. But when it came down to it, he was more sure every moment that he would choose Mia and Cora over most anything else he could think of.

He touched her cheek. "What are you thinking about?

When she looked up at him, he could swear he saw something in her eyes that reflected what was in his heart. For a long time he thought she wasn't going to answer him. But finally, she spoke.

"I was thinking about how lucky I was to come to Silver Glen and run into you again. My life was in chaos, but you were so calm and reassuring. For the first time I began to think that Cora and I were going to make it."

"Of course you were going to make it. You're a bright, capable woman. But everyone needs help once in a while."

She sat up. "Is that the only reason we're together? Because you like helping damsels in distress?"

He cupped her face in his hands. "It was my pleasure to do whatever I could for you and Cora. But no. We're together because of a magnetic attraction. You must have learned about that in science class."

Nibbling his fingers, she smiled wryly. "So you're calling this thing between us *opposites attract?*"

He kissed her softly and released her, unwilling to let things get out of hand with the baby nearby. "We're not opposites at all, Mia. Not where it really counts. We both value family. And roots. You wanted that connection badly enough to have a baby on your own."

Desire shimmered between them. They were enclosed in an intimate cocoon courtesy of the storm and the fire and the memories of last night and this morning.

Mia cocked her head, her expression reflecting his own physical need. "Cora is asleep."

He felt his neck heat. "We can't leave her here. And if we try to move her, she might wake up."

"I was thinking about how comfortable your sofa is."

His eyes darted to the furniture in question. He swallowed hard. "Really?" It was not a question about the couch.

Mia understood. "Really."

He helped her to her feet and held her hand as they crossed the thick carpet to the long, leather-covered divan. In hushed silence, they undressed each other. Shirts and pants. Socks and shoes. Unlike the night that cloaked activities in secret, this was the middle of the afternoon.

There was no hiding, metaphorical or otherwise. Mia's

gaze held his steadily, though he could see remnants of her innate shyness. When he knelt and drew her last piece of clothing down her legs, she stepped out of the lacy panties and stood before him bare as the day she was born.

He shed his boxers and felt a rush of heat scald his spine when Mia immediately took his shaft in her hands and stroked him from root to tip. He saw wonder in her eyes, the same wonder he felt. How could two such different people find common ground in such a primeval way?

The bare leather sofa seemed cold to the touch, so he grabbed a soft mohair afghan and spread it across the cushions. "Ladies first," he said.

When she stretched out and propped her foot on the back of the couch, the bottom fell out of his stomach at the sheer eroticism of the view. After rapidly taking care of protection, he came down on top of her, bracing himself on one arm to spare her his weight. Thunder still boomed overhead, rattling panes of glass in the windows. Mia had been silent through it all.

"I need this," he croaked, almost beyond speech. "I need you."

Her small, winsome smile warmed him from the inside out. "Then we're both going to get what we want."

He wanted to ask her to stay forever. To walk away from her old life. But that seemed incredibly selfish. So he tried to show her with his body that she was special to him. Ignoring the blistering urge to mate, he paid homage to her quiet beauty. Lingering kisses at her throat. Sharper nips at her collarbone.

Soon, though, Mia was not content to be passive. She found his mouth and kissed him recklessly. "I won't break, Dylan. And I don't want to wait. Let me feel you inside me."

It was an invitation he couldn't refuse. Bending her knee to gain access, he positioned himself. "I want to go on record as saying that I'm working under adverse conditions."

He watched as Mia stifled her giggle, biting her lip. "Duly noted," she whispered.

When he entered her, they went from amusement to awe. Eyes open, locked on hers, he moved inside her, feeling his world shift on its axis. Nothing in his life had ever felt so right, so natural. "Mia…" He had no clue what he was trying to say.

She held his gaze bravely, her arms linked around his neck. "I know, Dylan. I know."

How long it lasted, he couldn't say. A minute. An hour. A handful of seconds. Everything faded away. At last, even looking at her became too much of an effort. He closed his eyes, concentrating. Her sex gripped his, making him sweat.

The sofa creaked beneath the force of his movements. Wooly fibers scratched his legs. Sliding his hand beneath Mia's butt, he lifted her into his thrusts, hearing the choked inarticulate cries that told him she was close.

So sweet…she was so damned sweet and sexy.

Without warning, something inside him snapped. Wildly he plunged into her, straining for the goal and yet trying to hold back an inescapable tide. "Mia, Mia," he groaned.

The end, when it came, was swift, incredible and draining.

As he collapsed on top of her, he heard her whisper something, but his heart beat too loudly in his ears for him to hear.

Sixteen

Mia found herself in a predicament for which none of her studies had prepared her. She was in love with a man who clung stubbornly to the idea that she was only passing through. And for the life of her, she couldn't tell him he was wrong, though more and more every day, she wanted to. What Dylan offered was unbearably sweet. But it would mean giving up a great deal. And her sacrifice was predicated on the assumption that he wanted her for the long haul.

His weight was a pleasant burden. She honestly could not tell if he was asleep or not, but the momentary quiet gave her time to think. In her estimation, the sex they had shared was more than just momentarily satisfying. Their physical intimacy seemed born of a deeper connection.

Dylan's tenderness made her believe he cared even more than he had admitted to her.

But was she deceiving herself?

Moments later, Dylan stirred, lifting off her and standing up. The eye-level view of his sex was disconcerting.

He pulled her to her feet, tucking her against his chest. "We need to talk, Mia." His big body was warm and hard, making her feel both safe and aroused at the same time, a dangerous combination.

Her heart stuttered. "About what?"

"You. Me. Us."

"Okay." Her face was buried in his chest. To look at him would have taken more courage than she had at the moment. Her hands rested decorously at his waist, but she badly wanted to stroke his firm buttocks. The tone of his voice could have meant anything, but considering the way his erection nudged her abdomen, she had to hope that this *talk* was going to be a good thing.

Chilled suddenly, and more than a little embarrassed about their nudity in broad daylight, she stepped back, folding her arms across her breasts. "I need to clean up and get dressed. Cora will want to eat soon. Patience isn't her strong suit."

Dylan stood with his feet braced, shoulders squared, as he covered her from head to toe with a hot gaze. His smile made her toes curl. "It's probably for the best. Otherwise we might spend the whole day screwing our brains out."

"Dylan!"

He held up his hands. "Sorry. I'm weak and you're irresistible."

"No, I'm not." His praise made her heart sing, but she tried to keep her feet firmly planted on the ground.

"I'll be the judge of that." He glanced at the clock on the mantel. "If you don't mind being alone here with Cora, I really should run into town and see if the storm did any damage to the building. The insurance company had a tarp installed over the roof, but I don't know if it held in the wind."

"We'll be fine."

"I want to take you to dinner up at the hotel tonight. Table for two. Very private. So we can talk about your future. Our future."

She shivered inwardly, hoping for a miracle. "I'd like that. But what about Cora?"

"I'm pretty sure Zoe would love to babysit for a couple of hours, but I'll call her as I drive into town and check."

Mia picked up her clothes and held them in front of her. Dylan appeared entirely comfortable in his nakedness and in no hurry to rush off. She was not quite so sanguine. So she changed the subject. "At some point today or tomorrow morning I need you to glance at the forms I filled out for your quarterly tax report. I haven't submitted it yet because I wanted you to take a look and see if it's okay."

"I'm sure it's fine, but if it will make you feel better…"

"Thanks."

He took pity on her physical paralysis. "Go get dressed. I'll make sure Cora's okay until you get back."

As Dylan watched her walk away, he enjoyed the rear view. Making love to Mia was a revelation. She had more passion hidden beneath her quiet, reserved personality that anyone he had ever met. Tonight he would tell her he loved her and feel her out about the possibility of staying in Silver Glen permanently.

He was not fooling himself. There was a better-than-even chance that his relationship might not make it to September. Autumn in the Carolina mountains was spectacular. By then the bar would be up and running, and he would have something to distract him from the pain if Mia decided she couldn't stay.

And it would be pain. He already knew that. Hopefully, he was prepared for it.

He dressed rapidly and picked up Cora as she cried out. The baby looked up at him with eyes that were so much like her mother's. For a moment, Dylan felt sympathy for the anonymous man who would never know this precious child.

Being a father was about more than planting a seed. It meant sharing sleepless nights, dealing with croup and strep throat, and reading up on ways to care for diaper rash. *Daddy* was a full-time job, but one with enormous

benefits. Being with Cora had changed him…or at least
opened his eyes. He would do anything for that kid.

During tonight's dinner, he would lay out his plan. If
Mia was on the same page, perhaps during the next few
months they could decide if it was possible to mesh their
lives.

When Mia reappeared, his heart donkey-kicked him
in the chest. He spoke gruffly to cover the emotion that
threatened to choke him. "I'm leaving now." He handed
over the warm bundle of baby fat and drooling smiles.
"Unless you hear otherwise, we'll plan on leaving at six."

Mia bounced Cora on her shoulder. The kid was working up to a major screaming fit. "I'll be ready."

Her smile reached all the way down to his toes.

"Good. I'll look forward to it."

In his truck, away from the temptation that was Mia,
he wondered if he had it in him to watch a woman walk
away from him a second time. Tara's defection had hurt
his pride, but whenever it came time for Mia to leave, he'd
be in danger of getting down on the floor to beg.

His damaged business served as a welcome distrac-
tion even now. Fortunately, the Silver Dollar was in good
shape. Water had seeped in around one of the ground-floor
doors, but since repairs hadn't begun, it was no big deal.

He grabbed a cup of coffee from a shop near his business and took a moment to call Zoe, who was delighted to
be tapped as a babysitter. When he finished his drink, he
walked down one of the side streets, gazing in each window. Silver Glen boasted numerous unique shops.

He paused in front of an antique store. There in the
window was a collection of silver charms. One caught his
eye. A book. The tiny piece of silver seemed to encapsu-
late the very thing that had brought Mia into his life in

the beginning. On a whim, he went inside and bought the charm and a bracelet to match.

On the way home, his excitement mounted. Dinner with a beautiful woman. The possibility of sharing her bed later tonight. It didn't get much better than that.

When he entered the house, it was strangely quiet. He grabbed a water bottle out of the fridge and only then spotted the note on the kitchen table.

Dylan—

Cora and I are napping. Don't let us sleep past four-thirty. I'll need time to get ready.

Mia

He tucked the note in his shirt pocket, grinning. Neither he nor Mia had gotten much sleep last night. To keep himself from climbing into bed *with* her, he decided that now was as good a time as any to look over the tax stuff she wanted him to see.

His office was neat as a pin…far tidier than he ever managed to keep it. Gertie was banned from this room. The housekeeper rearranged his stacks and made it impossible for him to find things.

The laptop he'd given Mia was on the desk where she left it…and it was turned on. She must have gotten up abruptly to tend to Cora. He used the touch pad to wake things up and saw immediately that Mia's email was on the screen.

His first impulse was to click out of it. He wasn't the kind of man who snooped in other people's stuff. But even with only a brief glance, one word jumped off the screen. *Interview.* His gut tightened as he sat down to read the rest, unable to help himself.

The sender had merely replied to a message from Mia, so Dylan was able to scroll down and see what she had written. It sounded like she had sent more of these letters, all indicating her availability and asking about possible job openings.

Even as his stomach tightened, he told himself it made perfect sense. Mia hadn't kept any secrets from him. Of course she had been looking for future employment. Still, the email felt like a betrayal. An illogical response on his part, but true.

The original email had an attachment. He clicked on the word *résumé* and hit Print. Pages began spitting out of his printer. Gathering them up, he sat down in a chair and started to read…slowly, as always.

Any dreams he had begun to weave about keeping Mia in Silver Glen disintegrated into something that resembled the ashes of a hot fire. Mia had earned not one, but *two* PhDs from prestigious universities. Her work history was impressive, but what he found the most daunting were her research and writing credits.

Over two pages of the résumé were devoted to lists of Mia's articles published in academic journals, as well as papers she had presented at scientific conferences all over the U.S. and around the world.

He had fooled himself into thinking of Mia as a simple, down-to-earth mother of a new baby. Helping Mia and Cora had made him feel like a man. He liked having them look to him for support.

But the truth was far less cozy. He'd been right in the first place. Mia didn't belong in Silver Glen. And she would never belong to him. Even if she wanted him physically.

Calmly, he fed the pages into a shredder. Then he went to the living room and sat down to wait.

* * *

Mia had only napped forty-five minutes, but she awoke feeling refreshed and energetic. A peep in at Cora told her the baby still slept. If Mia was lucky, she might have time to pick out an outfit before her daughter demanded attention.

The impulse to dance around the room made her sheepish. Yes, she was going to have dinner with her lover. And yes, he wanted to talk to her…in private. But that could mean anything.

Her nap had left her mouth feeling cottony, so she headed to the kitchen for a glass of the iced tea Gertie kept on hand round the clock. When she was halfway across the living room, she stopped short, her hand to her chest. "Dylan. You startled me. I didn't expect you back so soon. Is everything at the Silver Dollar okay?"

"Everything at the saloon is fine. No change." He sat sprawled in an armchair, a beer in his right hand and his legs stretched out in front of him. He wasn't smiling. And he didn't look the least bit amorous.

Gradually, a feeling of alarm squashed Mia's euphoria. "What happened, then? You look…" She trailed off, unable to decide what was wrong with the picture.

The fingers of his left hand drummed on the arm of the chair. That slight movement was the only visible sign that he was upset. "I changed my mind about dinner," he said.

She sank into a seat opposite him, her heart at her feet. "I see."

"I doubt you do." Fatigue and bitterness nuanced his words.

"Then why don't you explain?"

He reached into the pocket of his pants and pulled out a folded check. Tossing it on the coffee table beside a small white box, he grimaced. "I hired you in good faith. So I've written that for six months' pay. It should be enough to help you and Cora make a new start in Raleigh. The other thing is a little gift that reminded me of you."

When she bit down hard on her lower lip, she tasted the rusty tang of blood. "I don't understand. I thought you wanted me here. I thought you wanted *me*."

His gaze was bleak. "What I want doesn't matter. You have a job offer. I saw the email. When I went to look at the tax forms." He stopped. She saw the muscles in his throat work. "I need you to leave, Mia. You don't belong here. Go home. Go back to the life you were meant for. Take what you need in the short-term and when you have an address, let me know and I'll ship the rest."

She rose to her feet, frantic. "I don't want to leave. I don't know what's happened, but please don't do this."

For a moment, she thought her plea had gotten through to him. His left hand curled into a fist, and his right hand gripped the beer bottle white-knuckled.

Long seconds ticked by.

Then, with every ounce of expression wiped from his face, he stood up, his gaze landing anywhere but on her. "I'm sleeping up at the hotel tonight. I'd like you to be gone by noon tomorrow. If you need Gertie's help in packing, her number's in the kitchen. Goodbye, Mia."

The six weeks that followed were some of the worst of Mia's life, harder even than when she had welcomed a newborn into her home. The drive back to Raleigh was a blur she barely remembered. Fortunately, Cora had been a doll, napping peacefully for most of the trip.

After one night in a chain motel, Mia hit rock-bottom. She didn't have the luxury of tearing Dylan's check into tiny pieces. If it had been only her, she would have slept in her car before she would have accepted his money. But she had Cora to think of, Cora to protect. Sometimes a parent had to make hard choices.

Once Mia took Dylan's check to the bank, the train was set in motion. With what was left in her checking and savings accounts, and with the generous termination settlement Dylan had given her, there was enough to put down deposits on a nice apartment.

For the moment, Cora slept on the carpet beside her mother. Mia purchased a sleeping bag for herself. Eventually she would get some things out of storage, but for now she was hiding out. Since she had already talked to her friends and told them she was staying in Silver Glen for a while, how could she explain her unexpected return?

From her phone, she emailed the department head who had offered an interview and told him a family situation had put her plans on hold. After that, all she did was play with her daughter and weep. The crying jags ended after the first week. It wasn't good for the baby to see her mother so unhappy. Mia decided that by living only in the present, she could pretend that everything was normal.

She lost weight. Only the prospect of her milk drying up induced her to eat at all. Nursing Cora was a lifeline. It kept her sane. Made her feel whole. She had to take in enough calories to keep feeding her daughter.

Sometimes, if it wasn't too hot, they went for a walk in the park. She had brought Cora's stroller with her from Dylan's house. Amongst other families pushing infants along the paths, she could almost pretend that she was going to be okay.

But at night, when Cora slept, dreams of Dylan kept Mia awake. Ironically, now that she would not have minded Cora's company in the middle of the night, the baby slept from eight in the evening until eight the next morning.

At the end of the second week, Dylan texted her and asked where to send her things. In a panic, she went to the phone store and had her number changed. Even that minimal contact with the man in Silver Glen, the man she loved who had broken her heart, threatened her fragile composure.

Her entire world had imploded, and she didn't know what to do. On the basis of one stupid email, Dylan had decided that Mia needed to go back to her career. But that wasn't his decision to make. Yes, she loved her work, and yes, it was important. But did that trump love? Why couldn't Dylan fight for her? Why couldn't he let her make her own decisions?

In truth, though, she couldn't see a clear answer. Short of Dylan moving to Raleigh—and that seemed wrong on many levels—she didn't see a solution. If Dylan's feelings for her had been stronger, she might have decided to put her career on hold. But even that seemed like a poor choice.

By the time August rolled toward a steamy end, heading for the Labor Day weekend and the official end of summer, Mia had managed to reach deep inside herself and draw on reserves of strength she hadn't known existed. For her child's sake, she had to pick up the pieces of her life.

Cora was growing rapidly and needed new clothes. One blistering afternoon after naptime, Mia loaded the baby into the car and found a mall, one in a part of town she had never frequented. She still couldn't bear the thought of running into anyone she knew.

By the time she wrestled the stroller out of the trunk, lifted Cora out of her car seat, and trudged across the hot pavement into the mall, she felt dizzy and sick. Instead of heading to a department store, she made her way to the food court. All she could think about was buying a large, icy-cold soda.

As she rummaged in her purse for her billfold, she staggered, putting out her hand and grabbing for support. The young man behind the counter stared. "You okay, ma'am?"

Mia licked her lips, trying to breathe. Yellow spots danced in front of her eyes. "Yes," she whispered. "No problem." And then her world went black….

Seventeen

Dylan was frantic. When Mia didn't respond to his text, he hired a private-detective agency to find her...to make sure she and the baby were okay. But everywhere they looked they hit a dead end. It was as if Mia had disappeared from the face of the earth.

She cashed his check. That knowledge gave him a tiny bit of comfort. At least he didn't have to worry that Mia and Cora were destitute. But when he tried to have her phone calls traced, he knew she had deliberately changed her number.

In the intervening weeks, as he missed Mia and Cora with a raw pain that kept him awake at night, he realized he had given up without a fight. And that was not like him. He had been wrong to make them leave. He began to think of solutions, and if none of those panned out, he was ready to pack up and move to Raleigh.

Desperation drove him to extreme measures. Though it was immoral if not downright illegal, he found a tech guru who was willing to hack into the computer Mia had used in Dylan's office. The man tapped into her email account, but there was only one outgoing email. A note informing the sender that she would not be interviewing for a job, the job Dylan had seen earlier.

If Mia wasn't trying to find a job, then what in the hell was she doing? He even checked hospitals throughout the

Raleigh/Durham area in case either Mia or Cora was ill or injured.

The computer geek had showed him how to access the email himself. Every morning and every evening, Dylan sat with the laptop, praying for something, anything. But apparently, Mia was not using her email at all.

His break came in an unexpected way. One morning, an email from her bank popped up with the heading "address change." Without compunction, he opened it, jotted down the information and ran to his bedroom to pack a bag. Six hours later, he parked in front of a nondescript block of apartments.

With his heart pounding and his chest tight, he searched for the numbers that identified the units. There it was.

When Mia opened the door, her face went pale with shock. "What are you doing here?" Animosity crackled in every syllable.

"I came to apologize," he said. "May I come in?"

In case she decided to be obstructive, he didn't wait for an answer, but instead, eased his way past her into the tiny efficiency apartment. He stopped short. Now it was his turn to be shocked. The space was virtually empty. A camp chair sat in the living room in front of him. A portable crib and a sleeping bag occupied the central section of the carpeted floor. There were no other items of furniture. No television, no sofa, no bed.

Dylan's net worth amounted to over three million dollars. Yet, the woman he loved was sleeping on the floor every night. Guilt for what he had done to her sickened him. Fury raged in his chest for his own stupidity. He had to convince Mia that he was sorry. That he was wrong to send her away. That he loved her too much to let her go. He had a feeling his negotiation skills were going to be tested to the limit.

Projecting a calm he didn't feel, he walked past Mia's

single chair and lowered himself to the floor, his back against a wall. "We need to talk."

She glared at him. "The last time you said that it was a prelude to kicking me out of your house."

Swallowing hard, he took the hit without trying to justify his actions. "Please, Mia. Let me say what I came to say." She looked ill, and that worried him more than anything.

"If that's what it takes to get rid of you, fine." Instead of taking the chair, she copied his pose, leaning against the adjacent wall.

Cora was asleep, so he kept his voice low. "I'm sorry for being an arrogant, insensitive jerk. It was presumptuous of me to think I knew what was best for you, for your life, for Cora."

"And what brought about this monumental change of heart?" Now he could see the grief in her gaze. Grief that could and should be laid firmly at his door.

"You left." He said it bluntly, willing her to understand.

"And?"

"And I realized how much I loved you. Well," he said, backtracking, "I was pretty sure about that *before* you left. But my empty house sealed the deal. I also realized that I had tried to play God with your future. As if you were not smart enough to choose your own path. And when you think about it, that makes me look pretty stupid."

"You're not stupid." Her response was automatic.

She'd said those same three words to him more than a decade ago and again when she returned to Silver Glen. The trouble was, he hadn't been able to hear them.

"Let's just say that I'm willing to learn from my mistakes."

"Okay. You're forgiven. Please leave."

"Not so fast," he said, stung by her rejection, though he undoubtedly deserved it. "I want a do-over."

"I don't know what that means."

As he studied her face, he was struck by the way her cheekbones stood out and by the dark smudges beneath her eyes. "You look terrible," he blurted out.

"Is that your idea of a do-over?"

For the first time he saw a glimmer of amusement on her face. "Sorry," he muttered. "I've been worried as hell about you."

"I'm not your responsibility."

They seemed to be going in circles. "Mia." He stopped, searched his heart, and did the best he could. He'd made a lot of mistakes in his life, but none he wanted to fix more than this one. "I didn't give you a choice before. I didn't ask what *you* wanted. That's why I'm here now. I need to know what *you* want. What will make *you* happy." He gave the tiny apartment a disparaging glance. "Surely not this place."

"I've moved on, Dylan. I'm making a new start. I'm not the same woman you booted out of your life eight weeks ago."

"Have you been sick?" He had to know.

She shrugged. "In a manner of speaking. When I left Silver Glen, I had a severe relapse into postpartum depression. But don't worry," she said quickly. "I'm under a doctor's care, and I'm going to be fine. I have three job interviews in the next two weeks. Cora and I are back on our feet."

"But are you happy?"

It hadn't escaped his notice that he'd told her he loved her and she never even acknowledged his declaration.

She looked down at her lap where her hands twisted and clenched. "I'm content. I think happiness is a bit of a myth. I'm focusing on Cora and her well-being. That's what matters to me now."

"Happiness is *not* a myth. It's real. And I'll ask you

again. What do *you* want, Mia? If I hadn't been such a jackass, what would have made you happy in Silver Glen?" She had never said she loved him, but she had hinted at it. Why wouldn't she express that emotion now? Had he hurt her too badly for her to ever trust him again?

"Please go, Dylan." Her face was the color of skim milk.

He scooted across the distance that separated them and sat beside her, hip to hip. "You're wearing the bracelet I gave you." He toyed with the book charm, his fingertips brushing the back of her hand.

"It entertains the baby."

He ignored her ridiculous explanation. "I want to marry you, Mia."

He felt her body jerk, but she didn't say a word. So he forged ahead doggedly. "I may as well spell it out, so you know where I stand. But keep in mind that all of this is subject to your approval…to *your* wants and needs."

Needing badly to connect with her, he took her hand in his, clasping her fingers and resting their linked hands on his thigh. She didn't pull away. So maybe there was still hope. "My family has the means to build a research facility in Silver Glen. We could bring in top-notch scientists from all over the world. You could run the whole thing, or we could outfit a lab just for you and the projects that are important to you. I can hire a manager for the Silver Dollar so I'll be free to keep Cora while you work. I'd like to adopt her if it's okay with you." He ran out of steam, his heart sinking to the soles of his feet. Mia had all the animation of a block of wood, not exactly the kind of response a man looks for when he proposes.

Finally, when he began to feel foolish and depressed all at the same time, Mia stood up to pace. She paused on the far side of the room. "I appreciate your apology and your proposal…or all of your proposals," she said quietly. "But I have to say no."

Was it possible for a man to feel his heart shatter?

Swallowing the lump of regret and grief in his throat, he stood as well. "Why, Mia? Why do you have to say no?" In his bed and in his arms, he could have sworn that she felt something for him.

She rubbed her temples with her fingertips, her posture defeated. "I'm pregnant, Dylan."

Mia's emotions were all over the map. When all the color leached from Dylan's face, he slid down the wall, his butt thumping the ground. "How? Is it another man?"

Rolling her eyes, she shook her head. "Now you *are* being stupid. Of course not. Do you remember that night when we made love half-asleep? Actually, it was toward morning. Neither of us thought to use protection."

She saw the moment when he remembered. Some expression crossed his face, one she couldn't discern. "I don't know what to say." His words were raspy as if he could barely speak.

"It isn't your fault. We were both in that bed. And you've made it abundantly clear that you don't intend to father any children. You'll have access, of course, if you want it."

"If I want it?" He parroted the words, clearly in shock.

"I know this is a lot to absorb, but your life won't change. You don't have to worry about anything. I can handle this."

He shook his head as if trying to dismiss the remnants of a bad dream. When he rose to his feet a second time, alarm skittered down her spine. His black scowl promised retribution. "Are you insane? Of course I want my child!"

She refused to be frightened by his bluster. They had to clear this up once and for all. "But what if your son or daughter takes after you? What if your child has dyslexia?

Or bad eyesight? Or a heart murmur? Or isn't coordinated? What if he or she does poorly in school?"

He put his hand over her mouth and drew her close. "You've made your point, Mia." His lopsided smile broadened with dawning wonder. "My God, a baby." He touched her flat belly with reverence. "We're going to be parents. Cora will have a sibling." He kissed her hard. A possessive mating of teeth and tongues and ragged breath that took the starch out of her knees.

Mia's eyes stung with tears when they separated, her throat tight. "I love you, Dylan, very much. But I have to be sure where you stand. You can't kick us to the curb every time I get an award or receive recognition for my work. I have to know that our relationship is one of equals."

He understood what she was saying. And he wasn't foolish enough to think everything would be easy. But none of that was critical in the end. "I'm so proud of you, Mia. I'll always be proud of you. But what matters to me now is far more important than your brain. I see the love in your heart. For Cora. For me. I want to be the man who makes *you* proud. Your friend. Your lover. Cora's father. I love you, Mia. For always."

She searched his face with a gaze full of hesitant wonder. "You really mean it, don't you? You understand."

"It's taken me a while," he said quietly. "But yes. I do."

She flung herself against him, her arms tightening around his neck in a stranglehold. "I adore you, Dylan Kavanagh."

Stroking her hair, he propped his chin on top of her head. "Pretty soon, word's going to get out about us and it will be pretty clear that *I'm* the smart one for snapping you up."

"You're such a flatterer. But I like it."

He pulled back and took her hands in his. "We'll get

married this weekend," he said. "My family knows every-one in Silver Glen. We can do it at the hotel, or a church if you'd prefer. Zoe can help you find a dress…."

Mia put a hand over *his* mouth. "This isn't going to be easy for you, is it? Letting me make decisions?"

He nipped her fingers with his teeth. "We'll probably argue a lot. And have wild, incredible makeup sex. I love you, Mia, more than you'll ever understand, even with that genius brain of yours."

He went still as she cupped his cheeks in her hands and searched his eyes for the truth. What she saw must have reassured her, because when she spoke, the words were confident and strong. "I want to spend time with our children before they start school. It's important to me. But with what you're suggesting about the lab, I can work from home, or utilize a flex schedule."

Dylan sobered. "*Our* children." The reality was sink-ing in at last. He and Mia had built a family. The rush of exhilaration weakened his knees. "Then you will have your wish. And in that case…" He stepped back enough to take her hands.

"Yes?"

He paused, swallowing hard. "I'd like to go back to school and finish a degree. With your help."

Mia hadn't known she could love him any more. "Will you believe me when I say it doesn't matter to me? I love you, Dylan Kavanagh. And I always will."

"Not for you," he said quietly, his eyes alight with hap-piness. "For me. For Cora. And for this one." He placed both of his hands on her stomach. "I have a feeling I'm going to have more than one genius on my hands, and I need to be able to keep up."

She laid her head against his chest, feeling the wonderfully steady beat of his heart. "You're going to be a wonderful father."

"And lover," he reminded helpfully.

"That, too."

Dylan glanced around the small room that had been her hideout for long, miserable weeks. "I think we're done here, Mia, my love. Let's take Cora and go home. You're both mine now. For keeps."

* * * * *

A sneaky peek at next month…

PASSIONATE AND DRAMATIC LOVE STORIES

My wish list for next month's titles…

In stores from 20th June 2014:

❏ Her Pregnancy Secret – Ann Major

& Matched to a Billionaire – Kat Cantrell

❏ Lured by the Rich Rancher – Kathie DeNosky

& The Sheik's Son – Kristi Gold

❏ A Taste of Temptation – Cat Schield

& When Opposites Attract… – Jules Bennett

2 stories in each book - only **£5.49!**

Available at WHSmith, Tesco, Asda, Eason, Amazon and Apple

Just can't wait?

Visit us Online

You can buy our books online a month before they hit the shops! **www.millsandboon.co.uk**

   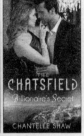
   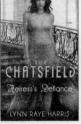

THE CHATSFIELD®

Enter the intriguing online world of
The Chatsfield and discover secret
stories behind closed doors…

www.thechatsfield.com

Check in online now for your exclusive
welcome pack!

The World of Mills & Boon

There's a Mills & Boon® series that's perfect for you. There are ten different series to choose from and new titles every month, so whether you're looking for glamorous seduction, Regency rakes, homespun heroes or sizzling erotica, we'll give you plenty of inspiration for your next read.

By Request — *Back by popular demand!*
12 stories every month

Cherish™ — *Experience the ultimate rush of falling in love.*
12 new stories every month

INTRIGUE... — *A seductive combination of danger and desire...*
7 new stories every month

Desire™ — *Passionate and dramatic love stories*
6 new stories every month

nocturne™ — *An exhilarating underworld of dark desires*
3 new stories every month

For exclusive member offers go to
millsandboon.co.uk/subscribe

MILLS & BOON®
Book Club

Join the Mills & Boon Book Club

Want to read more **Desire**™ books?
We're offering you **2 more** absolutely **FREE!**

We'll also treat you to these fabulous extras:

- 🌹 Exclusive offers and much more!

- 🌹 FREE home delivery

- 🌹 FREE books and gifts with our special rewards scheme

Get your free books now!

visit www.millsandboon.co.uk/bookclub
or call Customer Relations on 020 8288 2888